The Collected Supernatural and Weird Fiction of Edith Wharton Volume 2

The Collected Supernatural and Weird Fiction of Edith Wharton Volume 2

Seventeen Short Tales of the Strange and Unusual

Edith Wharton

LEONAUR

The Collected
Supernatural and Weird
Fiction of
Edith Wharton
Volume 2
Seventeen Short Tales
to Chill the Blood
by Edith Wharton

FIRST EDITION

Leonaur is an imprint of Oakpast Ltd

ISBN: 978-1-78282-549-4 (hardcover)
ISBN: 978-1-78282-550-0 (softcover)

http://www.leonaur.com

Publisher's Notes

The views expressed in this book are not necessarily those of the publisher.

Contents

All Souls'

Queer and inexplicable as the business was, on the surface it appeared fairly simple—at the time, at least; but with the passing of years, and owing to there not having been a single witness of what happened except Sara Clayburn herself, the stories about it have become so exaggerated, and often so ridiculously inaccurate, that it seems necessary that someone connected with the affair, though not actually present—I repeat that when it happened my cousin was (or thought she was) quite alone in her house—should record the few facts actually known.

In those days I was often at Whitegates (as the place had always been called)—I was there, in fact, not long before, and almost immediately after, the strange happenings of those thirty-six hours. Jim Clayburn and his widow were both my cousins, and because of that, and of my intimacy with them, both families think I am more likely than anybody else to be able to get at the facts, as far as they can be called facts, and as anybody can get at them. So I have written down, as clearly as I could, the gist of the various talks I had with cousin Sara, when she could be got to talk—it wasn't often—about what occurred during that mysterious weekend.

I read the other day in a book by a fashionable essayist that ghosts went out when electric light came in. What nonsense! The writer, though he is fond of dabbling, in a literary way, in the supernatural, hasn't even reached the threshold of his subject. As between turreted castles patrolled by headless victims with clanking chains, and the comfortable suburban house with a refrigerator and central heating where you feel, as soon as you're in it, *that there's something wrong,* give me the latter for sending a chill down the spine! And, by the way, haven't you noticed that it's generally not the high-strung and imaginative who see ghosts, but the calm matter-of-fact people who don't believe in them, and are sure they wouldn't mind if they did see one?

Well, that was the case with Sara Clayburn and her house. The house, in spite of its age—it was built, I believe, about 1780—was open, airy, high-ceilinged, with electricity, central heating and all the modern appliances: and its mistress was—well, very much like her house. And, anyhow, this isn't exactly a ghost story and I've dragged in the analogy only as a way of showing you what kind of woman my cousin was, and how unlikely it would have seemed that what happened at Whitegates should have happened just there—or to her.

When Jim Clayburn died the family all thought that, as the couple had no children, his widow would give up Whitegates and move cither to New York or Boston—for being of good Colonial stock, with many relatives and friends, she would have found a place ready for her in either. But Sara Clayburn seldom did what other people expected, and in this case she did exactly the contrary; she stayed at Whitegates.

'What, turn my back on the old house tear up all the family roots, and go and hang myself up in a bird-cage flat in one of those new skyscrapers in Lexington Avenue, with a bunch of chickweed and a cuttlefish to replace my good Connecticut mutton? No, thank you. Here I belong, and here I stay till my executors hand the place over to Jim's next-of-kin—that stupid fat Presley boy . . . Well, don't let's talk about him. But I tell you what- I'll keep him out of here as long as I can.' And she did—for being still in the early fifties when her husband died, and a muscular, resolute figure of a woman, she was more than a match for the fat Presley boy, and attended his funeral a few years ago, in correct mourning, with a faint smile under her veil.

Whitegates was a pleasant hospitable-looking house, on a height overlooking the stately windings of the Connecticut River; but it was five or six miles from Norrington, the nearest town, and its situation would certainly have seemed remote and lonely to modern servants. Luckily, however, Sara Clayburn had inherited from her mother-in-law two or three old standbys who seemed as much a part of the family tradition as the roof they lived under; and I never heard of her having any trouble in her domestic arrangements.

The house, in Colonial days, had been foursquare, with four spacious rooms on the ground floor, an oak-floored hall dividing them, the usual kitchen extension at the back, and a good attic under the roof. But Jim's grandparents, when interest in the 'Colonial' began to revive, in the early eighties, had added two wings, at right angles to the south front, so that the old 'circle' before the front door became a grassy court, enclosed *on* three sides, with a big elm in the middle. Thus the house was turned into a roomy dwelling, in which the last three generations of Clayburns had exercised a large hospitality; but the architect had respected the character of the old house, and the enlargement made it more comfortable without lessening its simplicity. There was a lot of land about it, and Jim Clayburn, like his fathers before him, farmed it, not without profit, and played a considerable and respected part in state politics. The Clayburns were always spoken of as a 'good influence' in the county, and the townspeople were glad when they learned that Sara did not mean to desert the place—'though it must be lonesome, winters, living all alone up there atop of that hill'—they remarked as the days shortened, and the first snow began to pile up under the quadruple row of elms along the common.

Well, if I've given you a sufficiently clear idea of Whitegates and the Clayburns—who shared with their old house a sort of reassuring orderliness and dignity—I'll efface myself, and tell the tale, not in my cousin's words, for they were too confused and fragmentary, but as I built it up gradually out of her half-avowals and nervous reticences. If the thing happened at all—and I must leave you to judge of that—I think it must have happened in this way . . .

1

The morning had been bitter, with a driving sleet—though it was only the last day of October—but after lunch a watery sun showed for a while through banked-up woolly clouds, and tempted Sara Clayburn out. She was an energetic walker, and given, at that season, to tramping three or four miles along the valley road, and coming back by way of Shaker's wood. She had made her usual round, and was following the main drive to the house when she overtook a plainly-dressed woman walking in the same direction. If the scene had not been so lonely—the way to Whitegates at the end of an autumn day was not a frequented one—Mrs Clayburn might not have paid any attention to the woman, for she was in no way noticeable; but when she caught up with the intruder my cousin was surprised to find that she was a stranger—for the mistress of Whitegates prided herself on knowing, at least by sight, most of her country neighbours. It was almost dark, and the woman's face was hardly visible, but Mrs Clayburn told me she recalled her as middle-aged, plain and rather pale.

Mrs Clayburn greeted her, and then added: 'You're going to the house?'

'Yes, ma'am,' the woman answered, in a voice that the Connecticut Valley in old days would have called 'foreign', but that would have been unnoticed by ears used to the modern multiplicity of tongues. 'No, I couldn't say where she came from,' Sara always said. 'What struck me as queer was that I didn't know her.'

She asked the woman, politely, what she wanted, and the woman answered: 'Only to see one of the girls.' The answer was natural enough, and Mrs Clayburn nodded and turned off from the drive to the lower part of the gardens, so that she saw no more of the visitor then or afterward. And, in fact, a half hour later something happened which put the stranger entirely out of her mind. The brisk and light-footed Mrs Clayburn, as she approached the house, slipped on a frozen puddle, turned her ankle and lay suddenly helpless.

Price, the butler, and Agnes, the dour old Scottish maid whom Sara had inherited from her mother-in-law, of course knew exactly what to do. In no time they had their mistress stretched out on a lounge, and Dr Selgrove had been called up from Norrington. When he arrived, he ordered Mrs Clayburn to bed, did the necessary examining and bandaging, and shook his head over her ankle, which he feared was fractured. He thought, however, that if she would swear not to get up, or even shift the position of her leg, he could spare her the discomfort of putting it in plaster. Mrs Clayburn agreed, the more promptly as the doctor warned her that any rash movement would prolong her immobility. Her quick imperious nature made the prospect trying, and she was annoyed with herself for having been so clumsy. But the mischief was done, and she immediately thought what an opportunity she would have for going over her accounts and catching up with her correspondence. So she settled down resignedly in her bed.

'And you won't miss much, you know, if you have to stay there a few days, it's beginning to snow, and it looks as if we were in for a good spell of it,' the doctor remarked, glancing through the window as he gathered up his implements. 'Well, we don't often get snow here as early as this; but winter's got to begin sometime,' he concluded philosophically. At the door he stopped to add: 'You don't want me to send up a nurse from Norrington? Not to nurse you, you know; there's nothing much to do till I see you again. But this is a pretty lonely place when the snow begins, and I thought maybe—'

Sara Clayburn laughed. 'Lonely? With my old servants? You forget how many winters I've spent here alone with them. Two of them were with me in my mother-in-law's time.'

'That's so,' Dr Selgrove agreed. 'You're a good deal luckier than most people, that way. Well, let me see; this is Saturday. We'll have to let the inflammation go down before we can X-ray you. Monday morning, first thing, I'll be here with the X-ray man. If you want me sooner, call me up.' And he was gone.

2

The foot, at first, had not been very painful; but toward the small hours Mrs Clayburn began to suffer. She was a bad patient, like most healthy and active people. Not being used to pain she did not know how to bear it, and the hours of wakefulness and immobility seemed endless. Agnes, before leaving her, had made everything as comfortable as possible. She had put a jug of lemonade within reach, and had even (Mrs Clayburn thought it odd afterward) insisted on bringing in a tray with sandwiches and a thermos of tea. 'In case you're hungry in the night, madam.'

'Thank you; but I'm never hungry in the night. And I certainly shan't be tonight—only thirsty. I think I'm feverish.'

'Well, there's the lemonade, madam.'

'That will do. Take the other things away, please.' (Sara had always hated the sight of unwanted food 'messing about' in her room.)

'Very well, madam. Only you might—'

'Please take it away,' Mrs Clayburn repeated irritably.

'Very good, madam.' But as Agnes went out, her mistress heard her set the tray down softly on a table behind the screen which shut off the door.

'Obstinate old goose!' she thought, rather touched by the old woman's insistence.

Sleep, once it had gone, would not return, and the long black hours moved more and more slowly. How late the dawn came in November! 'If only I could move my leg,' she grumbled.

She lay still and strained her ears for the first steps of the servants. Whitegates was an early house, its mistress setting the example; it would surely not be long now before one of the women came. She was tempted to ring for Agnes, but refrained. The woman had been up late, and this was Sunday morning, when the household was always allowed a little extra time. Mrs Clayburn reflected restlessly:

I was a fool not to let her leave the tea beside the bed, as she wanted to. I wonder if I could get up and get it?' But she remembered the doctor's warning, and dared not move. Anything rather than risk prolonging her imprisonment. . .

Ah, there was the stable clock striking. How loud it sounded in the snowy stillness! One—two—three—four—five . . .

What? Only five? Three hours and a quarter more before she could hope to hear the door handle turned . . . After a while she dozed off again, uncomfortably.

Another sound aroused her. Again the stable clock. She listened. But the room was still in deep darkness, and only six strokes fell . . . She thought of reciting something to put her to sleep; but she seldom read poetry, and being naturally a good sleeper, she could not remember any of the usual devices against insomnia. The whole of her leg felt like lead now. The bandages had grown terribly tight-her ankle must have swollen . . . She lay staring at the dark windows, watching for the first glimmer of dawn. At last she saw a pale filter of daylight through the shutters.

One by one the objects between the bed and the window recovered first their outline, then their bulk, and seemed to be stealthily regrouping themselves, after goodness knows what secret displacements during the night. Who that has lived in an old house could possibly believe that the furniture in it stays still all night? Mrs Clayburn almost fancied she saw one little slender-legged table slipping hastily back into its place.

'It knows Agnes is coming, and it's afraid,' she thought whimsically. Her bad night must have made her imaginative, for such nonsense as that about the furniture had never occurred to her before . . .

At length, after hours more, as it seemed, the stable clock struck eight. Only another quarter of an hour. She watched the hand moving slowly across the face of the little clock beside her bed . . . ten minutes . . . five . . . only five! Agnes was as punctual as destiny . . . in two minutes now she would come. The two minutes passed, and she did not come. Poor Agnes—she had looked pale and tired the night before. She had overslept herself, no doubt—or perhaps she felt ill, and would send the housemaid to replace her. Mrs Clayburn waited.

She waited half an hour; then she reached up to the bell at the head of the bed. Poor old Agnes—her mistress felt guilty about waking her. But Agnes did not appear—and after a considerable interval Mrs Clayburn, now with a certain impatience, rang again. She rang once; twice; three times—but still no one came.

Once more she waited; then she said to herself: 'There must be something wrong with the electricity.' Well—she could find out by switching on the bed lamp at her elbow (how admirably the room was equipped with every practical appliance!). She switched it on—but no light came. Electric current cut off; and it was Sunday, and nothing could be done about it till the next morning. Unless it turned out to be just a burnt-out fuse, which Price could remedy. Well, in a moment now someone would surely come to her door.

It was nine o'clock before she admitted to herself that something uncommonly strange must have happened in the house. She began to feel a nervous apprehension; but she was not the woman to encourage it. If only she had had the telephone put in her room, instead of out on the landing! She measured mentally the distance to be travelled, remembered Dr Selgrove's admonition, and wondered if her broken ankle would carry her there. She dreaded the prospect of being put in plaster, but she had to get to the telephone, whatever happened.

She wrapped herself in her dressing gown, found a walking stick, and, resting heavily on it, dragged herself to the door. In her bedroom the careful Agnes had closed and fastened the shutters, so that it was not much lighter there than at dawn; but outside in the corridor the cold whiteness of the snowy morning seemed almost reassuring. Mysterious things—dreadful things—were associated with darkness; and here was the wholesome prosaic daylight come again to banish them. Mrs Clayburn looked about her and listened. Silence. A deep nocturnal silence in that day-lit house, in which five people were presumably coming and going about their work. It was certainly strange . . . She looked out of the window, hoping to see someone crossing the court or coming along the drive.

But no one was in sight, and the snow seemed to have the place to itself: a quiet steady snow. It was still falling, with a businesslike regularity, muffling the outer world in layers on layers of thick white velvet, and intensifying the silence within. A noiseless world—were people so sure that absence of noise was what they wanted? Let them first try a lonely country house in a November snowstorm!

She dragged herself along the passage to the telephone. When she unhooked the receiver she noticed that her hand trembled.

She rang up the pantry—no answer. She rang again. Silence—more silence! It seemed to be piling itself up like the snow on the roof and in the gutters. Silence. How many people that she knew had any idea what silence was—and how loud it sounded when you really listened to it?

Again she waited: then she rang up 'Central'. No answer. She tried three times. After that she tried the pantry again . . . The telephone was cut off, then; like the electric current. Who was at work downstairs, isolating her thus from the world? Her heart began to hammer. Luckily there was a chair near the telephone, and she sat down to recover her strength—or was it her courage?

Agnes and the housemaid slept in the nearest wing. She would certainly get as far as that when she had pulled herself together. Had she the courage—? Yes, of course she had. She had always been regarded as a plucky woman; and had so regarded herself. But this silence—

It occurred to her that by looking from the window of a neighbouring bathroom she could see the kitchen chimney. There ought to be smoke coming from it at that hour; and if there were she thought she would be less afraid to go on. She got as far as the bathroom and looking through the window saw that no smoke came from the chimney. Her sense of loneliness grew more acute. Whatever had happened below stairs must have happened before the morning's work had begun. The cook had not had time to light the fire, the other servants had not yet begun their round. She sank down on the nearest chair, struggling against her fears. What next would she discover if she carried on her investigations?

The pain in her ankle made progress difficult; but she was aware of it now only as an obstacle to haste. No matter what it cost her in physical suffering, she must find out what was happening below stairs—or had happened. But first she would go to the maid's room. And if that were empty—well, somehow she would have to get herself downstairs.

She limped along the passage, and on the way steadied herself by resting her hand on a radiator. It was stone-cold. Yet in that well-ordered house in winter the central heating, though damped down at night, was never allowed to go out, and by eight in the morning a mellow warmth pervaded the rooms. The icy chill of the pipes startled her. It was the chauffeur who looked after the heating—so he too was involved in the mystery, whatever it was, as well as the house servants. But this only deepened the problem.

3

At Agnes's door Mrs Clayburn paused and knocked. She expected no answer, and there was none. She opened the door and went in. The room was dark and very cold. She went to the window and flung back the shutters; then she looked slowly around, vaguely apprehensive of what she might see. The room was empty but what frightened her was not so much its emptiness as its air of scrupulous and undisturbed order. There was no sign of anyone having lately dressed in it—or undressed the night before. And the bed had not been slept in.

Mrs Clayburn leaned against the wall for a moment; then she crossed the floor and opened the cupboard. That was where Agnes kept her dresses; and the dresses were there, neatly hanging in a row. On the shelf above were Agnes's few and unfashionable hats, rearrangements of her mistress's old ones. Mrs Clayburn, who knew them all, looked at the shelf, and saw that one was missing. And so was also the warm winter coat she had given to Agnes the previous winter.

The woman was out, then; had gone out, no doubt, the night before, since the bed was unslept in, the dressing and washing appliances untouched. Agnes, who never set foot out of the house after dark, who despised the movies as much as she did the wireless, and could never be persuaded that a little innocent amusement was a necessary clement in life, had deserted the house on a snowy winter night, while her mistress lay upstairs, suffering and helpless! Why had she gone, and where had she gone? When she was undressing Mrs Clayburn the night before, taking her orders, trying to make her more comfortable, was she already planning this mysterious nocturnal escape? Or had something—the mysterious and dreadful.

Something for the clue of which Mrs Clayburn was still groping occurred later in the evening, sending the maid downstairs and out of doors into the bitter night? Perhaps one of the men at the garage—where the chauffeur and gardener lived—had been suddenly taken ill, and someone had run up to the house for Agnes. Yes—that must be the explanation . . . Yet how much it left unexplained.

Next to Agnes's room was the linen room; beyond that was the housemaid's door. Mrs Clayburn went to it and knocked. 'Mary!' No one answered, and she went in. The room was in the same immaculate order as her maid's, and here too the bed was unslept in, and there were no signs of dressing or undressing. The two women had no doubt gone out together—gone where?

More and more the cold unanswering silence of the house weighed down on Mrs Clayburn. She had never thought of it as a big house, but now, in this snowy winter light, it seemed immense, and full of ominous corners around which one dared not look.

Beyond the housemaid's room were the back stairs. It was the nearest way down, and every step that Mrs Clayburn took was increasingly painful; but she decided to walk slowly back, the whole-length of the passage, and go down by the front stairs. She did not know why she did this; but she felt that at the moment she was past reasoning, and had better obey her instinct.

More than once she had explored the ground floor alone in the small hours, in search of unwonted midnight noises; but now it was not the idea of noises that frightened her, but that inexorable and hostile silence, the sense that the house had retained in full daylight its nocturnal mystery, and was watching her as she was watching it; that in entering those empty orderly rooms she might be disturbing-some unseen confabulation on which beings of flesh-and-blood had better not intrude.

The broad oak stairs were beautifully polished, and so slippery that she had to cling to the rail and let herself down tread by tread. And as she descended, the silence descended with her—heavier, denser, more absolute. She seemed to feel its steps just behind her, softly keeping time with hers, it had a quality she had never been aware of in any other silence, as though it were not merely an absence of sound, a thin barrier between the ear and the surging murmur of life just beyond, but an impenetrable substance made out of the worldwide cessation of all life and all movement.

Yes, that was what laid a chill on her: the feeling that there was no limit to this silence, no outer margin, nothing beyond it. By this time, she had reached the foot of the stairs and was limping across the hall to the drawing room. Whatever she found there, she was sure, would be mute and lifeless; but what would it be? The bodies of her dead servants, mown down by some homicidal maniac? And what if it were her turn next—if he were waiting for her behind the heavy curtains of the room she was about to enter? Well, she must find out—she must face whatever lay in wait. Not impelled by bravery—the last drop of courage had oozed out of her—but because anything, anything was better than to remain shut up in that snowbound house without knowing whether she was alone in it or not, 'I must find that out, I must find that out,' she repeated to herself in a sort of meaningless singsong.

The cold outer light flooded the drawing room. The shutters had not been closed, nor the curtains drawn. She looked about her. The room was empty, and every chair in its usual place. Her armchair was pushed up by the chimney, and the cold hearth was piled with the ashes of the fire at which she had warmed herself before starting on her ill-fated walk. Even her empty coffee cup stood on a table near the armchair. It was evident that the servants had not been in the room since she had left it the day before after luncheon. And suddenly the conviction entered into her that, as she found the drawing room, so she would find the rest of the house; cold, orderly—and empty. She would find nothing; she would find no one. She no longer felt any dread of ordinary human dangers lurking in those dumb spaces ahead of her. She knew she was utterly alone under her own roof. She sat down to rest her aching ankle, and looked slowly about her.

There were the other rooms to be visited, and she was determined to go through them all—but she knew in advance that they would give no answer to her question. She knew it, seemingly, from the quality of the silence which enveloped her. There was no break, no thinnest crack in it anywhere. It had the cold continuity of the snow which was still falling steadily outside.

She had no idea how long she waited before nerving herself to continue her inspection. She no longer felt the pain in her ankle, but was only conscious that she must not bear her weight on it, and therefore moved very slowly, supporting herself on each piece of furniture in her path. On the ground floor no shutter had been closed, no curtain drawn, and she progressed without difficulty from room to room: the library, her morning room, the dining room. In each of them, every piece of furniture was in its usual place. In the dining room, the table had been laid for her dinner of the previous evening, and the candelabra, with candles unlit, stood reflected in the dark mahogany. She was not the kind of woman to nibble a poached egg on a tray when she was alone, but always came down to the dining room, and had what she called a civilised meal.

The back premises remained to be visited. From the dining room she entered the pantry, and there too everything was in irreproachable order. She opened the door and looked down the back passage with its neat linoleum floor covering. The deep silence accompanied her; she still felt it moving watchfully at her side, as though she were its prisoner and it might throw itself upon her if she attempted to escape. She limped on toward the kitchen. That of course would be empty too, and immaculate. But she must see it.

She leaned a minute in the embrasure of a window in the passage. 'It's like the *Mary Celeste*—a *Mary Celeste* on *terra firma,*' she thought, recalling the unsolved sea mystery of her childhood. 'No one ever knew what happened on board the *Mary Celeste.* And perhaps no one will ever know what has happened here. Even I shan't know.'

At the thought her latent fear seemed to take on a new quality. It was like an icy liquid running through every vein, and lying in a pool about her heart. She understood now that she had never before known what fear was, and that most of the people she had met had probably never known either. For this sensation was something quite different...

It absorbed her so completely that she was not aware how long she remained leaning there. But suddenly a new impulse pushed her forward, and she walked on toward the scullery. She went there first because there was a service slide in the wall, through which she might peep into the kitchen without being seen; and some indefinable instinct told her that the kitchen held the clue to the mystery. She still felt strongly that whatever had happened in the house must have its source and centre in the kitchen.

In the scullery, as she had expected, everything was clean and tidy. Whatever had happened, no one in the house appeared to have been taken by surprise; there was nowhere any sign of confusion or disorder. 'It looks as if they'd known beforehand, and put everything straight,' she thought. She glanced at the wall facing the door, and saw that the slide was open. And then, as she was approaching it, the silence was broken. A voice was speaking in the kitchen—a man's voice, low but emphatic, and which she had never heard before.

She stood still, cold with fear. But this fear was again a different one. Her previous terrors had been speculative, conjectural, a ghostly emanation of the surrounding silence. This was a plain everyday dread of evildoers. Oh, God, why had she not remembered her husband's revolver, which ever since his death had lain in a drawer in her room?

She turned to retreat across the smooth slippery floor but halfway her stick slipped from her, and crashed down on the tiles. The noise seemed to echo on and on through the emptiness, and she stood still, aghast. Now that she had betrayed her presence, flight was useless. Whoever was beyond the kitchen door would be upon her in a second...

But to her astonishment the voice went on speaking. It was as though neither the speaker nor his listeners had heard her. The invisible stranger spoke so low that she could not make out what he was saying, but the tone was passionately earnest, almost threatening. The next moment she realised that he was speaking in a foreign language, a language unknown to her. Once more her terror was surmounted by the urgent desire to know what was going on, so close to her yet unseen. She crept to the slide, peered cautiously through into the kitchen, and saw that it was as orderly and empty as the other rooms. But in the middle of the carefully scoured table stood a portable wireless, and the voice she heard came out of it . . . She must have fainted then, she supposed; at any rate she felt so weak and dizzy that her memory of what next happened remained indistinct.

But in the course of time she groped her way back to the pantry, and there found a bottle of spirits—brandy or whisky, she could not remember which. She found a glass, poured herself a stiff drink, and while it was flushing through her veins, managed, she never knew with how many shuddering delays, to drag herself through the deserted ground floor, up the stairs, and down the corridor to her own room. There, apparently, she fell across the threshold, again unconscious . . .

When she came to, she remembered, her first care had been to lock herself in; then to recover her husband's revolver. It was not loaded, but she found some cartridges, and succeeded in loading it. Then she remembered that Agnes, on leaving her the evening before, had refused to carry away the tray with the tea and sandwiches, and she fell on them with a sudden hunger. She recalled also noticing that a flask of brandy had been put beside the thermos, and being vaguely surprised. Agnes's departure, then, had been deliberately planned, and she had known that her mistress, who never touched spirits, might have need of a stimulant before she returned. Mrs Clayburn poured some of the brandy into her tea, and swallowed it greedily-After that (she told me later) she remembered that she had managed to start a fire in her grate, and after warming herself, had got back into her bed, piling on it all the coverings she could find.

The afternoon passed in a haze of pain, out of which there emerged now and then a dim shape of tear—the fear that she might lie there alone and untended till she died of cold, and of the terror of her solitude. For she was sure by this time that the house was empty—completely empty, from garret to cellar. She knew it was so, she could not tell why; but again she felt that it must be because of the peculiar quality of the silence—the silence which had dogged her steps wherever she went, and was now folded down on her like a pall. She was sure that the nearness of any other human being, however dumb and secret, would have made a faint crack in the texture of that silence, flawed it as a sheet of glass is flawed by a pebble thrown against it. . . .

4

'Is that easier?' the doctor asked, lifting himself from bending over her ankle. He shook his head disapprovingly. 'Looks to me as if you'd disobeyed orders—eh? Been moving about, haven't you? And I guess Dr Selgrove told you to keep quiet till he saw you again, didn't he?'

The speaker was a stranger, whom Mrs Clayburn knew only by name. Her own doctor had been called away that morning to the bedside of an old patient in Baltimore, and had asked this young man, who was beginning to be known at Norrington, to replace him. The newcomer was shy, and somewhat familiar, as the shy often are, and Mrs Clayburn decided that she did not much like him. But before she could convey this by the tone of her reply (and she was past mistress of the shades of disapproval) she heard Agnes speaking—yes, Agnes, the same, the usual Agnes, standing behind the doctor, neat and stern-looking as ever. 'Mrs Clayburn must have got up and walked about in the night instead of ringing for me, as she'd ought to,' Agnes intervened severely.

This was too much! In spite of the pain, which was now exquisite, Mrs Clayburn laughed. 'Ringing for you? How could I, with the electricity cut off?'

'The electricity cut off?' Agnes's surprise was masterly. 'Why, when was it cut off?' She pressed her finger on the bell beside the bed, and the call tinkled through the quiet room. 'I tried that bell before I left you last night, madam, because if there'd been anything wrong with it I'd have come and slept in the dressing room sooner than leave you here alone.'

Mrs Clayburn lay speechless, staring up at her. 'Last night? But last night I was all alone in the house.'

Agnes's firm features did not alter. She folded her hands resignedly across her trim apron. 'Perhaps the pain's made you a little confused, madam.' She looked at the doctor, who nodded.

'The pain in your foot must have been pretty bad,' he said.

'It was,' Mrs Clayburn replied. 'But it was nothing to the horror of being left alone in this empty house since the day before yesterday, with the heat and the electricity cut off, and the telephone not working.'

The doctor was looking at her in evident wonder. Agnes's sallow face flushed slightly, but only as if in indignation at an unjust charge. 'But, madam, I made up your fire with my own hands last night—and look, it's smouldering still. I was getting ready to start it again just now, when the doctor came.'

'That's so. She was down on her knees before it,' the doctor corroborated.

Again Mrs Clayburn laughed. Ingeniously as the tissue of lies was being woven about her, she felt she could still break through it. 'I made up the fire myself yesterday—there was no one else to do it,' she said, addressing the doctor, but keeping her eyes on her maid. 'I got up twice to put on more coal, because the house was like a sepulchre. The central heating must have been out since Saturday afternoon.'

At this incredible statement Agnes's face expressed only a polite distress; but the new doctor was evidently embarrassed at being drawn into an unintelligible controversy with which he had no time to deal. He said he had brought the X-ray photographer with him, but that the ankle was too much swollen to be photographed at present. He asked Mrs Clayburn to excuse his haste, as he had all Dr Selgrove's patients to visit besides his own, and promised to come back that evening to decide whether she could be X-rayed then, and whether, as he evidently feared, the ankle would have to be put in plaster. Then, handing his prescriptions to Agnes, he departed.

Mrs Clayburn spent a feverish and suffering day. She did not feel well enough to carry on the discussion with Agnes; she did not ask to see the other servants. She grew drowsy, and understood that her mind was confused with fever. Agnes and the housemaid waited on her as attentively as usual, and by the time the doctor returned in the evening her temperature had fallen; but she decided not to speak of what was on her mind until Dr Selgrove reappeared. He was to be back the following evening; and the new doctor preferred to wait for him before deciding to put the ankle in plaster—though he feared this was now inevitable.

5

That afternoon Mrs Clayburn had me summoned by telephone, and I arrived at Whitegates the following day. My cousin, who looked pale and nervous, merely pointed to her toot, which had been put in plaster, and thanked me for coming to keep her company. She explained that Dr Selgrove had been taken suddenly ill in Baltimore, and would not be back for several days, but that the young man who replaced him seemed fairly competent. She made no allusion to the strange incidents I have set down, but I felt at once that she had received a shock which her accident, however painful, could not explain.

Finally, one evening, she told me the story of her strange weekend, as it had presented itself to her unusually clear and accurate mind, and as I have recorded it above. She did not tell me this till several weeks after my arrival; but she was still upstairs at the time, and obliged to divide her days between her bed and a lounge. During those endless intervening weeks, she told me, she had thought the whole matter over: and though the events of the mysterious thirty-six hours were still vivid to her, they had already lost something of their haunting terror, and she had finally decided not to reopen the question with Agnes, or to touch on it in speaking to the other servants.

Dr Selgrove's illness had been not only serious but prolonged. He had not yet returned, and it was reported that as soon as he was well enough he would go on a West Indian cruise, and not resume his practice at Norrington till the spring. Dr Selgrove, as my cousin was perfectly aware, was the only person who could prove that thirty-six hours had elapsed between his visit and that of his successor; and the latter, a shy young man, burdened by the heavy additional practice suddenly thrown on his shoulders, told me (when I risked a little private talk with him) that in the haste of Dr Selgrove's departure the only instructions he had given about Mrs Clayburn were summed up in the brief memorandum: 'Broken ankle. Have X-rayed.'

Knowing my cousin's authoritative character, I was surprised at her decision not to speak to the servants of what had happened; but on thinking it over I concluded she was right. They were all exactly as they had been before that unexplained episode: efficient, devoted, respectful and respectable. She was dependent on them and felt at home with them, and she evidently preferred to put the whole matter out of her mind, as far as she could. She was absolutely certain that something strange had happened in her house, and I was more than ever convinced that she had received a shock which the accident of a broken ankle was not sufficient to account for; but in the end I agreed that nothing was to be gained by cross-questioning the servants or the new doctor.

I was at Whitegates off and on that winter and during the following summer, and when I went home to New York for good early in October I left my cousin in her old health and spirits. Dr Selgrove had been ordered to Switzerland tor the summer, and this further postponement of his return to his practice seemed to have put the happenings of the strange weekend out of her mind. Her life was going on as peacefully and normally as usual, and I left her without anxiety, and indeed without a thought of the mystery, which was now nearly a year old.

I was living then in a small flat in New York by myself, and I had hardly settled into it when, very late one evening—on the last day of October—I heard my bell ring. As it was my maid's evening out, and I was alone, I went to the door myself, and on the threshold, to my amazement, I saw Sara Clayburn. She was wrapped in a fur cloak, with a hat drawn down over her forehead, and a face so pale and haggard that I saw something dreadful must have happened to her. 'Sara,' I gasped, not knowing what I was saying, 'where in the world have you come from at this hour?'

'From Whitegates. I missed the last train and came by car.' She came in and sat down on the bench near the door. I saw that she could hardly stand, and sat down beside her, putting my arm about her. 'For heaven's sake, tell me what's happened.'

She looked at me without seeming to see me. 'I telephoned to Nixon's and hired a car. It took me five hours and a quarter to get here.' She looked about her. 'Can you take me in for the night? I've left my luggage downstairs.'

'For as many nights as you like. But you look so ill—'

She shook her head. 'No; I'm not ill. I'm only frightened—deathly frightened,' she repeated in a whisper.

Her voice was so strange, and the hands I was pressing between mine were so cold, that I drew her to her feet and led her straight to my little guest room. My flat was in an old-fashioned building, not many storeys high, and I was on more human terms with the staff than is possible in one of the modern Babels. I telephoned down to have my cousin's bags brought up, and meanwhile I filled a hot water bottle, warmed the bed, and got her into it as quickly as I could. I had never seen her as unquestioning and submissive, and that alarmed me even more than her pallor. She was not the woman to let herself be undressed and put to bed like a baby; but she submitted without a word, as though aware that she had reached the end of her tether.

'It's good to be here,' she said in a quieter tone, as I tucked her up and smoothed the pillows. 'Don't leave me yet, will you—not just yet.'

'I'm not going to leave you for more than a minute—just to get you a cup of tea,' I reassured her; and she lay still. I left the door open, so that she could hear me stirring about in the little pantry across the passage, and when I brought her the tea she swallowed it gratefully, and a little colour came into her face. I sat with her in silence for some time; but at last she began: 'You see it's exactly a year—'

I should have preferred to have her put off till the next morning whatever she had to tell me; but I saw from her burning eyes that she was determined to rid her mind of what was burdening it, and that until she had done so it would be useless to proffer the sleeping draft I had ready.

'A year since what?' I asked stupidly, not yet associating her precipitate arrival with the mysterious occurrences of the previous year at Whitegates.

She looked at me in surprise. 'A year since I met that woman. Don't you remember—the strange woman who was coming up the drive the afternoon when I broke my ankle? I didn't think of it at the time, but it was on All Souls' eve that I met her.'

Yes, I said, I remembered that it was.

'Well—and this is All Souls' eve, isn't it? I'm not as good as you are on Church dates, but I thought it was.'

'Yes. This is All Souls' eve.'

'I thought so .... Well, this afternoon I went out for my usual walk. I'd been writing letters, and paying bills, and didn't start till late; not till it was nearly dusk. But it was a lovely clear evening. And as I got near the gate, there was the woman coming in—the same woman ... going toward the house ... '

I pressed my cousin's hand, which was hot and feverish now. 'If it was dusk, could you be perfectly sure it was the same woman?' I asked.

'Oh, perfectly sure, the evening was so clear. I knew her and she knew me; and I could see she was angry at meeting me. I stopped her and asked: "Where are you going?" just as I had asked her last year. And she said, in the same queer half-foreign voice: "Only to see one of the girls", as she had before. Then I felt angry all of a sudden, and I said: "You shan't set foot in my house again. Do you hear me? I order you to leave." And she laughed; yes, she laughed—very low, but distinctly. By that time, it had got quite dark, as if a sudden storm was sweeping up over the sky, so that though she was so near me I could hardly see her.

'We were standing by the clump of hemlocks at the turn of the drive, and as I went up to her, furious at her impertinence, she passed behind the hemlocks, and when I followed her she wasn't there ... No; I swear to you she wasn't there ... And in the darkness I hurried back to the house, afraid that she would slip by me and get there first. And the queer thing was that as I reached the door the black cloud vanished, and there was the transparent twilight again. In the house everything seemed as usual, and the servants were busy about their work; but I couldn't get it out of my head that the woman, under the shadow of that cloud, had somehow got there before me.' She paused for breath, and began again. 'In the hall I stopped at the telephone and rang up Nixon, and told him to send me a car at once to go to New York, with a man he knew to drive me. And Nixon came with the car himself...'

Her head sank back on the pillow and she looked at me like a frightened child. 'It was good of Nixon,' she said.

'Yes; it was very good of him. But when they saw you leaving—the servants, I mean ...'

'Yes. Well, when I got upstairs to my room I rang for Agnes. She came, looking just as cool and quiet as usual. And when I told her I was starting for New York in half an hour—I said it was on account of a sudden business call—well, then her presence of mind failed her for the first time. She forgot to look surprised, she even forgot to make an objection—and you know what an objector Agnes is. And as I watched her I could see a little secret spark of relief in her eyes, though she was so on her guard. And she just said: "Very well, madam," and asked me what I wanted to take with me. Just as if I were in the habit of dashing off to New York after dark on an autumn night to meet a business engagement! No, she made a mistake not to show any surprise—and not even to ask me why I didn't take my own car. And her losing her head in that way frightened me more than anything else. For I saw she was so thankful I was going that she hardly dared speak, for fear she should betray herself, or I should change my mind.'

After that Mrs Clayburn lay a long while silent, breathing less unrestfully; and at last she closed her eyes, as though she felt more at ease now that she had spoken, and wanted to sleep. As I got up quietly to leave her, she turned her head a little and murmured: 'I shall never go back to Whitegates again.' Then she shut her eyes and I saw that she was falling asleep.

I have set down above, I hope without omitting anything essential, the record of my cousin's strange experience as she told it to me. Of what happened at Whitegates that is all I can personally vouch for. The rest-and of course there is a rest—is sure conjecture; and I give it only as such.

My cousin's maid, Agnes, was from the Isle of Skye, and the Hebrides, as everyone knows, are full of the supernatural—whether in the shape of ghostly presences, or the almost ghostlier sense of unseen watchers peopling the long nights of those stormy solitudes. My cousin, at any rate, always regarded Agnes as the—perhaps unconscious, at any rate irresponsible—channel through which communications from the other side of the veil reached the submissive household at Whitegates. Though Agnes had been with Mrs Clayburn for a long time without any peculiar incident revealing this affinity with the unknown forces, the power to communicate with them may all the while have been latent in the woman, only awaiting a kindred touch; and that touch may have been given by the unknown visitor whom my cousin, two years in succession, had met coming up the drive at Whitegates on the eve of All Souls'. Certainly the date bears out my hypothesis; for I suppose that, even in this unimaginative age, a few people still remember that All Souls' eve is the night when the dead can walk—and when, by the same token, other spirits, piteous or malevolent, are also freed from the restrictions which secure the earth to the living on the other days of the year.

If the recurrence of this date is more than a coincidence—and for my part I think it is—then I take it that the strange woman who twice came up the drive at Whitegates on All Souls' eve was either a 'fetch', or else, more probably and more alarmingly, a living woman inhabited by a witch. The history of witchcraft, as is well known, abounds in such cases, and such a messenger might well have been delegated by the powers who rule in these matters to summon Agnes and her fellow servants to a midnight 'Coven' in some neighbouring-solitude. To learn what happens at covens, and the reason of the irresistible fascination they exercise over the timorous and superstitious, one need only address oneself to the immense body of literature dealing with these mysterious rites. Anyone who has once felt the faintest curiosity to assist at a coven apparently soon finds the curiosity increase to desire, the desire to an uncontrollable longing, which, when the opportunity presents itself, breaks down ail inhibitions; for those who have once taken part in a coven will move heaven and earth to take part again.

Such is my—conjectural—explanation of the strange happenings at Whitegates. My cousin always said she could not believe that incidents which might fit into the desolate landscape of the Hebrides could occur in the cheerful and populous Connecticut Valley; but if she did not believe, she at least feared—such moral paradoxes are not uncommon—and though she insisted that there must be some natural explanation of the mystery, she never returned to investigate it.

'No, no,' she said with a little shiver, whenever I touched on the subject of her going back to Whitegates, 'I don't want ever to risk seeing that woman again . . .' And she never went back.

The Angel at the Grave

1

The House stood a few yards back from the elm-shaded village street, in that semi-publicity sometimes cited as a democratic protest against old-world standards of domestic exclusiveness. This candid exposure to the public eye is more probably a result of the gregariousness which, in the New England bosom, oddly coexists with a shrinking from direct social contact; most of the inmates of such houses preferring that furtive intercourse which is the result of observations through shuttered windows and a categorical acquaintance with the neighbouring clotheslines.

The House, however, faced its public with a difference. For sixty years it had written itself with a capital letter, had self-consciously squared itself in the eye of an admiring nation. The most searching inroads of village intimacy hardly counted in a household that opened on the universe; and a lady whose door-bell was at any moment liable to be rung by visitors from London or Vienna was not likely to flutter upstairs when she observed a neighbor "stepping over."

The solitary inmate of the Anson House owed this induration of the social texture to the most conspicuous accident in her annals: the fact that she was the only granddaughter of the great Orestes Anson. She had been born, as it were, into a museum, and cradled in a glass case with a label; the first foundations of her consciousness being built on the rock of her grandfather's celebrity. To a little girl who acquires her earliest knowledge of literature through a *Reader* embellished with fragments of her ancestor's prose, that personage necessarily fills an heroic space in the foreground of life.

To communicate with one's past through the impressive medium of print, to have, as it were, a footing in every library in the country, and an acknowledged kinship with that world-diffused clan, the descendants of the great, was to be pledged to a standard of manners that amazingly simplified the lesser relations of life. The village street on which Paulina Anson's youth looked out led to all the capitals of Europe; and over the roads of intercommunication unseen caravans bore back to the elm-shaded House the tribute of an admiring world.

Fate seemed to have taken a direct share in fitting Paulina for her part as the custodian of this historic dwelling. It had long been secretly regarded as a "visitation" by the great man's family that he had left no son and that his daughters were not "intellectual." The ladies themselves were the first to lament their deficiency, to own that nature had denied them the gift of making the most of their opportunities. A profound veneration for their parent and an unswerving faith in his doctrines had not amended their congenital incapacity to understand what he had written.

Laura, who had her moments of mute rebellion against destiny, had sometimes thought how much easier it would have been if their progenitor had been a poet; for she could recite, with feeling, portions of *The Culprit Fay* and of the poems of Mrs. Hemans; and Phoebe, who was more conspicuous for memory than imagination, kept an album filled with "selections." But the great man was a philosopher; and to both daughters respiration was difficult on the cloudy heights of metaphysic. The situation would have been intolerable but for the fact that, while Phoebe and Laura were still at school, their father's fame had passed from the open ground of conjecture to the chill privacy of certitude. Dr. Anson had in fact achieved one of those anticipated immortalities not uncommon at a time when people were apt to base their literary judgments on their emotions, and when to affect plain food and despise England went a long way toward establishing a man's intellectual pre-eminence.

Thus, when the daughters were called on to strike a filial attitude about their parent's pedestal, there was little to do but to pose gracefully and point upward; and there are spines to which the immobility of worship is not a strain. A legend had by this time crystallized about the great Orestes, and it was of more immediate interest to the public to hear what brand of tea he drank, and whether he took off his boots in the hall, than to rouse the drowsy echo of his dialectic. A great man never draws so near his public as when it has become unnecessary to read his books and is still interesting to know what he eats for breakfast.

As recorders of their parent's domestic habits, as pious scavengers of his waste-paper basket, the Misses Anson were unexcelled. They always had an interesting anecdote to impart to the literary pilgrim, and the tact with which, in later years, they intervened between the public and the growing inaccessibility of its idol, sent away many an enthusiast satisfied to have touched the veil before the sanctuary. Still it was felt, especially by old Mrs. Anson, who survived her husband for some years, that Phoebe and Laura were not worthy of their privileges.

There had been a third daughter so unworthy of hers that she had married a distant cousin, who had taken her to live in a new Western community where the *Works of Orestes Anson* had not yet become a part of the civic consciousness; but of this daughter little was said, and she was tacitly understood to be excluded from the family heritage of fame. In time, however, it appeared that the traditional penny with which she had been cut off had been invested to unexpected advantage; and the interest on it, when she died, returned to the Anson House in the shape of a granddaughter who was at once felt to be what Mrs. Anson called a "compensation." It was Mrs. Anson's firm belief that the remotest operations of nature were governed by the centripetal force of her husband's greatness and that Paulina's exceptional intelligence could be explained only on the ground that she was designed to act as the guardian of the family temple.

The House, by the time Paulina came to live in it, had already acquired the publicity of a place of worship; not the perfumed chapel of a romantic idolatry but the cold clean empty meeting-house of ethical enthusiasms. The ladies lived on its outskirts, as it were, in cells that left the central fane undisturbed. The very position of the furniture had come to have a ritual significance: the sparse ornaments were the offerings of kindred intellects, the steel engravings by Raphael Morghen marked the Via Sacra of a European tour, and the black-walnut desk with its bronze inkstand modelled on the Pantheon was the altar of this bleak temple of thought.

To a child compact of enthusiasms, and accustomed to pasture them on the scanty herbage of a new social soil, the atmosphere of the old house was full of floating nourishment. In the compressed perspective of Paulina's outlook it stood for a monument of ruined civilizations, and its white portico opened on legendary distances. Its very aspect was impressive to eyes that had first surveyed life from the jig-saw "residence" of a raw-edged Western town. The high-ceilinged rooms, with their panelled walls, their polished mahogany, their portraits of triple-stocked ancestors and of ringleted "females" in crayon, furnished the child with the historic scenery against which a young imagination constructs its vision of the past. To other eyes the cold spotless thinly-furnished interior might have suggested the shuttered mind of a maiden-lady who associates fresh air and sunlight with dust and discoloration; but it is the eye which supplies the colouring-matter, and Paulina's brimmed with the richest hues.

Nevertheless, the House did not immediately dominate her. She had her confused out-reachings toward other centres of sensation, her vague intuition of a heliocentric system; but the attraction of habit, the steady pressure of example, gradually fixed her roving allegiance and she bent her neck to the yoke. Vanity had a share in her subjugation; for it had early been discovered that she was the only person in the family who could read her grandfather's works. The fact that she had perused them with delight at an age when (even presupposing a metaphysical bias) it was impossible for her to understand them, seemed to her aunts and grandmother sure evidence of predestination. Paulina was to be the interpreter of the oracle, and the philosophic fumes so vertiginous to meaner minds would throw her into the needed condition of clairvoyance.

Nothing could have been more genuine than the emotion on which this theory was based. Paulina, in fact, delighted in her grandfather's writings. His sonorous periods, his mystic vocabulary, his bold flights into the rarefied air of the abstract, were thrilling to a fancy unhampered by the need of definitions. This purely verbal pleasure was supplemented later by the excitement of gathering up crumbs of meaning from the rhetorical board. What could have been more stimulating than to construct the theory of a girlish world out of the fragments of this Titanic cosmogony? Before Paulina's opinions had reached the stage when ossification sets in their form was fatally predetermined.

The fact that Dr. Anson had died and that his apotheosis had taken place before his young priestess's induction to the temple, made her ministrations easier and more inspiring. There were no little personal traits—such as the great man's manner of helping himself to salt, or the guttural cluck that started the wheels of speech—to distract the eye of young veneration from the central fact of his divinity. A man whom one knows only through a crayon portrait and a dozen yellowing, tomes on free-will and intuition is at least secure from the belittling effects of intimacy.

Paulina thus grew up in a world readjusted to the fact of her grandfather's greatness; and as each organism draws from its surroundings the kind of nourishment most needful to its growth, so from this somewhat colorless conception she absorbed warmth, brightness and variety. Paulina was the type of woman who transmutes thought into sensation and nurses a theory in her bosom like a child.

In due course Mrs. Anson "passed away"—no one died in the Anson vocabulary—and Paulina became more than ever the foremost figure of the commemorative group. Laura and Phoebe, content to leave their father's glory in more competent hands, placidly lapsed into needlework and fiction, and their niece stepped into immediate prominence as the chief "authority" on the great man. Historians who were "getting up" the period wrote to consult her and to borrow documents; ladies with inexplicable yearnings begged for an interpretation of phrases which had "influenced" them, but which they had not quite understood; critics applied to her to verify some doubtful citation or to decide some disputed point in chronology; and the great tide of thought and investigation kept up a continuous murmur on the quiet shores of her life.

An explorer of another kind disembarked there one day in the shape of a young man to whom Paulina was primarily a kissable girl, with an after-thought in the shape of a grandfather. From the outset it had been impossible to fix Hewlett Winsloe's attention on Dr. Anson. The young man behaved with the innocent profanity of infants sporting on a tomb. His excuse was that he came from New York, a Cimmerian outskirt which survived in Paulina's geography only because Dr. Anson had gone there once or twice to lecture. The curious thing was that she should have thought it worthwhile to find excuses for young Winsloe.

The fact that she did so had not escaped the attention of the village; but people, after a gasp of awe, said it was the most natural thing in the world that a girl like Paulina Anson should think of marrying. It would certainly seem a little odd to see a man in the House, but young Winsloe would of course understand that the doctor's books were not to be disturbed, and that he must go down to the orchard to smoke—. The village had barely framed this *modus vivendi* when it was convulsed by the announcement that young Winsloe declined to live in the House on any terms. Hang going down to the orchard to smoke! He meant to take his wife to New York. The village drew its breath and watched.

Did Persephone, snatched from the warm fields of Enna, peer

half-consentingly down the abyss that opened at her feet? Paulina, it must be owned, hung a moment over the black gulf of temptation. She would have found it easy to cope with a deliberate disregard of her grandfather's rights; but young Winsloe's unconsciousness of that shadowy claim was as much a natural function as the falling of leaves on a grave. His love was an embodiment of the perpetual renewal which to some tender spirits seems a crueller process than decay.

On women of Paulina's mould this piety toward implicit demands, toward the ghosts of dead duties walking unappeased among usurping passions, has a stronger hold than any tangible bond. People said that she gave up young Winsloe because her aunts disapproved of her leaving them; but such disapproval as reached her was an emanation from the walls of the House, from the bare desk, the faded portraits, the dozen yellowing tomes that no hand but hers ever lifted from the shelf.

2

After that the House possessed her. As if conscious of its victory, it imposed a conqueror's claims. It had once been suggested that she should write a life of her grandfather, and the task from which she had shrunk as from a too-oppressive privilege now shaped itself into a justification of her course. In a burst of filial pantheism she tried to lose herself in the vast ancestral consciousness. Her one refuge from scepticism was a blind faith in the magnitude and the endurance of the idea to which she had sacrificed her life, and with a passionate instinct of self-preservation she laboured to fortify her position.

The preparations for the *Life* led her through by-ways that the most scrupulous of the previous biographers had left unexplored. She accumulated her material with a blind animal patience unconscious of fortuitous risks. The years stretched before her like some vast blank page spread out to receive the record of her toil; and she had a mystic conviction that she would not die till her work was accomplished.

The aunts, sustained by no such high purpose, withdrew in turn to their respective divisions of the Anson "plot," and Paulina remained alone with her task. She was forty when the book was completed. She had travelled little in her life, and it had become more and more difficult to her to leave the House even for a day; but the dread of entrusting her document to a strange hand made her decide to carry it herself to the publisher. On the way to Boston she had a sudden vision of the loneliness to which this last parting condemned her. All her youth, all her dreams, all her renunciations lay in that neat bundle on her knee. It was not so much her grandfather's life as her own that she had written; and the knowledge that it would come back to her in all the glorification of print was of no more help than, to a mother's grief, the assurance that the lad she must part with will return with epaulets.

She had naturally addressed herself to the firm which had published her grandfather's works. Its founder, a personal friend of the philosopher's, had survived the Olympian group of which he had been a subordinate member, long enough to bestow his octogenarian approval on Paulina's pious undertaking. But he had died soon afterward; and Miss Anson found herself confronted by his grandson, a person with a brisk commercial view of his trade, who was said to have put "new blood" into the firm.

This gentleman listened attentively, fingering her manuscript as though literature were a tactile substance; then, with a confidential twist of his revolving chair, he emitted the verdict: "We ought to have had this ten years sooner."

Miss Anson took the words as an allusion to the repressed avidity of her readers. "It has been a long time for the public to wait," she solemnly assented.

The publisher smiled. "They haven't waited," he said.

She looked at him strangely. "Haven't waited?"

"No—they've gone off; taken another train. Literature's like a big railway-station now, you know: there's a train starting every minute. People are not going to hang round the waiting-room. If they can't get to a place when they want to they go somewhere else."

The application of this parable cost Miss Anson several minutes of throbbing silence. At length she said: "Then I am to understand that the public is no longer interested in—in my grandfather?" She felt as though heaven must blast the lips that risked such a conjecture.

"Well, it's this way. He's a name still, of course. People don't exactly want to be caught not knowing who he is; but they don't want to spend two dollars finding out, when they can look him up for nothing in any biographical dictionary."

Miss Anson's world reeled. She felt herself adrift among mysterious forces, and no more thought of prolonging the discussion than of opposing an earthquake with argument. She went home carrying the manuscript like a wounded thing. On the return journey she found herself travelling straight toward a fact that had lurked for months in the background of her life, and that now seemed to await her on the very threshold: the fact that fewer visitors came to the House. She owned to herself that for the last four or five years the number had steadily diminished. Engrossed in her work, she had noted the change only to feel thankful that she had fewer interruptions. There had been a time when, at the travelling season, the bell rang continuously, and the ladies of the House lived in a chronic state of "best silks" and expectancy. It would have been impossible then to carry on any consecutive work; and she now saw that the silence which had gathered round her task had been the hush of death.

Not of *his* death! The very walls cried out against the implication. It was the world's enthusiasm, the world's faith, the world's loyalty that had died. A corrupt generation that had turned aside to worship the brazen serpent. Her heart yearned with a prophetic passion over the lost sheep straying in the wilderness. But all great glories had their interlunar period; and in due time her grandfather would once more flash full-orbed upon a darkling world.

The few friends to whom she confided her adventure reminded her with tender indignation that there were other publishers less subject to the fluctuations of the market; but much as she had braved for her grandfather she could not again brave that particular probation. She found herself, in fact, incapable of any immediate effort. She had lost her way in a labyrinth of conjecture where her worst dread was that she might put her hand upon the clue.

She locked up the manuscript and sat down to wait. If a pilgrim had come just then the priestess would have fallen on his neck; but she continued to celebrate her rites alone. It was a double solitude; for she had always thought a great deal more of the people who came to see the House than of the people who came to see her. She fancied that the neighbours kept a keen eye on the path to the House; and there were days when the figure of a stranger strolling past the gate seemed to focus upon her the scorching sympathies of the village. For a time she thought of travelling; of going to Europe, or even to Boston; but to leave the House now would have seemed like deserting her post.

Gradually her scattered energies centred themselves in the fierce resolve to understand what had happened. She was not the woman to live long in an unmapped country or to accept as final her private interpretation of phenomena. Like a traveller in unfamiliar regions she began to store for future guidance the minutest natural signs. Unflinchingly she noted the accumulating symptoms of indifference that marked her grandfather's descent toward posterity. She passed from the heights on which he had been grouped with the sages of his day to the lower level where he had come to be "the friend of Emerson," "the correspondent of Hawthorne," or (later still) "the Dr. Anson" mentioned in their letters. The change had taken place as slowly and imperceptibly as a natural process. She could not say that any ruthless hand had stripped the leaves from the tree: it was simply that, among the evergreen glories of his group, her grandfather's had proved deciduous.

She had still to ask herself why. If the decay had been a natural process, was it not the very pledge of renewal? It was easier to find such arguments than to be convinced by them. Again and again she tried to drug her solicitude with analogies; but at last she saw that such expedients were but the expression of a growing incredulity. The best way of proving her faith in her grandfather was not to be afraid of his critics. She had no notion where these shadowy antagonists lurked; for she had never heard of the great man's doctrine being directly combated. Oblique assaults there must have been, however, Parthian shots at the giant that none dared face; and she thirsted to close with such assailants. The difficulty was to find them.

She began by re-reading the *Works*; thence she passed to the writers of the same school, those whose rhetoric bloomed perennial in *First Readers* from which her grandfather's prose had long since faded. Amid that clamour of far-off enthusiasms she detected no controversial note. The little knot of Olympians held their views in common with an early-Christian promiscuity. They were continually proclaiming their admiration for each other, the public joining as chorus in this guileless antiphon of praise; and she discovered no traitor in their midst.

What then had happened? Was it simply that the main current of thought had set another way? Then why did the others survive? Why were they still marked down as tributaries to the philosophic stream? This question carried her still farther afield, and she pressed on with the passion of a champion whose reluctance to know the worst might be construed into a doubt of his cause. At length—slowly but inevitably—an explanation shaped itself. Death had overtaken the doctrines about which her grandfather had draped his cloudy rhetoric. They had disintegrated and been re-absorbed, adding their little pile to the dust drifted about the mute lips of the Sphinx. The great man's contemporaries had survived not by reason of what they taught, but of what they were; and he, who had been the mere mask through which they mouthed their lesson, the instrument on which their tune was played, lay buried deep among the obsolete tools of thought.

The discovery came to Paulina suddenly. She looked up one evening from her reading and it stood before her like a ghost. It had entered her life with stealthy steps, creeping close before she was aware of it. She sat in the library, among the carefully-tended books and portraits; and it seemed to her that she had been walled alive into a tomb hung with the effigies of dead ideas. She felt a desperate longing to escape into the outer air, where people toiled and loved, and living sympathies went hand in hand. It was the sense of wasted labour that oppressed her; of two lives consumed in that ruthless process that uses generations of effort to build a single cell. There was a dreary parallel between her grandfather's fruitless toil and her own unprofitable sacrifice. Each in turn had kept vigil by a corpse.

3

The bell rang—she remembered it afterward—with a loud thrilling note. It was what they used to call the "visitor's ring"; not the tentative tinkle of a neighbour dropping in to borrow a sauce-pan or discuss parochial incidents, but a decisive summons from the outer world.

Miss Anson put down her knitting and listened. She sat upstairs now, making her rheumatism an excuse for avoiding the rooms below. Her interests had insensibly adjusted themselves to the perspective of her neighbours' lives, and she wondered—as the bell re-echoed—if it could mean that Mrs. Heminway's baby had come. Conjecture had time to ripen into certainty, and she was limping toward the closet where her cloak and bonnet hung, when her little maid fluttered in with the announcement: "A gentleman to see the house."

"The *House*?"

"Yes, m'm. I don't know what he means," faltered the messenger, whose memory did not embrace the period when such announcements were a daily part of the domestic routine.

Miss Anson glanced at the proffered card. The name it bore—*Mr. George Corby*—was unknown to her, but the blood rose to her languid cheek. "Hand me my Mechlin cap, Katy," she said, trembling a little, as she laid aside her walking stick. She put her cap on before the mirror, with rapid unsteady touches. "Did you draw up the library blinds?" she breathlessly asked.

She had gradually built up a wall of commonplace between herself and her illusions, but at the first summons of the past filial passion swept away the frail barriers of expediency.

She walked downstairs so hurriedly that her stick clicked like a girlish heel; but in the hall she paused, wondering nervously if Katy had put a match to the fire. The autumn air was cold and she had the reproachful vision of a visitor with elderly ailments shivering by her inhospitable hearth. She thought instinctively of the stranger as a survivor of the days when such a visit was a part of the young enthusiast's itinerary.

The fire was unlit and the room forbiddingly cold; but the figure which, as Miss Anson entered, turned from a lingering scrutiny of the book-shelves, was that of a fresh-eyed sanguine youth clearly independent of any artificial caloric. She stood still a moment, feeling herself the victim of some anterior impression that made this robust presence an insubstantial thing; but the young man advanced with an air of genial assurance which rendered him at once more real and more reminiscent.

"Why this, you know," he exclaimed, "is simply immense!"

The words, which did not immediately present themselves as slang to Miss Anson's unaccustomed ear, echoed with an odd familiarity through the academic silence.

"The room, you know, I mean," he explained with a comprehensive gesture. "These jolly portraits, and the books—that's the old gentleman himself over the mantelpiece, I suppose?—and the elms outside, and—and the whole business. I do like a congruous background—don't you?"

His hostess was silent. No one but Hewlett Winsloe had ever spoken of her grandfather as "the old gentleman."

"It's a hundred times better than I could have hoped," her visitor continued, with a cheerful disregard of her silence. "The seclusion, the remoteness, the philosophic atmosphere—there's so little of that kind of flavour left! I should have simply hated to find that he lived over a grocery, you know.—I had the deuce of a time finding out where he *did* live," he began again, after another glance of parenthetical enjoyment. "But finally I got on the trail through some old book on Brook Farm. I was bound I'd get the environment right before I did my article."

Miss Anson, by this time, had recovered sufficient self-possession to seat herself and assign a chair to her visitor.

"Do I understand," she asked slowly, following his rapid eye about the room, "that you intend to write an article about my grandfather?"

"That's what I'm here for," Mr. Corby genially responded; "that is, if you're willing to help me; for I can't get on without your help," he added with a confident smile.

There was another pause, during which Miss Anson noticed a fleck of dust on the faded leather of the writing-table and a fresh spot of discoloration in the right-hand upper corner of Raphael Morghen's "Parnassus."

"Then you believe in him?" she said, looking up. She could not tell what had prompted her; the words rushed out irresistibly.

"Believe in him?" Corby cried, springing to his feet. "Believe in Orestes Anson? Why, I believe he's simply the greatest—the most stupendous—the most phenomenal figure we've got!"

The colour rose to Miss Anson's brow. Her heart was beating passionately. She kept her eyes fixed on the young man's face, as though it might vanish if she looked away.

"You—you mean to say this in your article?" she asked.

"Say it? Why, the facts will say it," he exulted. "The baldest kind of a statement would make it clear. When a man is as big as that he doesn't need a pedestal!"

Miss Anson sighed. "People used to say that when I was young," she murmured. "But now—"

Her visitor stared. "When you were young? But how did they know—when the thing hung fire as it did? When the whole edition was thrown back on his hands?"

"The whole edition—what edition?" It was Miss Anson's turn to stare.

"Why, of his pamphlet—*the* pamphlet—the one thing that counts, that survives, that makes him what he is! For heaven's sake," he tragically adjured her, "don't tell me there isn't a copy of it left!"

Miss Anson was trembling slightly. "I don't think I understand what you mean," she faltered, less bewildered by his vehemence than by the strange sense of coming on an unexplored region in the very heart of her dominion.

"Why, his account of the *amphioxus*, of course! You can't mean that his family didn't know about it—that *you* don't know about it? I came across it by the merest accident myself, in a letter of vindication that he wrote in 1830 to an old scientific paper; but I understood there were journals—early journals; there must be references to it somewhere in the 'twenties. He must have been at least ten or twelve years ahead of

Yarrell; and he saw the whole significance of it, too—he saw where it led to. As I understand it, he actually anticipated in his pamphlet Saint Hilaire's theory of the universal type, and supported the hypothesis by describing the notochord of the *amphioxus* as a cartilaginous vertebral column. The specialists of the day jeered at him, of course, as the specialists in Goethe's time jeered at the plant-metamorphosis. As far as I can make out, the anatomists and zoologists were down on Dr. Anson to a man; that was why his cowardly publishers went back on their bargain. But the pamphlet must be here somewhere—he writes as though, in his first disappointment, he had destroyed the whole edition; but surely there must be at least one copy left?"

His scientific jargon was as bewildering as his slang; and there were even moments in his discourse when Miss Anson ceased to distinguish between them; but the suspense with which he continued to gaze on her acted as a challenge to her scattered thoughts.

"The *amphioxus*," she murmured, half-rising. "It's an animal, isn't it—a fish? Yes, I think I remember." She sank back with the inward look of one who retraces some lost line of association.

Gradually the distance cleared, the details started into life. In her researches for the biography she had patiently followed every ramification of her subject, and one of these overgrown paths now led her back to the episode in question. The great Orestes's title of "Doctor" had in fact not been merely the spontaneous tribute of a national admiration; he had actually studied medicine in his youth, and his diaries, as his granddaughter now recalled, showed that he had passed through a brief phase of anatomical ardour before his attention was diverted to super-sensual problems.

It had indeed seemed to Paulina, as she scanned those early pages, that they revealed a spontaneity, a freshness of feeling somehow absent from his later lucubrations—as though this one emotion had reached him directly, the others through some intervening medium. In the excess of her commemorative zeal she had even struggled through the unintelligible pamphlet to which a few lines in the journal had bitterly directed her. But the subject and the phraseology were alien to her and unconnected with her conception of the great man's genius; and after a hurried perusal she had averted her thoughts from the episode as from a revelation of failure.

At length she rose a little unsteadily, supporting herself against the writing-table. She looked hesitatingly about the room; then she drew a key from her old-fashioned reticule and unlocked a drawer beneath one of the book-cases. Young Corby watched her breathlessly. With a tremulous hand she turned over the dusty documents that seemed to fill the drawer. "Is this it?" she said, holding out a thin discoloured volume.

He seized it with a gasp. "Oh, by George," he said, dropping into the nearest chair.

She stood observing him strangely as his eye devoured the mouldy pages.

"Is this the only copy left?" he asked at length, looking up for a moment as a thirsty man lifts his head from his glass.

"I think it must be. I found it long ago, among some old papers that my aunts were burning up after my grandmother's death. They said it was of no use—that he'd always meant to destroy the whole edition and that I ought to respect his wishes. But it was something he had written; to burn it was like shutting the door against his voice—against something he had once wished to say, and that nobody had listened to. I wanted him to feel that I was always here, ready to listen, even when others hadn't thought it worthwhile; and so I kept the pamphlet, meaning to carry out his wish and destroy it before my death."

Her visitor gave a groan of retrospective anguish. "And but for me—but for today—you would have?"

"I should have thought it my duty."

"Oh, by George—by George," he repeated, subdued afresh by the inadequacy of speech.

She continued to watch him in silence. At length he jumped up and impulsively caught her by both hands.

"He's bigger and bigger!" he almost shouted. "He simply leads the field! You'll help me go to the bottom of this, won't you? We must turn out all the papers—letters, journals, memoranda. He must have made notes. He must have left some record of what led up to this. We must leave nothing unexplored. By Jove," he cried, looking up at her with his bright convincing smile, "do you know you're the granddaughter of a Great Man?"

Her colour flickered like a girl's. "Are you—sure of him?" she whispered, as though putting him on his guard against a possible betrayal of trust.

"Sure! Sure! My dear lady—" he measured her again with his quick confident glance. "Don't *you* believe in him?"

She drew back with a confused murmur. "I— used to." She had left her hands in his: their pressure seemed to send a warm current to her heart. "It ruined my life!" she cried with sudden passion. He looked at her perplexedly.

"I gave up everything," she went on wildly, "to keep him alive. I sacrificed myself—others—I nursed his glory in my bosom and it died—and left me—left me here alone." She paused and gathered her courage with a gasp. "Don't make the same mistake!" she warned him.

He shook his head, still smiling. "No danger of that! You're not alone, my dear lady. He's here with you—he's come back to you to-day. Don't you see what's happened? Don't you see that it's your love that has kept him alive? If you'd abandoned your post for an instant—let things pass into other hands—if your wonderful tenderness hadn't perpetually kept guard—this might have been—must have been—irretrievably lost." He laid his hand on the pamphlet. "And then—then he *would* have been dead!"

"Oh," she said, "don't tell me too suddenly!" And she turned away and sank into a chair.

The young man stood watching her in an awed silence. For a long time she sat motionless, with her face hidden, and he thought she must be weeping.

At length he said, almost shyly: "You'll let me come back, then? You'll help me work this thing out?"

She rose calmly and held out her hand. "I'll help you," she declared.

"I'll come tomorrow, then. Can we get to work early?"

"As early as you please."

"At eight o'clock, then," he said briskly. "You'll have the papers ready?"

"I'll have everything ready." She added with a half-playful hesitancy: "And the fire shall be lit for you."

He went out with his bright nod. She walked to the window and watched his buoyant figure hastening down the elm-shaded street. When she turned back into the empty room she looked as though youth had touched her on the lips.

Mr. Jones

1.

Lady Jane Lynke was unlike other people: when she heard that she had inherited Bells, the beautiful old place which had belonged to the Lynkes of Thudeney for something like six hundred years, the fancy took her to go and see it unannounced. She was staying at a friend's nearby, in Kent, and the next morning she borrowed a motor and slipped away alone to Thudeney-Blazes, the adjacent village.

It was a lustrous motionless day. Autumn bloom lay on the Sussex downs, on the heavy trees of the weald, on streams moving indolently, far off across the marshes. Farther still, Dungeness, a fitful streak, floated on an immaterial sky which was perhaps, after all, only sky.

In the softness Thudeney-Blazes slept: a few aged houses bowed about a duck-pond, a silvery spire, orchards thick with dew. Did Thudeney-Blazes ever wake?

Lady Jane left the motor to the care of the geese on a miniature common, pushed open a white gate into a field (the griffoned portals being padlocked), and struck across the park toward a group of carved chimney-stacks. No one seemed aware of her.

In a dip of the land, the long low house, its ripe brick masonry overhanging a moat deeply sunk about its roots, resembled an aged cedar spreading immemorial red branches. Lady Jane held her breath and gazed.

A silence distilled from years of solitude lay on lawns and gardens. No one had lived at Bells since the last Lord Thudeney, then a penniless younger son, had forsaken it sixty years before to seek his fortune in Canada. And before that, he and his widowed mother, distant poor relations, were housed in one of the lodges, and the great place, even in their day, had been as mute and solitary as the family vault.

Lady Jane, daughter of another branch, to which an earldom and considerable possessions had accrued, had never seen Bells, hardly heard its name. A succession of deaths, and the whim of an old man she had never known, now made her heir to all this beauty; and as she stood and looked she was glad she had come to it from so far, from impressions so remote and different. "It would be dreadful to be used to it—to be thinking already about the state of the roof, or the cost of a heating system."

Till this her thirty-fifth year, Lady Jane had led an active, independent and decided life. One of several daughters, moderately but sufficiently provided for, she had gone early from home, lived in London lodgings, travelled in tropic lands, spent studious summers in Spain and Italy, and written two or three brisk business-like little books about cities usually dealt with sentimentally. And now, just back from a summer in the south of France, she stood ankle deep in wet bracken, and gazed at Bells lying there under a September sun that looked like moonlight.

"I shall never leave it!" she ejaculated, her heart swelling as if she had taken the vow to a lover.

She ran down the last slope of the park and entered the faded formality of gardens with clipped yews as ornate as architecture, and holly hedges as solid as walls. Adjoining the house rose a low deep-buttressed chapel. Its door was ajar, and she thought this of good augury: her forebears were waiting for her. In the porch she remarked fly-blown notices of services, an umbrella stand, a dishevelled doormat: no doubt the chapel served as the village church. The thought gave her a sense of warmth and neighbourliness.

Across the damp flags of the chancel, monuments and brasses showed through a traceried screen. She examined them curiously. Some hailed her with vocal memories, others whispered out of the remote and the unknown: it was a shame to know so little about her own family. But neither Crofts nor Lynkes had ever greatly distinguished themselves; they had gathered substance simply by holding on to what they had, and slowly accumulating privileges and acres. "Mostly by clever marriages," Lady Jane thought with a faint contempt.

At that moment her eyes lit on one of the less ornate monuments: a plain sarcophagus of gray marble niched in the wall and surmounted by the bust of a young man with a fine arrogant head, a Byronic throat and tossed-back curls.

"Peregrine Vincent Theobald Lynke, Baron Clouds, fifteenth Viscount Thudeney of Bells, Lord of the Manors of Thudeney, Thudeney-Blazes, Upper Lynke, Lynke-Linnet—" so it ran, with the usual tedious enumeration of honours, titles, court and county offices, ending with; "Born on May 1st, 1790, perished of the plague at Aleppo in 1828." And underneath, in small cramped characters, as if crowded as an afterthought into an insufficient space: "Also His Wife."

That was all. No name, dates, honours, epithets, for the Viscountess Thudeney. Did she too die of the plague at Aleppo? Or did the "also" imply her actual presence in the sarcophagus which her husband's pride had no doubt prepared for his own last sleep, little guessing that some Syrian drain was to receive him? Lady Jane racked her memory in vain. All she knew was that the death without issue of this Lord Thudeney had caused the property to revert to the Croft-Lynkes, and so, in the end, brought her to the chancel step where, shyly, she knelt a moment, vowing to the dead to carry on their trust.

She passed on to the entrance court, and stood at last at the door of her new home, a blunt tweed figure in heavy mud-stained shoes. She felt as intrusive as a tripper, and her hand hesitated on the door-bell. "I ought to have brought someone with me," she thought; an odd admission on the part of a young woman who, when she was doing her books of travel, had prided herself on forcing single-handed the most closely guarded doors. But those other places, as she looked back, seemed easy and accessible compared to Bells.

She rang, and a tinkle answered, carried on by a flurried echo which seemed to ask what in the world was happening. Lady Jane, through the nearest window, caught the spectral *vista* of a long room with shrouded furniture. She could not see its farther end, but she had the feeling that someone stationed there might very well be seeing her.

"Just at first," she thought, "I shall have to invite people here—to take the chill off."

She rang again, and the tinkle again prolonged itself; but no one came.

At last she reflected that the caretakers probably lived at the back of the house, and pushing open a door in the courtyard wall she worked her way around to what seemed a stableyard. Against the purple brick sprawled a neglected magnolia, bearing one late flower as big as a planet. Lady Jane rang at a door marked "Service." This bell, though also languid, had a wakefuller sound, as if it were more used to being rung, and still knew what was likely to follow; and after a delay during which Lady Jane again had the sense of being peered at—from above, through a lowered blind—a bolt shot, and a woman looked out. She was youngish, unhealthy, respectable and frightened; and she blinked at Lady Jane like someone waking out of sleep.

"Oh," said Lady Jane—"do you think I might visit the house?"

"The house?"

"I'm staying near here—I'm interested in old houses. Mightn't I take a look?"

The young woman drew back. "The house isn't shown."

"Oh, but not to—not to—" Jane weighed the case. "You see," she explained, "I know some of the family: the Northumberland branch."

"You're related, madam?"

"Well—distantly, yes." It was exactly what she had not meant to say; but there seemed no other way.

The woman twisted her apron-strings in perplexity.

"Come, you know," Lady Jane urged, producing half-a-crown. The woman turned pale.

"I couldn't, madam; not without asking." It was clear that she was sorely tempted.

"Well, ask, won't you?" Lady Jane pressed the tip into a hesitating hand. The young woman shut the door and vanished. She was away so long that the visitor concluded her half-crown had been pocketed, and there was an end; and she began to be angry with herself, which was more often her habit than to be so with others.

"Well, for a fool, Jane, you're a complete one," she grumbled.

A returning footstep, listless, reluctant—the tread of one who was not going to let her in. It began to be rather comic.

The door opened, and the young woman said in her dull sing-song: "Mr. Jones says that no one is allowed to visit the house."

She and Lady Jane looked at each other for a moment, and Lady Jane read the apprehension in the other's eyes.

"Mr. Jones? Oh?—Yes; of course, keep it. . . ." She waved away the woman's hand.

"Thank you, madam." The door closed again, and Lady Jane stood and gazed up at the inexorable face of her old home.

2.

"But you didn't get in? You actually came back without so much as a peep?"

Her story was received, that evening at dinner, with mingled mirth and incredulity.

"But, my dear! You mean to say you asked to see the house, and they wouldn't let you? *who* wouldn't?" Lady Jane's hostess insisted.

"Mr. Jones."

"Mr. Jones?"

"He said no one was allowed to visit it."

"Who on earth is Mr. Jones?"

"The caretaker, I suppose. I didn't see him."

"Didn't see him either? But I never heard such nonsense! Why in the world didn't you insist?"

"Yes; why didn't you?" they all chorused; and she could only answer, a little lamely: "I think I was afraid."

"Afraid? *You*, darling?" There was fresh hilarity. "Of Mr. Jones?"

"I suppose so." She joined in the laugh, yet she knew it was true: she had been afraid.

Edward Stramer, the novelist, an old friend of her family, had been listening with an air of abstraction, his eyes on his empty coffee-cup. Suddenly, as the mistress of the house pushed back her chair, he looked across the table at Lady Jane. "It's odd: I've just remembered something. Once, when I was a youngster, I tried to see Bells; over thirty years ago it must have been." He glanced at his host. "Your mother drove me over. And we were not let in."

There was a certain flatness in this conclusion, and someone remarked that Bells had always been known as harder to get into than any house thereabouts.

"Yes," said Stramer; "but the point is that we were refused in exactly the same words. Mr. Jones said no one was allowed to visit the house."

"Ah—he was in possession already? Thirty years ago? Unsociable fellow, Jones. Well, Jane, you've got a good watchdog."

They moved to the drawing-room, and the talk drifted to other topics. But Stramer came and sat down beside Lady Jane. "It is queer, though, that at such a distance of time we should have been given exactly the same answer."

She glanced up at him curiously. "Yes; and you didn't try to force your way in either?"

"Oh no: it was not possible."

"So I felt," she agreed.

"Well, next week, my dear, I hope we shall see it all, in spite of Mr. Jones," their hostess intervened, catching their last words as she moved toward the piano.

"I wonder if we shall see Mr. Jones," said Stramer.

3.

Bells was not nearly as large as it looked; like many old houses it was very narrow, and but one storey high, with servant's rooms in the low attics, and much space wasted in crooked passages and superfluous stairs. If she closed the great saloon, Jane thought, she might live there comfortably with the small staff which was the most she could afford. It was a relief to find the place less important than she had feared.

For already, in that first hour of arrival, she had decided to give up everything else for Bells. Her previous plans and ambitions—except such as might fit in with living there—had fallen from her like a discarded garment, and things she had hardly thought about, or had shrugged away with the hasty subversiveness of youth, were already laying quiet hands on her; all the lives from which her life had issued, with what they bore of example or admonishment. The very shabbiness of the house moved her more than splendours, made it, after its long abandonment, seem full of the careless daily coming and going of people long dead, people to whom it had not been a museum, or a page of history, but cradle, nursery, home, and sometimes, no doubt, a prison.

If those marble lips in the chapel could speak! If she could hear some of their comments on the old house which had spread its silent shelter over their sins and sorrows, their follies and submissions! A long tale, to which she was about to add another chapter, subdued and humdrum beside some of those earlier annals, yet probably freer and more varied than the unchronicled lives of the great-aunts and great-grandmothers buried there so completely that they must hardly have known when they passed from their beds to their graves. "Piled up like dead leaves," Jane thought, "layers and layers of them, to preserve something forever budding underneath."

Well, all these piled-up lives had at least preserved the old house in its integrity; and that was worthwhile. She was satisfied to carry on such a trust.

She sat in the garden looking up at those rosy walls, iridescent with damp and age. She decided which windows should be hers, which rooms given to the friends from Kent who were motoring over, Stramer among them, for a modest house-warming; then she got up and went in.

The hour had come for domestic questions; for she had arrived alone, unsupported even by the old family housemaid her mother had offered her. She preferred to start afresh, convinced that her small household could be staffed from the neighbourhood. Mrs. Clemm, the rosy-cheeked old person who had curtsied her across the threshold, would doubtless know.

Mrs. Clemm, summoned to the library, curtsied again. She wore black silk, gathered and spreading as to skirt, flat and perpendicular as to bodice. On her glossy false front was a black lace cap with ribbons which had faded from violet to ash-colour, and a heavy watch-chain descended from the lava brooch under her crochet collar. Her small round face rested on the collar like a red apple on a white plate: neat, smooth, circular, with a pursed-up mouth, eyes like black seeds, and round ruddy cheeks with the skin so taut that one had to look close to see that it was as wrinkled as a piece of old crackly.

Mrs. Clemm was sure there would be no trouble about servants. She herself could do a little cooking: though her hand might be a bit out. But there was her niece to help; and she was quite of her ladyship's opinion, that there was no need to get in strangers. They were mostly a poor lot; and besides, they might not take to Bells. There were persons who didn't. Mrs. Clemm smiled a sharp little smile, like the scratch of a pin, as she added that she hoped her ladyship wouldn't be one of them.

As for under-servants. . . .well, a boy, perhaps? She had a great-nephew she might send for. But about women—under-housemaids—if her ladyship thought they couldn't manage as they were; well, she really didn't know. Thudeney-Blazes? Oh, she didn't think so. . . . There was more dead than living at Thudeney-Blazes. . . . everyone was leaving there. . . .or in the churchyard. . . .one house after another being shut. . . .death was everywhere, wasn't it, my lady? Mrs. Clemm said it with another of her short sharp smiles, which provoked the appearance of a frosty dimple.

"But my niece Georgiana is a hard worker, my lady; her that let you in the other day. . . ."

"That didn't," Lady Jane corrected.

"Oh, my lady, it was too unfortunate. If only your ladyship had have said. . . .poor Georgiana had ought to have seen; but she never *did* have her wits about her, not for answering the door."

"But she was only obeying orders. She went to ask Mr. Jones."

Mrs. Clemm was silent. Her small hands, wrinkled and resolute, fumbled with the folds of her apron, and her quick eyes made the circuit of the room and then came back to Lady Jane's.

"Just so, my lady; but, as I told her, she'd ought to have known—"

"And who is Mr. Jones?"

Mrs. Clemm's smile snapped out again, deprecating, respectful. "Well, my lady, he's more dead than living, too...if I may say so," was her surprising answer.

"Is he? I'm sorry to hear that; but who is he?"

"Well, my lady, he's. . . .he's my great-uncle, as it were. . . .my grandmother's own brother, as you might say."

"Ah; I see." Lady Jane considered her with growing curiosity. "He must have reached a great age, then."

"Yes, my lady; he has that. Though I'm not," Mrs. Clemm added, the dimple showing, "as old myself as your ladyship might suppose. Living at Bells all these years has been ageing to me; it would be to anybody."

"I suppose so. And yet," Lady Jane continued, "Mr. Jones has survived; has stood it well—as you certainly have?"

"Oh. Not as well as I have," Mrs. Clemm interjected, as if resentful of the comparison.

"At any rate, he still mounts guard; mounts it as well as he did thirty years ago."

"Thirty years ago?" Mrs. Clemm echoed, her hands dropping from her apron to her sides.

"Wasn't he here thirty years ago?"

"Oh, yes, my lady; certainly; he's never once been away that I know of."

"What a wonderful record! And what exactly are his duties?"

Mrs. Clemm paused again, her hands still motionless in the folds of her skirt. Lady Jane noticed that the fingers were tightly clenched, as if to check an involuntary gesture.

"He began as pantry-boy; then footman; then butler, my lady; but it's hard to say, isn't it, what an old servant's duties are, when he's stayed on in the same house so many years?"

"Yes; and that house always empty."

"Just so, my lady. Everything came to depend on him; one thing after another. His late lordship thought the world of him."

"His late lordship? But he was never here! He spent all his life in Canada."

Mrs. Clemm seemed slightly disconcerted. "Certainly, my lady."

(Her voice said: "Who are you, to set me right as to the chronicles of Bells?") "But by letter, my lady; I can show you the letters. And there was his lordship before, the sixteenth Viscount. He *did* come here once."

"Ah, did he?" Lady Jane was embarrassed to find how little she knew of them all. She rose from her seat. "They were lucky, all these absentees, to have someone to watch over their interests so faithfully. I should like to see Mr. Jones—to thank him. Will you take me to him now?"

"Now?" Mrs. Clemm moved back a step or two; Lady Jane fancied her cheeks paled a little under their ruddy varnish. "Oh, not today, my lady."

"Why? Isn't he well enough?"

"Not nearly. He's between life and death, as it were," Mrs. Clemm repeated, as if the phrase were the nearest approach she could find to a definition of Mr. Jones's state.

"He wouldn't even know who I was?"

Mrs. Clemm considered a moment. "I don't say *that*, my lady;" her tone implied that to do so might appear disrespectful. "He'd know you, my lady; but you wouldn't know *him*." She broke off and added hastily: "I mean, for what he is: he's in no state for you to see him."

"He's so very ill? Poor man! And is everything possible being done?"

"Oh, everything; and more too, my lady. But perhaps," Mrs. Clemm suggested, with a clink of keys, "this would be a good time for your ladyship to take a look about the house. If your ladyship has no objection, I should like to begin with the linen."

4.

"And Mr. Jones?" Stramer queried, a few days later, as they sat, Lady Jane and the party from Kent, about an improvised tea-table in a recess of one of the great holly-hedges.

The day was as hushed and warm as that on which she had first come to Bells, and Lady Jane looked up with a smile of ownership at the old walls which seemed to smile back, the windows which now looked at her with friendly eyes.

"Mr. Jones? Who's Mr. Jones?" the others asked; only Stramer recalled their former talk.

Lady Jane hesitated. "Mr. Jones is my invisible guardian; or rather, the guardian of Bells."

They remembered then. "Invisible? You don't mean to say you haven't seen him yet?"

"Not yet; perhaps I never shall. He's very old—and very ill, I'm afraid."

"And he still rules here?"

"Oh, absolutely. The fact is," Lady Jane added "I believe he's the only person left who really knows all about Bells."

"Jane, my *dear*! That big shrub over there against the wall! I verily believe it's *Templetonia retusa*. It *is*! Did anyone ever hear of it standing an English winter?" Gardeners all, they dashed towards the shrub in its sheltered angle. "I shall certainly try it on a south wall at Dipway," cried the hostess from Kent.

Tea over, they moved on to inspect the house. The short autumn day was drawing to a close; but the party had been able to come only for an afternoon, instead of staying over the week-end, and having lingered so long in the gardens they had only time, indoors, to puzzle out what they could through the shadows. Perhaps, Lady Jane thought, it was the best hour to see a house like Bells, so long abandoned, and not yet warmed into new life.

The fire she had had lit in the saloon sent its radiance to meet them, giving the great room an air of expectancy and welcome. The portraits, the Italian cabinets, the shabby armchairs and rugs, all looked as if life had but lately left them; and Lady Jane said to herself: "Perhaps Mrs. Clemm is right in advising me to live here and close the blue parlour."

"My dear, what a fine room! Pity it faces north. Of course you'll have to shut it in winter. It would cost a fortune to heat."

Lady Jane hesitated. "I don't know: I *had* meant to. But there seems to be no other. . . ."

"No other? In all this house?" They laughed; and one of the visitors, going ahead and crossing a panelled anteroom, cried out: "But here! A delicious room; windows south—yes, and west. The warmest of the house. This is perfect."

They followed, and the blue room echoed with exclamations. "Those charming curtains with the parrots. . . .and the blue of that petit point fire-screen! But, Jane, of course you must live here. Look at this citron-wood desk!"

Lady Jane stood on the threshold. "It seems that the chimney smokes hopelessly."

"Hopelessly? Nonsense! Have you consulted anybody? I'll send you a wonderful man..."

"Besides, if you put in one of those one-pipe heaters. . . .At Dipway. . . ."

Stramer was looking over Lady Jane's shoulder. "What does Mr. Jones say about it?"

"He says no one has ever been able to use this room; not for ages. It was the housekeeper who told me. She's his great-niece, and seems simply to transmit his oracles."

Stramer shrugged. "Well, he's lived at Bells longer than you have. Perhaps he's right."

"How absurd!" one of the ladies cried. "The housekeeper and Mr. Jones probably spend their evenings here, and don't want to be disturbed. Look—ashes on the hearth! What did I tell you?"

Lady Jane echoed the laugh as they turned away. They had still to see the library, damp and dilapidated, the panelled dining-room, the breakfast-parlour, and such bedrooms as had any old furniture left; not many, for the late lords of Bells, at one time or another, had evidently sold most of its removable treasures.

When the visitors came down their motors were waiting. A lamp had been placed in the hall, but the rooms beyond were lit only by the broad clear band of western sky showing through uncurtained casements. On the doorstep one of the ladies exclaimed that she had lost her handbag—no, she remembered; she had laid it on the desk in the blue room. Which way was the blue room?

"I'll get it," Jane said, turning back. She heard Stramer following. He asked if he should bring the lamp.

"Oh, no; I can see."

She crossed the threshold of the blue room, guided by the light from its western window; then she stopped. Someone was in the room already; she felt rather than saw another presence. Stramer, behind her, paused also; he did not speak or move. What she saw, or thought she saw, was simply an old man with bent shoulders turning away from the citron-wood desk. Almost before she had received the impression there was no one there; only the slightest stir of the needlework curtain over the farther door. She heard no step or other sound.

"There's the bag," she said, as if the act of speaking, and saying something obvious were a relief.

In the hall her glance crossed Stramer's, but failed to find there the reflection of what her own had registered.

He shook hands, smiling. "Well, goodbye. I commit you to Mr.

Jones's care; only don't let him say that *you're* not shown to visitors."

She smiled: "Come back and try," and then shivered a little as the lights of the last motor vanished beyond the great black hedges.

5.

Lady Jane had exulted in her resolve to keep Bells to herself till she and the old house should have had time to make friends. But after a few days she recalled the uneasy felling which had come over her as she stood on the threshold after her first tentative ring. Yes; she had been right in thinking she would have to have people about her to take the chill off. The house was too old, too mysterious, too much withdrawn into its own secret past, for her poor little present to fit into it without uneasiness.

But it was not a time of year when, among Lady Jane's friends, it was easy to find people free. Her own family were all in the north, and impossible to dislodge. One of her sisters, when invited, simply sent her back a list of shooting-dates; and her mother wrote: "Why not come to us? What can you have to do all alone in that empty house at this time of year? Next summer we're all coming."

Having tried one or two friends with the same result, Lady Jane bethought her of Stramer. He was finishing a novel, she knew, and at such times he liked to settle down somewhere in the country where he could be sure of not being disturbed. Bells was a perfect asylum, and though it was probable that some other friend had anticipated her, and provided the requisite seclusion, Lady Jane decided to invite him. "Do bring your work and stay till it's finished—and don't be in a hurry to finish. I promise that no one shall bother you—" and she added, half-nervously: "Not even Mr. Jones." As she wrote she felt an absurd impulse to blot the words out. "He might not like it," she thought; and the "he" did not refer to Stramer.

Was the solitude already making her superstitious? She thrust the letter into an envelope, and carried it herself to the post-office at Thudeney-Blazes. Two days later a wire from Stramer announced his arrival.

He came on a cold stormy afternoon, just before dinner, and as they went up to dress Lady Jane called after him: "We shall sit in the blue parlour this evening." The housemaid Georgiana was crossing the passage with hot water for the visitor. She stopped and cast a vacant glance at Lady Jane. The latter met it, and said carelessly: "You hear Georgiana? The fire in the blue parlour."

While Lady Jane was dressing she heard a knock, and saw Mrs. Clemm's round face just inside the door, like a red apple on a garden wall.

"Is there anything wrong about the saloon, my lady? Georgiana understood—"

"That I want the fire in the blue parlour. Yes. What's wrong with the saloon is that one freezes there."

"But the chimney smokes in the blue parlour."

"Well, we'll give it a trial, and if it does I'll send for someone to arrange it."

"Nothing can be done, my lady. Everything has been tried, and—"

Lady Jane swung about suddenly. She had heard Stramer singing a cheerful hunting-song in a cracked voice, in his dressing-room at the other end of the corridor.

"That will do, Mrs. Clemm. I want the fire in the blue parlour."

"Yes, my lady." The door closed on the housekeeper.

"So you decided on the saloon after all?" Stramer said, as Lady Jane led the way there after their brief repast.

"Yes, I hope you won't be frozen. Mr. Jones swears that the chimney in the blue parlour isn't safe; so, until I can fetch the mason over from Strawbridge—"

"Oh, I see." Stramer drew up to the blaze in the great fire-place. "We're very well off here; though heating this room is going to be ruinous. Meanwhile, I note that Mr. Jones still rules."

Lady Jane gave a slight laugh.

"Tell me," Stramer continued, as she bent over the mixing of the Turkish coffee, "what is there about him? I'm getting curious."

Lady Jane laughed again, and heard the embarrassment in her laugh. "So am I."

"Why—you don't mean to say you haven't seen him yet?"

"No. He's still too ill."

"What's the matter with him? What does the doctor say?"

"He won't see the doctor."

"But, look here—if things take a worse turn—I don't know; but mightn't you be held to have been negligent?"

"What can I do? Mrs. Clemm says he has a doctor who treats him by correspondence. I don't see that I can interfere."

"Isn't there some one beside Mrs. Clemm whom you can consult?"

She considered: certainly, as yet, she had not made much effort to get into relation with her neighbours. "I expected the vicar to call. But

I've enquired: there's no vicar any longer at Thudeney-Blazes. A curate comes from Strawbridge every other Sunday. And the one who comes now is new: nobody about the place seems to know him."

"But I thought the chapel here was in use? It looked so when you showed it to us the other day."

"I thought so too. It used to be the parish church of Lynke-Linnet and Lower-Lynke; but it seems that was years ago. The parishioners objected to coming so far; and there weren't enough of them. Mrs. Clemm says that nearly everybody has died off or left. It's the same at Thudeney-Blazes."

Stramer glanced about the great room, with its circle of warmth and light by the hearth, and the sullen shadows huddled at its farther end, as if hungrily listening. "With this emptiness at the centre, life was bound to cease gradually on the outskirts."

Lady Jane followed his glance. "Yes; it's all wrong. I must try to wake the place up."

"Why not open it to the public? Have a visitors' day?"

She thought a moment. In itself the suggestion was distasteful; she could imagine few things that would bore her more. Yet to do so might be a duty, a first step toward re-establishing relations between the lifeless house and its neighbourhood. Secretly, she felt that even the coming and going of indifferent unknown people would help to take the chill from those rooms, to brush from their walls the dust of too-heavy memories.

"Who's that?" asked Stramer. Lady Jane started in spite of herself, and glanced over her shoulder; but he was only looking past her at a portrait which a dart of flame from the hearth had momentarily called from its obscurity.

"That's a Lady Thudeney." She got up and went toward the picture with a lamp. "Might be an Opie, don't you think? It's a strange face, under the smirk of the period."

Stramer took the lamp and held it up. The portrait was that of a young woman in a short-waisted muslin gown caught beneath the breast by a cameo. Between clusters of beribboned curls a long fair oval looked out dumbly, inexpressively, in a stare of frozen beauty. "It's as if the house had been too empty even then," Lady Jane murmured. "I wonder which she was? . . . . Oh, I know: it must be 'Also His Wife'."

Stramer stared.

"It's the only name on her monument. The wife of Peregrine Vincent Theobald, who perished of the plague at Aleppo in 1828. Perhaps she was very fond of him, and this was painted when she was an inconsolable widow."

"They didn't dress like that as late as 1828." Stramer holding the lamp closer, deciphered the inscription on the border of the lady's India scarf; "Juliana, Viscountess Thudeney, 1818". "She must have been inconsolable before his death, then."

Lady Jane smiled. "Let's hope she grew less so after it."

Stramer passed the lamp across the canvas. "Do you see where she was painted? In the blue parlour. Look: the old panelling; and she's leaning on the citron-wood desk. They evidently used the room in winter then." The lamp paused on the background of the picture: a window framing snow-laden paths and hedges in icy perspective.

"Curious," Stramer said—"and rather melancholy: to be painted against that wintry desolation. I wish you could find out more about her. Have you dipped into your archives?"

"No. Mr. Jones—"

"He won't allow that either?"

"Yes; but he's lost the key of the muniment-room. Mrs. Clemm has been trying to get a locksmith."

"Surely the neighbourhood can still produce one?"

"There *was* one at Thudeney-Blazes; but he died the week before I came."

"Of course!"

"Of course?"

"Well, in Mrs. Clemm's hands keys get lost, chimneys smoke, locksmith's die. . . ." Stramer stood, light in hand, looking down the shadowy length of the saloon. "I say, let's go and see what's happening now in the blue parlour."

Lady Jane laughed: a laugh seemed easy with another voice nearby to echo it. "Let's—"

She followed him out of the saloon, across the hall in which a single candle burned on a far-off table, and past the stairway yawning like a black funnel above them. In the doorway of the blue parlour Stramer paused. "Now, then, Mr. Jones!"

It was stupid, but Lady Jane's heart gave a jerk: she hoped the challenge would not evoke the shadowy figure she had half seen that other day.

"Lord, it's cold!" Stramer stood looking about him. "Those ashes are still on the hearth. Well, it's all very queer." He crossed over to the citron-wood desk. "There's where she sat for her picture—and in this very armchair—look!"

"Oh, don't!" Lady Jane exclaimed. The words slipped out unawares.

"Don't—what?"

"Try those drawers—" she wanted to reply; for his hand was stretched toward the desk.

"I'm frozen; I think I'm starting a cold. Do come away," she grumbled, backing toward the door.

Stramer lighted her out without comment. As the lamplight slid along the walls Lady Jane fancied that the needle-work curtain over the farther door stirred as it had that other day. But it may have been the wind rising outside. . . .

The saloon seemed like home when they got back to it.

"There *is* no Mr. Jones!"

Stramer proclaimed it triumphantly when they met the next morning. Lady Jane had motored off early to Strawbridge in quest of a mason and a locksmith. The quest had taken longer than she had expected, for everybody in Strawbridge was busy on jobs nearer by, and unaccustomed to the idea of going to Bells, with which the town seemed to have had no communication within living memory. The younger workmen did not even know where the place was, and the best Lady Jane could do was to coax a locksmith's apprentice to come with her, on the understanding that he would be driven back to the nearest station as soon as his job was over. As for the mason, he had merely taken note of her request, and promised half-heartedly to send somebody when he could. "Rather off our beat, though."

She returned, discouraged and somewhat weary, as Stramer was coming downstairs after his morning's work.

"No Mr. Jones?" she echoed.

"Not a trace! I've been trying the old Glamis experiment—situating his room by its window. Luckily the house is smaller. . . ."

Lady Jane smiled. "Is this what you call locking yourself up with your work?"

"I can't work: that's the trouble. Not till this is settled. Bells is a fidgety place."

"Yes," she agreed.

"Well, I wasn't going to be beaten; so I went to try to find the head-gardener."

"But there isn't—"

"No. Mrs. Clemm told me. The head-gardener died last year. That woman positively glows with life whenever she announces a death.

Have you noticed?"

Yes: Lady Jane had.

"Well—I said to myself that if there wasn't a head-gardener there must be an underling; at least one. I'd seen somebody in the distance, raking leaves, and I ran him down. Of course he'd never seen Mr. Jones."

"You mean that poor old half-blind Jacob? He couldn't see anybody."

"Perhaps not. At any rate, he told me that Mr. Jones wouldn't let the leaves be buried for leaf-mould—I forget why. Mr. Jones's authority extends even to the gardens."

"Yet you say he doesn't exist!"

"Wait. Jacob is half-blind, but he's been here for years, and knows more about the place than you'd think. I got him talking about the house, and I pointed to one window after another, and he told me each time whose the room was, or had been. But he couldn't situate Mr. Jones."

"I beg your ladyship's pardon—" Mrs. Clemm was on the threshold, cheeks shining, skirt rustling, her eyes like drills. "The locksmith your ladyship brought back; I understand it was for the lock of the muniment-room—"

"Well?"

"He's lost one of his tools, and can't do anything without it. So he's gone. The butcher's boy gave him a lift back."

Lady Jane caught Stramer's faint chuckle. She stood and stared at Mrs. Clemm, and Mrs. Clemm stared back, deferential but unflinching.

"Gone? Very well; I'll motor after him."

"Oh, my lady, it's too late. The butcher's boy had his motor-cycle... Besides, what could he do?"

"Break the lock," exclaimed Lady Jane, exasperated.

"Oh, my lady—" Mrs. Clemm's intonation marked the most respectful incredulity. She waited another moment, and then withdrew, while Lady Jane and Stramer considered each other.

"But this is absurd," Lady Jane declared when they had lunched, waited on, as usual, by the flustered Georgiana. "I'll break in that door myself, if I have to.—Be careful please, Georgiana," she added; "I was speaking of doors, not dishes." For Georgiana had let fall with a crash the dish she was removing from the table. She gathered up the pieces in her tremulous fingers, and vanished. Jane and Stramer returned to the saloon.

"Queer!" the novelist commented.

"Yes." Lady Jane, facing the door, started slightly. Mrs. Clemm was there again; but this time subdued, unrustling, bathed in that odd pallor which enclosed but seemed unable to penetrate the solid crimson of her cheeks.

"I beg pardon, my lady. The key is found." Her hand, as she held it out, trembled like Georgiana's.

7.

"It's not here," Stramer announced a couple of hours later.

"What isn't?" Lady Jane queried, looking up from a heap of disordered papers. Her eyes blinked at him through the fog of yellow dust raised by her manipulations.

"The clue.—I've got all the 1800 to 1840 papers here; and there's a gap."

She moved over to the table above which he was bending. "A gap?"

"A big one. Nothing between 1815 and 1835. No mention of Peregrine or Juliana."

They looked at each other across the tossed papers, and suddenly Stramer exclaimed: "Someone has been here before us—just lately."

Lady Jane stared, incredulous, and then followed the direction of his downward pointing hand.

"Do you wear flat heelless shoes?" he questioned.

"And of that size? Even my feet are too small to fit into those footprints. Luckily there wasn't time to sweep the floor!"

Lady Jane felt a slight chill, a chill of a different and more inward quality than the shock of stuffy coldness which had met them as they entered the unaired attic set apart for the storing of the Thudeney archives.

"But how absurd! Of course when Mrs. Clemm found we were coming up she came—or sent someone—to open the shutters."

"That's not Mrs. Clemm's foot, or the other woman's. She must have sent a man—an old man with a shaky uncertain step. Look how it wanders."

"Mr. Jones, then!" said Lady Jane, half impatiently.

"Mr. Jones. And he got what he wanted, and put it—where?"

"Ah, *that*—! I'm freezing, you know; let's give this up for the present." She rose, and Stramer followed her without protest; the muniment-room was really untenable.

"I must catalogue all this stuff someday, I suppose," Lady Jane continued, as they went down the stairs. "But meanwhile, what do you say to a good tramp, to get the dust out of our lungs?"

He agreed, and turned back to his room to get some letters he wanted to post at Thudeney-Blazes.

Lady Jane went down alone. It was a fine afternoon, and the sun, which had made the dust-clouds of the muniment-room so dazzling, sent a long shaft through the west window of the blue parlour, and across the floor of the hall.

Certainly Georgiana kept the oak floors remarkably well; considering how much else she had to do, it was surp—

Lady Jane stopped as if an unseen hand had jerked her violently back. On the smooth parquet before her she had caught the trace of dusty footprints—the prints of broad-soled heelless shoes—making for the blue parlour and crossing its threshold. She stood still with the same inward shiver that she had felt upstairs; then, avoiding the footprints, she too stole very softly toward the blue parlour, pushed the door wider, and saw, in the long dazzle of autumn light, as if translucid, edged with the glitter, an old man at the desk.

"Mr. Jones!"

A step came up behind her: Mrs. Clemm with the post-bag. "You called, my lady?"

"I. . . .yes. . . ."

When she turned back to the desk there was no one there.

She faced about on the housekeeper. "Who was that?"

"Where, my lady?"

Lady Jane, without answering, moved toward the needlework curtain, in which she had detected the same faint tremor as before. "Where does that door go to—behind the curtain?"

"Nowhere, my lady. I mean; there is no door."

Mrs. Clemm had followed; her step sounded quick and assured. She lifted up the curtain with a firm hand. Behind it was a rectangle of roughly plastered wall, where an opening had visibly been bricked up.

"When was that done?"

"The wall built up? I couldn't say. I've never known it otherwise," replied the housekeeper.

The two women stood for an instant measuring each other with level eyes; then the housekeeper's were slowly lowered, and she let the curtain fall from her hand. "There are a great many things in old houses that nobody knows about," she said.

"There shall be as few as possible in mine," said Lady Jane.

"My lady!" The housekeeper stepped quickly in front of her. "My lady, what are you doing?" she gasped.

Lady Jane had turned back to the desk at which she had just seen—or fancied she had seen—the bending figure of Mr. Jones.

"I am going to look through these drawers," she said.

The housekeeper still stood in pale immobility between her and the desk. "No, my lady—no. You won't do that."

"Because—?"

Mrs. Clemm crumpled up her black silk apron with a despairing gesture. "Because—if you *will* have it—that's where Mr. Jones keeps his private papers. I know he'd oughtn't to. . . ."

"Ah—then it was Mr. Jones I saw here?"

The housekeeper's arms sank to her sides and her mouth hung open on an unspoken word. "You *saw* him." The question came out in a confused whisper; and before Lady Jane could answer, Mrs. Clemm's arms rose again, stretched before her face as if to fend off a blaze of intolerable light, or some forbidden sight she had long since disciplined herself not to see. Thus screening her eyes she hurried across the hall to the door of the servant's wing.

Lady Jane stood for a moment looking after her; then, with a slightly shaking hand, she opened the desk and hurriedly took out from it all the papers—a small bundle—that it contained. With them she passed back into the saloon.

As she entered it her eye was caught by the portrait of the melancholy lady in the short-waisted gown, whom she and Stramer had christened "Also His Wife." The lady's eyes, usually so empty of all awareness save of her own frozen beauty, seemed suddenly waking to an anguished participation in the scene.

"Fudge!" muttered Lady Jane, shaking off the spectral suggestion as she turned to meet Stramer on the threshold.

8.

The missing papers were all there. Stramer and she spread them out hurriedly on a table and at once proceeded to gloat over their find. Not a particularly important one, indeed; in the long history of the Lynkes and Crofts it took up hardly more space than the little handful of documents did, in actual bulk, among the stacks of the muniment room. But the fact that these papers filled a gap in the chronicles of the house, and situated the sad-faced beauty as veritably the wife of the Peregrine Vincent Theobald Lynke who had "perished of the plague at Aleppo in 1828"—this was a discovery sufficiently exciting to whet amateur appetites, and to put out of Lady Jane's mind the strange incident which had attended the opening of the cabinet.

For a while she and Stramer sat silently and methodically going through their respective piles of correspondence; but presently Lady Jane, after glancing over one of the yellowing pages, uttered a startled exclamation.

"How strange! Mr. Jones again—always Mr. Jones!"

Stramer looked up from the papers he was sorting. "You too? I've got a lot of letters here addressed to a Mr. Jones by Peregrine Vincent, who seems to have been always disporting himself abroad, and chronically in want of money. Gambling debts, apparently. . . .ah and women. . . .a dirty record altogether. . . ."

"Yes? My letter is not written to a Mr. Jones; but it's about one. Listen." Lady Jane began to read. "'Bells, February 20th, 1826. . . .' (It's from poor 'Also His Wife' to her husband.)

> My dear Lord, acknowledging as I ever do the burden of the sad impediment which denies me the happiness of being more frequently in your company, I yet fail to conceive how anything in my state obliges that close seclusion in which Mr. Jones persists—and by your express orders, so he declares—in confining me. Surely, my lord, had you found it possible to spend more time with me since the day of our marriage, you would yourself have seen it to be unnecessary to put this restraint upon me.
> It is true, alas, that my unhappy infirmity denies me the happiness to speak with you, or to hear the accents of the voice I should love above all others could it but reach me; but, my dear husband, I would have you consider that my mind is in no way affected by this obstacle, but goes out to you, as my heart does, in a perpetual eagerness of attention, and that to sit in this great house alone, day after day, month after month, deprived of your company, and debarred also from any intercourse but that of the servants you have chosen to put about me, is a fate more cruel than I deserve and more painful than I can bear.
> I have entreated Mr. Jones, since he seems all-powerful with you, to represent this to you, and to transmit this my last request—for should I fail I am resolved to make no other—that

> you should consent to my making the acquaintance of a few of your friends and neighbours, among whom I cannot but think there must be some kind hearts that would take pity on my unhappy situation, and afford me such companionship as would give me more courage to bear your continual absence. . . .

Lady Jane folded up the letter. "Deaf and dumb—ah, poor creature! That explains the look—"

"And this explains the marriage," Stramer continued, unfolding a stiff parchment document. "Here are the Viscountess Thudeney's marriage settlements. She appears to have been a Miss Portallo, daughter of Obadiah Portallo Esquire, of Purflew Castle, Caermarthenshire, and Bombay House, Twickenham, East India merchant, senior member of the banking house of Portallo and Prest—and so on and so on. And the figures run up into hundreds of thousands."

"It's rather ghastly—putting the two things together. All the millions and—imprisonment in the blue parlour. I suppose her Viscount had to have the money, and was ashamed to have it known how he had got it. . . ." Lady Jane shivered. "Think of it—day after day, winter after winter, year after year...speechless, soundless, alone. . . .under Mr. Jones's guardianship. Let me see: what year were they married?"

"In 1817."

"And only a year later that portrait was painted. And she had the frozen look already."

Stramer mused: "Yes; it's grim enough. But the strangest figure in the whole case is still—Mr. Jones."

"Mr. Jones—yes. Her keeper," Lady Jane mused "I suppose he must have been this one's ancestor. The office seems to have been hereditary at Bells."

"Well—I don't know."

Stramer's voice was so odd that Lady Jane looked up at him with a stare of surprise. "What if it were the same one?" suggested Stramer with a queer smile.

"The same?" Lady Jane laughed. "You're not good at figures are you? If poor Lady Thudeney's Mr. Jones were alive now he'd be—"

"I didn't say ours was alive now," said Stramer.

"Oh—why, what. . . .?" she faltered.

But Stramer did not answer; his eyes had been arrested by the precipitate opening of the door behind his hostess, and the entry of Georgiana, a livid, dishevelled Georgiana, more than usually bereft of her faculties, and gasping out something inarticulate.

"Oh, my lady—it's my aunt—she won't answer me," Georgiana stammered in a voice of terror.

Lady Jane uttered an impatient exclamation. "Answer you? Why—what do you want her to answer?"

"Only whether she's alive, my lady," said Georgiana with streaming eyes.

Lady Jane continued to look at her severely. "Alive? Alive? Why on earth shouldn't she be?"

"She might as well be dead—by the way she just lies there."

"Your aunt dead? I saw her alive enough in the blue parlour half an hour ago," Lady Jane returned. She was growing rather *blasé* with regard to Georgiana's panics; but suddenly she felt this to be of a different nature from any of the others. "Where is it your aunt's lying?"

"In her own bedroom, on her bed," the other wailed, "and won't say why."

Lady Jane got to her feet, pushing aside the heaped-up papers, and hastening to the door with Stramer in her wake.

As they went up the stairs she realized that she had seen the housekeeper's bedroom only once, on the day of her first obligatory round of inspection, when she had taken possession of Bells. She did not even remember very clearly where it was, but followed Georgiana down the passage and through a door which communicated, rather surprisingly, with a narrow walled-in staircase that was unfamiliar to her. At its top she and Stramer found themselves on a small landing upon which two doors opened. Through the confusion of her mind Lady Jane noticed that these rooms, with their special staircase leading down to what had always been called his lordship's suite, must obviously have been occupied by his lordship's confidential servants. In one of them, presumably, had been lodged the original Mr. Jones, the Mr. Jones of the yellow letters, the letters purloined by Lady Jane. As she crossed the threshold, Lady Jane remembered the housekeeper's attempt to prevent her touching the contents of the desk.

Mrs. Clemm's room, like herself, was neat, glossy and extremely cold. Only Mrs. Clemm herself was no longer like Mrs. Clemm. The red-apple glaze had barely faded from her cheeks, and not a lock was disarranged in the unnatural lustre of her false front; even her cap ribbons hung symmetrically along either cheek. But death had happened to her, and had made her into someone else. At first glance it was impossible to say if the unspeakable horror in her wide-open eyes were only the reflection of that change, or of the agent by whom it had come. Lady Jane, shuddering, paused a moment while Stramer went up to the bed.

"Her hand is warm still—but no pulse." He glanced about the room. "A glass anywhere?" The cowering Georgiana took a hand-glass from the neat chest of drawers, and Stramer held it over the housekeeper's drawn-back lip. . . .

"She's dead," he pronounced.

"Oh, poor thing! But how—?" Lady Jane drew near, and was kneeling down, taking the inanimate hand in hers, when Stramer touched her on the arm, then silently raised a finger of warning. Georgiana was crouching in the farther corner of the room, her face buried in her lifted arms.

"Look here," Stramer whispered. He pointed to Mrs. Clemm's throat, and Lady Jane, bending over, distinctly saw a circle of red marks on it—the marks of recent bruises. She looked again into the awful eyes.

"She's been strangled," Stramer whispered.

Lady Jane, with a shiver of fear, drew down the housekeeper's lids. Georgiana, her face hidden, was still sobbing convulsively in the corner. There seemed, in the air of the cold orderly room, something that forbade wonderment and silenced conjecture. Lady Jane and Stramer stood and looked at each other without speaking.

At length Stramer crossed over to Georgiana, and touched her on the shoulder. She appeared unaware of the touch, and he grasped her shoulder and shook it. "Where is Mr. Jones?" he asked.

The girl looked up, her face blurred and distorted with weeping, her eyes dilated as if with the vision of some latent terror. "Oh, sir, she's not really dead, is she?"

Stramer repeated his question in a loud authoritative tone; and slowly she echoed it in a scarce-heard whisper. "Mr. Jones—?"

"Get up, my girl, and send him here to us at once, or tell us where to find him."

Georgiana, moved by the old habit of obedience, struggled to her feet and stood unsteadily, her heaving shoulders braced against the wall. Stramer asked her sharply if she had not heard what he had said.

"Oh, poor thing, she's so upset—" Lady Jane intervened compassionately. "Tell me, Georgiana: where shall we find Mr. Jones?"

The girl turned to her with eyes as fixed as the dead woman's. "You won't find him a anywhere," she slowly said.

"Why not?"

"Because he's not here."

"Not here? Where is he, then?" Stramer broke in.

Georgiana did not seem to notice the interruption. She continued to stare at Lady Jane with Mrs. Clemm's awful eyes. "He's in his grave in the churchyard—these years and years he is. . . . .Long before ever I was born. . . .my aunt hadn't ever seen him herself, not since she was a tiny child. . . .That's the terror of it. . . .that's why she always had to do what he told her to. . . .because you couldn't ever answer him back. . . ." Her horrified gaze turned from Lady Jane to the stony face and fast-glazing pupils of the dead woman. "You hadn't ought to have meddled with his papers, my lady. . . . That's what he's punished her for. . . . When it came to those papers he wouldn't ever listen to human reason. . . .he wouldn't. . . ." Then, flinging her arms above her head, Georgiana straightened herself to her full height before falling in a swoon at Stramer's feet.

Pomegranate Seed

1

Charlotte Ashby paused on her doorstep. Dark had descended on the brilliancy of the March afternoon, and the grinding, rasping street life of the city was at its highest. She turned her back on it, standing for a moment in the old-fashioned, marble-flagged vestibule before she inserted her key in the lock. The sash curtains drawn across the panes of the inner door softened the light within to a warm blur through which no details showed. It was the hour when, in the first months of her marriage to Kenneth Ashby, she had most liked to return to that quiet house in a street long since deserted by business and fashion. The contrast between the soulless roar of New York, its devouring blaze of lights, the oppression of its congested traffic, congested houses, lives, minds and this veiled sanctuary she called home, always stirred her profoundly. In the very heart of the hurricane she had found her tiny islet—or thought she had. And now, in the last months, everything was changed, and she always wavered on the doorstep and had to force herself to enter.

While she stood there she called up the scene within: the hall hung with old prints, the ladder-like stairs, and on the left her husband's long shabby library, full of books and pipes and worn armchairs inviting to meditation. How she had loved that room! Then, upstairs, her own drawing room, in which, since the death of Kenneth's first wife, neither furniture nor hangings had been changed, because there had never been money enough, but which Charlotte had made her own by moving furniture about and adding more books, another lamp, a table for the new reviews. Even on the occasion of her only visit to the first Mrs. Ashby—a distant, self-centered woman, whom she had known very slightly—she had looked about her with an innocent envy, feeling it to be exactly the drawing room she would have liked for herself; and now for more than a year it had been hers to deal with as she chose—the room to which she hastened back at dusk on winter days, where she sat reading by the fire, or answering notes at the pleasant roomy desk, or going over her stepchildren's copybooks, till she heard her husband's step.

Sometimes friends dropped in; sometimes—oftener—she was alone; and she liked that best, since it was another way of being with Kenneth, thinking over what he had said when they parted in the morning, imagining what he would say when he sprang up the stairs, found her by herself and caught her to him.

Now, instead of this, she thought of one thing only—the letter she might or might not find on the hall table. Until she had made sure whether or not it was there, her mind had no room for anything else. The letter was always the same—a square greyish envelope with "Kenneth Ashby, Esquire," written on it in bold but faint characters. From the first it had struck Charlotte as peculiar that anyone who wrote such a firm hand should trace the letters so lightly; the address was always written as though there were not enough ink in the pen, or the writer's wrist were too weak to bear upon it.

Another curious thing was that, in spite of its masculine curves, the writing was so visibly feminine. Some hands are sexless, some masculine, at first glance; the writing on the grey envelope, for all its strength and assurance, was without doubt a woman's. The envelope never bore anything but the recipient's name; no stamp, no address. The letter was presumably delivered by hand—but by whose? No doubt it was slipped into the letter box, whence the parlourmaid, when she closed the shutters and lit the lights, probably extracted it. At any rate, it was always in the evening, after dark, that Charlotte saw it lying there. She thought of the letter in the singular, as "it," because, though there had been several since her marriage—seven, to be exact—they were so alike in appearance that they had become merged in one another in her mind, become one letter, become "it."

The first had come the day after their return from their honeymoon—a journey prolonged to the West Indies, from which they had returned to New York after an absence of more than two months. Re-entering the house with her husband, late on that first evening—they had dined at his mother's—she had seen, alone on the hall table, the grey envelope. Her eye fell on it before Kenneth's, and her first thought was: "Why, I've seen that writing before"; but where she could not recall. The memory was just definite enough for her to identify the script whenever it looked up at her faintly from the same pale envelope; but on that first day she would have thought no more of the letter if, when her husband's glance lit on it, she had not chanced to be looking at him.

It all happened in a flash—his seeing the letter, putting out his hand for it, raising it to his short-sighted eyes to decipher the faint writing, and then abruptly withdrawing the arm he had slipped through Charlotte's, and moving away to the hanging light, his back turned to her. She had waited—waited for a sound, an exclamation; waited for him to open the letter; but he had slipped it into his pocket without a word and followed her into the library. And there they had sat down by the fire and lit their cigarettes, and he had remained silent, his head thrown back broodingly against the armchair, his eyes fixed on the hearth, and presently had passed his hand over his forehead and said: "Wasn't it unusually hot at my mother's tonight? I've got a splitting head. Mind if I take myself off to bed?"

That was the first time. Since then Charlotte had never been present when he had received the letter. It usually came before he got home from his office, and she had to go upstairs and leave it lying there. But even if she had not seen it, she would have known it had come by the change in his face when he joined her—which, on those evenings, he seldom did before they met for dinner. Evidently, whatever the letter contained, he wanted to be by himself to deal with it; and when he reappeared he looked years older, looked emptied of life and courage, and hardly conscious of her presence.

Sometimes he was silent for the rest of the evening; and if he spoke, it was usually to hint some criticism of her household arrangements, suggest some change in the domestic administration, to ask, a little nervously, if she didn't think Joyce's nursery governess was rather young and flighty, or if she herself always saw to it that Peter—whose throat was delicate—was properly wrapped up when he went to school.

At such times Charlotte would remember the friendly warnings she had received when she became engaged to Kenneth Ashby: "Marrying a heartbroken widower! Isn't that rather risky? You know Elsie Ashby absolutely dominated him"; and how she had jokingly replied: "He may be glad of a little liberty for a change." And in this respect she had been right. She had needed no one to tell her, during the first months, that her husband was perfectly happy with her. When they came back from their protracted honeymoon the same friends said:

"What have you done to Kenneth? He looks twenty years younger"; and this time she answered with careless joy: "I suppose I've got him out of his groove."

But what she noticed after the grey letters began to come was not so much his nervous tentative fault-finding—which always seemed to be uttered against his will—as the look in his eyes when he joined her after receiving one of the letters. The look was not unloving, not even indifferent; it was the look of a man who had been so far away from ordinary events that when he returns to familiar things they seem strange. She minded that more than the fault-finding.

Though she had been sure from the first that the handwriting on the grey envelope was a woman's, it was long before she associated the mysterious letters with any sentimental secret. She was too sure of her husband's love, too confident of filling his life, for such an idea to occur to her. It seemed far more likely that the letters—which certainly did not appear to cause him any sentimental pleasure—were addressed to the busy lawyer than to the private person. Probably they were from some tiresome client—women, he had often told her, were nearly always tiresome as clients—who did not want her letters opened by his secretary and therefore had them carried to his house. Yes; but in that case the unknown female must be unusually troublesome, judging from the effect her letters produced.

Then again, though his professional discretion was exemplary, it was odd that he had never uttered an impatient comment, never remarked to Charlotte, in a moment of expansion, that there was a nuisance of a woman who kept badgering him about a case that had gone against her. He had made more than one semi-confidence of the kind—of course without giving names or details; but concerning this mysterious correspondent his lips were sealed.

There was another possibility: what is euphemistically called an "old entanglement." Charlotte Ashby was a sophisticated woman. She had few illusions about the intricacies of the human heart; she knew that there were often old entanglements. But when she had married Kenneth Ashby, her friends, instead of hinting at such a possibility, had said: "You've got your work cut out for you. Marrying a Don Juan is a sinecure to it. Kenneth's never looked at another woman since he first saw Elsie Corder. During all the years of their marriage he was more like an unhappy lover than a comfortably contented husband. He'll never let you move an armchair or change the place of a lamp; and whatever you venture to do, he'll mentally compare with what Elsie would have done in your place."

Except for an occasional nervous mistrust as to her ability to manage the children—a mistrust gradually dispelled by her good humour and the children's obvious fondness for her—none of these forebodings had come true. The desolate widower, of whom his nearest friends said that only his absorbing professional interests had kept him from suicide after his first wife's death, had fallen in love, two years later, with Charlotte Gorse, and after an impetuous wooing had married her and carried her off on a tropical honeymoon. And ever since he had been as tender and lover-like as during those first radiant weeks.

Before asking her to marry him he had spoken to her frankly of his great love for his first wife and his despair after her sudden death; but even then he had assumed no stricken attitude, or implied that life offered no possibility of renewal. He had been perfectly simple and natural, and had confessed to Charlotte that from the beginning he had hoped the future held new gifts for him. And when, after their marriage, they returned to the house where his twelve years with his first wife had been spent, he had told Charlotte at once that he was sorry he couldn't afford to do the place over for her, but that he knew every woman had her own views about furniture and all sorts of household arrangements a man would never notice, and had begged her to make any changes she saw fit without bothering to consult him.

As a result, she made as few as possible; but his way of beginning their new life in the old setting was so frank and unembarrassed that it put her immediately at her ease, and she was almost sorry to find that the portrait of Elsie Ashby, which used to hang over the desk in his library, had been transferred in their absence to the children's nursery. Knowing herself to be the indirect cause of this banishment, she spoke of it to her husband; but he answered: "Oh, I thought they ought to grow up with her looking down on them."

The answer moved Charlotte, and satisfied her; and as time went by she had to confess that she felt more at home in her house, more at ease and in confidence with her husband, since that long coldly beautiful face on the library wall no longer followed her with guarded eyes. It was as if Kenneth's love had penetrated to the secret she hardly acknowledged to her own heart—her passionate need to feel herself the sovereign even of his past.

With all this stored-up happiness to sustain her, it was curious that she had lately found herself yielding to a nervous apprehension. But there the apprehension was; and on this particular afternoon—perhaps because she was more tired than usual, or because of the trouble of finding a new cook or, for some other ridiculously trivial reason, moral or physical—she found herself unable to react against the feeling. Latchkey in hand, she looked back down the silent street to the whirl and illumination of the great thoroughfare beyond, and up at the sky already aflare with the city's nocturnal life.

"Outside there," she thought, "skyscrapers, advertisements, telephones, wireless, airplanes, movies, motors, and all the rest of the twentieth century; and on the other side of the door something I can't explain, can't relate to them. Something as old as the world, as mysterious as life . . . . Nonsense! What am I worrying about? There hasn't been a letter for three months now—not since the day we came back from the country after Christmas . . . . Queer that they always seem to come after our holidays! . . . Why should I imagine there's going to be one tonight!"

No reason why, but that was the worst of it—one of the worst!—that there were days when she would stand there cold and shivering with the premonition of something inexplicable, intolerable, to be faced on the other side of the curtained panes; and when she opened the door and went in, there would be nothing; and on other days when she felt the same premonitory chill, it was justified by the sight of the grey envelope. So that ever since the last had come she had taken to feeling cold and premonitory every evening, because she never opened the door without thinking the letter might be there.

Well, she'd had enough of it: that was certain. She couldn't go on like that. If her husband turned white and had a headache on the days when the letter came, he seemed to recover afterward; but she couldn't. With her the strain had become chronic, and the reason was not far to seek. Her husband knew from whom the letter came and what was in it; he was prepared beforehand for whatever he had to deal with, and master of the situation, however bad; whereas she was shut out in the dark with her conjectures.

"I can't stand it! I can't stand it another day!" she exclaimed aloud, as she put her key in the lock. She turned the key and went in; and there, on the table, lay the letter.

2

She was almost glad of the sight. It seemed to justify everything, to put a seal of definiteness on the whole blurred business. A letter for her husband; a letter from a woman—no doubt another vulgar case of "old entanglement." What a fool she had been ever to doubt it, to rack her brains for less obvious explanations! She took up the envelope with a steady contemptuous hand, looked closely at the faint letters, held it against the light and just discerned the outline of the folded sheet within. She knew that now she would have no peace till she found out what was written on that sheet.

Her husband had not come in; he seldom got back from his office before half-past six or seven, and it was not yet six. She would have time to take the letter up to the drawing room, hold it over the tea kettle which at that hour always simmered by the fire in expectation of her return, solve the mystery and replace the letter where she had found it. No one would be the wiser, and her gnawing uncertainty would be over. The alternative, of course, was to question her husband; but to do that seemed even more difficult. She weighed the letter between thumb and finger, looked at it again under the light, started up the stairs with the envelope—and came down again and laid it on the table.

"No, I evidently can't," she said, disappointed.

What should she do, then? She couldn't go up alone to that warm welcoming room, pour out her tea, look over her correspondence, glance at a book or review—not with that letter lying below and the knowledge that in a little while her husband would come in, open it and turn into the library alone, as he always did on the days when the grey envelope came.

Suddenly she decided. She would wait in the library and see for herself; see what happened between him and the letter when they thought themselves unobserved. She wondered the idea had never occurred to her before. By leaving the door ajar, and sitting in the corner behind it, she could watch him unseen . . . . Well, then, she would watch him! She drew a chair into the corner, sat down, her eyes on the crack, and waited.

As far as she could remember, it was the first time she had ever tried to surprise another person's secret, but she was conscious of no compunction. She simply felt as if she were fighting her way through a stifling fog that she must at all costs get out of.

At length she heard Kenneth's latchkey and jumped up. The impulse to rush out and meet him had nearly made her forget why she was there; but she remembered in time and sat down again. From her post she covered the whole range of his movements—saw him enter the hall, draw the key from the door and take off his hat and overcoat.

Then he turned to throw his gloves on the hall table, and at that moment he saw the envelope. The light was full on his face, and what Charlotte first noted there was a look of surprise. Evidently he had not expected the letter—had not thought of the possibility of its being there that day. But though he had not expected it, now that he saw it he knew well enough what it contained. He did not open it immediately, but stood motionless, the colour slowly ebbing from his face.

Apparently he could not make up his mind to touch it; but at length he put out his hand, opened the envelope, and moved with it to the light. In doing so he turned his back on Charlotte, and she saw only his bent head and slightly stooping shoulders. Apparently all the writing was on one page, for he did not turn the sheet but continued to stare at it for so long that he must have reread it a dozen times—or so it seemed to the woman breathlessly watching him. At length she saw him move; he raised the letter still closer to his eyes, as though he had not fully deciphered it. Then he lowered his head, and she saw his lips touch the sheet.

"Kenneth!" she exclaimed, and went on out into the hall.

The letter clutched in his hand, her husband turned and looked at her. "Where were you?" he said, in a low bewildered voice, like a man waked out of his sleep.

"In the library, waiting for you." She tried to steady her voice: "What's the matter! What's in that letter? You look ghastly."

Her agitation seemed to calm him, and he instantly put the envelope into his pocket with a slight laugh. "Ghastly? I'm sorry. I've had a hard day in the office—one or two complicated cases. I look dog-tired, I suppose."

"You didn't look tired when you came in. It was only when you opened that letter ——"

He had followed her into the library, and they stood gazing at each other. Charlotte noticed how quickly he had regained his self-control; his profession had trained him to rapid mastery of face and voice. She saw at once that she would be at a disadvantage in any attempt to surprise his secret, but at the same moment she lost all desire to manoeuvre, to trick him into betraying anything he wanted to conceal. Her wish was still to penetrate the mystery, but only that she might help him to bear the burden it implied. "Even if it *is* another woman," she thought.

"Kenneth," she said, her heart beating excitedly, "I waited here on purpose to see you come in. I wanted to watch you while you opened that letter."

His face, which had paled, turned to dark red; then it paled again. "That letter? Why especially that letter?"

"Because I've noticed that whenever one of those letters comes it seems to have such a strange effect on you."

A line of anger she had never seen before came out between his eyes, and she said to herself: "The upper part of his face is too narrow; this is the first time I ever noticed it."

She heard him continue, in the cool and faintly ironic tone of the prosecuting lawyer making a point: "Ah, so you're in the habit of watching people open their letters when they don't know you're there?"

"Not in the habit. I never did such a thing before. But I had to find out what she writes to you, at regular intervals, in those grey envelopes."

He weighed this for a moment; then: "The intervals have not been regular," he said.

"Oh, I dare say you've kept a better account of the dates than I have," she retorted, her magnanimity vanishing at his tone. "All I know is that every time that woman writes to you ——"

"Why do you assume it's a woman?"

"It's a woman's writing. Do you deny it?"

He smiled. "No, I don't deny it. I asked only because the writing is generally supposed to look more like a man's."

Charlotte passed this over impatiently. "And this woman—what does she write to you about?"

Again he seemed to consider a moment. "About business."

"Legal business?"

"In a way, yes. Business in general."

"You look after her affairs for her?"

"Yes."

"You've looked after them for a long time?"

"Yes. A very long time."

"Kenneth, dearest, won't you tell me who she is?"

"No. I can't." He paused, and brought out, as if with a certain hesitation: "Professional secrecy."

The blood rushed from Charlotte's heart to her temples. "Don't say that—don't!"

"Why not?"

"Because I saw you kiss the letter."

The effect of the words was so disconcerting that she instantly repented having spoken them. Her husband, who had submitted to her cross-questioning with a sort of contemptuous composure, as though he were humouring an unreasonable child, turned on her a face of terror and distress. For a minute he seemed unable to speak; then, collecting himself, with an effort, he stammered out: "The writing is very faint; you must have seen me holding the letter close to my eyes to try to decipher it."

"No; I saw you kissing it." He was silent. "Didn't I see you kissing it?"

He sank back into indifference. "Perhaps."

"Kenneth! You stand there and say that—to me?"

"What possible difference can it make to you? The letter is on business, as I told you. Do you suppose I'd lie about it? The writer is a very old friend whom I haven't seen for a long time."

"Men don't kiss business letters, even from women who are very old friends, unless they have been their lovers, and still regret them."

He shrugged his shoulders slightly and turned away, as if he considered the discussion at an end and were faintly disgusted at the turn it had taken.

"Kenneth!" Charlotte moved toward him and caught hold of his arm.

He paused with a look of weariness and laid his hand over hers. "Won't you believe me?" he asked gently.

"How can I? I've watched these letters come to you—for months now they've been coming. Ever since we came back from the West Indies—one of them greeted me the very day we arrived. And after each one of them I see their mysterious effect on you, I see you disturbed, unhappy, as if someone were trying to estrange you from me."

"No, dear; not that. Never!"

She drew back and looked at him with passionate entreaty. "Well, then, prove it to me, darling. It's so easy!"

He forced a smile. "It's not easy to prove anything to a woman who's once taken an idea into her head."

"You've only got to show me the letter."

His hand slipped from hers and he drew back and shook his head.

"You won't?"

"I can't."

"Then the woman who wrote it is your mistress."

"No, dear. No."

"Not now, perhaps. I suppose she's trying to get you back, and you're struggling, out of pity for me. My poor Kenneth!"

"I swear to you she never was my mistress."

Charlotte felt the tears rushing to her eyes. "Ah, that's worse, then—that's hopeless! The prudent ones are the kind that keep their hold on a man. We all know that." She lifted her hands and hid her face in them.

Her husband remained silent; he offered neither consolation nor denial, and at length, wiping away her tears, she raised her eyes almost timidly to his.

"Kenneth, think! We've been married such a short time. Imagine what you're making me suffer. You say you can't show me this letter. You refuse even to explain it."

"I've told you the letter is on business. I will swear to that too."

"A man will swear to anything to screen a woman. If you want me to believe you, at least tell me her name. If you'll do that, I promise you I won't ask to see the letter."

There was a long interval of suspense, during which she felt her heart beating against her ribs in quick admonitory knocks, as if warning her of the danger she was incurring.

"I can't," he said at length.

"Not even her name?"

"No."

"You can't tell me anything more?"

"No."

Again a pause; this time they seemed both to have reached the end of their arguments and to be helplessly facing each other across a baffling waste of incomprehension.

Charlotte stood breathing rapidly, her hands against her breast. She felt as if she had run a hard race and missed the goal. She had meant to move her husband and had succeeded only in irritating him; and this error of reckoning seemed to change him into a stranger, a mysterious incomprehensible being whom no argument or entreaty of hers could reach. The curious thing was that she was aware in him of no hostility or even impatience, but only of a remoteness, an inaccessibility, far more difficult to overcome. She felt herself excluded, ignored, blotted out of his life. But after a moment or two, looking at him more calmly, she saw that he was suffering as much as she was. His distant guarded face was drawn with pain; the coming of the grey envelope, though it always cast a shadow, had never marked him as deeply as this discussion with his wife.

Charlotte took heart; perhaps, after all, she had not spent her last shaft. She drew nearer and once more laid her hand on his arm. "Poor Kenneth! If you knew how sorry I am for you—"

She thought he winced slightly at this expression of sympathy, but he took her hand and pressed it.

"I can think of nothing worse than to be incapable of loving long," she continued, "to feel the beauty of a great love and to be too unstable to bear its burden."

He turned on her a look of wistful reproach. "Oh, don't say that of me. Unstable!"

She felt herself at last on the right tack, and her voice trembled with excitement as she went on: "Then what about me and this other woman? Haven't you already forgotten Elsie twice within a year?"

She seldom pronounced his first wife's name; it did not come naturally to her tongue. She flung it out now as if she were flinging some dangerous explosive into the open space between them, and drew back a step, waiting to hear the mine go off.

Her husband did not move; his expression grew sadder, but showed no resentment. "I have never forgotten Elsie," he said.

Charlotte could not repress a faint laugh. "Then, you poor dear, between the three of us—"

"There are not—" he began; and then broke off and put his hand to his forehead.

"Not what?"

"I'm sorry; I don't believe I know what I'm saying. I've got a blinding headache." He looked wan and furrowed enough for the statement to be true, but she was exasperated by his evasion.

"Ah, yes; the grey envelope headache!"

She saw the surprise in his eyes. "I'd forgotten how closely I've been watched," he said coldly. "If you'll excuse me, I think I'll go up and try an hour in the dark, to see if I can get rid of this neuralgia."

She wavered; then she said, with desperate resolution: "I'm sorry your head aches. But before you go I want to say that sooner or later this question must be settled between us. Someone is trying to separate us, and I don't care what it costs me to find out who it is." She looked him steadily in the eyes. "If it costs me your love, I don't care! If I can't have your confidence I don't want anything from you."

He still looked at her wistfully. "Give me time."

"Time for what? It's only a word to say."

"Time to show you that you haven't lost my love or my confidence."

"Well, I'm waiting."

He turned toward the door, and then glanced back hesitatingly. "Oh, do wait, my love," he said, and went out of the room.

She heard his tired step on the stairs and the closing of his bedroom door above. Then she dropped into a chair and buried her face in her folded arms. Her first movement was one of compunction; she seemed to herself to have been hard, unhuman, unimaginative. "Think of telling him that I didn't care if my insistence cost me his love! The lying rubbish!" She started up to follow him and unsay the meaningless words. But she was checked by a reflection. He had had his way, after all; he had eluded all attacks on his secret, and now he was shut up alone in his room, reading that other woman's letter.

3

She was still reflecting on this when the surprised parlourmaid came in and found her. No, Charlotte said, she wasn't going to dress for dinner; Mr. Ashby didn't want to dine. He was very tired and had gone up to his room to rest; later she would have something brought on a tray to the drawing room. She mounted the stairs to her bedroom. Her dinner dress was lying on the bed, and at the sight the quiet routine of her daily life took hold of her and she began to feel as if the strange talk she had just had with her husband must have taken place in another world, between two beings who were not Charlotte Gorse and Kenneth Ashby, but phantoms projected by her fevered imagination. She recalled the year since her marriage—her husband's constant devotion; his persistent, almost too insistent tenderness; the feeling he had given her at times of being too eagerly dependent on her, too searchingly close to her, as if there were not air enough between her soul and his. It seemed preposterous, as she recalled all this, that a few moments ago she should have been accusing him of an intrigue with another woman! But, then, what—

Again she was moved by the impulse to go up to him, beg his pardon and try to laugh away the misunderstanding. But she was restrained by the fear of forcing herself upon his privacy. He was troubled and unhappy, oppressed by some grief or fear; and he had shown her that he wanted to fight out his battle alone. It would be wiser, as well as more generous, to respect his wish. Only, how strange, how unbearable, to be there, in the next room to his, and feel herself at the other end of the world! In her nervous agitation she almost regretted not having had the courage to open the letter and put it back on the hall table before he came in. At least she would have known what his secret was, and the bogy might have been laid. For she was beginning now to think of the mystery as something conscious, malevolent: a secret persecution before which he quailed, yet from which he could not free himself. Once or twice in his evasive eyes she thought she had detected a desire for help, an impulse of confession, instantly restrained and suppressed. It was as if he felt she could have helped him if she had known, and yet had been unable to tell her!

There flashed through her mind the idea of going to his mother. She was very fond of old Mrs. Ashby, a firm-fleshed clear-eyed old lady, with an astringent bluntness of speech which responded to the forthright and simple in Charlotte's own nature. There had been a tacit bond between them ever since the day when Mrs. Ashby Senior, coming to lunch for the first time with her new daughter-in-law, had been received by Charlotte downstairs in the library, and glancing up at the empty wall above her son's desk, had remarked laconically: "Elsie gone, eh?" adding, at Charlotte's murmured explanation: "Nonsense. Don't have her back. Two's company."

Charlotte, at this reading of her thoughts, could hardly refrain from exchanging a smile of complicity with her mother-in-law; and it seemed to her now that Mrs. Ashby's almost uncanny directness might pierce to the core of this new mystery. But here again she hesitated, for the idea almost suggested a betrayal. What right had she to call in anyone, even so close a relation, to surprise a secret which her husband was trying to keep from her? "Perhaps, by and by, he'll talk to his mother of his own accord," she thought, and then ended: "But what does it matter? He and I must settle it between us."

She was still brooding over the problem when there was a knock on the door and her husband came in. He was dressed for dinner and seemed surprised to see her sitting there, with her evening dress lying unheeded on the bed.

"Aren't you coming down?"

"I thought you were not well and had gone to bed," she faltered.

He forced a smile. "I'm not particularly well, but we'd better go down." His face, though still drawn, looked calmer than when he had fled upstairs an hour earlier.

"There it is; he knows what's in the letter and has fought his battle out again, whatever it is," she reflected, "while I'm still in darkness."

She rang and gave a hurried order that dinner should be served as soon as possible—just a short meal, whatever could be got ready quickly, as both she and Mr. Ashby were rather tired and not very hungry.

Dinner was announced, and they sat down to it. At first neither seemed able to find a word to say; then Ashby began to make conversation with an assumption of ease that was more oppressive than his silence. "How tired he is! How terribly overtired!" Charlotte said to herself, pursuing her own thoughts while he rambled on about municipal politics, aviation, an exhibition of modern French painting, the health of an old aunt and the installing of the automatic telephone. "Good heavens, how tired he is!"

When they dined alone they usually went into the library after dinner, and Charlotte curled herself up on the divan with her knitting while he settled down in his armchair under the lamp and lit a pipe. But this evening, by tacit agreement, they avoided the room in which their strange talk had taken place, and went up to Charlotte's drawing room.

They sat down near the fire, and Charlotte said: "Your pipe?" after he had put down his hardly tasted coffee.

He shook his head. "No, not tonight."

"You must go to bed early; you look terribly tired. I'm sure they overwork you at the office."

"I suppose we all overwork at times."

She rose and stood before him with sudden resolution. "Well, I'm not going to have you use up your strength slaving in that way. It's absurd. I can see you're ill." She bent over him and laid her hand on his forehead. "My poor old Kenneth. Prepare to be taken away soon on a long holiday."

He looked up at her, startled. "A holiday?"

"Certainly. Didn't you know I was going to carry you off at Easter? We're going to start in a fortnight on a month's voyage to somewhere or other. On any one of the big cruising steamers." She paused and bent closer, touching his forehead with her lips. "I'm tired, too, Kenneth."

He seemed to pay no heed to her last words, but sat, his hands on his knees, his head drawn back a little from her caress, and looked up at her with a stare of apprehension. "Again? My dear, we can't; I can't possibly go away."

"I don't know why you say 'again,' Kenneth; we haven't taken a real holiday this year."

"At Christmas we spent a week with the children in the country."

"Yes, but this time I mean away from the children, from servants, from the house. From everything that's familiar and fatiguing. Your mother will love to have Joyce and Peter with her."

He frowned and slowly shook his head. "No, dear; I can't leave them with my mother."

"Why, Kenneth, how absurd! She adores them. You didn't hesitate to leave them with her for over two months when we went to the West Indies."

He drew a deep breath and stood up uneasily. "That was different."

"Different? Why?"

"I mean, at that time I didn't realise—" He broke off as if to choose his words and then went on: "My mother adores the children, as you say. But she isn't always very judicious. Grandmothers always spoil children. And sometimes she talks before them without thinking." He turned to his wife with an almost pitiful gesture of entreaty. "Don't ask me to, dear."

Charlotte mused. It was true that the elder Mrs. Ashby had a fearless tongue, but she was the last woman in the world to say or hint anything before her grandchildren at which the most scrupulous parent could take offense. Charlotte looked at her husband in perplexity.

"I don't understand."

He continued to turn on her the same troubled and entreating gaze. "Don't try to," he muttered.

"Not try to?"

"Not now—not yet." He put up his hands and pressed them against his temples. "Can't you see that there's no use in insisting? I can't go away, no matter how much I might want to."

Charlotte still scrutinized him gravely. "The question is, *do* you want to?"

He returned her gaze for a moment; then his lips began to tremble, and he said, hardly above his breath: "I want—anything you want."

"And yet ——"

"Don't ask me. I can't leave—I can't!"

"You mean that you can't go away out of reach of those letters!"

Her husband had been standing before her in an uneasy half-hesitating attitude; now he turned abruptly away and walked once or twice up and down the length of the room, his head bent, his eyes fixed on the carpet.

Charlotte felt her resentfulness rising with her fears. "It's that," she persisted. "Why not admit it? You can't live without them."

He continued his troubled pacing of the room; then he stopped short, dropped into a chair and covered his face with his hands. From the shaking of his shoulders, Charlotte saw that he was weeping. She had never seen a man cry, except her father after her mother's death, when she was a little girl; and she remembered still how the sight had frightened her. She was frightened now; she felt that her husband was being dragged away from her into some mysterious bondage, and that she must use up her last atom of strength in the struggle for his freedom, and for hers.

"Kenneth—Kenneth!" she pleaded, kneeling down beside him. "Won't you listen to me? Won't you try to see what I'm suffering? I'm not unreasonable, darling, really not. I don't suppose I should ever have noticed the letters if it hadn't been for their effect on you. It's not my way to pry into other people's affairs; and even if the effect had been different—yes, yes, listen to me—if I'd seen that the letters made you happy, that you were watching eagerly for them, counting the days between their coming, that you wanted them, that they gave you something I haven't known how to give—why, Kenneth, I don't say I shouldn't have suffered from that, too; but it would have been in a different way, and I should have had the courage to hide what I felt, and the hope that someday you'd come to feel about me as you did about the writer of the letters.

"But what I can't bear is to see how you dread them, how they make you suffer, and yet how you can't live without them and won't go away lest you should miss one during your absence. Or perhaps," she added, her voice breaking into a cry of accusation—"perhaps it's because she's actually forbidden you to leave. Kenneth, you must answer me! Is that the reason? Is it because she's forbidden you that you won't go away with me?"

She continued to kneel at his side, and raising her hands, she drew his gently down. She was ashamed of her persistence, ashamed of uncovering that baffled disordered face, yet resolved that no such scruples should arrest her. His eyes were lowered, the muscles of his face quivered; she was making him suffer even more than she suffered herself. Yet this no longer restrained her.

"Kenneth, is it that? She won't let us go away together?"

Still he did not speak or turn his eyes to her; and a sense of defeat swept over her. After all, she thought, the struggle was a losing one. "You needn't answer. I see I'm right," she said.

Suddenly, as she rose, he turned and drew her down again. His hands caught hers and pressed them so tightly that she felt her rings cutting into her flesh. There was something frightened, convulsive in his hold; it was the clutch of a man who felt himself slipping over a precipice. He was staring up at her now as if salvation lay in the face she bent above him. "Of course we'll go away together. We'll go wherever you want," he said in a low confused voice; and putting his arm about her, he drew her close and pressed his lips on hers.

4

Charlotte had said to herself: "I shall sleep tonight," but instead she sat before her fire into the small hours, listening for any sound that came from her husband's room. But he, at any rate, seemed to be resting after the tumult of the evening. Once or twice she stole to the door and in the faint light that came in from the street through his open window she saw him stretched out in heavy sleep—the sleep of weakness and exhaustion. "He's ill," she thought "he's undoubtedly ill. And it's not overwork; it's this mysterious persecution."

She drew a breath of relief. She had fought through the weary fight and the victory was hers—at least for the moment. If only they could have started at once—started for anywhere! She knew it would be useless to ask him to leave before the holidays; and meanwhile the secret influence—as to which she was still so completely in the dark—would continue to work against her, and she would have to renew the struggle day after day till they started on their journey. But after that everything would be different. If once she could get her husband away under other skies, and all to herself, she never doubted her power to release him from the evil spell he was under. Lulled to quiet by the thought, she too slept at last.

When she woke, it was long past her usual hour, and she sat up in bed surprised and vexed at having overslept herself. She always liked to be down to share her husband's breakfast by the library fire; but a glance at the clock made it clear that he must have started long since for his office. To make sure, she jumped out of bed and went into his room, but it was empty. No doubt he had looked in on her before leaving, seen that she still slept, and gone downstairs without disturbing her; and their relations were sufficiently lover-like for her to regret having missed their morning hour.

She rang and asked if Mr. Ashby had already gone. Yes, nearly an hour ago, the maid said. He had given orders that Mrs. Ashby should not be waked and that the children should not come to her till she sent for them . . . . Yes, he had gone up to the nursery himself to give the order. All this sounded usual enough, and Charlotte hardly knew why she asked: "And did Mr. Ashby leave no other message?"

Yes, the maid said, he did; she was so sorry she'd forgotten. He'd told her, just as he was leaving, to say to Mrs. Ashby that he was going to see about their passages, and would she please be ready to sail tomorrow?

Charlotte echoed the woman's "Tomorrow," and sat staring at her incredulously. "Tomorrow—you're sure he said to sail tomorrow?"

"Oh, ever so sure, ma'am. I don't know how I could have forgotten to mention it."

"Well, it doesn't matter. Draw my bath, please." Charlotte sprang up, dashed through her dressing, and caught herself singing at her image in the glass as she sat brushing her hair. It made her feel young again to have scored such a victory. The other woman vanished to a speck on the horizon, as this one, who ruled the foreground, smiled back at the reflection of her lips and eyes. He loved her, then—he loved her as passionately as ever. He had divined what she had suffered, had understood that their happiness depended on their getting away at once, and finding each other again after yesterday's desperate groping in the fog.

The nature of the influence that had come between them did not much matter to Charlotte now; she had faced the phantom and dispelled it. "Courage—that's the secret! If only people who are in love weren't always so afraid of risking their happiness by looking it in the eyes." As she brushed back her light abundant hair it waved electrically above her head, like the palms of victory. Ah, well, some women knew how to manage men, and some didn't—and only the fair—she gaily paraphrased—deserve the brave! Certainly she was looking very pretty.

The morning danced along like a cockleshell on a bright sea—such a sea as they would soon be speeding over. She ordered a particularly good dinner, saw the children off to their classes, had her trunks brought down, consulted with the maid about getting out summer clothes—for of course they would be heading for heat and sunshine—and wondered if she oughtn't to take Kenneth's flannel suits out of camphor. "But how absurd," she reflected, "that I don't yet know where we're going!" She looked at the clock, saw that it was close on noon, and decided to call him up at his office. There was a slight delay; then she heard his secretary's voice saying that Mr. Ashby had looked in for a moment early, and left again almost immediately . . . . Oh, very well; Charlotte would ring up later. How soon was he likely to be back? The secretary answered that she couldn't tell; all they knew in the office was that when he left he had said he was in a hurry because he had to go out of town.

Out of town! Charlotte hung up the receiver and sat blankly gazing into new darkness. Why had he gone out of town? And where had he gone? And of all days, why should he have chosen the eve of their suddenly planned departure? She felt a faint shiver of apprehension. Of course he had gone to see that woman—no doubt to get her permission to leave. He was as completely in bondage as that; and Charlotte had been fatuous enough to see the palms of victory on her forehead. She burst into a laugh and, walking across the room, sat down again before her mirror. What a different face she saw! The smile on her pale lips seemed to mock the rosy vision of the other Charlotte. But gradually her colour crept back.

After all, she had a right to claim the victory, since her husband was doing what she wanted, not what the other woman exacted of him. It was natural enough, in view of his abrupt decision to leave the next day, that he should have arrangements to make, business matters to wind up; it was not even necessary to suppose that his mysterious trip was a visit to the writer of the letters. He might simply have gone to see a client who lived out of town. Of course they would not tell Charlotte at the office; the secretary had hesitated before imparting even such meagre information as the fact of Mr. Ashby's absence. Meanwhile she would go on with her joyful preparations, content to learn later in the day to what particular island of the blest she was to be carried.

The hours wore on, or rather were swept forward on a rush of eager preparations. At last the entrance of the maid who came to draw the curtains roused Charlotte from her labours, and she saw to her surprise that the clock marked five. And she did not yet know where they were going the next day! She rang up her husband's office and was told that Mr. Ashby had not been there since the early morning. She asked for his partner, but the partner could add nothing to her information, for he himself, his suburban train having been behind time, had reached the office after Ashby had come and gone. Charlotte stood perplexed; then she decided to telephone to her mother-in-law.

Of course Kenneth, on the eve of a month's absence, must have gone to see his mother. The mere fact that the children—in spite of his vague objections—would certainly have to be left with old Mrs. Ashby, made it obvious that he would have all sorts of matters to decide with her. At another time Charlotte might have felt a little hurt at being excluded from their conference, but nothing mattered now but that she had won the day, that her husband was still hers and not another woman's. Gaily she called up Mrs. Ashby, heard her friendly voice, and began: "Well, did Kenneth's news surprise you? What do you think of our elopement?"

Almost instantly, before Mrs. Ashby could answer, Charlotte knew what her reply would be. Mrs. Ashby had not seen her son, she had had no word from him and did not know what her daughter-in-law meant. Charlotte stood silent in the intensity of her surprise. "But then, where *has* he been?" she thought. Then, recovering herself, she explained their sudden decision to Mrs. Ashby, and in doing so, gradually regained her own self-confidence, her conviction that nothing could ever again come between Kenneth and herself.

Mrs. Ashby took the news calmly and approvingly. She, too, had thought that Kenneth looked worried and overtired, and she agreed with her daughter-in-law that in such cases change was the surest remedy. "I'm always so glad when he gets away. Elsie hated traveling; she was always finding pretexts to prevent his going anywhere. With you, thank goodness, it's different."

Nor was Mrs. Ashby surprised at his not having had time to let her know of his departure. He must have been in a rush from the moment the decision was taken; but no doubt he'd drop in before dinner. Five minutes' talk was really all they needed. "I hope you'll gradually cure Kenneth of his mania for going over and over a question that could be settled in a dozen words. He never used to be like that, and if he carried the habit into his professional work he'd soon lose all his clients . . . . Yes, do come in for a minute, dear, if you have time; no doubt he'll turn up while you're here." The tonic ring of Mrs. Ashby's voice echoed on reassuringly in the silent room while Charlotte continued her preparations.

Toward seven the telephone rang, and she darted to it. Now she would know! But it was only from the conscientious secretary, to say that Mr. Ashby hadn't been back, or sent any word, and before the office closed she thought she ought to let Mrs. Ashby know. "Oh, that's all right. Thanks a lot!" Charlotte called out cheerfully, and hung up the receiver with a trembling hand. But perhaps by this time, she reflected, he was at his mother's. She shut her drawers and cupboards, put on her hat and coat and called up to the nursery that she was going out for a minute to see the children's grandmother.

Mrs. Ashby lived nearby, and during her brief walk through the cold spring dusk Charlotte imagined that every advancing figure was her husband's. But she did not meet him on the way, and when she entered the house she found her mother-in-law alone. Kenneth had neither telephoned nor come. Old Mrs. Ashby sat by her bright fire, her knitting needles flashing steadily through her active old hands, and her mere bodily presence gave reassurance to Charlotte. Yes, it was certainly odd that Kenneth had gone off for the whole day without letting any of them know; but, after all, it was to be expected. A busy lawyer held so many threads in his hands that any sudden change of plan would oblige him to make all sorts of unforeseen arrangements and adjustments. He might have gone to see some client in the suburbs and been detained there; his mother remembered his telling her that he had charge of the legal business of a queer old recluse somewhere in New Jersey, who was immensely rich but too mean to have a telephone. Very likely Kenneth had been stranded there.

But Charlotte felt her nervousness gaining on her. When Mrs. Ashby asked her at what hour they were sailing the next day and she had to say she didn't know—that Kenneth had simply sent her word he was going to take their passages—the uttering of the words again brought home to her the strangeness of the situation. Even Mrs. Ashby conceded that it was odd; but she immediately added that it only showed what a rush he was in.

"But, mother, it's nearly eight o'clock! He must realise that I've got to know when we're starting tomorrow."

"Oh, the boat probably doesn't sail till evening. Sometimes they have to wait till midnight for the tide. Kenneth's probably counting on that. After all, he has a level head."

Charlotte stood up. "It's not that. Something has happened to him."

Mrs. Ashby took off her spectacles and rolled up her knitting. "If you begin to let yourself imagine things ——"

"Aren't you in the least anxious?"

"I never am till I have to be. I wish you'd ring for dinner, my dear. You'll stay and dine? He's sure to drop in here on his way home."

Charlotte called up her own house. No, the maid said, Mr. Ashby hadn't come in and hadn't telephoned. She would tell him as soon as he came that Mrs. Ashby was dining at his mother's. Charlotte followed her mother-in-law into the dining room and sat with parched throat before her empty plate, while Mrs. Ashby dealt calmly and efficiently with a short but carefully prepared repast. "You'd better eat something, child, or you'll be as bad as Kenneth . . . . Yes, a little more asparagus, please, Jane."

She insisted on Charlotte's drinking a glass of sherry and nibbling a bit of toast; then they returned to the drawing room, where the fire had been made up, and the cushions in Mrs. Ashby's armchair shaken out and smoothed. How safe and familiar it all looked; and out there, somewhere in the uncertainty and mystery of the night, lurked the answer to the two women's conjectures, like an indistinguishable figure prowling on the threshold.

At last Charlotte got up and said: "I'd better go back. At this hour Kenneth will certainly go straight home."

Mrs. Ashby smiled indulgently. "It's not very late, my dear. It doesn't take two sparrows long to dine."

"It's after nine." Charlotte bent down to kiss her. "The fact is, I can't keep still."

Mrs. Ashby pushed aside her work and rested her two hands on the arms of her chair. "I'm going with you," she said, helping herself up.

Charlotte protested that it was too late, that it was not necessary, that she would call up as soon as Kenneth came in, but Mrs. Ashby had already rung for her maid. She was slightly lame, and stood resting on her stick while her wraps were brought. "If Mr. Kenneth turns up, tell him he'll find me at his own house," she instructed the maid as the two women got into the taxi which had been summoned. During the short drive Charlotte gave thanks that she was not returning home alone. There was something warm and substantial in the mere fact of Mrs. Ashby's nearness, something that corresponded with the clearness of her eyes and the texture of her fresh firm complexion. As the taxi drew up she laid her hand encouragingly on Charlotte's. "You'll see; there'll be a message."

The door opened at Charlotte's ring and the two entered. Charlotte's heart beat excitedly; the stimulus of her mother-in-law's confidence was beginning to flow through her veins.

"You'll see—you'll see," Mrs. Ashby repeated.

The maid who opened the door said no, Mr. Ashby had not come in, and there had been no message from him.

"You're sure the telephone's not out of order?" his mother suggested; and the maid said, well, it certainly wasn't half an hour ago; but she'd just go and ring up to make sure. She disappeared, and Charlotte turned to take off her hat and cloak. As she did so her eyes lit on the hall table, and there lay a grey envelope, her husband's name faintly traced on it. "Oh!" she cried out, suddenly aware that for the first time in months she had entered her house without wondering if one of the grey letters would be there.

"What is it, my dear?" Mrs. Ashby asked with a glance of surprise.

Charlotte did not answer. She took up the envelope and stood staring at it as if she could force her gaze to penetrate to what was within. Then an idea occurred to her. She turned and held out the envelope to her mother-in-law.

"Do you know that writing?" she asked.

Mrs. Ashby took the letter. She had to feel with her other hand for her eyeglasses, and when she had adjusted them she lifted the envelope to the light. "Why!" she exclaimed; and then stopped. Charlotte noticed that the letter shook in her usually firm hand. "But this is addressed to Kenneth," Mrs. Ashby said at length, in a low voice. Her tone seemed to imply that she felt her daughter-in-law's question to be slightly indiscreet.

"Yes, but no matter," Charlotte spoke with sudden decision. "I want to know—do you know the writing?"

Mrs. Ashby handed back the letter. "No," she said distinctly.

The two women had turned into the library. Charlotte switched on the electric light and shut the door. She still held the envelope in her hand.

"I'm going to open it," she announced.

She caught her mother-in-law's startled glance. "But, dearest—a letter not addressed to you? My dear, you can't!"

"As if I cared about that—now!" She continued to look intently at Mrs. Ashby. "This letter may tell me where Kenneth is."

Mrs. Ashby's glossy bloom was effaced by a quick pallor; her firm cheeks seemed to shrink and wither. "Why should it? What makes you believe —— It can't possibly ——"

Charlotte held her eyes steadily on that altered face. "Ah, then you *do* know the writing?" she flashed back.

"Know the writing? How should I? With all my son's correspondents . . . . What I do know is—" Mrs. Ashby broke off and looked at her daughter-in-law entreatingly, almost timidly.

Charlotte caught her by the wrist. "Mother! What do you know? Tell me! You must!"

"That I don't believe any good ever came of a woman's opening her husband's letters behind his back."

The words sounded to Charlotte's irritated ears as flat as a phrase culled from a book of moral axioms. She laughed impatiently and dropped her mother-in-law's wrist. "Is that all? No good can come of this letter, opened or unopened. I know that well enough. But whatever ill comes, I mean to find out what's in it." Her hands had been trembling as they held the envelope, but now they grew firm, and her voice also. She still gazed intently at Mrs. Ashby.

"This is the ninth letter addressed in the same hand that has come for Kenneth since we've been married. Always these same grey envelopes. I've kept count of them because after each one he has been like a man who has had some dreadful shock. It takes him hours to shake off their effect. I've told him so. I've told him I must know from whom they come, because I can see they're killing him. He won't answer my questions; he says he can't tell me anything about the letters; but last night he promised to go away with me—to get away from them."

Mrs. Ashby, with shaking steps, had gone to one of the armchairs and sat down in it, her head drooping forward on her breast. "Ah," she murmured.

"So now you understand ——"

"Did he tell you it was to get away from them?"

"He said, to get away—to get away. He was sobbing so that he could hardly speak. But I told him I knew that was why."

"And what did he say?"

"He took me in his arms and said he'd go wherever I wanted."

"Ah, thank God!" said Mrs. Ashby. There was a silence, during which she continued to sit with bowed head, and eyes averted from her daughter-in-law. At last she looked up and spoke. "Are you sure there have been as many as nine?"

"Perfectly. This is the ninth. I've kept count."

"And he has absolutely refused to explain?"

"Absolutely."

Mrs. Ashby spoke through pale contracted lips. "When did they begin to come? Do you remember?"

Charlotte laughed again. "Remember? The first one came the night we got back from our honeymoon."

"All that time?" Mrs. Ashby lifted her head and spoke with sudden energy. "Then—yes, open it."

The words were so unexpected that Charlotte felt the blood in her temples, and her hands began to tremble again. She tried to slip her finger under the flap of the envelope, but it was so tightly stuck that she had to hunt on her husband's writing table for his ivory letter opener. As she pushed about the familiar objects his own hands had so lately touched, they sent through her the icy chill emanating from the little personal effects of someone newly dead. In the deep silence of the room the tearing of the paper as she slit the envelope sounded like a human cry. She drew out the sheet and carried it to the lamp.

"Well?" Mrs. Ashby asked below her breath.

Charlotte did not move or answer. She was bending over the page with wrinkled brows, holding it nearer and nearer to the light. Her sight must be blurred, or else dazzled by the reflection of the lamplight on the smooth surface of the paper, for, strain her eyes as she would, she could discern only a few faint strokes, so faint and faltering as to be nearly undecipherable.

"I can't make it out," she said.

"What do you mean, dear?"

"The writing's too indistinct . . . . Wait."

She went back to the table and, sitting down close to Kenneth's reading lamp, slipped the letter under a magnifying glass. All this time she was aware that her mother-in-law was watching her intently.

"Well?" Mrs. Ashby breathed.

"Well, it's no clearer. I can't read it."

"You mean the paper is an absolute blank?"

"No, not quite. There is writing on it. I can make out something like 'mine'—oh, and 'come.' It might be 'come.'"

Mrs. Ashby stood up abruptly. Her face was even paler than before. She advanced to the table and, resting her two hands on it, drew a deep breath. "Let me see," she said, as if forcing herself to a hateful effort.

Charlotte felt the contagion of her whiteness. "She knows," she thought. She pushed the letter across the table. Her mother-in-law lowered her head over it in silence, but without touching it with her pale wrinkled hands.

Charlotte stood watching her as she herself, when she had tried to read the letter, had been watched by Mrs. Ashby. The latter fumbled for her glasses, held them to her eyes, and bent still closer to the outspread page, in order, as it seemed, to avoid touching it. The light of the lamp fell directly on her old face, and Charlotte reflected what depths of the unknown may lurk under the clearest and most candid lineaments. She had never seen her mother-in-law's features express any but simple and sound emotions—cordiality, amusement, a kindly sympathy; now and again a flash of wholesome anger. Now they seemed to wear a look of fear and hatred, of incredulous dismay and almost cringing defiance. It was as if the spirits warring within her had distorted her face to their own likeness. At length she raised her head. "I can't—I can't," she said in a voice of childish distress.

"You can't make it out either?"

She shook her head, and Charlotte saw two tears roll down her cheeks.

"Familiar as the writing is to you?" Charlotte insisted with twitching lips.

Mrs. Ashby did not take up the challenge. "I can make out nothing—nothing."

"But you do know the writing?"

Mrs. Ashby lifted her head timidly; her anxious eyes stole with a glance of apprehension around the quiet familiar room. "How can I tell? I was startled at first . . . ."

"Startled by the resemblance?"

"Well, I thought ——"

"You'd better say it out, mother! You knew at once it was *her* writing?"

"Oh, wait, my dear—wait."

"Wait for what?"

Mrs. Ashby looked up; her eyes, traveling slowly past Charlotte, were lifted to the blank wall behind her son's writing table.

Charlotte, following the glance, burst into a shrill laugh of accusation. "I needn't wait any longer! You've answered me now! You're looking straight at the wall where her picture used to hang!"

Mrs. Ashby lifted her hand with a murmur of warning. "Sh-h."

"Oh, you needn't imagine that anything can ever frighten me again!" Charlotte cried.

Her mother-in-law still leaned against the table. Her lips moved plaintively. "But we're going mad—we're both going mad. We both know such things are impossible."

Her daughter-in-law looked at her with a pitying stare. "I've known for a long time now that everything was possible."

"Even this?"

"Yes, exactly this."

"But this letter—after all, there's nothing in this letter ——"

"Perhaps there would be to him. How can I tell? I remember his saying to me once that if you were used to a handwriting the faintest stroke of it became legible. Now I see what he meant. He *was* used to it.

"But the few strokes that I can make out are so pale. No one could possibly read that letter."

Charlotte laughed again. "I suppose everything's pale about a ghost," she said stridently.

"Oh, my child—my child—don't say it!"

"Why shouldn't I say it, when even the bare walls cry it out? What difference does it make if her letters are illegible to you and me? If even you can see her face on that blank wall, why shouldn't he read her writing on this blank paper? Don't you see that she's everywhere in this house, and the closer to him because to everyone else she's become invisible?" Charlotte dropped into a chair and covered her face with her hands. A turmoil of sobbing shook her from head to foot. At length a touch on her shoulder made her look up, and she saw her mother-in-law bending over her. Mrs. Ashby's face seemed to have grown still smaller and more wasted, but it had resumed its usual quiet look. Through all her tossing anguish, Charlotte felt the impact of that resolute spirit.

"Tomorrow—tomorrow. You'll see. There'll be some explanation tomorrow."

Charlotte cut her short. "An explanation? Who's going to give it, I wonder?"

Mrs. Ashby drew back and straightened herself heroically. "Kenneth himself will," she cried out in a strong voice. Charlotte said nothing, and the old woman went on: "But meanwhile we must act; we must notify the police. Now, without a moment's delay. We must do everything—everything."

Charlotte stood up slowly and stiffly; her joints felt as cramped as an old woman's. "Exactly as if we thought it could do any good to do anything?"

Resolutely Mrs. Ashby cried: "Yes!" and Charlotte went up to the telephone and unhooked the receiver.

The Confessional

When I was a young man I thought a great deal of local colour. At that time, it was still a pigment of recent discovery, and supposed to have a peculiarly stimulating effect on the mental eye. As an aid to the imagination its value was perhaps overrated; but as an object of pursuit to that vagrant faculty, it had all the merits claimed for it. I certainly never hunted any game better worth my powder; and to a young man with rare holidays and long working hours, its value was enhanced by the fact that one might bring it down at any turn, if only one kept one's eye alert and one's hand on the trigger.

Even the large manufacturing city where, for some years, my young enthusiasms were chained to an accountant's desk, was not without its romantic opportunities. Many of the mill-hands at Dunstable were Italians, and a foreign settlement had formed itself in that unsavoury and unsanitary portion of the town known as the Point. The Point, like more aristocratic communities, had its residential and commercial districts, its church, its theatre and its restaurant. When the craving for local colour was on me it was my habit to resort to the restaurant, a low-browed wooden building with the appetising announcement:

Aristiù di montone

pasted in one of its fly-blown window-panes. Here the consumption of tough macaroni or of an ambiguous *frittura* sufficed to transport me to the Cappello d'Oro in Venice, while my cup of coffee and a wasp-waisted cigar with a straw in it turned my greasy table-cloth into the marble top of one of the little round tables under the arcade of the Caffè Pedrotti at Padua. This feat of the imagination was materially aided by Agostino, the hollow-eyed and low-collared waiter, whose slimy napkin never lost its Latin flourish and whose zeal for my comfort was not infrequently displayed by his testing the warmth of my soup with his finger. Through Agostino I became acquainted with the inner history of the colony, heard the details of its feuds and vendettas, and learned to know by sight the leading characters in these domestic dramas.

The restaurant was frequented by the chief personages of the community: the overseer of the Italian hands at the Meriton Mills, the doctor, his wife the *levatrice* (a plump Neapolitan with greasy ringlets, a plush picture-hat, and a charm against the evil-eye hanging in a crease of her neck) and lastly by Don Egidio, the *parocco* of the little church across the street. The doctor and his wife came only on feast days, but the overseer and Don Egidio were regular patrons. The former was a quiet saturnine-looking man, of accomplished manners but reluctant speech, and I depended for my diversion chiefly on Don Egidio, whose large loosely-hung lips were always ajar for conversation.

The remarks issuing from them were richly tinged by the gutturals of the Bergamasque dialect, and it needed but a slight acquaintance with Italian types to detect the Lombard peasant under the priest's rusty cassock. This inference was confirmed by Don Egidio's telling me that he came from a village of Val Camonica, the radiant valley which extends northward from the lake of Iseo to the Adamello glaciers. His stepfather had been a labourer on one of the fruit-farms of a Milanese count who owned large estates in the Val Camonica; and that gentleman, taking a fancy to the lad, whom he had seen at work in his orchards, had removed him to his villa on the lake of Iseo and had subsequently educated him for the Church.

It was doubtless to this picturesque accident that Don Egidio owed the mingling of ease and simplicity that gave an inimitable charm to his stout shabby presence. It was as though some wild mountain-fruit had been transplanted to the count's orchards and had mellowed under cultivation without losing its sylvan flavour. I have never seen the social art carried farther without suggestion of artifice. The fact that Don Egidio's amenities were mainly exercised on the mill-hands composing his parish proved the genuineness of his gift. It is easier to simulate gentility among gentlemen than among navvies; and the plain man is a touchstone who draws out all the alloy in the gold.

Among his parishioners Don Egidio ruled with the cheerful despotism of the good priest. On cardinal points he was inflexible, but in minor matters he had that elasticity of judgment which enables the Catholic discipline to fit itself to every inequality of the human conscience. There was no appeal from his verdict; but his judgment-seat was a revolving chair from which he could view the same act at various angles. His influence was acknowledged not only by his flock, but by the policeman at the corner, the "bar-keep'" in the dive, the ward politician in the corner grocery. The general verdict of Dunstable was that the Point would have been hell without the priest. It was perhaps not precisely heaven with him; but such light of the upper sky as pierced its murky atmosphere was reflected from Don Egidio's countenance. It is hardly possible for anyone to exercise such influence without taking pleasure in it; and on the whole the priest was probably a contented man; though it does not follow that he was a happy one. On this point the first stages of our acquaintance yielded much food for conjecture.

At first sight Don Egidio was the image of cheerfulness. He had all the physical indications of a mind at ease: the leisurely rolling gait, the ready laugh, the hospitable eye of the man whose sympathies are always on the latch. It took me some time to discover under his surface garrulity the impenetrable reticence of his profession, and under his enjoyment of trifles a levelling melancholy which made all enjoyment trifling. Don Egidio's aspect and conversation were so unsuggestive of psychological complexities that I set down this trait to poverty or home-sickness. There are few classes of men more frugal in tastes and habit than the village priest in Italy; but Don Egidio, by his own account, had been introduced, at an impressionable age, to a way of living that must have surpassed his wildest dreams of self-indulgence. To whatever privations his parochial work had since accustomed him, the influences of that earlier life were too perceptible in his talk not to have made a profound impression on his tastes; and he remained, for all his apostolic simplicity, the image of the family priest who has his seat at the rich man's table.

It chanced that I had used one of my short European holidays to explore afoot the romantic passes connecting the Valtelline with the lake of Iseo; and my remembrance of that enchanting region made it seem impossible that Don Egidio should ever look without a reminiscent pang on the grimy perspective of his parochial streets. The transition was too complete, too ironical, from those rich glades and Titianesque acclivities to the brick hovels and fissured sidewalks of the Point.

This impression was confirmed when Don Egidio, in response to my urgent invitation, paid his first visit to my modest lodgings. He called one winter evening, when a wood-fire in its happiest humor was giving a factitious lustre to my book-shelves and bringing out the values of the one or two old prints and Chinese porcelains that accounted for the perennial shabbiness of my wardrobe.

"Ah," said he with a murmur of satisfaction, as he laid aside his shiny hat and bulging umbrella, "it is a long time since I have been in a *casa signorile*."

My remembrance of his own room (he lodged with the doctor and the *levatrice*) saved this epithet from the suggestion of irony and kept me silent while he sank into my armchair with the deliberation of a tired traveller lowering himself gently into a warm bath.

"Good! good!" he repeated, looking about him. "Books, porcelains, objects of *virtù*—I am glad to see that there are still such things in the world!" And he turned a genial eye on the glass of Marsala that I had poured out for him.

Don Egidio was the most temperate of men and never exceeded his one glass; but he liked to sit by the hour puffing at my Cabanas, which I suspected him of preferring to the black weed of his native country. Under the influence of my tobacco he became even more blandly garrulous, and I sometimes fancied that of all the obligations of his calling none could have placed such a strain on him as that of preserving the secrets of the confessional.

He often talked of his early life at the count's villa, where he had been educated with his patron's two sons till he was of age to be sent to the seminary; and I could see that the years spent in simple and familiar intercourse with his benefactors had been the most vivid chapter in his experience. The Italian peasant's inarticulate tenderness for the beauty of his birthplace had been specialized in him by contact with cultivated tastes, and he could tell me not only that the count had a "stupendous" collection of pictures, but that the chapel of the villa contained a sepulchral monument by Bambaja, and that the art-critics were divided as to the authenticity of the Leonardo in the family palace at Milan.

On all these subjects he was inexhaustibly voluble; but there was one point which he always avoided, and that was his reason for coming to America. I remember the round turn with which he brought me up when I questioned him.

"A priest," said he, "is a soldier and must obey orders like a soldier." He set down his glass of Marsala and strolled across the room. "I had not observed," he went on, "that you have here a photograph of the

Sposalizio of the Brera. What a picture! È *stupendo*!" and he turned back to his seat and smilingly lit a fresh cigar.

I saw at once that I had hit on a point where his native garrulity was protected by the chain-mail of religious discipline that every Catholic priest wears beneath his cassock. I had too much respect for my friend to wish to penetrate his armor, and now and then I almost fancied he was grateful to me for not putting his reticence to the test.

Don Egidio must have been past sixty when I made his acquaintance; but it was not till the close of an exceptionally harsh winter, some five or six years after our first meeting, that I began to think of him as an old man. It was as though the long-continued cold had cracked and shrivelled him. He had grown bent and hollow-chested and his lower lip shook like an unhinged door. The summer heat did little to revive him, and in September, when I came home from my vacation, I found him just recovering from an attack of pneumonia. That autumn he did not care to venture often into the night air, and now and then I used to go and sit with him in his little room, to which I had contributed the unheard-of luxuries of an easy-chair and a gas-stove.

My engagements, however, made these visits infrequent, and several weeks had elapsed without my seeing the *parocco* when, one snowy November morning, I ran across him in the railway-station. I was on my way to New York for the day and had just time to wave a greeting to him as I jumped into the railway-carriage; but a moment later, to my surprise, I saw him stiffly clambering into the same train. I found him seated in the common car, with his umbrella between his knees and a bundle done up in a red cotton handkerchief on the seat at his side. The caution with which, at my approach, he transferred this bundle to his arms caused me to glance at it in surprise; and he answered my look by saying with a smile:

"They are flowers for the dead—the most exquisite flowers—from the greenhouses of Mr. Meriton—*si figuri*!" And he waved a descriptive hand. "One of my lads, Gianpietro, is employed by the gardener there, and every year on this day he brings me a beautiful bunch of flowers—for such a purpose it is no sin," he added, with the charming Italian pliancy of judgment.

"And why are you travelling in this snowy weather, *signor parocco*?" I asked, as he ended with a cough.

He fixed me gravely with his simple shallow eye. "Because it is the day of the dead, my son," he said, "and I go to place these on the grave of the noblest man that ever lived."

"You are going to New York?"

"To Brooklyn—"

I hesitated a moment, wishing to question him, yet uncertain whether his replies were curtailed by the persistency of his cough or by the desire to avoid interrogation.

"This is no weather to be travelling with such a cough," I said at length.

He made a deprecating gesture.

"I have never missed the day—not once in eighteen years. But for me he would have no one!" He folded his hands on his umbrella and looked away from me to hide the trembling of his lip.

I resolved on a last attempt to storm his confidence. "Your friend is buried in Calvary cemetery?"

He signed an assent.

"That is a long way for you to go alone, *signor parocco*. The streets are sure to be slippery and there is an icy wind blowing. Give me your flowers and let me send them to the cemetery by a messenger. I give you my word they shall reach their destination safely."

He turned a quiet look on me. "My son, you are young," he said, "and you don't know how the dead need us." He drew his breviary from his pocket and opened it with a smile. "*Mi scusi?*" he murmured.

The business which had called me to town obliged me to part from him as soon as the train entered the station, and in my dash for the street I left his unwieldy figure labouring far behind me through the crowd on the platform. Before we separated, however, I had learned that he was returning to Dunstable by the four o'clock train, and had resolved to despatch my business in time to travel home with him. When I reached Wall Street I was received with the news that the man I had appointed to meet was ill and detained in the country. My business was "off" and I found myself with the rest of the day at my disposal.

I had no difficulty in deciding how to employ my time. I was at an age when, in such contingencies, there is always a feminine alternative; and even now I don't know how it was that, on my way to a certain hospitable luncheon-table, I suddenly found myself in a cab which was carrying me at full-speed to the Twenty-Third Street ferry. It was not till I had bought my ticket and seated myself in the varnished tunnel of the ferry-boat that I was aware of having been diverted from my purpose by an overmastering anxiety for Don Egidio. I rapidly calculated that he had not more than an hour's advance on me, and that, allowing for my greater agility and for the fact that I had a cab at my call, I was likely to reach the cemetery in time to see him under shelter before the gusts of sleet that were already sweeping across the river had thickened to a snow-storm.

At the gates of the cemetery I began to take a less sanguine view of my attempt. The commemorative anniversary had filled the silent avenues with visitors, and I felt the futility of my quest as I tried to fix the gatekeeper's attention on my delineation of a stout Italian priest with a bad cough and a bunch of flowers tied up in a red cotton handkerchief. The gate-keeper showed that delusive desire to oblige that is certain to send its victims in the wrong direction; but I had the presence of mind to go exactly contrary to his indication, and thanks to this precaution I came, after half an hour's search, on the figure of my poor *parocco*, kneeling on the wet ground in one of the humblest by-ways of the great necropolis. The mound before which he knelt was strewn with the spoils of Mr. Meriton's conservatories, and on the weather-worn tablet at its head I read the inscription:

IL CONTE SIVIANO
DA MILANO.
Super flumina Babylonis, illic sedimus et flevimus.

So engrossed was Don Egidio that for some moments I stood behind him unobserved; and when he rose and faced me, grief had left so little room for any minor emotion that he looked at me almost without surprise.

"Don Egidio," I said, "I have a carriage waiting for you at the gate. You must come home with me."

He nodded quietly and I drew his hand through my arm.

He turned back to the grave. "One moment, my son," he said. "It may be for the last time." He stood motionless, his eyes on the heaped-up flowers which were already bruised and blackened by the cold. "To leave him alone—after sixty years! But God is everywhere—" he murmured as I led him away.

On the journey home he did not care to talk, and my chief concern was to keep him wrapped in my greatcoat and to see that his bed was made ready as soon as I had restored him to his lodgings. The *levatrice* brought a quilted coverlet from her own room and hovered over him as gently as though he had been of the sex to require her services; while Agostino, at my summons, appeared with a bowl of hot soup that was heralded down the street by a reviving waft of garlic. To these ministrations I left the *parocco*, intending to call for news of him the next evening; but an unexpected pressure of work kept me late at my desk, and the following day some fresh obstacle delayed me.

On the third afternoon, as I was leaving the office, an agate-eyed infant from the Point hailed me with a message from the doctor. The *parocco* was worse and had asked for me. I jumped into the nearest car and ten minutes later was running up the doctor's greasy stairs.

To my dismay I found Don Egidio's room cold and untenanted; but I was reassured a moment later by the appearance of the *levatrice*, who announced that she had transferred the blessed man to her own apartment, where he could have the sunlight and a good bed to lie in. There in fact he lay, weak but smiling, in a setting which contrasted oddly enough with his own monastic surroundings: a cheerful grimy room, hung with anecdotic chromos, photographs of lady-patients proudly presenting their offspring to the camera, and innumerable Neapolitan *santolini* decked out with shrivelled palm-leaves.

The *levatrice* whispered that the good man had the pleurisy, and that, as she phrased it, he was nearing his last mile-stone. I saw that he was in fact in a bad way, but his condition did not indicate any pressing danger, and I had the presentiment that he would still, as the saying is, put up a good fight. It was clear, however, that he knew what turn the conflict must take, and the solemnity with which he welcomed me showed that my summons was a part of that spiritual strategy with which the Catholic opposes the surprise of death.

"My son," he said, when the *levatrice* had left us, "I have a favour to ask you. You found me yesterday bidding goodbye to my best friend." His cough interrupted him. "I have never told you," he went on, "the name of the family in which I was brought up. It was Siviano, and that was the grave of the count's eldest son, with whom I grew up as a brother. For eighteen years he has lain in that strange ground—*in terra aliena*—and when I die, there will be no one to care for his grave."

I saw what he waited for. "I will care for it, *signor parocco*."

"I knew I should have your promise, my child; and what you promise you keep. But my friend is a stranger to you—you are young and at your age life is a mistress who kisses away sad memories. Why should you remember the grave of a stranger? I cannot lay such a claim on you. But I will tell you his story—and then I think that neither joy nor grief will let you forget him; for when you rejoice you will remember how he sorrowed; and when you sorrow the thought of him will be like a friend's hand in yours."

You tell me (Don Egidio began) that you know our little lake; and if you have seen it you will understand why it always used to remind me of the "garden enclosed" of the Canticles.

Hortus inclusus; columba mea in foraminibus petræ: the words used to come back to me whenever I returned from a day's journey across the mountains, and looking down saw the blue lake far below, hidden in its hills like a happy secret in a stern heart. We were never envious of the glory of the great lakes. They are like the show pictures that some nobleman hangs in his public gallery; but our Iseo is the treasure that he hides in his inner chamber.

You tell me you saw it in summer, when it looks up like a saint's eye, reflecting the whole of heaven. It was then too that I first saw it. My future friend, the old count, had found me at work on one of his fruit-farms up the valley, and hearing that I was ill-treated by my stepfather—a drunken pedlar from the Val Mastellone, whom my poor mother a year or two earlier had come across at the fair of Lovere—he had taken me home with him to Iseo. I used to serve mass in our hill-village of Cerveno, and the village children called me "the little priest" because when my work was done I often crept back to the church to get away from my stepfather's blows and curses. "I will make a real priest of him," the count declared; and that afternoon, perched on the box of his travelling-carriage, I was whirled away from the dark scenes of my childhood into a world, where, as it seemed to me, everyone was as happy as an angel on a *presepio*.

I wonder if you remember the count's villa? It lies on the shore of the lake, facing the green knoll of Monte Isola, and overlooked by the village of Siviano and by the old parish-church where I said mass for fifteen happy years. The village hangs on a ledge of the mountain; but the villa dips its foot in the lake, smiling at its reflection like a bather lingering on the brink. What Paradise it seemed to me that day! In our church up the valley there hung an old brown picture, with a Saint Sabastian in the foreground; and behind him the most wonderful palace, with terraced gardens adorned with statues and fountains, where fine folk in resplendent dresses walked up and down without heeding the blessed martyr's pangs. The count's villa, with its terraces, its roses, its marble steps descending to the lake, reminded me of that palace; only instead of being inhabited by wicked people engrossed in their selfish pleasures it was the home of the kindest friends that ever took a poor lad by the hand.

The old count was a widower when I first knew him. He had been twice married, and his first wife had left him two children, a son and a daughter. The eldest, Donna Marianna, was then a girl of twenty, who kept her father's house and was a mother to the two lads. She was not handsome or learned, and had no taste for the world; but she was like the lavender-plant in a poor man's window—just a little grey flower, but a sweetness that fills the whole house. Her brother, Count Roberto, had been ailing from his birth, and was a studious lad with a melancholy musing face such as you may see in some of Titian's portraits of young men. He looked like an exiled prince dressed in mourning. There was one child by the second marriage, Count Andrea, a boy of my own age, handsome as a Saint George, but not as kind as the others.

No doubt, being younger, he was less able to understand why an uncouth peasant lad should have been brought to his father's table; and the others were so fearful of hurting my feelings that, but for his teasing, I might never have mended my clumsy manners or learned how to behave in the presence of my betters. Count Andrea was not sparing in such lessons, and Count Roberto, in spite of his weak arms, chastised his brother roundly when he thought the discipline had been too severe; but for my part it seemed to me natural enough that such a godlike being should lord it over a poor clodhopper like myself.

Well—I will not linger over the beginning of my new life for my story has to do with its close. Only I should like to make you understand what the change meant to me—an ignorant peasant lad, coming from hard words and blows and a smoke-blackened hut in the hills to that great house full of rare and beautiful things, and of beings who seemed to me even more rare and beautiful. Do you wonder I was ready to kiss the ground they trod, and would have given the last drop of my blood to serve them?

In due course I was sent to the seminary at Lodi; and on holidays I used to visit the family in Milan. Count Andrea was growing up to be one of the handsomest young men imaginable, but a trifle wild; and the old count married him in haste to the daughter of a Venetian noble, who brought as her dower a great estate in Istria. The Countess Gemma, as this lady was called, was as light as thistledown and had an eye like a baby's; but while she was cooing for the moon her pretty white hands were always stealing toward something within reach that she had not been meant to have.

The old count was not alert enough to follow these manoeuvres;

and the countess hid her designs under a torrent of guileless chatter, as pick-pockets wear long sleeves to conceal their movements. Her only fault, he used to say, was that one of her aunts had married an Austrian; and this event having taken place before she was born he laughingly acquitted her of any direct share in it. She confirmed his good opinion of her by giving her husband two sons; and Roberto showing no inclination to marry, these boys naturally came to be looked on as the heirs of the house.

Meanwhile I had finished my course of studies, and the old count, on my twenty-first birthday, had appointed me priest of the parish of Siviano. It was the year of Count Andrea's marriage and there were great festivities at the villa. Three years later the old count died, to the sorrow of his two eldest children. Donna Marianna and Count Roberto closed their apartments in the palace at Milan and withdrew for a year to Siviano. It was then that I first began to know my friend. Before that I had loved him without understanding him; now I learned of what metal he was made.

His bookish tastes inclined him to a secluded way of living; and his younger brother perhaps fancied that he would not care to assume the charge of the estate. But if Andrea thought this he was disappointed. Roberto resolutely took up the tradition of his father's rule, and, as if conscious of lacking the old count's easy way with the peasants, made up for it by a redoubled zeal for their welfare. I have seen him toil for days to adjust some trifling difficulty that his father would have set right with a ready word; like the sainted bishop who, when a beggar asked him for a penny, cried out: "Alas, my brother, I have not a penny in my purse; but here are two gold pieces, if they can be made to serve you instead!"

We had many conferences over the condition of his people, and he often sent me up the valley to look into the needs of the peasantry on the fruit-farms. No grievance was too trifling for him to consider it, no abuse too deep-seated for him to root it out; and many an hour that other men of his rank would have given to books or pleasure was devoted to adjusting a quarrel about boundary-lines or to weighing the merits of a complaint against the tax-collector. I often said that he was as much his people's priest as I; and he smiled and answered that every landowner was a king and that in old days the king was always a priest.

Donna Marianna was urgent with him to marry, but he always declared that he had a family in his tenantry, and that, as for a wife, she had never let him feel the want of one. He had that musing temper which gives a man a name for coldness; though in fact he may all the while be storing fuel for a great conflagration. But to me he whispered another reason for not marrying. A man, he said, does not take wife and rejoice while his mother is on her death-bed; and Italy, his mother, lay dying, with the foreign vultures waiting to tear her apart.

You are too young to know anything of those days, my son; and how can anyone understand them who did not live through them? Italy lay dying indeed; but Lombardy was her heart, and the heart still beat, and sent the faint blood creeping to her cold extremities. Her torturers, weary of their work, had allowed her to fall into a painless stupor; but just as she was sinking from sleep to death, heaven sent Radetsky to scourge her back to consciousness; and at the first sting of his lash she sprang maimed and bleeding to her feet.

Ah, those days, those days, my son! Italy—Italy—was the word on our lips; but the thought in our hearts was just *Austria.* We clamoured for liberty, unity, the franchise; but under our breath we prayed only to smite the white-coats. Remove the beam from our eye, we cried, and we shall see our salvation clearly enough! We priests in the north were all liberals and worked with the nobles and the men of letters. Gioberti was our breviary and his Holiness the new Pope was soon to be the Tancred of our crusade. But meanwhile, mind you, all this went on in silence, underground as it were, while on the surface Lombardy still danced, feasted, married, and took office under the Austrian.

In the iron-mines up our valley there used to be certain miners who stayed below ground for months at a time; and, like one of these, Roberto remained buried in his purpose, while life went its way overhead. Though I was not in his confidence I knew well enough where his thoughts were, for he went among us with the eye of a lover, the visionary look of one who hears a Voice. We all heard that Voice, to be sure, mingling faintly with the other noises of life; but to Roberto it was already as the roar of mighty waters, drowning every other sound with its thunder.

On the surface, as I have said, things looked smooth enough. An Austrian cardinal throned in Milan and an Austrian-hearted Pope ruled in Rome. In Lombardy, Austria crouched like a beast of prey, ready to spring at our throats if we stirred or struggled. The Moderates, to whose party Count Roberto belonged, talked of prudence, compromise, the education of the masses; but if their words were a velvet sheath their thought was a dagger. For many years, as you know, the Milanese had maintained an outward show of friendliness with their rulers. The nobles had accepted office under the viceroy, and in the past there had been frequent intermarriage between the two aristocracies. But now, one by one, the great houses had closed their doors against official society. Though some of the younger and more careless, those who must dance and dine at any cost, still went to the palace and sat beside the enemy at the opera, fashion was gradually taking sides against them, and those who had once been laughed at as old fogeys were now applauded as patriots.

Among these, of course, was Count Roberto, who for several years had refused to associate with the Austrians, and had silently resented his easy-going brother's disregard of political distinctions. Andrea and Gemma belonged to the moth tribe, who flock to the brightest light; and Gemma's Istrian possessions, and her family's connection with the Austrian nobility, gave them a pretext for fluttering about the vice-regal candle. Roberto let them go their way, but his own course was a tacit protest against their conduct. They were always welcome at the palazzo Siviano; but he and Donna Marianna withdrew from society in order to have an excuse for not showing themselves at the Countess Gemma's entertainments. If Andrea and Gemma were aware of his disapproval they were clever enough to ignore it; for the rich elder brother who paid their debts and never meant to marry was too important a person to be quarrelled with on political grounds.

They seemed to think that if he married it would be only to spite them; and they were persuaded that their future depended on their giving him no cause to take such reprisals. I shall never be more than a plain peasant at heart and I have little natural skill in discerning hidden motives; but the experience of the confessional gives every priest a certain insight into the secret springs of action, and I often wondered that the worldly wisdom of Andrea and Gemma did not help them to a clearer reading of their brother's character. For my part I knew that, in Roberto's heart, no great passion could spring from a mean motive; and I had always thought that if he ever loved any woman as he loved Italy, it must be from his country's hand that he received his bride. And so it came about.

Have you ever noticed, on one of those still autumn days before a storm, how here and there a yellow leaf will suddenly detach itself from the bough and whirl through the air as though some warning of the gale had reached it? So it was then in Lombardy. All round was the silence of decay; but now and then a word, a look, a trivial incident, fluttered ominously through the stillness. It was in '45. Only a year earlier the glorious death of the Bandiera brothers had sent a long shudder through Italy. In the Romagna, Renzi and his comrades had tried to uphold by action the protest set forth in the "Manifesto of Rimini"; and their failure had sowed the seed which d'Azeglio and Cavour were to harvest. Everywhere the forces were silently gathering; and nowhere was the hush more profound, the least reverberation more audible, than in the streets of Milan.

It was Count Roberto's habit to attend early mass in the cathedral; and one morning, as he was standing in the aisle, a young girl passed him with her father. Roberto knew the father, a beggarly Milanese of the noble family of Intelvi, who had cut himself off from his class by accepting an appointment in one of the government offices. As the two went by he saw a group of Austrian officers looking after the girl, and heard one of them say: "Such a choice morsel as that is too good for slaves;" and another answer with a laugh: "Yes, it's a dish for the master's table!"

The girl heard too. She was as white as a wind-flower and he saw the words come out on her cheek like the red mark from a blow. She whispered to her father, but he shook his head and drew her away without so much as a glance at the Austrians. Roberto heard mass and then hastened out and placed himself in the porch of the cathedral. A moment later the officers appeared, and they too stationed themselves near the doorway. Presently the girl came out on her father's arm. Her admirers stepped forward to greet Intelvi; and the cringing wretch stood there exchanging compliments with them, while their insolent stare devoured his daughter's beauty. She, poor thing, shook like a leaf, and her eyes, in avoiding theirs, suddenly encountered Roberto's. Her look was a wounded bird that flew to him for shelter. He carried it away in his breast and its live warmth beat against his heart. He thought that Italy had looked at him through those eyes; for love is the wiliest of masqueraders and has a thousand disguises at his command.

Within a month Faustina Intelvi was his wife. Donna Marianna and I rejoiced; for we knew he had chosen her because he loved her, and she seemed to us almost worthy of such a choice. As for Count Andrea and his wife, I leave you to guess what ingredients were mingled in the kiss with which they welcomed the bride. They were all smiles at Roberto's marriage, and had only words of praise for his wife. Donna Marianna, who had sometimes taxed me with suspecting their motives, rejoiced in this fresh proof of their magnanimity; but for my part I could have wished to see them a little less kind. All such twilight fears, however, vanished in the flush of my friend's happiness. Over some natures love steals gradually, as the morning light widens across a valley; but it had flashed on Roberto like the leap of dawn to a snow-peak. He walked the world with the wondering step of a blind man suddenly restored to sight; and once he said to me with a laugh: "Love makes a Columbus of every one of us!"

And the countess—? The countess, my son, was eighteen, and her husband was forty. Count Roberto had the heart of a poet, but he walked with a limp and his skin was sallow. Youth plucks the fruit for its colour rather than its flavour; and first love does not serenade its mistress on a church-organ. In Italy girls are married as land is sold; if two estates adjoin two lives are united. As for the portionless girl, she is a knick-knack that goes to the highest bidder. Faustina was handed over to her purchaser as if she had been a picture for his gallery; and the transaction doubtless seemed as natural to her as to her parents. She walked to the altar like an Iphigenia; but pallor becomes a bride, and it looks well for a daughter to weep on leaving her mother. Perhaps it would have been different if she had guessed that the threshold of her new home was carpeted with love and its four corners hung with tender thoughts of her; but her husband was a silent man, who never called attention to his treasures.

The great palace in Milan was a gloomy house for a girl to enter. Roberto and his sister lived in it as if it had been a monastery, going nowhere and receiving only those who laboured for the Cause. To Faustina, accustomed to the easy Austrian society, the Sunday evening receptions at the palazzo Siviano must have seemed as dreary as a scientific congress. It pleased Roberto to regard her as a victim of barbarian insolence, an embodiment of his country desecrated by the desire of the enemy; but though, like any handsome penniless girl, Faustina had now and then been exposed to a free look or a familiar word, I doubt if she connected such incidents with the political condition of Italy.

She knew, of course, that in marrying Siviano she was entering a house closed against the Austrian. One of Siviano's first cares had been to pension his father-in-law, with the stipulation that Intelvi should resign his appointment and give up all relations with the government; and the old hypocrite, only too glad to purchase idleness on such terms, embraced the liberal cause with a zeal which left his daughter no excuse for half-heartedness. But he found it less easy than he had expected to recover a footing among his own people. In spite of his patriotic bluster the Milanese held aloof from him; and being the kind of man who must always take his glass in company he gradually drifted back to his old associates. It was impossible to forbid Faustina to visit her parents; and in their house she breathed an air that was at least tolerant of Austria.

But I must not let you think that the young countess appeared ungrateful or unhappy. She was silent and shy, and it needed a more enterprising temper than Roberto's to break down the barrier between them. They seemed to talk to one another through a convent-grating, rather than across a hearth; but if Roberto had asked more of her than she could give, outwardly she was a model wife. She chose me at once as her confessor and I watched over the first steps of her new life. Never was younger sister tenderer to her elder than she to Donna Marianna; never was young wife more mindful of her religious duties, kinder to her dependents, more charitable to the poor; yet to be with her was like living in a room with shuttered windows. She was always the caged bird, the transplanted flower: for all Roberto's care she never bloomed or sang.

Donna Marianna was the first to speak of it. "The child needs more light and air," she said.

"Light? Air?" Roberto repeated. "Does she not go to mass every morning? Does she not drive on the Corso every evening?"

Donna Marianna was not called clever, but her heart was wiser than most women's heads.

"At our age, brother," said she, "the windows of the mind face north and look out on a landscape full of lengthening shadows. Faustina needs another outlook. She is as pale as a hyacinth grown in a cellar."

Roberto himself turned pale and I saw that she had uttered his own thought.

"You want me to let her go to Gemma's!" he exclaimed.

"Let her go wherever there is a little careless laughter."

"Laughter—now!" he cried, with a gesture toward the sombre line of portraits above his head.

"Let her laugh while she can, my brother."

That evening after dinner he called Faustina to him.

"My child," he said, "go and put on your jewels. Your sister Gemma gives a ball tonight and the carriage waits to take you there. I am too much of a recluse to be at ease in such scenes, but I have sent word to your father to go with you."

Andrea and Gemma welcomed their young sister-in-law with effusion, and from that time she was often in their company. Gemma forbade any mention of politics in her drawing-room, and it was natural that Faustina should be glad to escape from the solemn conclaves of the palazzo Siviano to a house where life went as gaily as in that villa above Florence where Boccaccio's careless story-tellers took refuge from the plague. But meanwhile the political distemper was rapidly spreading, and in spite of Gemma's Austrian affiliations it was no longer possible for her to receive the enemy openly. It was whispered that her door was still ajar to her old friends; but the rumour may have risen from the fact that one of the Austrian cavalry officers stationed at Milan was her own cousin, the son of the aunt on whose misalliance the old count had so often bantered her. No one could blame the Countess Gemma for not turning her own flesh and blood out of doors; and the social famine to which the officers of the garrison were reduced made it natural that young Welkenstern should press the claims of consanguinity.

All this must have reached Roberto's ears; but he made no sign and his wife came and went as she pleased. When they returned the following year to the old dusky villa at Siviano she was like the voice of a brook in a twilight wood: one could not look at her without ransacking the spring for new similes to paint her freshness. With Roberto it was different. I found him older, more preoccupied and silent; but I guessed that his preoccupations were political, for when his eye rested on his wife it cleared like the lake when a cloud-shadow lifts from it.

Count Andrea and his wife occupied an adjoining villa; and during the *villeggiatura* the two households lived almost as one family. Roberto, however, was often absent in Milan, called thither on business of which the nature was not hard to guess. Sometimes he brought back guests to the villa; and on these occasions Faustina and Donna Marianna went to Count Andrea's for the day. I have said that I was not in his confidence; but he knew my sympathies were with the liberals and now and then he let fall a word of the work going on underground. Meanwhile the new Pope had been elected, and from Piedmont to Calabria we hailed in him the Banner that was to lead our hosts to war.

So time passed and we reached the last months of '47. The villa on Iseo had been closed since the end of August. Roberto had no great liking for his gloomy palace in Milan, and it had been his habit to spend nine months of the year at Siviano; but he was now too much engrossed in his work to remain away from Milan, and his wife and sister had joined him there as soon as the midsummer heat was over. During the autumn he had called me once or twice to the city to consult me on business connected with his fruit-farms; and in the course of our talks he had sometimes let fall a hint of graver matters. It was in July of that year that a troop of Croats had marched into Ferrara, with muskets and cannon loaded. The lighted matches of their cannon had fired the sleeping hate of Austria, and the whole country now echoed the Lombard cry: "Out with the barbarian!" All talk of adjustment, compromise, reorganization, shrivelled on lips that the live coal of patriotism had touched. Italy for the Italians, and then—monarchy, federation, republic, it mattered not what!

The oppressor's grip had tightened on our throats and the clear-sighted saw well enough that Metternich's policy was to provoke a rebellion and then crush it under the Croat heel. But it was too late to cry prudence in Lombardy. With the first days of the new year the tobacco riots had drawn blood in Milan. Soon afterward the Lions' Club was closed, and edicts were issued forbidding the singing of Pio Nono's hymn, the wearing of white and blue, the collecting of subscriptions for the victims of the riots. To each prohibition Milan returned a fresh defiance. The ladies of the nobility put on mourning for the rioters who had been shot down by the soldiery.

Half the members of the Guardia Nobile resigned and Count Borromeo sent back his Golden Fleece to the emperor. Fresh regiments were continually pouring into Milan and it was no secret that Radetsky was strengthening the fortifications. Late in January several leading liberals were arrested and sent into exile, and two weeks later martial law was proclaimed in Milan. At the first arrests several members of the liberal party had hastily left Milan, and I was not surprised to hear, a few days later, that orders had been given to reopen the villa at Siviano. The count and countess arrived there early in February.

It was seven months since I had seen the countess, and I was struck with the change in her appearance.

She was paler than ever, and her step had lost its lightness. Yet she did not seem to share her husband's political anxieties; one would have said that she was hardly aware of them. She seemed wrapped in a veil of lassitude, like Iseo on a still grey morning, when dawn is blood-red on the mountains but a mist blurs its reflection in the lake. I felt as though her soul were slipping away from me, and longed to win her back to my care; but she made her ill-health a pretext for not coming to confession, and for the present I could only wait and carry the thought of her to the altar. She had not been long at Siviano before I discovered that this drooping mood was only one phase of her humour. Now and then she flung back the cowl of melancholy and laughed life in the eye; but next moment she was in shadow again, and her muffled thoughts had given us the slip. She was like the lake on one of those days when the wind blows twenty ways and every promontory holds a gust in ambush.

Meanwhile there was a continual coming and going of messengers between Siviano and the city. They came mostly at night, when the household slept, and were away again with the last shadows; but the news they brought stayed and widened, shining through every cranny of the old house. The whole of Lombardy was up. From Pavia to Mantua, from Como to Brescia, the streets ran blood like the arteries of one great body. At Pavia and Padua the universities were closed. The frightened viceroy was preparing to withdraw from Milan to Verona, and Radetsky continued to pour his men across the Alps, till a hundred thousand were massed between the Piave and the Ticino. And now every eye was turned to Turin.

Ah, how we watched for the blue banner of Piedmont on the mountains! Charles Albert was pledged to our cause; his whole people had armed to rescue us, the streets echoed with *avanti, Savoia!* and yet Savoy was silent and hung back. Each day was a life-time strained to the cracking-point with hopes and disappointments. We reckoned the hours by rumors, the very minutes by hearsay. Then suddenly—ah, it was worth living through!—word came to us that Vienna was in revolt. The points of the compass had shifted and our sun had risen in the north. I shall never forget that day at the villa. Roberto sent for me early, and I found him smiling and resolute, as becomes a soldier on the eve of action. He had made all his preparations to leave for Milan and was awaiting a summons from his party.

The whole household felt that great events impended, and Donna Marianna, awed and tearful, had pleaded with her brother that they should all receive the sacrament together the next morning. Roberto and his sister had been to confession the previous day, but the Countess Faustina had again excused herself. I did not see her while I was with the count, but as I left the house she met me in the laurel-walk. The morning was damp and cold, and she had drawn a black scarf over her hair, and walked with a listless dragging step; but at my approach she lifted her head quickly and signed to me to follow her into one of the recesses of clipped laurel that bordered the path.

"Don Egidio," she said, "you have heard the news?"

I assented.

"The count goes to Milan tomorrow?"

"It seems probable, your Excellency."

"There will be fighting—we are on the eve of war, I mean?"

"We are in God's hands, your excellency."

"In God's hands!" she murmured. Her eyes wandered and for a moment we stood silent; then she drew a purse from her pocket. "I was forgetting," she exclaimed. "This is for that poor girl you spoke to me about the other day—what was her name? The girl who met the Austrian soldier at the fair at Peschiera—"

"Ah, Vannina," I said; "but she is dead, your Excellency."

"Dead!" She turned white and the purse dropped from her hand. I picked it up and held it out to her, but she put back my hand. "That is for masses, then," she said; and with that she moved away toward the house.

I walked on to the gate; but before I had reached it I heard her step behind me.

"Don Egidio!" she called; and I turned back.

"You are coming to say mass in the chapel tomorrow morning?"

"That is the count's wish."

She wavered a moment. "I am not well enough to walk up to the village this afternoon," she said at length. "Will you come back later and hear my confession here?"

"Willingly, your Excellency."

"Come at sunset then." She looked at me gravely. "It is a long time since I have been to confession," she added.

"My child, the door of heaven is always unlatched."

She made no answer and I went my way.

I returned to the villa a little before sunset, hoping for a few words with Roberto. I felt with Faustina that we were on the eve of war, and the uncertainty of the outlook made me treasure every moment of my friend's company. I knew he had been busy all day, but hoped to find that his preparations were ended and that he could spare me a half hour. I was not disappointed; for the servant who met me asked me to follow him to the count's apartment. Roberto was sitting alone, with his back to the door, at a table spread with maps and papers. He stood up and turned an ashen face on me.

"Roberto!" I cried, as if we had been boys together.

He signed to me to be seated.

"Egidio," he said suddenly, "my wife has sent for you to confess her?"

"The countess met me on my way home this morning and expressed a wish to receive the sacrament tomorrow morning with you and Donna Marianna, and I promised to return this afternoon to hear her confession."

Roberto sat silent, staring before him as though he hardly heard. At length he raised his head and began to speak.

"You have noticed lately that my wife has been ailing?" he asked.

"Everyone must have seen that the countess is not in her usual health. She has seemed nervous, out of spirits—I have fancied that she might be anxious about your excellency."

He leaned across the table and laid his wasted hand on mine. "Call me Roberto," he said.

There was another pause before he went on. "Since I saw you this morning," he said slowly, "something horrible has happened. After you left I sent for Andrea and Gemma to tell them the news from Vienna and the probability of my being summoned to Milan before night. You know as well as I that we have reached a crisis. There will be fighting within twenty-four hours, if I know my people; and war may follow sooner than we think. I felt it my duty to leave my affairs in Andrea's hands, and to entrust my wife to his care. Don't look startled," he added with a faint smile. "No reasonable man goes on a journey without setting his house in order; and if things take the turn I expect it may be some months before you see me back at Siviano.—But it was not to hear this that I sent for you."

He pushed his chair aside and walked up and down the room with his short limping step. "My God!" he broke out wildly, "how can I say it?—When Andrea had heard me, I saw him exchange a glance with his wife, and she said with that infernal sweet voice of hers, 'Yes, Andrea, it is our duty.'

"'Your duty?' I asked. 'What is your duty?'

"Andrea wetted his lips with his tongue and looked at her again; and her look was like a blade in his hand.

"'Your wife has a lover,' he said.

"She caught my arm as I flung myself on him. He is ten times stronger than I, but you remember how I made him howl for mercy in the old days when he used to bully you.

"'Let me go,' I said to his wife. 'He must live to unsay it.'

"Andrea began to whimper. 'Oh, my poor brother, I would give my heart's blood to unsay it!'

"'The secret has been killing us,' she chimed in.

"'The secret? Whose secret? How dare you —?'

"Gemma fell on her knees like a tragedy actress. 'Strike me—kill me—it is I who am the offender! It was at my house that she met him—'

"'Him?'

"'Franz Welkenstern—my cousin,' she wailed.

"I suppose I stood before them like a stunned ox, for they repeated the name again and again, as if they were not sure of my having heard it.—Not hear it!" he cried suddenly, dropping into a chair and hiding his face in his hands. "Shall I ever on earth hear anything else again?"

He sat a long time with his face hidden and I waited. My head was like a great bronze bell with one thought for the clapper.

After a while he went on in a low deliberate voice, as though his words were balancing themselves on the brink of madness. With strange composure he repeated each detail of his brother's charges: the meetings in the Countess Gemma's drawing-room, the innocent friendliness of the two young people, the talk of mysterious visits to a villa outside the Porta Ticinese, the ever-widening circle of scandal that had spread about their names. At first, Andrea said, he and his wife had refused to listen to the reports which reached them. Then, when the talk became too loud, they had sent for Welkenstern, remonstrated with him, implored him to exchange into another regiment; but in vain. The young officer indignantly denied the reports and declared that to leave his post at such a moment would be desertion.

With a laborious accuracy Roberto went on, detailing one by one each incident of the hateful story, till suddenly he cried out, springing from his chair—"And now to leave her with this lie unburied!"

His cry was like the lifting of a grave-stone from my breast. "You must not leave her!" I exclaimed.

He shook his head. "I am pledged."

"This is your first duty."

"It would be any other man's; not an Italian's."

I was silent: in those days the argument seemed unanswerable.

At length I said: "No harm can come to her while you are away. Donna Marianna and I are here to watch over her. And when you come back—"

He looked at me gravely. "*If* I come back—"

"Roberto!"

"We are men, Egidio; we both know what is coming. Milan is up already; and there is a rumour that Charles Albert is moving. This year the spring rains will be red in Italy."

"In your absence not a breath shall touch her!"

"And if I never come back to defend her? They hate her as hell hates, Egidio!—They kept repeating, 'He is of her own age and youth draws youth—.' She is in their way, Egidio!"

"Consider, my son. They do not love her, perhaps; but why should they hate her at such cost? She has given you no child."

"No child!" He paused. "But what if—? She has ailed lately!" he cried, and broke off to grapple with the stabbing thought.

"Roberto! Roberto!" I adjured him.

He jumped up and gripped my arm.

"Egidio! You believe in her?"

"She's as pure as a lily on the altar!"

"Those eyes are wells of truth—and she has been like a daughter to Marianna.—Egidio! do I look like an old man?"

"Quiet yourself, Roberto," I entreated.

"Quiet myself? With this sting in my blood? A lover—and an Austrian lover! Oh, Italy, Italy, my bride!"

"I stake my life on her truth," I cried, "and who knows better than I? Has her soul not lain before me like the bed of a clear stream?"

"And if what you saw there was only the reflection of your faith in her?"

"My son, I am a priest, and the priest penetrates to the soul as the angel passed through the walls of Peter's prison. I see the truth in her heart as I see Christ in the host!"

"No, no, she is false!" he cried.

I sprang up terrified. "Roberto, be silent!"

He looked at me with a wild incredulous smile. "Poor simple man of God!" he said.

"I would not exchange my simplicity for yours—the dupe of envy's first malicious whisper!"

"Envy—you think that?"

"Is it questionable?"

"You would stake your life on it?"

"My life!"

"Your faith?"

"My faith!"

"Your vows as a priest?"

"My vows—" I stopped and stared at him. He had risen and laid his hand on my shoulder.

"You see now what I would be at," he said quietly. "I must take your place presently—"

"My place —?"

"When my wife comes down. You understand me."

"Ah, now you are quite mad!" I cried breaking away from him.

"Am I?" he returned, maintaining his strange composure. "Consider a moment. She has not confessed to you before since our return from Milan—"

"Her ill-health—"

He cut me short with a gesture. "Yet today she sends for you—"

"In order that she may receive the sacrament with you on the eve of your first separation."

"If that is her only reason her first words will clear her. I must hear those words, Egidio!"

"You are quite mad," I repeated.

"Strange," he said slowly. "You stake your life on my wife's innocence, yet you refuse me the only means of vindicating it!"

"I would give my life for any one of you—but what you ask is not mine to give."

"The priest first—the man afterward?" he sneered.

"Long afterward!"

He measured me with a contemptuous eye. "We laymen are ready to give the last shred of flesh from our bones, but you priests intend to keep your cassocks whole."

"I tell you my cassock is not mine," I repeated.

"And, by God," he cried, "you are right; for it's mine! Who put it on your back but my father? What kept it there but my charity? Peasant! beggar! Hear his holiness pontificate!" "Yes," I said, "I was a peasant and a beggar when your father found me; and if he had left me one I might have been excused for putting my hand to any ugly job that my betters required of me; but he made me a priest, and so set me above all of you, and laid on me the charge of your souls as well as mine."

He sat down shaken with dreadful tears. "Ah," he broke out, "would you have answered me thus when we were boys together, and I stood between you and Andrea?"

"If God had given me the strength."

"You call it strength to make a woman's soul your stepping-stone to heaven?"

"Her soul is in my care, not yours, my son. She is safe with me."

"She? But I? I go out to meet death, and leave a worse death behind me!" He leaned over and clutched my arm. "It is not for myself I plead but for her—for her, Egidio! Don't you see to what a hell you condemn her if I don't come back? What chance has she against that slow unsleeping hate? Their lies will fasten themselves to her and suck out her life. You and Marianna are powerless against such enemies."

"You leave her in God's hands, my son."

"Easily said—but, ah, priest, if you were a man! What if their poison works in me and I go to battle thinking that every Austrian bullet may be sent by her lover's hand? What if I die not only to free Italy but to free my wife as well?"

I laid my hand on his shoulder. "My son, I answer for her. Leave your faith in her in my hands and I will keep it whole."

He stared at me strangely. "And what if your own fail you?"

"In her? Never. I call every saint to witness!"

"And yet—and yet—ah, this is a blind," he shouted; "you know all and perjure yourself to spare me!"

At that, my son, I felt a knife in my breast. I looked at him in anguish and his gaze was a wall of metal. Mine seemed to slip away from it, like a clawless thing struggling up the sheer side of a precipice.

"You know all," he repeated, "and you dare not let me hear her!"

"I dare not betray my trust."

He waved the answer aside.

"Is this a time to quibble over church discipline? If you believed in her you would save her at any cost!"

I said to myself, "Eternity can hold nothing worse than this for me—" and clutched my resolve again like a cross to my bosom.

Just then there was a hand on the door and we heard Donna Marianna.

"Faustina has sent to know if the *signar parocco* is here."

"He is here. Bid her come down to the chapel." Roberto spoke quietly, and closed the door on her so that she should not see his face. We heard her patter away across the brick floor of the *salone*.

Roberto turned to me. "Egidio!" he said; and all at once I was no more than a straw on the torrent of his will.

The chapel adjoined the room in which we sat. He opened the

door, and in the twilight I saw the light glimmering before the Virgin's shrine and the old carved confessional standing like a cowled watcher in its corner. But I saw it all in a dream; for nothing in heaven or earth was real to me but the iron grip on my shoulder.

"Quick!" he said and drove me forward. I heard him shoot back the bolt of the outer door and a moment later I stood alone in the garden. The sun had set and the cold spring dusk was falling. Lights shone here and there in the long front of the villa; the statues glimmered grey among the thickets. Through the window-pane of the chapel I caught the faint red gleam of the Virgin's lamp; but I turned my back on it and walked away.

All night I lay like a heretic on the fire. Before dawn there came a call from the villa. The count had received a second summons from Milan and was to set out in an hour. I hurried down the cold dewy path to the lake. All was new and hushed and strange as on the day of resurrection; and in the dark twilight of the garden alleys the statues stared at me like the shrouded dead.

In the *salone*, where the old count's portrait hung, I found the family assembled. Andrea and Gemma sat together, a little pinched, I thought, but decent and self-contained, like mourners who expect to inherit. Donna Marianna drooped near them, with something black over her head and her face dim with weeping. Roberto received me calmly and then turned to his sister.

"Go fetch my wife," he said.

While she was gone there was silence. We could hear the cold drip of the garden-fountain and the patter of rats in the wall. Andrea and his wife stared out of window and Roberto sat in his father's carved seat at the head of the long table. Then the door opened and Faustina entered.

When I saw her I stopped breathing. She seemed no more than the shell of herself, a hollow thing that grief has voided. Her eyes returned our images like polished agate, but conveyed to her no sense of our presence. Marianna led her to a seat, and she crossed her hands and nailed her dull gaze on Roberto. I looked from one to another, and in that spectral light it seemed to me that we were all souls come to judgment and naked to each other as to God. As to my own wrongdoing, it weighed on me no more than dust. The only feeling I had room for was fear—a fear that seemed to fill my throat and lungs and bubble coldly over my drowning head.

Suddenly Roberto began to speak. His voice was clear and steady, and I clutched at his words to drag myself above the surface of my terror. He touched on the charge that had been made against his wife—he did not say by whom—the foul rumour that had made itself heard on the eve of their first parting. Duty, he said, had sent him a double summons; to fight for his country and for his wife. He must clear his wife's name before he was worthy to draw sword for Italy. There was no time to tame the slander before throttling it; he had to take the shortest way to its throat. At this point he looked at me and my soul shook. Then he turned to Andrea and Gemma.

"When you came to me with this rumour," he said quietly, "you agreed to consider the family honour satisfied if I could induce Don Egidio to let me take his place and overhear my wife's confession, and if that confession convinced me of her innocence. Was this the understanding?"

Andrea muttered something and Gemma tapped a sullen foot.

"After you had left," Roberto continued, "I laid the case before Don Egidio and threw myself on his mercy." He looked at me fixedly. "So strong was his faith in my wife's innocence that for her sake he agreed to violate the sanctity of the confessional. I took his place."

Marianna sobbed and crossed herself and a strange look flitted over Faustina's face.

There was a moment's pause; then Roberto, rising, walked across the room to his wife and took her by the hand.

"Your seat is beside me, Countess Siviano," he said, and led her to the empty chair by his own.

Gemma started to her feet, but her husband pulled her down again.

"Jesus! Mary!" We heard Donna Marianna moan.

Roberto raised his wife's hand to his lips. "You forgive me," he said, "the means I took to defend you?" And turning to Andrea he added slowly: "I declare my wife innocent and my honour satisfied. You swear to stand by my decision?"

What Andrea stammered out, what hissing serpents of speech Gemma's clinched teeth bit back, I never knew—for my eyes were on Faustina, and her face was a wonder to behold.

She had let herself be led across the room like a blind woman, and had listened without change of feature to her husband's first words; but as he ceased her frozen gaze broke and her whole body seemed to melt against his breast. He put his arm out, but she slipped to his feet and Marianna hastened forward to raise her up. At that moment we heard the stroke of oars across the quiet water and saw the count's boat touch the landing-steps. Four strong oarsmen from Monte Isola were to row him down to Iseo, to take horse for Milan, and his servant, knapsack on shoulder, knocked warningly at the terrace window.

"No time to lose, excellency!" he cried.

Roberto turned and gripped my hand. "Pray for me," he said low; and with a brief gesture to the others ran down the terrace to the boat.

Marianna was bathing Faustina with happy tears.

"Look up, dear! Think how soon he will come back! And there is the sunrise—see!"

Andrea and Gemma had slunk away like ghosts at cock-crow, and a red dawn stood over Milan.

If that sun rose red it set scarlet. It was the first of the Five Days in Milan—the Five Glorious Days, as they are called. Roberto reached the city just before the gates closed. So much we knew—little more. We heard of him in the Broletto (whence he must have escaped when the Austrians blew in the door) and in the Casa Vidiserti, with Casati, Cattaneo and the rest; but after the barricading began we could trace him only as having been seen here and there in the thick of the fighting, or tending the wounded under Bertani's orders. His place, one would have said, was in the council-chamber, with the soberer heads; but that was an hour when every man gave his blood where it was most needed, and Cernuschi, Dandolo, Anfossi, della Porta fought shoulder to shoulder with students, artisans and peasants.

Certain it is that he was seen on the fifth day; for among the volunteers who swarmed after Manara in his assault on the Porta Tosa was a servant of palazzo Siviano; and this fellow swore he had seen his master charge with Manara in the last assault—had watched him, sword in hand, press close to the gates, and then, as they swung open before the victorious dash of our men, had seen him drop and disappear in the inrushing tide of peasants that almost swept the little company off its feet. After that we heard nothing. There was savage work in Milan in those days, and more than one well-known figure lay lost among the heaps of dead hacked and disfeatured by Croat blades.

At the villa, we waited breathless. News came to us hour by hour: the very wind seemed to carry it, and it was swept to us on the incessant rush of the rain. On the twenty-third Radetsky had fled from Milan, to face Venice rising in his path. On the twenty-fourth the first Piedmontese had crossed the Ticino, and Charles Albert himself was in Pavia on the twenty-ninth. The bells of Milan had carried the word from Turin to Naples, from Genoa to Ancona, and the whole country was pouring like a flood-tide into Lombardy. Heroes sprang up from the bloody soil as thick as wheat after rain, and every day carried some new name to us; but never the one for which we prayed and waited. Weeks passed. We heard of Pastrengo, Goito, Rivoli; of Radetsky hemmed into the Quadrilateral, and our troops closing in on him from Rome, Tuscany and Venetia. Months passed—and we heard of Custozza. We saw Charles Albert's broken forces flung back from the Mincio to the Oglio, from the Oglio to the Adda. We followed the dreadful retreat from Milan, and saw our rescuers dispersed like dust before the wind. But all the while no word came to us of Roberto.

These were dark days in Lombardy; and nowhere darker than in the old villa on Iseo. In September Donna Marianna and the young countess put on black, and Count Andrea and his wife followed their example. In October the countess gave birth to a daughter. Count Andrea then took possession of the palazzo Siviano, and the two women remained at the villa. I have no heart to tell you of the days that followed. Donna Marianna wept and prayed incessantly, and it was long before the baby could snatch a smile from her.

As for the Countess Faustina, she went among us like one of the statues in the garden. The child had a wet-nurse from the village, and it was small wonder there was no milk for it in that marble breast. I spent much of my time at the villa, comforting Donna Marianna as best I could; but sometimes, in the long winter evenings, when we three sat in the dimly-lit *salone*, with the old count's portrait overhead, and I looked up and saw the Countess Faustina in the tall carved seat beside her husband's empty chair, my spine grew chill and I felt a cold wind in my hair.

The end of it was that in the spring I went to see my bishop and laid my sin before him. He was a saintly and merciful old man, and gave me a patient hearing.

"You believed the lady innocent?" he asked when I had ended.

"*Monsignore*, on my soul!"

"You thought to avert a great calamity from the house to which you owed more than your life?"

"It was my only thought."

He laid his hand on my shoulder.

"Go home, my son. You shall learn my decision."

Three months later I was ordered to resign my living and go to America, where a priest was needed for the Italian mission church in New York. I packed my possessions and set sail from Genoa. I knew no more of America than any peasant up in the hills. I fully expected to be speared by naked savages on landing; and for the first few months after my arrival I wished at least once a day that such a blessed fate had befallen me. But it is no part of my story to tell you what I suffered in those early days. The Church had dealt with me mercifully, as is her wont, and her punishment fell far below my deserts. . . .

I had been some four years in New York, and no longer thought of looking back from the plough, when one day word was brought me that an Italian professor lay ill and had asked for a priest. There were many Italian refugees in New York at that time, and the greater number, being well-educated men, earned a living by teaching their language, which was then included among the accomplishments of fashionable New York. The messenger led me to a poor boarding-house and up to a small bare room on the top floor. On the visiting-card nailed to the door I read the name "De Roberti, Professor of Italian." Inside, a grey-haired haggard man tossed on the narrow bed. He turned a glazed eye on me as I entered, and I recognized Roberto Siviano.

I steadied myself against the door-post and stood staring at him without a word.

"What's the matter?" asked the doctor who was bending over the bed. I stammered that the sick man was an old friend.

"He wouldn't know his oldest friend just now," said the doctor. "The fever's on him; but it will go down toward sunset."

I sat down at the head of the bed and took Roberto's hand in mine.

"Is he going to die?" I asked.

"I don't believe so; but he wants nursing."

"I will nurse him."

The doctor nodded and went out. I sat in the little room, with Roberto's burning hand in mine. Gradually his skin cooled, the fingers grew quiet, and the flush faded from his sallow cheek-bones. Toward dusk he looked up at me and smiled.

"Egidio," he said quietly.

I administered the sacrament, which he received with the most fervent devotion; then he fell into a deep sleep.

During the weeks that followed I had no time to ask myself the meaning of it all. My one business was to keep him alive if I could. I fought the fever day and night, and at length it yielded. For the most part he raved or lay unconscious; but now and then he knew me for a moment, and whispered "Egidio" with a look of peace.

I had stolen many hours from my duties to nurse him; and as soon as the danger was past I had to go back to my parish work. Then it was that I began to ask myself what had brought him to America; but I dared not face the answer.

On the fourth day I snatched a moment from my work and climbed to his room. I found him sitting propped against his pillows, weak as a child but clear-eyed and quiet. I ran forward, but his look stopped me.

"*Signor parocco*," he said, "the doctor tells me that I owe my life to your nursing, and I have to thank you for the kindness you have shown to a friendless stranger."

"A stranger?" I gasped.

He looked at me steadily. "I am not aware that we have met before," he said.

For a moment I thought the fever was on him; but a second glance convinced me that he was master of himself.

"Roberto!" I cried, trembling.

"You have the advantage of me," he said civilly. "But my name is Roberti, not Roberto."

The floor swam under me and I had to lean against the wall.

"You are not Count Roberto Siviano of Milan?"

"I am Tommaso de Roberti, professor of Italian, from Modena."

"And you have never seen me before?"

"Never that I know of."

"Were you never at Siviano, on the lake of Iseo?" I faltered.

He said calmly: "I am unacquainted with that part of Italy."

My heart grew cold and I was silent.

"You mistook me for a friend, I suppose?" he added.

"Yes," I cried, "I mistook you for a friend;" and with that I fell on my knees by his bed and cried like a child.

Suddenly I felt a touch on my shoulder. "Egidio," said he in a broken voice, "look up."

I raised my eyes, and there was his old smile above me, and we clung to each other without a word. Presently, however, he drew back, and put me quietly aside.

"Sit over there, Egidio. My bones are like water and I am not good for much talking yet."

"Let us wait, Roberto. Sleep now—we can talk tomorrow."

"No. What I have to say must be said at once." He examined me thoughtfully. "You have a parish here in New York?"

I assented.

"And my work keeps me here. I have pupils. It is too late to make a change."

"A change?"

He continued to look at me calmly. "It would be difficult for me," he explained, "to find employment in a new place."

"But why should you leave here?"

"I shall have to," he returned deliberately, "if you persist in recognizing in me your former friend Count Siviano."

"Roberto!"

He lifted his hand. "Egidio," he said, "I am alone here, and without friends. The companionship, the sympathy of my parish priest would be a consolation in this strange city; but it must not be the companionship of the *parocco* of Siviano. You understand?"

"Roberto," I cried, "it is too dreadful to understand!"

"Be a man, Egidio," said he with a touch of impatience. "The choice lies with you, and you must make it now. If you are willing to ask no questions, to name no names, to make no allusions to the past, let us live as friends together, in God's name! If not, as soon as my legs can carry me I must be off again. The world is wide, luckily—but why should we be parted?"

I was on my knees at his side in an instant. "We must never be parted!" I cried. "Do as you will with me. Give me your orders and I obey—have I not always obeyed you?"

I felt his hand close sharply on mine. "Egidio!" he admonished me.

"No—no—I shall remember. I shall say nothing—"

"Think nothing?"

"Think nothing," I said with a last effort.

"God bless you!" he answered.

My son, for eight years I kept my word to him. We met daily almost, we ate and walked and talked together, we lived like David and Jonathan—but without so much as a glance at the past. How he had escaped from Milan—how he had reached New York—I never knew. We talked often of Italy's liberation—as what Italians would not?—but never touched on his share in the work. Once only a word slipped from him; and that was when one day he asked me how it was that I had been sent to America. The blood rushed to my face, and before I could answer he had raised a silencing hand.

"I see," he said; "it was *your* penance too."

During the first years he had plenty of work to do, but he lived so frugally that I guessed he had some secret use for his earnings. It was easy to conjecture what it was. All over the world Italian exiles were toiling and saving to further the great cause. He had political friends in New York, and sometimes he went to other cities to attend meetings and make addresses. His zeal never slackened; and but for me he would often have gone hungry that some shivering patriot might dine. I was with him heart and soul, but I had the parish on my shoulders, and perhaps my long experience of men had made me a little less credulous than Christian charity requires; for I could have sworn that some of the heroes who hung on him had never had a whiff of Austrian blood, and would have fed out of the same trough with the white-coats if there had been polenta enough to go round. Happily, my friend had no such doubts. He believed in the patriots as devoutly as in the cause; and if some of his hard-earned dollars travelled no farther than the nearest wine-cellar or cigar-shop, he never suspected the course they took.

His health was never the same after the fever; and by and by he began to lose his pupils, and the patriots cooled off as his pockets fell in. Toward the end I took him to live in my shabby attic. He had grown weak and had a troublesome cough, and he spent the greater part of his days indoors. Cruel days they must have been to him, but he made no sign, and always welcomed me with a cheerful word. When his pupils dropped off, and his health made it difficult for him to pick up work outside, he set up a letter-writer's sign, and used to earn a few pennies by serving as amanuensis to my poor parishioners; but it went against him to take their money, and half the time he did the work for nothing. I knew it was hard for him to live on charity, as he called it, and I used to find what jobs I could for him among my friends the *negozianti*, who would send him letters to copy, accounts to make up and what not; but we were all poor together, and the master had licked the platter before the dog got it.

So lived that just man, my son; and so, after eight years of exile, he died one day in my arms. God had let him live long enough to see Solferino and Villa-franca; and was perhaps never more merciful than in sparing him Monte Rotondo and Mentana. But these are things of which it does not become me to speak. The new Italy does not wear the face of our visions; but it is written that God shall know His own, and it cannot be that He shall misread the hearts of those who dreamed of fashioning her in His image.

As for my friend, he is at peace, I doubt not; and his just life and holy death intercede for me, who sinned for his sake alone.

The Eyes

1

We had been put in the mood for ghosts, that evening, after an excellent dinner at our old friend Culwin's, by a tale of Fred Murchard's—the narrative of a strange personal visitation.

Seen through the haze of our cigars, and by the drowsy gleam of a coal fire, Culwin's library, with its oak walls and dark old bindings, made a good setting for such evocations; and ghostly experiences at first hand being, after Murchard's brilliant opening, the only kind acceptable to us, we proceeded to take stock of our group and tax each member for a contribution. There were eight of us, and seven contrived, in a manner more or less adequate, to fulfil the condition imposed. It surprised us all to find that we could muster such a show of supernatural impressions, for none of us, excepting Murchard himself and young Phil Frenham—whose story was the slightest of the lot—had the habit of sending our souls into the invisible. So that, on the whole, we had every reason to be proud of our seven "exhibits," and none of us would have dreamed of expecting an eighth from our host.

Our old friend, Mr. Andrew Culwin, who had sat back in his armchair, listening and blinking through the smoke circles with the cheerful tolerance of a wise old idol, was not the kind of man likely to be favoured with such contacts, though he had imagination enough to enjoy, without envying, the superior privileges of his guests. By age and by education he belonged to the stout Positivist tradition, and his habit of thought had been formed in the days of the epic struggle between physics and metaphysics. But he had been, then and always, essentially a spectator, a humorous detached observer of the immense muddled variety show of life, slipping out of his seat now and then for a brief dip into the convivialities at the back of the house, but never, as far as one knew, showing the least desire to jump on the stage and do a "turn."

Among his contemporaries there lingered a vague tradition of his having, at a remote period, and in a romantic clime, been wounded in a duel; but this legend no more tallied with what we younger men knew of his character than my mother's assertion that he had once been "a charming little man with nice eyes" corresponded to any possible reconstitution of his dry thwarted physiognomy.

"He never can have looked like anything but a bundle of sticks," Murchard had once said of him. "Or a phosphorescent log, rather," someone else amended; and we recognised the happiness of this description of his small squat trunk, with the red blink of the eyes in a face like mottled bark. He had always been possessed of a leisure which he had nursed and protected, instead of squandering it in vain activities.

His carefully guarded hours had been devoted to the cultivation of a fine intelligence and a few judiciously chosen habits; and none of the disturbances common to human experience seemed to have crossed his sky. Nevertheless, his dispassionate survey of the universe had not raised his opinion of that costly experiment, and his study of the human race seemed to have resulted in the conclusion that all men were superfluous, and women necessary only because some one had to do the cooking. On the importance of this point his convictions were absolute, and gastronomy was the only science which he revered as dogma. It must be owned that his little dinners were a strong argument in favour of this view, besides being a reason—though not the main one—for the fidelity of his friends.

Mentally he exercised a hospitality less seductive but no less stimulating. His mind was like a forum, or some open meeting-place for the exchange of ideas: somewhat cold and draughty, but light, spacious and orderly—a kind of academic grove from which all the leaves had fallen. In this privileged area a dozen of us were wont to stretch our muscles and expand our lungs; and, as if to prolong as much as possible the tradition of what we felt to be a vanishing institution, one or two neophytes were now and then added to our band.

Young Phil Frenham was the last, and the most interesting, of these recruits, and a good example of Murchard's somewhat morbid assertion that our old friend "liked 'em juicy." It was indeed a fact that Culwin, for all his mental dryness, specially tasted the lyric qualities in youth. As he was far too good an Epicurean to nip the flowers of soul which he gathered for his garden, his friendship was not a disintegrating influence: on the contrary, it forced the young idea to robuster bloom. And in Phil Frenham he had a fine subject for experimentation. The boy was really intelligent, and the soundness of his nature was like the pure paste under a delicate glaze. Culwin had fished him out of a thick fog of family dullness, and pulled him up to a peak in Darien; and the adventure hadn't hurt him a bit.

Indeed, the skill with which Culwin had contrived to stimulate his curiosities without robbing them of their young bloom of awe seemed to me a sufficient answer to Murchard's ogreish metaphor. There was nothing hectic in Frenham's efflorescence, and his old friend had not laid even a finger-tip on the sacred stupidities. One wanted no better proof of that than the fact that Frenham still reverenced them in Culwin.

"There's a side of him you fellows don't see. *I* believe that story about the duel!" he declared; and it was of the very essence of this belief that it should impel him—just as our little party was dispersing—to turn back to our host with the absurd demand: "And now you've got to tell us about *your* ghost!"

The outer door had closed on Murchard and the others; only Frenham and I remained; and the vigilant servant who presided over Culwin's destinies, having brought a fresh supply of soda-water, had been laconically ordered to bed.

Culwin's sociability was a night-blooming flower, and we knew that he expected the nucleus of his group to tighten around him after midnight. But Frenham's appeal seemed to disconcert him comically, and he rose from the chair in which he had just reseated himself after his farewells in the hall.

"*My* ghost? Do you suppose I'm fool enough to go to the expense of keeping one of my own, when there are so many charming ones in my friends' closets?—Take another cigar," he said, revolving toward me with a laugh.

Frenham laughed too, pulling up his slender height before the chimney-piece as he turned to face his short bristling friend.

"Oh," he said, "you'd never be content to share if you met one you really liked."

Culwin had dropped back into his armchair, his shock head embedded in its habitual hollow, his little eyes glimmering over a fresh cigar.

"Liked—*liked?* Good Lord!" he growled.

"Ah, you *have*, then!" Frenham pounced on him in the same instant, with a sidewise glance of victory at me; but Culwin cowered gnomelike among his cushions, dissembling himself in a protective cloud of smoke.

"What's the use of denying it? You've seen everything, so of course you've seen a ghost!" his young friend persisted, talking intrepidly into the cloud. "Or, if you haven't seen one, it's only because you've seen two!"

The form of the challenge seemed to strike our host. He shot his head out of the mist with a queer tortoise-like motion he sometimes had, and blinked approvingly at Frenham.

"Yes," he suddenly flung at us on a shrill jerk of laughter; "it's only because I've seen two!"

The words were so unexpected that they dropped down and down into a fathomless silence, while we continued to stare at each other over Culwin's head, and Culwin stared at his ghosts. At length Frenham, without speaking, threw himself into the chair on the other side of the hearth, and leaned forward with his listening smile. . . .

2

"Oh, of course they're not show ghosts—a collector wouldn't think anything of them. . . . Don't let me raise your hopes. . . . their one merit is their numerical strength: the exceptional fact of their being *two*. But, as against this, I'm bound to admit that at any moment I could probably have exorcised them both by asking my doctor for a prescription, or my oculist for a pair of spectacles. Only, as I never could make up my mind whether to go to the doctor or the oculist—whether I was afflicted by an optical or a digestive delusion—I left them to pursue their interesting double life, though at times they made mine exceedingly comfortable. . . .

"Yes—uncomfortable; and you know how I hate to be uncomfortable! But it was part of my stupid pride, when the thing began, not to admit that I could be disturbed by the trifling matter of seeing two—

"And then I'd no reason, really, to suppose I was ill. As far as I knew I was simply bored—horribly bored. But it was part of my boredom—I remember—that I was feeling so uncommonly well, and didn't know how on earth to work off my surplus energy. I had come back from a long journey—down in South America and Mexico—and had settled down for the winter near New York, with an old aunt who had known Washington Irving and corresponded with N. P. Willis. She lived, not far from Irvington, in a damp Gothic villa, overhung by Norway spruces, and looking exactly like a memorial emblem done in hair. Her personal appearance was in keeping with this image, and her own hair—of which there was little left—might have been sacrificed to the manufacture of the emblem.

"I had just reached the end of an agitated year, with considerable arrears to make up in money and emotion; and theoretically it seemed as though my aunt's mild hospitality would be as beneficial to my nerves as to my purse. But the deuce of it was that as soon as I felt myself safe and sheltered my energy began to revive; and how was I to work it off inside of a memorial emblem? I had, at that time, the agreeable illusion that sustained intellectual effort could engage a man's whole activity; and I decided to write a great book—I forget about what. My aunt, impressed by my plan, gave up to me her Gothic library, filled with classics in black cloth and daguerreotypes of faded celebrities; and I sat down at my desk to make myself a place among their number. And to facilitate my task she lent me a cousin to copy my manuscript.

"The cousin was a nice girl, and I had an idea that a nice girl was just what I needed to restore my faith in human nature, and principally in myself. She was neither beautiful nor intelligent—poor Alice Nowell!—but it interested me to see any woman content to be so uninteresting, and I wanted to find out the secret of her content. In doing this I handled it rather rashly, and put it out of joint—oh, just for a moment! There's no fatuity in telling you this, for the poor girl had never seen anyone but cousins ...

"Well, I was sorry for what I'd done, of course, and confoundedly bothered as to how I should put it straight. She was staying in the house, and one evening, after my aunt had gone to bed, she came down to the library to fetch a book she'd mislaid, like any artless heroine on the shelves behind us. She was pink-nosed and flustered, and it suddenly occurred to me that her hair, though it was fairly thick and pretty, would look exactly like my aunt's when she grew older. I was glad I had noticed this, for it made it easier for me to do what was right; and when I had found the book she hadn't lost I told her I was leaving for Europe that week.

"Europe was terribly far off in those days, and Alice knew at once what I meant. She didn't take it in the least as I'd expected—it would have been easier if she had. She held her book very tight, and turned away a moment to wind up the lamp on my desk—it had a ground glass shade with vine leaves, and glass drops around the edge, I remember. Then she came back, held out her hand, and said: 'Goodbye.' And as she said it she looked straight at me and kissed me. I had never felt anything as fresh and shy and brave as her kiss. It was worse than any reproach, and it made me ashamed to deserve a reproach from her. I said to myself: 'I'll marry her, and when my aunt dies she'll leave us this house, and I'll sit here at the desk and go on with my book; and Alice will sit over there with her embroidery and look at me as she's looking now. And life will go on like that for any number of years.' The prospect frightened me a little, but at the time it didn't frighten me as much as doing anything to hurt her; and ten minutes later she had my seal ring on my finger, and my promise that when I went abroad she should go with me.

"You'll wonder why I'm enlarging on this familiar incident. It's because the evening on which it took place was the very evening on which I first saw the queer sight I've spoken of. Being at that time an ardent believer in a necessary sequence between cause and effect I naturally tried to trace some kind of link between what had just happened to me in my aunt's library, and what was to happen a few hours later on the same night; and so the coincidence between the two events always remained in my mind.

"I went up to bed with rather a heavy heart, for I was bowed under the weight of the first good action I had ever consciously committed; and young as I was, I saw the gravity of my situation. Don't imagine from this that I had hitherto been an instrument of destruction. I had been merely a harmless young man, who had followed his bent and declined all collaboration with Providence. Now I had suddenly undertaken to promote the moral order of the world, and I felt a good deal like the trustful spectator who has given his gold watch to the conjurer, and doesn't know in what shape he'll get it back when the trick is over. . . . Still, a glow of self-righteousness tempered my fears, and I said to myself as I undressed that when I'd got used to being good it probably wouldn't make me as nervous as it did at the start. And by the time I was in bed, and had blown out my candle, I felt that I really *was* getting used to it, and that, as far as I'd got, it was not unlike sinking down into one of my aunt's very softest wool mattresses.

"I closed my eyes on this image, and when I opened them it must have been a good deal later, for my room had grown cold, and the night was intensely still. I was waked suddenly by the feeling we all know—the feeling that there was something near me that hadn't been there when I fell asleep. I sat up and strained my eyes into the darkness.

The room was pitch black, and at first I saw nothing; but gradually a vague glimmer at the foot of the bed turned into two eyes staring back at me. I couldn't see the face attached to them—on account of the darkness, I imagined—but as I looked the eyes grew more and more distinct: they gave out a light of their own.

"The sensation of being thus gazed at was far from pleasant, and you might suppose that my first impulse would have been to jump out of bed and hurl myself on the invisible figure attached to the eyes. But it wasn't—my impulse was simply to lie still ... I can't say whether this was due to an immediate sense of the uncanny nature of the apparition—to the certainty that if I did jump out of bed I should hurl myself on nothing—or merely to the benumbing effect of the eyes themselves. They were the very worst eyes I've ever seen: a man's eyes—but what a man! My first thought was that he must be frightfully old. The orbits were sunk, and the thick red-lined lids hung over the eyeballs like blinds of which the cords are broken. One lid drooped a little lower than the other, with the effect of a crooked leer; and between these pulpy folds of flesh, with their scant bristle of lashes, the eyes themselves, small glassy disks with an agate-like rim about the pupils, looked like sea-pebbles in the grip of a starfish.

"But the age of the eyes was not the most unpleasant thing about them. What turned me sick was their expression of vicious security. I don't know how else to describe the fact that they seemed to belong to a man who had done a lot of harm in his life, but had always kept just inside the danger lines. They were not the eyes of a coward, but of someone much too clever to take risks; and my gorge rose at their look of base astuteness. Yet even that wasn't the worst; for as we continued to scan each other I saw in them a tinge of faint derision, and felt myself to be its object.

"At that I was seized by an impulse of rage that jerked me out of bed and pitched me straight on the unseen figure at its foot. But of course there wasn't any figure there, and my fists struck at emptiness. Ashamed and cold, I groped about for a match and lit the candles. The room looked just as usual—as I had known it would; and I crawled back to bed, and blew out the lights.

"As soon as the room was dark again the eyes reappeared; and I now applied myself to explaining them on scientific principles. At first I thought the illusion might have been caused by the glow of the last embers in the chimney; but the fire-place was on the other side of my bed, and so placed that the fire could not possibly be reflected in my toilet glass, which was the only mirror in the room. Then it occurred to me that I might have been tricked by the reflection of the embers in some polished bit of wood or metal; and though I couldn't discover any object of the sort in my line of vision, I got up again, groped my way to the hearth, and covered what was left of the fire. But as soon as I was back in bed the eyes were back at its foot.

"They were an hallucination, then: that was plain. But the fact that they were not due to any external dupery didn't make them a bit pleasanter to see. For if they were a projection of my inner consciousness, what the deuce was the matter with that organ? I had gone deeply enough into the mystery of morbid pathological states to picture the conditions under which an exploring mind might lay itself open to such a midnight admonition; but I couldn't fit it to my present case. I had never felt more normal, mentally and physically; and the only unusual fact in my situation—that of having assured the happiness of an amiable girl—did not seem of a kind to summon unclean spirits about my pillow. But there were the eyes still looking at me. . . .

"I shut mine, and tried to evoke a vision of Alice Nowell's. They were not remarkable eyes, but they were as wholesome as fresh water, and if she had had more imagination—or longer lashes—their expression might have been interesting. As it was, they did not prove very efficacious, and in a few moments I perceived that they had mysteriously changed into the eyes at the foot of the bed. It exasperated me more to feel these glaring at me through my shut lids than to see them, and I opened my eyes again and looked straight into their hateful stare. . . .

"And so it went on all night. I can't tell you what that night was, nor how long it lasted. Have you ever lain in bed, hopelessly wide awake, and tried to keep your eyes shut, knowing that if you opened 'em you'd see something you dreaded and loathed? It sounds easy, but it's devilish hard. Those eyes hung there and drew me. I had the *vertige de l'abime*, and their red lids were the edge of my abyss. . . . I had known nervous hours before: hours when I'd felt the wind of danger in my neck; but never this kind of strain. It wasn't that the eyes were so awful; they hadn't the majesty of the powers of darkness. But they had—how shall I say?—a physical effect that was the equivalent of a bad smell: their look left a smear like a snail's. And I didn't see what business they had with me, anyhow—and I stared and stared, trying to find out. . . .

"I don't know what effect they were trying to produce; but the effect they *did* produce was that of making me pack my portmanteau and bolt to town early the next morning. I left a note for my aunt, explaining that I was ill and had gone to see my doctor; and as a matter of fact I did feel uncommonly ill—the night seemed to have pumped all the blood out of me. But when I reached town I didn't go to the doctor's. I went to a friend's rooms, and threw myself on a bed, and slept for ten heavenly hours. When I woke it was the middle of the night, and I turned cold at the thought of what might be waiting for me. I sat up, shaking, and stared into the darkness; but there wasn't a break in its blessed surface, and when I saw that the eyes were not there I dropped back into another long sleep.

"I had left no word for Alice when I fled, because I meant to go back the next morning. But the next morning I was too exhausted to stir. As the day went on the exhaustion increased, instead of wearing off like the lassitude left by an ordinary night of insomnia: the effect of the eyes seemed to be cumulative, and the thought of seeing them again grew intolerable. For two days I struggled with my dread; but on the third evening I pulled myself together and decided to go back the next morning. I felt a good deal happier as soon as I'd decided, for I knew that my abrupt disappearance, and the strangeness of my not writing, must have been very painful for poor Alice. That night I went to bed with an easy mind, and fell asleep at once; but in the middle of the night I woke, and there were the eyes ...

"Well, I simply couldn't face them; and instead of going back to my aunt's I bundled a few things into a trunk and jumped onto the first steamer for England. I was so dead tired when I got on board that I crawled straight into my berth, and slept most of the way over; and I can't tell you the bliss it was to wake from those long stretches of dreamless sleep and look fearlessly into the darkness, *knowing* that I shouldn't see the eyes . . . .

"I stayed abroad for a year, and then I stayed for another; and during that time I never had a glimpse of them. That was enough reason for prolonging my stay if I'd been on a desert island. Another was, of course, that I had perfectly come to see, on the voyage over, the folly, complete impossibility, of my marrying Alice Nowell. The fact that I had been so slow in making this discovery annoyed me, and made me want to avoid explanations. The bliss of escaping at one stroke from the eyes, and from this other embarrassment, gave my freedom an extraordinary zest; and the longer I savoured it the better I liked its taste.

"The eyes had burned such a hole in my consciousness that for a long time I went on puzzling over the nature of the apparition, and wondering nervously if it would ever come back. But as time passed I lost this dread, and retained only the precision of the image. Then that faded in its turn.

"The second year found me settled in Rome, where I was planning, I believe, to write another great book—a definitive work on Etruscan influences in Italian art. At any rate, I'd found some pretext of the kind for taking a sunny apartment in the Piazza di Spagna and dabbling about indefinitely in the Forum; and there, one morning, a charming youth came to me. As he stood there in the warm light, slender and smooth and hyacinthine, he might have stepped from a ruined altar—one to Antinous, say—but he'd come instead from New York, with a letter (of all people) from Alice Nowell. The letter—the first I'd had from her since our break—was simply a line introducing her young cousin, Gilbert Noyes, and appealing to me to befriend him.

"It appeared, poor lad, that he 'had talent,' and 'wanted to write'; and, an obdurate family having insisted that his calligraphy should take the form of double entry, Alice had intervened to win him six months' respite, during which he was to travel on a meagre pittance, and somehow prove his ultimate ability to increase it by his pen. The quaint conditions of the test struck me first: it seemed about as conclusive as a mediaeval 'ordeal.' Then I was touched by her having sent him to me. I had always wanted to do her some service, to justify myself in my own eyes rather than hers; and here was a beautiful embodiment of my chance.

"Well, I imagine it's safe to lay down the general principle that predestined geniuses don't, as a rule, appear before one in the spring sunshine of the Forum looking like one of its banished gods. At any rate, poor Noyes wasn't a predestined genius. But he *was* beautiful to see, and charming as a comrade too. It was only when he began to talk literature that my heart failed me. I knew all the symptoms so well—the things he had 'in him,' and the things outside him that impinged! There's the real test, after all. It was always—punctually, inevitably, with the inexorableness of a mechanical law—it was *always* the wrong thing that struck him. I grew to find a certain grim fascination in deciding in advance exactly which wrong thing he'd select; and I acquired an astonishing skill at the game. . . .

"The worst of it was that his *betise* wasn't of the too obvious sort. Ladies who met him at picnics thought him intellectual; and even at dinners he passed for clever. I, who had him under the microscope, fancied now and then that he might develop some kind of a slim talent, something that he could make 'do' and be happy on; and wasn't that, after all, what I was concerned with? He was so charming—he continued to be so charming—that he called forth all my charity in support of this argument; and for the first few months I really believed there was a chance for him ...

"Those months were delightful. Noyes was constantly with me, and the more I saw of him the better I liked him. His stupidity was a natural grace—it was as beautiful, really, as his eye-lashes. And he was so gay, so affectionate, and so happy with me, that telling him the truth would have been about as pleasant as slitting the throat of some artless animal. At first I used to wonder what had put into that radiant head the detestable delusion that it held a brain. Then I began to see that it was simply protective mimicry—an instinctive ruse to get away from family life and an office desk. Not that Gilbert didn't—dear lad!—believe in himself.

"There wasn't a trace of hypocrisy in his composition. He was sure that his 'call' was irresistible, while to me it was the saving grace of his situation that it *wasn't*, and that a little money, a little leisure, a little pleasure would have turned him into an inoffensive idler. Unluckily, however, there was no hope of money, and with the grim alternative of the office desk before him he couldn't postpone his attempt at literature. The stuff he turned out was deplorable, and I see now that I knew it from the first. Still, the absurdity of deciding a man's whole future on a first trial seemed to justify me in withholding my verdict, and perhaps even in encouraging him a little, on the ground that the human plant generally needs warmth to flower.

"At any rate, I proceeded on that principle, and carried it to the point of getting his term of probation extended. When I left Rome he went with me, and we idled away a delicious summer between Capri and Venice. I said to myself: 'If he has anything in him, it will come out now; and it *did*. He was never more enchanting and enchanted. There were moments of our pilgrimage when beauty born of murmuring sound seemed actually to pass into his face—but only to issue forth in a shallow flood of the palest ink. . . .

"Well the time came to turn off the tap; and I knew there was no hand but mine to do it. We were back in Rome, and I had taken him to stay with me, not wanting him to be alone in his dismal *pension* when he had to face the necessity of renouncing his ambition. I hadn't, of course, relied solely on my own judgment in deciding to advise him to drop literature. I had sent his stuff to various people—editors and critics—and they had always sent it back with the same chilling lack of comment. Really there was nothing on earth to say about it—

"I confess I never felt more shabbily than I did on the day when I decided to have it out with Gilbert. It was well enough to tell myself that it was my duty to knock the poor boy's hopes into splinters—but I'd like to know what act of gratuitous cruelty hasn't been justified on that plea? I've always shrunk from usurping the functions of Providence, and when I have to exercise them I decidedly prefer that it shouldn't be on an errand of destruction. Besides, in the last issue, who was I to decide, even after a year's trial, if poor Gilbert had it in him or not?

"The more I looked at the part I'd resolved to play, the less I liked it; and I liked it still less when Gilbert sat opposite me, with his head thrown back in the lamplight, just as Phil's is now. . . . I'd been going over his last manuscript, and he knew it, and he knew that his future hung on my verdict—we'd tacitly agreed to that. The manuscript lay between us, on my table—a novel, his first novel, if you please!—and he reached over and laid his hand on it, and looked up at me with all his life in the look.

"I stood up and cleared my throat, trying to keep my eyes away from his face and on the manuscript.

"'The fact is, my dear Gilbert,' I began—

"I saw him turn pale, but he was up and facing me in an instant.

"'Oh, look here, don't take on so, my dear fellow! I'm not so awfully cut up as all that!' His hands were on my shoulders, and he was laughing down on me from his full height, with a kind of mortally-stricken gaiety that drove the knife into my side.

"He was too beautifully brave for me to keep up any humbug about my duty. And it came over me suddenly how I should hurt others in hurting him: myself first, since sending him home meant losing him; but more particularly poor Alice Nowell, to whom I had so uneasily longed to prove my good faith and my immense desire to serve her. It really seemed like failing her twice to fail Gilbert—

"But my intuition was like one of those lightning flashes that encircle the whole horizon, and in the same instant I saw what I might be letting myself in for if I didn't tell the truth. I said to myself: 'I shall have him for life'—and I'd never yet seen anyone, man or woman, whom I was quite sure of wanting on those terms. Well, this impulse of egotism decided me. I was ashamed of it, and to get away from it I took a leap that landed me straight in Gilbert's arms.

"'The thing's all right, and you're all wrong!' I shouted up at him; and as he hugged me, and I laughed and shook in his incredulous clutch, I had for a minute the sense of self-complacency that is supposed to attend the footsteps of the just. Hang it all, making people happy *has* its charms—

"Gilbert, of course, was for celebrating his emancipation in some spectacular manner; but I sent him away alone to explode his emotions, and went to bed to sleep off mine. As I undressed I began to wonder what their after-taste would be—so many of the finest don't keep! Still, I wasn't sorry, and I meant to empty the bottle, even if it *did* turn a trifle flat.

"After I got into bed I lay for a long time smiling at the memory of his eyes—his blissful eyes...Then I fell asleep, and when I woke the room was deathly cold, and I sat up with a jerk—and there were *the other eyes*. . . .

"It was three years since I'd seen them, but I'd thought of them so often that I fancied they could never take me unawares again. Now, with their red sneer on me, I knew that I had never really believed they would come back, and that I was as defenceless as ever against them. . . . As before, it was the insane irrelevance of their coming that made it so horrible. What the deuce were they after, to leap out at me at such a time? I had lived more or less carelessly in the years since I'd seen them, though my worst indiscretions were not dark enough to invite the searchings of their infernal glare; but at this particular moment I was really in what might have been called a state of grace; and I can't tell you how the fact added to their horror. . . .

"But it's not enough to say they were as bad as before: they were worse. Worse by just so much as I'd learned of life in the interval; by all the damnable implications my wider experience read into them. I saw now what I hadn't seen before: that they were eyes which had grown hideous gradually, which had built up their baseness coral-wise, bit by bit, out of a series of small turpitudes slowly accumulated through the industrious years. Yes—it came to me that what made them so bad was that they'd grown bad so slowly ...

"There they hung in the darkness, their swollen lids dropped across the little watery bulbs rolling loose in the orbits, and the puff of fat flesh making a muddy shadow underneath—and as their filmy stare moved with my movements, there came over me a sense of their tacit complicity, of a deep hidden understanding between us that was worse than the first shock of their strangeness. Not that I understood them; but that they made it so clear that someday I should. . . . Yes, that was the worst part of it, decidedly; and it was the feeling that became stronger each time they came back to me. . . .

"For they got into the damnable habit of coming back. They reminded me of vampires with a taste for young flesh, they seemed so to gloat over the taste of a good conscience. Every night for a month they came to claim their morsel of mine: since I'd made Gilbert happy they simply wouldn't loosen their fangs. The coincidence almost made me hate him, poor lad, fortuitous as I felt it to be. I puzzled over it a good deal, but couldn't find any hint of an explanation except in the chance of his association with Alice Nowell. But then the eyes had let up on me the moment I had abandoned her, so they could hardly be the emissaries of a woman scorned, even if one could have pictured poor Alice charging such spirits to avenge her. That set me thinking, and I began to wonder if they would let up on me if I abandoned Gilbert. The temptation was insidious, and I had to stiffen myself against it; but really, dear boy! he was too charming to be sacrificed to such demons. And so, after all, I never found out what they wanted. . . ."

3

The fire crumbled, sending up a flash which threw into relief the narrator's gnarled red face under its grey-black stubble. Pressed into the hollow of the dark leather armchair, it stood out an instant like an intaglio of yellowish red-veined stone, with spots of enamel for the eyes; then the fire sank and in the shaded lamp-light it became once more a dim Rembrandtish blur.

Phil Frenham, sitting in a low chair on the opposite side of the hearth, one long arm propped on the table behind him, one hand supporting his thrown-back head, and his eyes steadily fixed on his old friend's face, had not moved since the tale began. He continued to maintain his silent immobility after Culwin had ceased to speak, and it was I who, with a vague sense of disappointment at the sudden drop of the story, finally asked: "But how long did you keep on seeing them?"

Culwin, so sunk into his chair that he seemed like a heap of his own empty clothes, stirred a little, as if in surprise at my question. He appeared to have half-forgotten what he had been telling us.

"How long? Oh, off and on all that winter. It was infernal. I never got used to them. I grew really ill."

Frenham shifted his attitude silently, and as he did so his elbow struck against a small mirror in a bronze frame standing on the table behind him. He turned and changed its angle slightly; then he resumed his former attitude, his dark head thrown back on his lifted palm, his eyes intent on Culwin's face. Something in his stare embarrassed me, and as if to divert attention from it I pressed on with another question:

"And you never tried sacrificing Noyes?"

"Oh, no. The fact is I didn't have to. He did it for me, poor infatuated boy!"

"Did it for you? How do you mean?"

"He wore me out—wore everybody out. He kept on pouring out his lamentable twaddle, and hawking it up and down the place till he became a thing of terror. I tried to wean him from writing—oh, ever so gently, you understand, by throwing him with agreeable people, giving him a chance to make himself felt, to come to a sense of what he *really* had to give. I'd foreseen this solution from the beginning—felt sure that, once the first ardour of authorship was quenched, he'd drop into his place as a charming parasitic thing, the kind of chronic Cherubino for whom, in old societies, there's always a seat at table, and a shelter behind the ladies' skirts. I saw him take his place as 'the poet': the poet who doesn't write. One knows the type in every drawing-room.

"Living in that way doesn't cost much—I'd worked it all out in my mind, and felt sure that, with a little help, he could manage it for the next few years; and meanwhile he'd be sure to marry. I saw him married to a widow, rather older, with a good cook and a well-run house. And I actually had my eye on the widow. . . . .Meanwhile I did everything to facilitate the transition—lent him money to ease his conscience, introduced him to pretty women to make him forget his vows. But nothing would do him: he had but one idea in his beautiful obstinate head. He wanted the laurel and not the rose, and he kept on repeating Gautier's axiom, and battering and filing at his limp prose till he'd spread it out over Lord knows how many thousand sloppy pages. Now and then he would send a pailful to a publisher, and of course it would always come back.

"At first it didn't matter—he thought he was 'misunderstood.' He took the attitudes of genius, and whenever an opus came home he wrote another to keep it company. Then he had a reaction of despair, and accused me of deceiving him, and Lord knows what. I got angry at that, and told him it was he who had deceived himself. He'd come to me determined to write, and I'd done my best to help him. That was the extent of my offence, and I'd done it for his cousin's sake, not his.

"That seemed to strike home, and he didn't answer for a minute. Then he said: 'My time's up and my money's up. What do you think I'd better do?'

"'I think you'd better not be an ass,' I said.

"He turned red, and asked: 'What do you mean by being an ass?'

"I took a letter from my desk and held it out to him.

"'I mean refusing this offer of Mrs. Ellinger's: to be her secretary at a salary of five thousand dollars. There may be a lot more in it than that.'

"He flung out his hand with a violence that struck the letter from mine. 'Oh, I know well enough what's in it!' he said, scarlet to the roots of his hair.

"'And what's your answer, if you know?' I asked.

"He made none at the minute, but turned away slowly to the door. There, with his hand on the threshold, he stopped to ask, almost under his breath: 'Then you really think my stuff's no good?'

"I was tired and exasperated, and I laughed. I don't defend my laugh—it was in wretched taste. But I must plead in extenuation that the boy was a fool, and that I'd done my best for him—I really had.

"He went out of the room, shutting the door quietly after him. That afternoon I left for Frascati, where I'd promised to spend the Sunday with some friends. I was glad to escape from Gilbert, and by the same token, as I learned that night, I had also escaped from the eyes. I dropped into the same lethargic sleep that had come to me before when their visitations ceased; and when I woke the next morning, in my peaceful painted room above the ilexes, I felt the utter weariness and deep relief that always followed on that repairing slumber. I put in two blessed nights at Frascati, and when I got back to my rooms in Rome I found that Gilbert had gone. . . . Oh, nothing tragic had happened—the episode never rose to *that*. He'd simply packed his manuscripts and left for America—for his family and the Wall Street desk. He left a decent little note to tell me of his decision, and behaved altogether, in the circumstances, as little like a fool as it's possible for a fool to behave. . . . "

4

Culwin paused again, and again Frenham sat motionless, the dusky contour of his young head reflected in the mirror at his back.

"And what became of Noyes afterward?" I finally asked, still disquieted by a sense of incompleteness, by the need of some connecting thread between the parallel lines of the tale.

Culwin twitched his shoulders. "Oh, nothing became of him—because he became nothing. There could be no question of 'becoming' about it. He vegetated in an office, I believe, and finally got a clerkship in a consulate, and married drearily in China. I saw him once in Hong Kong, years afterward. He was fat and hadn't shaved. I was told he drank. He didn't recognize me."

"And the eyes?" I asked, after another pause which Frenham's continued silence made oppressive.

Culwin, stroking his chin, blinked at me meditatively through the shadows. "I never saw them after my last talk with Gilbert. Put two and two together if you can. For my part, I haven't found the link."

He rose stiffly, his hands in his pockets, and walked over to the table on which reviving drinks had been set out.

"You must be parched after this dry tale. Here, help yourself, my dear fellow. Here, Phil—" He turned back to the hearth.

Frenham still sat in his low chair, making no response to his host's hospitable summons. But as Culwin advanced toward him, their eyes met in a long look; after which, to my intense surprise, the young man, turning suddenly in his seat, flung his arms across the table, and dropped his face upon them.

Culwin, at the unexpected gesture, stopped short, a flush on his face.

"Phil—what the deuce? Why, have the eyes scared *you?* My dear boy—my dear fellow—I never had such a tribute to my literary ability, never!"

He broke into a chuckle at the thought, and halted on the hearth-rug, his hands still in his pockets, gazing down in honest perplexity at the youth's bowed head. Then, as Frenham still made no answer, he moved a step or two nearer.

"Cheer up, my dear Phil! It's years since I've seen them—apparently I've done nothing lately bad enough to call them out of chaos. Unless my present evocation of them has made *you* see them; which would be their worst stroke yet!"

His bantering appeal quivered off into an uneasy laugh, and he moved still nearer, bending over Frenham, and laying his gouty hands on the lad's shoulders.

"Phil, my dear boy, really—what's the matter? Why don't you answer? *Have* you seen the eyes?"

Frenham's face was still pressed against his arms, and from where I stood behind Culwin I saw the latter, as if under the rebuff of this unaccountable attitude, draw back slowly from his friend. As he did so, the light of the lamp on the table fell full on his perplexed congested face, and I caught its sudden reflection in the mirror behind Frenham's head.

Culwin saw the reflection also. He paused, his face level with the mirror, as if scarcely recognising the countenance in it as his own. But as he looked his expression gradually changed, and for an appreciable space of time he and the image in the glass confronted each other with a glare of slowly gathering hate. Then Culwin let go of Frenham's shoulders, and drew back a step, covering his eyes with his hands. . . .

Frenham, his face still hidden, did not stir.

The Fullness of Life

1

For hours she had lain in a kind of gentle torpor, not unlike that sweet lassitude which masters one in the hush of a midsummer noon, when the heat seems to have silenced the very birds and insects, and, lying sunk in the tasselled meadow-grasses, one looks up through a level roofing of maple-leaves at the vast shadowless, and unsuggestive blue. Now and then, at ever-lengthening intervals, a flash of pain darted through her, like the ripple of sheet-lightning across such a midsummer sky; but it was too transitory to shake her stupor, that calm, delicious, bottomless stupor into which she felt herself sinking more and more deeply, without a disturbing impulse of resistance, an effort of reattachment to the vanishing edges of consciousness.

The resistance, the effort, had known their hour of violence; but now they were at an end. Through her mind, long harried by grotesque visions, fragmentary images of the life that she was leaving, tormenting lines of verse, obstinate presentments of pictures once beheld, indistinct impressions of rivers, towers, and cupolas, gathered in the length of journeys half forgotten—through her mind there now only moved a few primal sensations of colourless well-being; a vague satisfaction in the thought that she had swallowed her noxious last draught of medicine . . . and that she should never again hear the creaking of her husband's boots—those horrible boots—and that no one would come to bother her about the next day's dinner . . . or the butcher's book. . . .

"It is all over," said the nurse, drawing down the eyelids with official composure.

The clock struck three. They remembered it afterward. Someone opened the window and let in a blast of that strange, neutral air which walks the earth between darkness and dawn; someone else led the husband into another room. He walked vaguely, like a blind man, on his creaking boots. . .

2

She stood, as it seemed, on a threshold, yet no tangible gateway was in front of her. Only a wide *vista* of light, mild yet penetrating as the gathered glimmer of innumerable stars, expanded gradually before her eyes, in blissful contrast to the cavernous darkness from which she had of late emerged.

Her gaze lost itself in the ethereal remoteness of the mountains.

"How beautiful! How satisfying!" she murmured. "Perhaps now I shall really know what it is to live."

As she spoke she felt a sudden thickening of her heart-beats, and looking up she was aware that before her stood the Spirit of Life.

"Have you never really known what it is to live?" the Spirit of Life asked her.

"I have never known," she replied, "that fullness of life which we all feel ourselves capable of knowing; though my life has not been without scattered hints of it, like the scent of earth which comes to one sometimes far out at sea."

"And what do you call the fullness of life?" the Spirit asked again.

"Oh, I can't tell you, if you don't know," she said, almost reproachfully. "Many words are supposed to define it—love and sympathy are those in commonest use, but I am not even sure that they are the right ones, and so few people really know what they mean."

"You were married," said the Spirit, "yet you did not find the fullness of life in your marriage?"

"Oh, dear, no," she replied, with an indulgent scorn, "my marriage was a very incomplete affair."

"And yet you were fond of your husband?"

"You have hit upon the exact word; I was fond of him, yes, just as I was fond of my grandmother, and the house that I was born in, and my old nurse. Oh, I was fond of him, and we were counted a very happy couple. But I have sometimes thought that a woman's nature is like a great house full of rooms: there is the hall, through which everyone passes in going in and out; the drawing- room, where one receives formal visits; the sitting-room, where the members of the family come and go as they list; but beyond that, far beyond, are other rooms, the handles of whose doors perhaps are never turned; no one knows the way to them, no one knows whither they lead; and in the innermost room, the holy of holies, the soul sits alone and waits for a footstep that never comes."

"And your husband," asked the Spirit, after a pause, "never got beyond the family sitting-room?"

"Never," she returned, impatiently; "and the worst of it was that he was quite content to remain there. He thought it perfectly beautiful, and sometimes, when he was admiring its commonplace furniture, insignificant as the chairs and tables of a hotel parlour, I felt like crying out to him: 'Fool, will you never guess that close at hand are rooms full of treasures and wonders, such as the eye of man hath not seen, rooms that no step has crossed, but that might be yours to live in, could you but find the handle of the door?'"

"Then," the Spirit continued, "those moments of which you lately spoke, which seemed to come to you like scattered hints of the fullness of life, were not shared with your husband?"

"Oh, no—never. He was different. His boots creaked, and he always slammed the door when he went out, and he never read anything but railway novels and the sporting advertisements in the papers—and—and, in short, we never understood each other in the least."

"To what influence, then, did you owe those exquisite sensations?"

"I can hardly tell. Sometimes to the perfume of a flower; sometimes to a verse of Dante or of Shakespeare; sometimes to a picture or a sunset, or to one of those calm days at sea, when one seems to be lying in the hollow of a blue pearl; sometimes, but rarely, to a word spoken by someone who chanced to give utterance, at the right moment, to what I felt but could not express."

"Someone whom you loved?" asked the Spirit.

"I never loved anyone, in that way," she said, rather sadly, "nor was I thinking of any one person when I spoke, but of two or three who, by touching for an instant upon a certain chord of my being, had called forth a single note of that strange melody which seemed sleeping in my soul. It has seldom happened, however, that I have owed such feelings to people; and no one ever gave me a moment of such happiness as it was my lot to feel one evening in the Church of Or San Michele, in Florence."

"Tell me about it," said the Spirit.

"It was near sunset on a rainy spring afternoon in Easter week. The clouds had vanished, dispersed by a sudden wind, and as we entered the church the fiery panes of the high windows shone out like lamps through the dusk. A priest was at the high altar, his white cope a livid spot in the incense-laden obscurity, the light of the candles flickering up and down like fireflies about his head; a few people knelt nearby. We stole behind them and sat down on a bench close to the tabernacle of Orcagna.

"Strange to say, though Florence was not new to me, I had never been in the church before; and in that magical light I saw for the first time the inlaid steps, the fluted columns, the sculptured bas-reliefs and canopy of the marvellous shrine. The marble, worn and mellowed by the subtle hand of time, took on an unspeakable rosy hue, suggestive in some remote way of the honey-coloured columns of the Parthenon, but more mystic, more complex, a colour not born of the sun's inveterate kiss, but made up of cryptal twilight, and the flame of candles upon martyrs' tombs, and gleams of sunset through symbolic panes of chrysoprase and ruby; such a light as illumines the missals in the library of Siena, or burns like a hidden fire through the Madonna of Gian Bellini in the Church of the Redeemer, at Venice; the light of the Middle Ages, richer, more solemn, more significant than the limpid sunshine of Greece.

"The church was silent, but for the wail of the priest and the occasional scraping of a chair against the floor, and as I sat there, bathed in that light, absorbed in rapt contemplation of the marble miracle which rose before me, cunningly wrought as a casket of ivory and enriched with jewel-like incrustations and tarnished gleams of gold, I felt myself borne onward along a mighty current, whose source seemed to be in the very beginning of things, and whose tremendous waters gathered as they went all the mingled streams of human passion and endeavour. Life in all its varied manifestations of beauty and strangeness seemed weaving a rhythmical dance around me as I moved, and wherever the spirit of man had passed I knew that my foot had once been familiar.

"As I gazed the mediaeval bosses of the tabernacle of Orcagna seemed to melt and flow into their primal forms so that the folded lotus of the Nile and the Greek acanthus were braided with the runic knots and fish-tailed monsters of the North, and all the plastic terror and beauty born of man's hand from the Ganges to the Baltic quivered and mingled in Orcagna's apotheosis of Mary. And so the river bore me on, past the alien face of antique civilizations and the familiar wonders of Greece, till I swam upon the fiercely rushing tide of the Middle Ages, with its swirling eddies of passion, its heaven-reflecting pools of poetry and art; I heard the rhythmic blow of the craftsmen's hammers in the goldsmiths' workshops and on the walls of churches, the party-cries of armed factions in the narrow streets, the organ-roll of Dante's verse, the crackle of the fagots around Arnold of Brescia, the twitter of the swallows to which St. Francis preached, the laughter of the ladies listening on the hillside to the quips of the *Decameron*, while plague-struck Florence howled beneath them—all this and much more I heard, joined in strange unison with voices earlier and more remote, fierce, passionate, or tender, yet subdued to such awful harmony that I thought of the song that the morning stars sang together and felt as though it were sounding in my ears. My heart beat to suffocation, the tears burned my lids, the joy, the mystery of it seemed too intolerable to be borne. I could not understand even then the words of the song; but I knew that if there had been someone at my side who could have heard it with me, we might have found the key to it together.

"I turned to my husband, who was sitting beside me in an attitude of patient dejection, gazing into the bottom of his hat; but at that moment he rose, and stretching his stiffened legs, said, mildly: 'Hadn't we better be going? There doesn't seem to be much to see here, and you know the *table d'hote* dinner is at half-past six o'clock."

Her recital ended, there was an interval of silence; then the Spirit of Life said: "There is a compensation in store for such needs as you have expressed."

"Oh, then you *do* understand?" she exclaimed. "Tell me what compensation, I entreat you!"

"It is ordained," the Spirit answered, "that every soul which seeks in vain on earth for a kindred soul to whom it can lay bare its inmost being shall find that soul here and be united to it for eternity."

A glad cry broke from her lips. "Ah, shall I find him at last?" she cried, exultant.

"He is here," said the Spirit of Life.

She looked up and saw that a man stood near whose soul (for in that unwonted light she seemed to see his soul more clearly than his face) drew her toward him with an invincible force.

"Are you really he?" she murmured.

"I am he," he answered.

She laid her hand in his and drew him toward the parapet which overhung the valley.

"Shall we go down together," she asked him, "into that marvellous country; shall we see it together, as if with the self-same eyes, and tell each other in the same words all that we think and feel?"

"So," he replied, "have I hoped and dreamed."

"What?" she asked, with rising joy. "Then you, too, have looked for me?"

"All my life."

"How wonderful! And did you never, never find anyone in the other world who understood you?"

"Not wholly—not as you and I understand each other."

"Then you feel it, too? Oh, I am happy," she sighed.

They stood, hand in hand, looking down over the parapet upon the shimmering landscape which stretched forth beneath them into sapphirine space, and the Spirit of Life, who kept watch near the threshold, heard now and then a floating fragment of their talk blown backward like the stray swallows which the wind sometimes separates from their migratory tribe.

"Did you never feel at sunset—"

"Ah, yes; but I never heard anyone else say so. Did you?"

"Do you remember that line in the third canto of the *Inferno*?"

"Ah, that line—my favourite always. Is it possible—"

"You know the stooping Victory in the frieze of the Nike Apteros?"

"You mean the one who is tying her sandal? Then you have noticed, too, that all Botticelli and Mantegna are dormant in those flying folds of her drapery?"

"After a storm in autumn have you never seen—"

"Yes, it is curious how certain flowers suggest certain painters—the perfume of the incarnation, Leonardo; that of the rose, Titian; the tuberose, Crivelli—"

"I never supposed that anyone else had noticed it."

"Have you never thought—"

"Oh, yes, often and often; but I never dreamed that anyone else had."

"But surely you must have felt—"

"Oh, yes, yes; and you, too—"

"How beautiful! How strange—"

Their voices rose and fell, like the murmur of two fountains answering each other across a garden full of flowers. At length, with a certain tender impatience, he turned to her and said:

"Love, why should we linger here? All eternity lies before us. Let us go down into that beautiful country together and make a home for ourselves on some blue hill above the shining river."

As he spoke, the hand she had forgotten in his was suddenly withdrawn, and he felt that a cloud was passing over the radiance of her soul.

"A home," she repeated, slowly, "a home for you and me to live in for all eternity?"

"Why not, love? Am I not the soul that yours has sought?"

"Y-yes—yes, I know—but, don't you see, home would not be like home to me, unless—"

"Unless?" he wonderingly repeated.

She did not answer, but she thought to herself, with an impulse of whimsical inconsistency, "Unless you slammed the door and wore creaking boots."

But he had recovered his hold upon her hand, and by imperceptible degrees was leading her toward the shining steps which descended to the valley.

"Come, O my soul's soul," he passionately implored; "why delay a moment? Surely you feel, as I do, that eternity itself is too short to hold such bliss as ours. It seems to me that I can see our home already. Have I not always seen it in my dreams? It is white, love, is it not, with polished columns, and a sculptured cornice against the blue? Groves of laurel and oleander and thickets of roses surround it; but from the terrace where we walk at sunset, the eye looks out over woodlands and cool meadows where, deep-bowered under ancient boughs, a stream goes delicately toward the river. Indoors our favourite pictures hang upon the walls and the rooms are lined with books. Think, dear, at last we shall have time to read them all. With which shall we begin? Come, help me to choose. Shall it be *Faust* or the *Vita Nuova*, the *Tempest* or *Les Caprices de Marianne*, or the thirty-first canto of the *Paradise*, or *Epipsychidion* or *Lycidas*? Tell me, dear, which one?"

As he spoke he saw the answer trembling joyously upon her lips; but it died in the ensuing silence, and she stood motionless, resisting the persuasion of his hand.

"What is it?" he entreated.

"Wait a moment," she said, with a strange hesitation in her voice. "Tell me first, are you quite sure of yourself? Is there no one on earth whom you sometimes remember?"

"Not since I have seen you," he replied; for, being a man, he had indeed forgotten.

Still she stood motionless, and he saw that the shadow deepened on her soul.

"Surely, love," he rebuked her, "it was not that which troubled you? For my part I have walked through Lethe. The past has melted like a cloud before the moon. I never lived until I saw you."

She made no answer to his pleadings, but at length, rousing herself with a visible effort, she turned away from him and moved toward the Spirit of Life, who still stood near the threshold.

"I want to ask you a question," she said, in a troubled voice.

"Ask," said the Spirit.

"A little while ago," she began, slowly, "you told me that every soul which has not found a kindred soul on earth is destined to find one here."

"And have you not found one?" asked the Spirit.

"Yes; but will it be so with my husband's soul also?"

"No," answered the Spirit of Life, "for your husband imagined that he had found his soul's mate on earth in you; and for such delusions eternity itself contains no cure."

She gave a little cry. Was it of disappointment or triumph?

"Then—then what will happen to him when he comes here?"

"That I cannot tell you. Some field of activity and happiness he will doubtless find, in due measure to his capacity for being active and happy."

She interrupted, almost angrily: "He will never be happy without me."

"Do not be too sure of that," said the Spirit.

She took no notice of this, and the Spirit continued: "He will not understand you here any better than he did on earth."

"No matter," she said; "I shall be the only sufferer, for he always thought that he understood me."

"His boots will creak just as much as ever—"

"No matter."

"And he will slam the door—"

"Very likely."

"And continue to read railway novels—"

She interposed, impatiently: "Many men do worse than that."

"But you said just now," said the Spirit, "that you did not love him."

"True," she answered, simply; "but don't you understand that I shouldn't feel at home without him? It is all very well for a week or two—but for eternity! After all, I never minded the creaking of his boots, except when my head ached, and I don't suppose it will ache *here*; and he was always so sorry when he had slammed the door, only he never *could* remember not to. Besides, no one else would know how to look after him, he is so helpless. His inkstand would never be filled, and he would always be out of stamps and visiting-cards. He would never remember to have his umbrella re-covered, or to ask the price of anything before he bought it. Why, he wouldn't even know what novels to read. I always had to choose the kind he liked, with a murder or a forgery and a successful detective."

She turned abruptly to her kindred soul, who stood listening with a mien of wonder and dismay.

"Don't you see," she said, "that I can't possibly go with you?"

"But what do you intend to do?" asked the Spirit of Life.

"What do I intend to do?" she returned, indignantly. "Why, I mean to wait for my husband, of course. If he had come here first *he* would have waited for me for years and years; and it would break his heart not to find me here when he comes." She pointed with a contemptuous gesture to the magic vision of hill and vale sloping away to the translucent mountains. "He wouldn't give a fig for all that," she said, "if he didn't find me here."

"But consider," warned the Spirit, "that you are now choosing for eternity. It is a solemn moment."

"Choosing!" she said, with a half-sad smile. "Do you still keep up here that old fiction about choosing? I should have thought that *you* knew better than that. How can I help myself? He will expect to find me here when he comes, and he would never believe you if you told him that I had gone away with someone else—never, never."

"So be it," said the Spirit. "Here, as on earth, each one must decide for himself."

She turned to her kindred soul and looked at him gently, almost wistfully. "I am sorry," she said. "I should have liked to talk with you again; but you will understand, I know, and I dare say you will find someone else a great deal cleverer—"

And without pausing to hear his answer she waved him a swift farewell and turned back toward the threshold.

"Will my husband come soon?" she asked the Spirit of Life.

"That you are not destined to know," the Spirit replied.

"No matter," she said, cheerfully; "I have all eternity to wait in."

And still seated alone on the threshold, she listens for the creaking of his boots.

The Hermit and the Wild Woman

1

The Hermit lived in a cave in the hollow of a hill. Below him was a glen, with a stream in a coppice of oaks and alders, and on the farther side of the valley, half a day's journey distant, another hill, steep and bristling, which raised aloft a little walled town with Ghibelline swallow-tails notched against the sky.

When the Hermit was a lad, and lived in the town, the crenellations of the walls had been square-topped, and a Guelf lord had flown his standard from the keep. Then one day a steel-coloured line of men-at-arms rode across the valley, wound up the hill and battered in the gates. Stones and Greek fire rained from the ramparts, shields clashed in the streets, blade sprang at blade in passages and stairways, pikes and lances dripped above huddled flesh, and all the still familiar place was a stew of dying bodies. The boy fled from it in horror. He had seen his father go forth and not come back, his mother drop dead from an arquebuse shot as she leaned from the platform of the tower, his little sister fall with a slit throat across the altar steps of the chapel—and he ran, ran for his life, through the slippery streets, over warm twitching bodies, between legs of soldiers carousing, out of the gates, past burning farmsteads, trampled wheat-fields, orchards stripped and broken, till the still woods received him and he fell face down on the unmutilated earth.

He had no wish to go back. His longing was to live hidden from life. Up the hillside he found a hollow in the rock, and built before it a porch of boughs bound together with withies. He fed on nuts and roots, and on trout which he caught with his hands under the stones in the stream. He had always been a quiet boy, liking to sit at his mother's feet and watch the flowers grow on her embroidery frame, while the chaplain read aloud the histories of the Desert Fathers from a great silver-clasped volume. He would rather have been bred a clerk and scholar than a knight's son, and his happiest moments were when he served mass for the chaplain in the early morning, and felt his heart flutter up and up like a lark, up and up till it was lost in infinite space and brightness. Almost as happy were the hours when he sat beside the foreign painter who came over the mountains to paint the chapel, and under whose brush celestial faces grew out of the rough wall as if he had sown some magic seed which flowered while you watched it.

With the appearing of every gold-rimmed face the boy felt he had won another friend, a friend who would come and bend above him at night, keeping off the ugly visions which haunted his pillow—visions of the gnawing monsters about the church-porch, evil-faced bats and dragons, giant worms and winged bristling hogs, a devil's flock who crept down from the stone-work at night and hunted the souls of sinful children through the town. With the growth of the picture the bright mailed angels thronged so close about the boy's bed that between their interwoven wings not a snout or a claw could force itself; and he would turn over sighing on his pillow, which felt as soft and warm as if it had been lined with down from those sheltering pinions.

All these thoughts came back to him now in his cave on the cliff-side. The stillness seemed to enclose him with wings, to fold him away from life and evil. He was never restless or discontented. He loved the long silent empty days, each one as like the other as pearls in a well-matched string. Above all he liked to have time to save his soul. He had been greatly troubled about his soul since a band of Flagellants had passed through the town, exhibiting their gaunt scourged bodies and exhorting the people to turn from soft raiment and delicate fare, from marriage and money-getting and dancing and games, and think only how they might escape the devil's talons and the great red blaze of hell. For days that red blaze hung on the edge of the boy's thoughts like the light of a burning city across a plain.

There seemed to be so many pitfalls to avoid—so many things were wicked which one might have supposed to be harmless. How could a child of his age tell? He dared not for a moment think of anything else. And the scene of sack and slaughter from which he had fled gave shape and distinctness to that blood-red vision. Hell was like that, only a million million times worse. Now he knew how flesh looked when devils' pincers tore it, how the shrieks of the damned sounded, and how roasting bodies smelled. How could a Christian spare one moment of his days and nights from the long long struggle to keep safe from the wrath to come?

Gradually the horror faded, leaving only a tranquil pleasure in the minute performance of his religious duties. His mind was not naturally given to the contemplation of evil, and in the blessed solitude of his new life his thoughts dwelt more and more on the beauty of holiness. His desire was to be perfectly good, and to live in love and charity with his fellow-men; and how could one do this without fleeing from them?

At first his life was difficult, for in the winter season he was put to great straits to feed himself; and there were nights when the sky was like an iron vault, and a hoarse wind rattled the oakwood in the valley, and a great fear came on him that was worse than any cold. But in time it became known to his townsfolk and to the peasants in the neighbouring valleys that he had withdrawn to the wilderness to lead a godly life; and after that his worst hardships were over, for pious persons brought him gifts of oil and dried fruit, one good woman gave him seeds from her garden, another spun for him a hodden gown, and others would have brought him all manner of food and clothing, had he not refused to accept anything but for his bare needs.

The good woman who had given him the seeds showed him also how to build a little garden on the southern ledge of his cliff, and all one summer the Hermit carried up soil from the streamside, and the next he carried up water to keep his garden green. After that the fear of solitude quite passed from him, for he was so busy all day long that at night he had much ado to fight off the demon of sleep, which Saint Arsenius the Abbot has denounced as the chief foe of the solitary. His memory kept good store of prayers and litanies, besides long passages from the Mass and other offices, and he marked the hours of his day by different acts of devotion.

On Sundays and feast days, when the wind was set his way, he could hear the church bells from his native town, and these helped him to follow the worship of the faithful, and to bear in mind the seasons of the liturgical year; and what with carrying up water from the river, digging in the garden, gathering fagots for his fire, observing his religious duties, and keeping his thoughts continually upon the salvation of his soul, the Hermit knew not a moment's idleness.

At first, during his night vigils, he had felt a great fear of the stars, which seemed to set a cruel watch upon him, as though they spied out the frailty of his heart and took the measure of his littleness. But one day a wandering clerk, to whom he chanced to give a night's shelter, explained to him that, in the opinion of the most learned doctors of theology, the stars were inhabited by the spirits of the blessed, and this thought brought great consolation to the Hermit. Even on winter nights, when the eagle's wings clanged among the peaks, and he heard the long howl of wolves about the sheep-cotes in the valley, he no longer felt any fear, but thought of those sounds as representing the evil voices of the world, and hugged himself in the solitude of his cave. Sometimes, to keep himself awake, he composed lauds in honour of Christ and the saints, and they seemed to him so pleasant that he feared to forget them, so after much debate with himself he decided to ask a friendly priest from the valley, who sometimes visited him, to write down the lauds; and the priest wrote them down on comely sheepskin, which the Hermit dried and prepared with his own hands.

When the Hermit saw them written down they appeared to him so beautiful that he feared to commit the sin of vanity if he looked at them too often, so he hid them between two smooth stones in his cave, and vowed that he would take them out only once in the year, at Easter, when our Lord has risen and it is meet that Christians should rejoice. And this vow he faithfully kept; but, alas, when Easter drew near, he found he was looking forward to the blessed festival less because of our Lord's rising than because he should then be able to read his pleasant lauds written on fair sheepskin; and thereupon he took a vow that he would not look upon the lauds till he lay dying.

So the Hermit, for many years, lived to the glory of God and in great peace of mind.

2

One day he resolved to set forth on a visit to the Saint of the Rock, who lived on the other side of the mountains. Travellers had brought the Hermit report of this solitary, how he lived in great holiness and austerity in a desert place among the hills, where snow lay all winter, and in summer the sun beat down cruelly. The Saint, it appeared, had vowed that he would withdraw from the world to a spot where there was neither shade nor water, lest he should be tempted to take his ease and think less continually upon his Maker; but wherever he went he found a spreading tree or a gushing spring, till at last he climbed up to the bare heights where nothing grows, and where the only water comes from the melting of the snow in spring. Here he found a tall rock rising from the ground, and in it he scooped a hollow with his own hands, labouring for five years and wearing his fingers to the bone. Then he seated himself in the hollow, which faced the west, so that in winter he should have small warmth of the sun and in summer be consumed by it; and there he had sat without moving for years beyond number.

The Hermit was greatly drawn by the tale of such austerities, which in his humility he did not dream of emulating, but desired, for his soul's good, to contemplate and praise; so one day he bound sandals to his feet, cut an alder staff from the stream, and set out to visit the Saint of the Rock.

It was the pleasant spring season, when seeds are shooting and the bud is on the tree. The Hermit was troubled at the thought of leaving his plants without water, but he could not travel in winter by reason of the snows, and in summer he feared the garden would suffer even more from his absence. So he set out, praying that rain might fall while he was away, and hoping to return again in five days. The peasants labouring in the fields left their work to ask his blessing; and they would even have followed him in great numbers had he not told them that he was bound on a pilgrimage to the Saint of the Rock, and that it behoved him to go alone, as one solitary seeking another. So they respected his wish, and he went on and entered the forest. In the forest he walked for two days and slept for two nights.

He heard the wolves crying, and foxes rustling in the covert, and once, at twilight, a shaggy brown man peered at him through the leaves and galloped away with a soft padding of hoofs; but the Hermit feared neither wild beasts nor evil-doers, nor even the fauns and satyrs who linger in unhallowed forest depths where the Cross has not been raised; for he said: "If I die, I die to the glory of God, and if I live it must be to the same end." Only he felt a secret pang at the thought that he might die without seeing his lauds again. But the third day, without misadventure, he came out on another valley.

Then he began to climb the mountain, first through brown woods of beech and oak, then through pine and broom, and then across red stony ledges where only a pinched growth of lentisk and briar spread in patches over the rock. By this time, he thought to have reached his goal, but for two more days he fared on through the same scene, with the sky close over him and the green valleys of earth receding far below. Sometimes for hours he saw only the red glistering slopes tufted with thin bushes, and the hard blue heaven so close that it seemed his hand could touch it; then at a turn of the path the rocks rolled apart, the eye plunged down a long pine-clad defile, and beyond it the forest flowed in mighty undulations to a plain shining with cities and another mountain-range many days' journey away.

To some eyes this would have been a terrible spectacle, reminding the wayfarer of his remoteness from his kind, and of the perils which lurk in waste places and the weakness of man against them; but the Hermit was so mated to solitude, and felt such love for all things created, that to him the bare rocks sang of their Maker and the vast distance bore witness to His greatness. So His servant journeyed on unafraid.

But one morning, after a long climb over steep and difficult slopes, the wayfarer halted suddenly at a bend of the way; for beyond the defile at his feet there was no plain shining with cities, but a bare expanse of shaken silver that reached away to the rim of the world; and the Hermit knew it was the sea. Fear seized him then, for it was terrible to see that great plain move like a heaving bosom, and, as he looked on it, the earth seemed also to heave beneath him. But presently he remembered how Christ had walked the waves, and how even Saint Mary of Egypt, who was a great sinner, had crossed the waters of Jordan dry-shod to receive the Sacrament from the Abbot Zosimus; and then the Hermit's heart grew still, and he sang as he went down the mountain: "The sea shall praise Thee, O Lord."

All day he kept seeing it and then losing it; but toward night he came to a cleft of the hills, and lay down in a pine-wood to sleep. He had now been six days gone, and once and again he thought anxiously of his herbs; but he said to himself: "What though my garden perish, if I see a holy man face to face and praise God in his company?" So he was never long cast down.

Before daylight he was afoot under the stars; and leaving the wood where he had slept, began climbing the face of a tall cliff, where he had to clutch the jutting ledges with his hands, and with every step he gained, a rock seemed thrust forth to hurl him back. So, footsore and bleeding, he reached a little stony plain as the sun dropped to the sea; and in the red light he saw a hollow rock, and the Saint sitting in the hollow.

The Hermit fell on his knees, praising God; then he rose and ran across the plain to the rock. As he drew near he saw that the Saint was a very old man, clad in goatskin, with a long white beard. He sat motionless, his hands on his knees, and two red eye-sockets turned to the sunset. Near him was a young boy in skins who brushed the flies from his face; but they always came back, and settled on the rheum which ran from his eyes.

He did not appear to hear or see the approach of the Hermit, but sat quite still till the boy said: "Father, here is a pilgrim."

Then he lifted up his voice and asked angrily who was there and what the stranger sought.

The Hermit answered: "Father, the report of your holy practices came to me a long way off, and being myself a solitary, though not worthy to be named with you for godliness, it seemed fitting that I should cross the mountains to visit you, that we might sit together and speak in praise of solitude."

The Saint replied: "You fool, how can two sit together and praise solitude, since by so doing they put an end to the thing they pretend to honour?"

The Hermit, at that, was sorely abashed, for he had thought his speech out on the way, reciting it many times over; and now it appeared to him vainer than the crackling of thorns under a pot.

Nevertheless, he took heart and said: "True, Father; but may not two sinners sit together and praise Christ, who has taught them the blessings of solitude?"

But the other only answered: "If you had really learned the blessings of solitude you would not squander them in idle wandering." And, the Hermit not knowing how to reply, he said again: "If two sinners meet they can best praise Christ by going each his own way in silence."

After that he shut his lips and continued motionless while the boy brushed the flies from his eye-sockets; but the Hermit's heart sank, and for the first time he felt all the weariness of the way he had fared, and the great distance dividing him from home.

He had meant to take counsel with the Saint concerning his lauds, and whether he ought to destroy them; but now he had no heart to say another word, and turning away he began to descend the mountain. Presently he heard steps running behind him, and the boy came up and pressed a honey-comb in his hand.

"You have come a long way and must be hungry," he said; but before the Hermit could thank him he had hastened back to his task. So the Hermit crept down the mountain till he reached the wood where he had slept before; and there he made his bed again, but he had no mind to eat before sleeping, for his heart hungered more than his body; and his salt tears made the honey-comb bitter.

3

On the fourteenth day he came to the valley below his cliff, and saw the walls of his native town against the sky. He was footsore and heavy of heart, for his long pilgrimage had brought him only weariness and humiliation, and as no drop of rain had fallen he knew that his garden must have perished. So he climbed the cliff heavily and reached his cave at the angelus.

But there a great wonder awaited him. For though the scant earth of the hillside was parched and crumbling, his garden-soil reeked with moisture, and his plants had shot up, fresh and glistening, to a height they had never before attained. More wonderful still, the tendrils of the gourd had been trained about his door, and kneeling down he saw that the earth had been loosened between the rows of sprouting vegetables, and that every leaf sparkled with drops as though the rain had but newly ceased. Then it appeared to the Hermit that he beheld a miracle, but doubting his own deserts he refused to believe himself worthy of such grace, and went within doors to ponder on what had befallen him. And on his bed of rushes he saw a young woman sleeping, clad in an outlandish garment, with strange amulets about her neck.

The sight was very terrifying to the Hermit, for he recalled how often the demon, in tempting the Desert Fathers, had taken the form of a woman for their undoing; but he reflected that, since there was nothing pleasing to him in the sight of this female, who was brown as a nut and lean with wayfaring, he ran no great danger in looking at her. At first he took her for a wandering Egyptian, but as he looked he perceived, among the heathen charms, an Agnus Dei in her bosom; and this so surprised him that he bent over and called on her to wake.

She sprang up with a start, but seeing the Hermit's gown and staff, and his face above her, lay quiet and said to him: "I have watered your garden daily in return for the beans and oil that I took from your store."

"Who are you, and how do you come here?" asked the Hermit.

She said: "I am a wild woman and live in the woods."

And when he pressed her again to tell him why she had sought shelter in his cave, she said that the land to the south, whence she came, was full of armed companies and bands of marauders, and that great license and bloodshed prevailed there; and this the Hermit knew to be true, for he had heard of it on his homeward journey. The Wild Woman went on to tell him that she had been hunted through the woods like an animal by a band of drunken men-at-arms, Lanskne-chts from the north by their barbarous dress and speech, and at length, starving and spent, had come on his cave and hidden herself from her pursuers. "For," she said, "I fear neither wild beasts nor the woodland people, charcoal burners, Egyptians, wandering minstrels or chapmen; even the highway robbers do not touch me, because I am poor and brown; but these armed men flown with blood and wine are more terrible than wolves and tigers."

And the Hermit's heart melted, for he thought of his little sister lying with her throat slit across the altar steps, and of the scenes of blood and rapine from which he had fled away into the wilderness. So he said to the stranger that it was not meet he should house her in his cave, but that he would send a messenger to the town across the valley, and beg a pious woman there to give her lodging and work in her household. "For," said he, "I perceive by the blessed image about your neck that you are not a heathen wilding, but a child of Christ, though so far astray from Him in the desert."

"Yes," she said, "I am a Christian, and know as many prayers as you; but I will never set foot in city walls again, lest I be caught and put back into the convent."

"What," cried the Hermit with a start, "you are a runagate nun?" And he crossed himself, and again thought of the demon.

She smiled and said: "It is true I was once a cloistered woman, but I will never willingly be one again. Now drive me forth if you like; but I cannot go far, for I have a wounded foot, which I got in climbing the cliff with water for your garden." And she pointed to a deep cut in her foot.

At that, for all his fear, the Hermit was moved to pity, and washed the cut and bound it up; and as he did so he bethought him that perhaps his strange visitor had been sent to him not for his soul's undoing but for her own salvation. And from that hour he earnestly yearned to save her.

But it was not fitting that she should remain in his cave; so, having given her water to drink and a handful of lentils, he raised her up and putting his staff in her hand guided her to a hollow not far off in the face of the cliff. And while he was doing this he heard the sunset bells ring across the valley, and set about reciting the *Angelus Domini nuntiavit Mariae*; and she joined in very piously, with her hands folded, not missing a word.

Nevertheless, the thought of her wickedness weighed on him, and the next day when he went to carry her food he asked her to tell him how it came about that she had fallen into such abominable sin. And this is the story she told.

4

I was born (said she) in the north country, where the winters are long and cold, where snow sometimes falls in the valleys, and the high mountains for months are white with it. My father's castle is in a tall green wood, where the winds always rustle, and a cold river runs down from the ice-gorges. South of us was the wide plain, glowing with heat, but above us were stony passes where the eagle nests and the storms howl; in winter great fires roared in our chimneys, and even in summer there was always a cool air off the gorges. But when I was a child my mother went southward in the great empress's train and I went with her. We travelled many days, across plains and mountains, and saw Rome, where the Pope lives in a golden palace, and many other cities, till we came to the great emperor's court.

There for two years or more we lived in pomp and merriment, for it was a wonderful court, full of mimes, magicians, philosophers and poets; and the empress's ladies spent their days in mirth and music, dressed in light silken garments, walking in gardens of roses, and bathing in a great cool marble tank, while the emperor's eunuchs guarded the approach to the gardens. Oh, those baths in the marble tank, my Father! I used to lie awake through the whole hot southern night, and think of that plunge at sunrise under the last stars. For we were in a burning country, and I pined for the tall green woods and the cold stream of my father's valley; and when I had cooled my limbs in the tank I lay all day in the scant cypress shade and dreamed of my next bath.

My mother pined for the coolness till she died; then the empress put me in a convent and I was forgotten. The convent was on the side of a bare yellow hill, where bees made a hot buzzing in the thyme. Below was the sea, blazing with a million shafts of light; and overhead a blinding sky, which reflected the sun's glitter like a huge baldric of steel. Now the convent was built on the site of an old pleasure-house which a holy princess had given to our Order; and a part of the house was left standing with its court and garden. The nuns had built all about the garden; but they left the cypresses in the middle, and the long marble tank where the princess and her ladies had bathed.

The tank, however, as you may conceive, was no longer used as a bath; for the washing of the body is an indulgence forbidden to cloistered virgins; and our abbess, who was famed for her austerities, boasted that, like holy Sylvia the nun, she never touched water save to bathe her finger-tips before receiving the Sacrament. With such an example before them, the nuns were obliged to conform to the same pious rule, and many, having been bred in the convent from infancy, regarded all ablutions with horror, and felt no temptation to cleanse the filth from their flesh; but I, who had bathed daily, had the freshness of clear water in my veins, and perished slowly for want of it, like your garden herbs in a drought.

My cell did not look on the garden, but on the steep mule-path leading up the cliff, where all day long the sun beat as if with flails of fire, and I saw the sweating peasants toil up and down behind their thirsty asses, and the beggars whining and scraping their sores in the heat. Oh, how I hated to look out through the bars on that burning world! I used to turn away from it, sick with disgust, and lying on my hard bed, stare up by the hour at the ceiling of my cell. But flies crawled in hundreds on the ceiling, and the hot noise they made was worse than the glare.

Sometimes, at an hour when I knew myself unobserved, I tore off my stifling gown, and hung it over the grated window, that I might no longer see the shaft of hot sunlight lying across my cell, and the dust dancing in it like fat in the fire. But the darkness choked me, and I struggled for breath as though I lay at the bottom of a pit; so that at last I would spring up, and dragging down the dress, fling myself on my knees before the Cross, and entreat our Lord to give me the gift of holiness, that I might escape the everlasting fires of hell, of which this heat was like an awful foretaste. For if I could not endure the scorching of a summer's day, with what constancy could I meet the thought of the flame that dieth not?

This longing to escape the heat of hell made me apply myself to a devouter way of living, and I reflected that if my bodily distress were somewhat eased I should be able to throw myself with greater zeal into the practice of vigils and austerities. And at length, having set forth to the Abbess that the sultry air of my cell induced in me a grievous heaviness of sleep, I prevailed on her to lodge me in that part of the building which overlooked the garden.

For a few days I was quite happy, for instead of the dusty mountainside, and the sight of the sweating peasants and their asses, I looked out on dark cypresses and rows of budding vegetables. But presently I found I had not bettered myself. For with the approach of midsummer the garden, being all enclosed with buildings, grew as stifling as my cell. All the green things in it withered and dried off, leaving trenches of bare red earth, across which the cypresses cast strips of shade too narrow to cool the aching heads of the nuns who sought shelter there; and I began to think sorrowfully of my former cell, where now and then there came a sea-breeze, hot and languid, yet alive, and where at least I could look out upon the sea.

But this was not the worst; for when the dog-days came I found that the sun, at a certain hour, cast on the ceiling of my cell the reflection of the ripples on the garden-tank; and to say how I suffered from this sight is not within the power of speech. It was indeed agony to watch the clear water rippling and washing above my head, yet feel no solace of it on my limbs: as though I had been a senseless brazen image lying at the bottom of a well. But the image, if it felt no refreshment, would have suffered no torture; whereas every inch of my skin throbbed with thirst, and every vein was a mouth of Dives praying for a drop of water. Oh, Father, how shall I tell you the grievous pains that I endured? Sometimes I so feared the sight of the mocking ripples overhead that I hid my eyes from their approach, lying face down on my burning bed till I knew that they were gone; yet on cloudy days, when they did not come, the heat was even worse to bear.

By day I hardly dared trust myself in the garden, for the nuns walked there, and one fiery noon they found me hanging so close above the tank that they snatched me away, crying out that I had tried to destroy myself. The scandal of this reaching the abbess, she sent for me to know what demon had beset me; and when I wept and said, the longing to bathe my burning body, she broke into great anger and cried out: "Do you not know that this is a sin well-nigh as great as the other, and condemned by all the greatest saints? For a nun may be tempted to take her life through excess of self-scrutiny and despair of her own worthiness; but this desire to indulge the despicable body is one of the lusts of the flesh, to be classed with concupiscence and adultery." And she ordered me to sleep every night for a month in my heavy gown, with a veil upon my face.

Now, Father, I believe it was this penance that drove me to sin. For we were in the dog-days, and it was more than flesh could bear. And on the third night, after the portress had passed, and the lights were out, I rose and flung off my veil and gown, and knelt in my window fainting. There was no moon, but the sky was full of stars. At first the garden was all blackness; but as I looked I saw a faint twinkle between the cypress-trunks, and I knew it was the starlight on the tank. The water! The water! It was there close to me—only a few bolts and bars were between us.

The portress was a heavy sleeper, and I knew where her keys hung, on a nail just within the door of her cell. I stole thither, unlatched the door, seized the keys and crept barefoot down the corridor. The bolts of the cloister-door were stiff and heavy, and I dragged at them till the veins in my wrists were bursting. Then I turned the key and it cried out in the ward. I stood still, my whole body beating with fear lest the hinges too should have a voice—but no one stirred, and I pushed open the door and slipped out. The garden was as airless as a pit, but at least I could stretch my arms in it; and, oh, my Father, the sweetness of the stars! The stones in the path cut my feet as I ran, but I thought of the joy of bathing them in the tank, and that made the wounds sweet to me. . . . My Father, I have heard of the temptations which in times past assailed the holy Solitaries of the desert, flattering the reluctant flesh beyond resistance; but none, I think, could have surpassed in ecstasy that first touch of the water on my limbs.

To prolong the joy I let myself slip in slowly, resting my hands on the edge of the tank, and smiling to see my body, as I lowered it, break up the shining black surface and shatter the starbeams into splinters. And the water, my Father, seemed to crave me as I craved it. Its ripples rose about me, first in furtive touches, then in a long embrace that clung and drew me down; till at length they lay like kisses on my lips. It was no frank comrade like the mountain pools of my childhood, but a secret playmate compassionating my pains and soothing them with noiseless hands. From the first I thought of it as an accomplice—its whisper seemed to promise me secrecy if I would promise it love. And I went back and back to it, my Father; all day I lived in the thought of it; each night I stole to it with fresh thirst. . . . .

But at length the old portress died, and a young lay-sister took her place. She was a light sleeper, and keen-eared; and I knew the danger of venturing to her cell. I knew the danger, but when darkness came I felt the water drawing me. The first night I fought on my bed and held out; but the second I crept to her door. She made no motion when I entered, but rose up secretly and stole after me; and the second night she warned the abbess, and the two came on me as I stood by the tank.

I was punished with terrible penances: fasting, scourging, imprisonment, and the privation of drinking water; for the Abbess stood amazed at the obduracy of my sin, and was resolved to make me an example to my fellows. For a month I endured the pains of hell; then one night the Saracen pirates fell on our convent. On a sudden the darkness was full of flames and blood; but while the other nuns ran hither and thither, clinging to the abbess's feet or shrieking on the steps of the altar, I slipped through an unwatched postern and made my way to the hills. The next day the emperor's soldiery descended on the carousing heathen, slew them and burned their vessels on the beach; the abbess and nuns were rescued, the convent walls rebuilt, and peace restored to the holy precincts.

All this I heard from a shepherdess of the hills, who found me in my hiding, and brought me honeycomb and water. In her simplicity she offered to lead me home to the convent; but while she slept I laid off my wimple and scapular, and stealing her cloak fled away lest she should betray me. And since then I have wandered alone over the face of the world, living in woods and desert places, often hungry, often cold and sometimes fearful; yet resigned to any hardship, and with a front for any peril, if only I may sleep under the free heaven and wash the dust from my body in cool water.

5

The Hermit, as may be supposed, was much perturbed by this story, and dismayed that such sinfulness should cross his path. His first motion was to drive the woman forth, for he knew the heinousness of the craving for water, and how Saint Jerome, Saint Augustine and other holy doctors have taught that they who would purify the soul must not be distraught by the vain cares of bodily cleanliness; yet, remembering the lust that drew him to his lauds, he dared not judge his sister's fault too harshly.

Moreover, he was moved by the Wild Woman's story of the hardships she had suffered, and the godless company she had been driven to keep—Egyptians, jugglers, outlaws and even sorcerers, who are masters of the pagan lore of the East, and still practice their dark rites among the simple folk of the hills. Yet she would not have him think wholly ill of this vagrant people, from whom she had often received food and comfort; and her worst danger, as he learned with shame, had come from the *girovaghi* or wandering monks, who are the scourge and dishonour of Christendom; carrying their ribald idleness from one monastery to another, and leaving on their way a trail of thieving, revelry and worse.

Once or twice the Wild Woman had nearly fallen into their hands; but had been saved by her own quick wit and skill in woodcraft. Once, so she assured the Hermit, she had found refuge with a faun and his female, who fed and sheltered her in their cave, where she slept on a bed of leaves with their shaggy nurslings; and in this cave she had seen a stock or idol of wood, extremely seamed and ancient, before which the wood-creatures, when they thought she slept, laid garlands and the wild bees' honey-comb.

She told him also of a hill-village of weavers, where she lived many weeks, and learned to ply their trade in return for her lodging; and where wayfaring men in the guise of cobblers, charcoal-burners or goatherds came and taught strange doctrines at midnight in the poor hovels. What they taught she could not clearly tell, save that they believed each soul could commune directly with its Maker, without need of priest or intercessor; also she had heard from some of their disciples that there are two Gods, one of good and one of evil, and that the God of evil has his throne in the Pope's palace in Rome.

But in spite of these dark teachings they were a mild and merciful folk, full of loving-kindness toward poor persons and wayfarers; so that her heart grieved for them when one day a Dominican monk appeared in the village with a company of soldiers, and some of the weavers were seized and dragged to prison, while others, with their wives and babes, fled to the winter woods. She fled with them, fearing to be charged with their heresy, and for months they lay hid in desert places, the older and weaker, who fell sick from want and exposure, being devoutly ministered to by their brethren, and dying in the sure faith of heaven.

All this she related modestly and simply, not as one who joys in a godless life, but as having been drawn into it through misadventure; and she told the Hermit that when she heard the sound of church bells she never failed to say an *Ave* or a *Pater*, and that often, as she lay in the midnight darkness of the forest, she had hushed her fears by reciting the versicles from the Evening Hour:

Keep us, O Lord, as the apple of the eye,
Protect us under the shadow of Thy wings.

The wound in her foot healed slowly; and the Hermit, while it was mending, repaired daily to her cave, reasoning with her in love and charity, and exhorting her to return to the cloister. But this she persistently refused to do; and fearing lest she attempt to fly before her foot was healed, and so expose herself to hunger and ill-usage, he promised not to betray her presence, or to take any measures toward restoring her to her Order.

He began indeed to doubt whether she had any calling to the life enclosed; yet her gentleness and innocency of mind made him feel that she might be won back to holy living, if only her freedom were assured. So after many inward struggles (since his promise forbade his taking counsel with any concerning her) he resolved to let her remain in the cave till some light should come to him. And one day, visiting her about the hour of Nones (for it became his pious habit to say the evening office with her), he found her engaged with a little goatherd, who in a sudden seizure had fallen from a rock above her cave, and lay senseless and full of blood at her feet.

And the Hermit saw with wonder how skilfully she bound up his cuts and restored his senses, giving him to drink of a liquor she had distilled from the wild simples of the mountain; whereat the boy opened his eyes and praised God, as one restored by heaven. Now it was known that this lad was subject to possessions, and had more than once dropped lifeless while he heeded his flock; and the Hermit, knowing that only great saints or unclean necromancers can loosen devils, feared that the Wild Woman had exorcised the spirits by means of unholy spells. But she told him that the goatherd's sickness was caused only by the heat of the sun, and that, such seizures being common in the hot countries whence she came, she had learned from a wise woman how to stay them by a decoction of the *carduus benedictus*, made in the third night of the waxing moon, but without the aid of magic.

"But," she continued, "you need not fear my bringing scandal on your holy retreat, for by the arts of the same wise woman my own wound is well-nigh healed, and tonight at sunset I set forth on my travels."

The Hermit's heart grew heavy as she spoke, and it seemed to him that her own look was sorrowful. And suddenly his perplexities were lifted from him, and he saw what was God's purpose with the Wild Woman.

"Why," said he, "do you fly from this place, where you are safe from molestation, and can look to the saving of your soul? Is it that your feet weary for the road, and your spirits are heavy for lack of worldly discourse?"

She replied that she had no wish to travel, and felt no repugnance to solitude. "But," said she, "I must go forth to beg my bread, since in this wilderness there is none but yourself to feed me; and moreover, when it is known that I have healed the goatherd, curious folk and scandal-mongers may seek me out, and, learning whence I come, drag me back to the cloister."

Then the Hermit answered her and said: "In the early days, when the faith of Christ was first preached, there were holy women who fled to the desert and lived there in solitude, to the glory of God and the edification of their sex. If you are minded to embrace so austere a life, contenting you with such sustenance as the wilderness yields, and wearing out your days in prayer and vigil, it may be that you shall make amends for the great sin you have committed, and live and die in the peace of the Lord Jesus."

He spoke thus, knowing that if she left him and returned to her roaming, hunger and fear might drive her to fresh sin; whereas in a life of penance and reclusion her eyes might be opened to her iniquity, and her soul snatched back from ruin.

He saw that his words moved her, and she seemed about to consent, and embrace a life of holiness; but suddenly she fell silent, and looked down on the valley at their feet.

"A stream flows in the glen below us," she said. "Do you forbid me to bathe in it in the heat of summer?"

"It is not I that forbid you, my daughter, but the laws of God," said the Hermit; "yet see how miraculously heaven protects you—for in the hot season, when your lust is upon you, our stream runs dry, and temptation will be removed from you. Moreover, on these heights there is no excess of heat to madden the body, but always, before dawn and at the angelus, a cool breeze which refreshes it like water."

And after thinking long on this, and again receiving his promise not to betray her, the Wild Woman agreed to embrace a life of reclusion; and the Hermit fell on his knees, worshipping God and rejoicing to think that, if he saved his sister from sin, his own term of probation would be shortened.

6

Thereafter for two years the Hermit and the Wild Woman lived side by side, meeting together to pray on the great feast-days of the year, but on all other days dwelling apart, engaged in pious practices.

At first the Hermit, knowing the weakness of woman, and her little aptitude for the life apart, had feared that he might be disturbed by the nearness of his penitent; but she faithfully held to his commands, abstaining from all sight of him save on the Days of Obligation; and when they met, so modest and devout was her demeanour that she raised his soul to fresh fervency. And gradually it grew sweet to him to think that, nearby though unseen, was one who performed the same tasks at the same hours; so that, whether he tended his garden, or recited his chaplet, or rose under the stars to repeat the midnight office, he had a companion in all his labours and devotions.

Meanwhile the report had spread abroad that a holy woman who cast out devils had made her dwelling in the Hermit's cliff; and many sick persons from the valley sought her out, and went away restored by her. These poor pilgrims brought her oil and flour, and with her own hands she made a garden like the Hermit's, and planted it with corn and lentils; but she would never take a trout from the brook, or receive the gift of a snared wild-fowl, for she said that in her vagrant life the wild creatures of the wood had befriended her, and as she had slept in peace among them, so now she would never suffer them to be molested.

In the third year came a plague, and death walked the cities, and many poor peasants fled to the hills to escape it. These the Hermit and his penitent faithfully tended, and so skilful were the Wild Woman's ministrations that the report of them reached the town across the valley, and a deputation of burgesses came with rich offerings, and besought her to descend and comfort their sick. The Hermit, seeing her depart on so dangerous a mission, would have accompanied her, but she bade him remain and tend those who fled to the hills; and for many days his heart was consumed in prayer for her, and he feared lest every fugitive should bring him word of her death.

But at length she returned, wearied-out but whole, and covered with the blessings of the townsfolk; and thereafter her name for holiness spread as wide as the Hermit's.

Seeing how constant she remained in her chosen life, and what advance she had made in the way of perfection, the Hermit now felt that it behoved him to exhort her again to return to the convent; and more than once he resolved to speak with her, but his heart hung back. At length he bethought him that by failing in this duty he imperilled his own soul, and thereupon, on the next feast-day, when they met, he reminded her that in spite of her good works she still lived in sin and excommunicate, and that, now she had once more tasted the sweets of godliness, it was her duty to confess her fault and give herself up to her superiors.

She heard him meekly, but when he had spoken she was silent and her tears ran over; and looking at her he wept also, and said no more. And they prayed together, and returned each to his cave.

It was not till late winter that the plague abated; and the spring and early summer following were heavy with rains and great heat. When the Hermit visited his penitent at the feast of Pentecost, she appeared to him so weak and wasted that, when they had recited the *Veni, sancte spiritus*, and the proper psalms, he taxed her with too great rigour of penitential practices; but she replied that her weakness was not due to an excess of discipline, but that she had brought back from her labours among the sick a heaviness of body which the intemperance of the season no doubt increased. The evil rains continued, falling chiefly at night, while by day the land reeked with heat and vapours; so that lassitude fell on the Hermit also, and he could hardly drag himself down to the spring whence he drew his drinking-water.

Thus he fell into the habit of going down to the glen before cockcrow, after he had recited *Matins*; for at that hour the rain commonly ceased, and a faint air was stirring. Now because of the wet season the stream had not gone dry, and instead of replenishing his flagon slowly at the trickling spring, the Hermit went down to the waterside to fill it; and once, as he descended the steep slope of the glen, he heard the covert rustle, and saw the leaves stir as though something moved behind them. As he looked silence fell, and the leaves grew still; but his heart was shaken, for it seemed to him that what he had seen in the dusk had a human semblance, such as the wood-people wear. And he was loth to think that such unhallowed beings haunted the glen.

A few days passed, and again, descending to the stream, he saw a figure flit by him through the covert; and this time a deeper fear entered into him; but he put away the thought, and prayed fervently for all souls in temptation. And when he spoke with the Wild Woman again, on the feast of the Seven Maccabees, which falls on the first day of August, he was smitten with fear to see her wasted looks, and besought her to cease from labouring and let him minister to her in her weakness. But she denied him gently, and replied that all she asked of him was to keep her steadfastly in his prayers.

Before the feast of the Assumption the rains ceased, and the plague, which had begun to show itself, was stayed; but the ardency of the sun grew greater, and the Hermit's cliff was a fiery furnace. Never had such heat been known in those regions; but the people did not murmur, for with the cessation of the rain their crops were saved and the pestilence banished; and these mercies they ascribed in great part to the prayers and macerations of the two holy anchorets. Therefore on the eve of the Assumption they sent a messenger to the Hermit, saying that at daylight on the morrow the townspeople and all the dwellers in the valley would come forth, led by their bishop, who bore the Pope's blessing to the two solitaries, and who was mindful to celebrate the Mass of the Assumption in the Hermit's cave in the cliffside. At the blessed word the Hermit was well-nigh distraught with joy, for he felt this to be a sign from heaven that his prayers were heard, and that he had won the Wild Woman's grace as well as his own. And all night he prayed that on the morrow she might confess her fault and receive the Sacrament with him.

Before dawn he recited the psalms of the proper nocturn; then he girded on his gown and sandals, and went forth to meet the bishop in the valley.

As he went downward daylight stood on the mountains, and he thought he had never seen so fair a dawn. It filled the farthest heaven with brightness, and penetrated even to the woody crevices of the glen, as the grace of God had entered into the obscurest folds of his heart. The morning airs were hushed, and he heard only the sound of his own footfall, and the murmur of the stream which, though diminished, still poured a swift current between the rocks; but as he reached the bottom of the glen a sound of chanting came to him, and he knew that the pilgrims were at hand. His heart leapt up and his feet hastened forward; but at the streamside they were suddenly stayed, for in a pool where the water was still deep he saw the shining of a woman's body—and on a stone hard by lay the Wild Woman's gown and sandals.

Fear and rage possessed the Hermit's heart, and he stood as one smitten speechless, covering his eyes from the shame. But the song of the approaching pilgrims swelled ever louder and nearer, and finding voice he cried to the Wild Woman to come forth and hide herself from the people.

She made no answer, but in the dusk he saw her limbs sway with the swaying of the water, and her eyes were turned to him as if in mockery. At the sight blind fury filled him, and clambering over the rocks to the pool's edge he bent down and caught her by the shoulder. At that moment he could have strangled her with his hands, so abhorrent to him was the touch of her flesh; but as he cried out on her, heaping her with cruel names, he saw that her eyes returned his look without wavering; and suddenly it came to him that she was dead.

Then through all his anger and fear a great pang smote him; for here was his work undone, and one he had loved in Christ laid low in her sin, in spite of all his labours.

One moment pity possessed him; the next he bethought him how the people would find him bending above the body of a naked woman, whom he had held up to them as holy, but whom they might now well take for the secret instrument of his undoing; and beholding how at her touch all the slow edifice of his holiness was demolished, and his soul in mortal jeopardy, he felt the earth reel round him and his sight grew red.

Already the head of the procession had entered the glen, and the stillness shook with the great sound of the *Salve Regina.* When the Hermit opened his eyes once more the air was quivering with thronged candle-flames, which glittered on the gold thread of priestly vestments, and on the blazing monstrance beneath its canopy; and close above him was bent the bishop's face.

The Hermit struggled to his knees.

"My Father in God," he cried, "behold, for my sins I have been visited by a demon—" But as he spoke he perceived that those about him no longer heeded him, and that the bishop and all his clergy had fallen on their knees about the pool. Then the Hermit, following their gaze, saw that the brown waters of the pool covered the Wild Woman's limbs as with a garment, and that about her floating head a great light floated; and to the utmost edges of the throng a cry of praise went up, for many were there whom the Wild Woman had healed and comforted, and who read God's mercy in this wonder. But fresh fear fell on the Hermit, for he had cursed a dying saint, and denounced her aloud to all the people; and this new anguish, coming so close upon the other, smote down his weakened frame, so that his limbs failed him and he sank once more to the ground.

Again the earth reeled about him, and the bending faces grew remote; but as he forced his weak voice once more to proclaim his sins he felt the blessed touch of absolution, and the holy oils of the last voyage laid on his lips and eyes. Peace returned to him then, and with it a great longing to look once more upon his lauds, as he had dreamed of doing at his last hour; but he was too far gone to make this longing known, and so tried to banish it from his mind. Yet in his weakness the wish held him, and the tears ran down his face.

Then, as he lay there, feeling the earth slip from under him, and the Everlasting Arms replace it, he heard a great peal of voices that seemed to come down from the sky and mingle with the singing of the throng; and the words of the chant were the words of his own lauds, so long hidden in the secret of his breast, and now rejoicing above him through the spheres. And his soul rose on the chant, and soared with it to the seat of mercy.

The Lady's Maid's Bell

1

It was the autumn after I had the typhoid. I'd been three months in hospital, and when I came out I looked so weak and tottery that the two or three ladies I applied to were afraid to engage me. Most of my money was gone, and after I'd boarded for two months, hanging about the employment-agencies, and answering any advertisement that looked any way respectable, I pretty nearly lost heart, for fretting hadn't made me fatter, and I didn't see why my luck should ever turn. It did though—or I thought so at the time. A Mrs. Railton, a friend of the lady that first brought me out to the States, met me one day and stopped to speak to me: she was one that had always a friendly way with her. She asked me what ailed me to look so white, and when I told her, "Why, Hartley," says she, "I believe I've got the very place for you. Come in tomorrow and we'll talk about it."

The next day, when I called, she told me the lady she'd in mind was a niece of hers, a Mrs. Brympton, a youngish lady, but something of an invalid, who lived all the year round at her country-place on the Hudson, owing to not being able to stand the fatigue of town life.

"Now, Hartley," Mrs. Railton said, in that cheery way that always made me feel things must be going to take a turn for the better—"now understand me; it's not a cheerful place I'm sending you to. The house is big and gloomy; my niece is nervous, vaporish; her husband—well, he's generally away; and the two children are dead. A year ago, I would as soon have thought of shutting a rosy active girl like you into a vault; but you're not particularly brisk yourself just now, are you? and a quiet place, with country air and wholesome food and early hours, ought to be the very thing for you. Don't mistake me," she added, for I suppose I looked a trifle downcast; "you may find it dull, but you won't be unhappy. My niece is an angel.

"Her former maid, who died last spring, had been with her twenty years and worshipped the ground she walked on. She's a kind mistress to all, and where the mistress is kind, as you know, the servants are generally good-humoured, so you'll probably get on well enough with the rest of the household. And you're the very woman I want for my niece: quiet, well-mannered, and educated above your station. You read aloud well, I think? That's a good thing; my niece likes to be read to. She wants a maid that can be something of a companion: her last was, and I can't say how she misses her. It's a lonely life... Well, have you decided?"

"Why, ma'am," I said, "I'm not afraid of solitude."

"Well, then, go; my niece will take you on my recommendation. I'll telegraph her at once and you can take the afternoon train. She has no one to wait on her at present, and I don't want you to lose any time."

I was ready enough to start, yet something in me hung back; and to gain time I asked, "And the gentleman, ma'am?"

"The gentleman's almost always away, I tell you," said Mrs. Ralston, quick-like—"and when he's there," says she suddenly, "you've only to keep out of his way."

I took the afternoon train and got out at D—— station at about four o'clock. A groom in a dog-cart was waiting, and we drove off at a smart pace. It was a dull October day, with rain hanging close overhead, and by the time we turned into the Brympton Place woods the daylight was almost gone. The drive wound through the woods for a mile or two, and came out on a gravel court shut in with thickets of tall black-looking shrubs. There were no lights in the windows, and the house *did* look a bit gloomy.

I had asked no questions of the groom, for I never was one to get my notion of new masters from their other servants: I prefer to wait and see for myself. But I could tell by the look of everything that I had got into the right kind of house, and that things were done handsomely. A pleasant-faced cook met me at the back door and called the housemaid to show me up to my room. "You'll see madam later," she said. "Mrs. Brympton has a visitor."

I hadn't fancied Mrs. Brympton was a lady to have many visitors, and somehow the words cheered me. I followed the housemaid upstairs, and saw, through a door on the upper landing, that the main part of the house seemed well-furnished, with dark panelling and a number of old portraits. Another flight of stairs led us up to the servants' wing. It was almost dark now, and the housemaid excused herself for not having brought a light. "But there's matches in your room," she said, "and if you go careful you'll be all right. Mind the step at the end of the passage. Your room is just beyond."

I looked ahead as she spoke, and halfway down the passage, I saw a woman standing. She drew back into a doorway as we passed, and the housemaid didn't appear to notice her. She was a thin woman with a white face, and a darkish stuff gown and apron. I took her for the housekeeper and thought it odd that she didn't speak, but just gave me a long look as she went by. My room opened into a square hall at the end of the passage. Facing my door was another which stood open: the housemaid exclaimed when she saw it.

"There—Mrs. Blinder's left that door open again!" said she, closing it.

"Is Mrs. Blinder the housekeeper?"

"There's no housekeeper: Mrs. Blinder's the cook."

"And is that her room?"

"Laws, no," said the housemaid, cross-like. "That's nobody's room. It's empty, I mean, and the door hadn't ought to be open. Mrs. Brympton wants it kept locked."

She opened my door and led me into a neat room, nicely furnished, with a picture or two on the walls; and having lit a candle she took leave, telling me that the servants'-hall tea was at six, and that Mrs. Brympton would see me afterward.

I found them a pleasant-spoken set in the servants' hall, and by what they let fall I gathered that, as Mrs. Railton had said, Mrs. Brympton was the kindest of ladies; but I didn't take much notice of their talk, for I was watching to see the pale woman in the dark gown come in. She didn't show herself, however, and I wondered if she ate apart; but if she wasn't the housekeeper, why should she? Suddenly it struck me that she might be a trained nurse, and in that case her meals would of course be served in her room. If Mrs. Brympton was an invalid it was likely enough she had a nurse. The idea annoyed me, I own, for they're not always the easiest to get on with, and if I'd known, I shouldn't have taken the place. But there I was, and there was no use pulling a long face over it; and not being one to ask questions, I waited to see what would turn up.

When tea was over, the housemaid said to the footman: "Has Mr. Ranford gone?" and when he said yes, she told me to come up with her to Mrs. Brympton.

Mrs. Brympton was lying down in her bedroom. Her lounge stood near the fire and beside it was a shaded lamp. She was a delicate-looking lady, but when she smiled I felt there was nothing I wouldn't do for her. She spoke very pleasantly, in a low voice, asking me my name and age and so on, and if I had everything I wanted, and if I wasn't afraid of feeling lonely in the country.

"Not with you I wouldn't be, madam," I said, and the words surprised me when I'd spoken them, for I'm not an impulsive person; but it was just as if I'd thought aloud.

She seemed pleased at that, and said she hoped I'd continue in the same mind; then she gave me a few directions about her toilet, and said Agnes the housemaid would show me next morning where things were kept.

"I am tired tonight, and shall dine upstairs," she said. "Agnes will bring me my tray, that you may have time to unpack and settle yourself; and later you may come and undress me."

"Very well, ma'am," I said. "You'll ring, I suppose?"

I thought she looked odd.

"No—Agnes will fetch you," says she quickly, and took up her book again.

Well—that was certainly strange: a lady's maid having to be fetched by the housemaid whenever her lady wanted her! I wondered if there were no bells in the house; but the next day I satisfied myself that there was one in every room, and a special one ringing from my mistress's room to mine; and after that it did strike me as queer that, whenever Mrs. Brympton wanted anything, she rang for Agnes, who had to walk the whole length of the servants' wing to call me.

But that wasn't the only queer thing in the house. The very next day I found out that Mrs. Brympton had no nurse; and then I asked Agnes about the woman I had seen in the passage the afternoon before. Agnes said she had seen no one, and I saw that she thought I was dreaming. To be sure, it was dusk when we went down the passage, and she had excused herself for not bringing a light; but I had seen the woman plain enough to know her again if we should meet. I decided that she must have been a friend of the cook's, or of one of the other women-servants: perhaps she had come down from town for a night's visit, and the servants wanted it kept secret. Some ladies are very stiff about having their servants' friends in the house overnight. At any rate, I made up my mind to ask no more questions.

In a day or two, another odd thing happened. I was chatting one afternoon with Mrs. Blinder, who was a friendly disposed woman, and had been longer in the house than the other servants, and she asked me if I was quite comfortable and had everything I needed. I said I had no fault to find with my place or with my mistress, but I thought it odd that in so large a house there was no sewing-room for the lady's maid.

"Why," says she, "there *is* one; the room you're in is the old sewing-room."

"Oh," said I; "and where did the other lady's maid sleep?"

At that she grew confused, and said hurriedly that the servants' rooms had all been changed about last year, and she didn't rightly remember.

That struck me as peculiar, but I went on as if I hadn't noticed: "Well, there's a vacant room opposite mine, and I mean to ask Mrs. Brympton if I mayn't use that as a sewing-room."

To my astonishment, Mrs. Blinder went white, and gave my hand a kind of squeeze. "Don't do that, my dear," said she, trembling-like. "To tell you the truth, that was Emma Saxon's room, and my mistress has kept it closed ever since her death."

"And who was Emma Saxon?"

"Mrs. Brympton's former maid."

"The one that was with her so many years?" said I, remembering what Mrs. Railton had told me.

Mrs. Blinder nodded.

"What sort of woman was she?"

"No better walked the earth," said Mrs. Blinder. "My mistress loved her like a sister."

"But I mean—what did she look like?"

Mrs. Blinder got up and gave me a kind of angry stare. "I'm no great hand at describing," she said; "and I believe my pastry's rising." And she walked off into the kitchen and shut the door after her.

2

I had been near a week at Brympton before I saw my master. Word came that he was arriving one afternoon, and a change passed over the whole household. It was plain that nobody loved him below stairs. Mrs. Blinder took uncommon care with the dinner that night, but she snapped at the kitchen-maid in a way quite unusual with her; and Mr. Wace, the butler, a serious, slow-spoken man, went about his duties as if he'd been getting ready for a funeral. He was a great Bible-reader,

Mr. Wace was, and had a beautiful assortment of texts at his command; but that day he used such dreadful language that I was about to leave the table, when he assured me it was all out of Isaiah; and I noticed that whenever the master came Mr. Wace took to the prophets.

About seven, Agnes called me to my mistress's room; and there I found Mr. Brympton. He was standing on the hearth; a big fair bull-necked man, with a red face and little bad-tempered blue eyes: the kind of man a young simpleton might have thought handsome, and would have been like to pay dear for thinking it.

He swung about when I came in, and looked me over in a trice. I knew what the look meant, from having experienced it once or twice in my former places. Then he turned his back on me, and went on talking to his wife; and I knew what *that* meant, too. I was not the kind of morsel he was after. The typhoid had served me well enough in one way: it kept that kind of gentleman at arm's-length.

"This is my new maid, Hartley," says Mrs. Brympton in her kind voice; and he nodded and went on with what he was saying.

In a minute or two he went off, and left my mistress to dress for dinner, and I noticed as I waited on her that she was white, and chill to the touch.

Mr. Brympton took himself off the next morning, and the whole house drew a long breath when he drove away. As for my mistress, she put on her hat and furs (for it was a fine winter morning) and went out for a walk in the gardens, coming back quite fresh and rosy, so that for a minute, before her colour faded, I could guess what a pretty young lady she must have been, and not so long ago, either.

She had met Mr. Ranford in the grounds, and the two came back together, I remember, smiling and talking as they walked along the terrace under my window. That was the first time I saw Mr. Ranford, though I had often heard his name mentioned in the hall. He was a neighbour, it appeared, living a mile or two beyond Brympton, at the end of the village; and as he was in the habit of spending his winters in the country he was almost the only company my mistress had at that season. He was a slight tall gentleman of about thirty, and I thought him rather melancholy-looking till I saw his smile, which had a kind of surprise in it, like the first warm day in spring.

He was a great reader, I heard, like my mistress, and the two were forever borrowing books of one another, and sometimes (Mr. Wace told me) he would read aloud to Mrs. Brympton by the hour, in the big dark library where she sat in the winter afternoons. The servants all liked him, and perhaps that's more of a compliment than the masters suspect. He had a friendly word for every one of us, and we were all glad to think that Mrs. Brympton had a pleasant companionable gentleman like that to keep her company when the master was away. Mr. Ranford seemed on excellent terms with Mr. Brympton too; though I couldn't but wonder that two gentlemen so unlike each other should be so friendly. But then I knew how the real quality can keep their feelings to themselves.

As for Mr. Brympton, he came and went, never staying more than a day or two, cursing the dullness and the solitude, grumbling at everything, and (as I soon found out) drinking a deal more than was good for him. After Mrs. Brympton left the table he would sit half the night over the old Brympton port and madeira, and once, as I was leaving my mistress's room rather later than usual, I met him coming up the stairs in such a state that I turned sick to think of what some ladies have to endure and hold their tongues about.

The servants said very little about their master; but from what they let drop I could see it had been an unhappy match from the beginning. Mr. Brympton was coarse, loud and pleasure-loving; my mistress quiet, retiring, and perhaps a trifle cold. Not that she was not always pleasant-spoken to him: I thought her wonderfully forbearing; but to a gentleman as free as Mr. Brympton I daresay she seemed a little offish.

Well, things went on quietly for several weeks. My mistress was kind, my duties were light, and I got on well with the other servants. In short, I had nothing to complain of; yet there was always a weight on me. I can't say why it was so, but I know it was not the loneliness that I felt. I soon got used to that; and being still languid from the fever, I was thankful for the quiet and the good country air. Nevertheless, I was never quite easy in my mind. My mistress, knowing I had been ill, insisted that I should take my walk regular, and often invented errands for me:—a yard of ribbon to be fetched from the village, a letter posted, or a book returned to Mr. Ranford. As soon as I was out of doors my spirits rose, and I looked forward to my walks through the bare moist-smelling woods; but the moment I caught sight of the house again my heart dropped down like a stone in a well. It was not a gloomy house exactly, yet I never entered it but a feeling of gloom came over me.

Mrs. Brympton seldom went out in winter; only on the finest days did she walk an hour at noon on the south terrace. Excepting

Mr. Ranford, we had no visitors but the doctor, who drove over from D—— about once a week. He sent for me once or twice to give me some trifling direction about my mistress, and though he never told me what her illness was, I thought, from a waxy look she had now and then of a morning, that it might be the heart that ailed her. The season was soft and unwholesome, and in January we had a long spell of rain. That was a sore trial to me, I own, for I couldn't go out, and sitting over my sewing all day, listening to the drip, drip of the eaves, I grew so nervous that the least sound made me jump. Somehow, the thought of that locked room across the passage began to weigh on me.

Once or twice, in the long rainy nights, I fancied I heard noises there; but that was nonsense, of course, and the daylight drove such notions out of my head. Well, one morning Mrs. Brympton gave me quite a start of pleasure by telling me she wished me to go to town for some shopping. I hadn't known till then how low my spirits had fallen. I set off in high glee, and my first sight of the crowded streets and the cheerful-looking shops quite took me out of myself. Toward afternoon, however, the noise and confusion began to tire me, and I was actually looking forward to the quiet of Brympton, and thinking how I should enjoy the drive home through the dark woods, when I ran across an old acquaintance, a maid I had once been in service with. We had lost sight of each other for a number of years, and I had to stop and tell her what had happened to me in the interval. When I mentioned where I was living she rolled up her eyes and pulled a long face.

"What! The Mrs. Brympton that lives all the year at her place on the Hudson? My dear, you won't stay there three months."

"Oh, but I don't mind the country," says I, offended somehow at her tone. "Since the fever I'm glad to be quiet."

She shook her head. "It's not the country I'm thinking of. All I know is she's had four maids in the last six months, and the last one, who was a friend of mine, told me nobody could stay in the house."

"Did she say why?" I asked.

"No—she wouldn't give me her reason. But she says to me, '*Mrs. Ansey'*, she says, *'if ever a young woman as you know of thinks of going there, you tell her it's not worthwhile to unpack her boxes.'*"

"Is she young and handsome?" said I, thinking of Mr. Brympton.

"Not her! She's the kind that mothers engage when they've gay young gentlemen at college."

Well, though I knew the woman was an idle gossip, the words

stuck in my head, and my heart sank lower than ever as I drove up to Brympton in the dusk. There *was* something about the house—I was sure of it now. . . .

When I went in to tea I heard that Mr. Brympton had arrived, and I saw at a glance that there had been a disturbance of some kind. Mrs. Blinder's hand shook so that she could hardly pour the tea, and Mr. Wace quoted the most dreadful texts full of brimstone. Nobody said a word to me then, but when I went up to my room Mrs. Blinder followed me.

"Oh, my dear," says she, taking my hand, "I'm so glad and thankful you've come back to us!"

That struck me, as you may imagine. "Why," said I, "did you think I was leaving for good?"

"No, no, to be sure," said she, a little confused, "but I can't a-bear to have madam left alone for a day even." She pressed my hand hard, and, "Oh, Miss Hartley," says she, "be good to your mistress, as you're a Christian woman." And with that she hurried away, and left me staring.

A moment later Agnes called me to Mrs. Brympton. Hearing Mr. Brympton's voice in her room, I went round by the dressing-room, thinking I would lay out her dinner-gown before going in. The dressing-room is a large room with a window over the portico that looks toward the gardens. Mr. Brympton's apartments are beyond. When I went in, the door into the bedroom was ajar, and I heard Mr. Brympton saying angrily:—"One would suppose he was the only person fit for you to talk to."

"I don't have many visitors in winter," Mrs. Brympton answered quietly.

"You have *me!*" he flung at her, sneering.

"You are here so seldom," said she.

"Well—whose fault is that? You make the place about as lively as a family vault—"

With that I rattled the toilet-things, to give my mistress warning and she rose and called me in.

The two dined alone, as usual, and I knew by Mr. Wace's manner at supper that things must be going badly. He quoted the prophets something terrible, and worked on the kitchen-maid so that she declared she wouldn't go down alone to put the cold meat in the ice-box. I felt nervous myself, and after I had put my mistress to bed I was half-tempted to go down again and persuade Mrs. Blinder to sit up awhile over a game of cards. But I heard her door closing for the night, and so I went on to my own room. The rain had begun again, and the drip, drip, drip seemed to be dropping into my brain. I lay awake listening to it, and turning over what my friend in town had said. What puzzled me was that it was always the maids who left. . . .

After a while I slept; but suddenly a loud noise wakened me. My bell had rung. I sat up, terrified by the unusual sound, which seemed to go on jangling through the darkness. My hands shook so that I couldn't find the matches. At length I struck a light and jumped out of bed. I began to think I must have been dreaming; but I looked at the bell against the wall, and there was the little hammer still quivering.

I was just beginning to huddle on my clothes when I heard another sound. This time it was the door of the locked room opposite mine softly opening and closing. I heard the sound distinctly, and it frightened me so that I stood stock still. Then I heard a footstep hurrying down the passage toward the main house. The floor being carpeted, the sound was very faint, but I was quite sure it was a woman's step. I turned cold with the thought of it, and for a minute or two I dursn't breathe or move. Then I came to my senses.

"Alice Hartley," says I to myself, "someone left that room just now and ran down the passage ahead of you. The idea isn't pleasant, but you may as well face it. Your mistress has rung for you, and to answer her bell you've got to go the way that other woman has gone."

Well—I did it. I never walked faster in my life, yet I thought I should never get to the end of the passage or reach Mrs. Brympton's room. On the way I heard nothing and saw nothing: all was dark and quiet as the grave. When I reached my mistress's door the silence was so deep that I began to think I must be dreaming, and was half-minded to turn back. Then a panic seized me, and I knocked.

There was no answer, and I knocked again, loudly. To my astonishment the door was opened by Mr. Brympton. He started back when he saw me, and in the light of my candle his face looked red and savage.

"You!" he said, in a queer voice. *"How many of you are there, in God's name?"*

At that I felt the ground give under me; but I said to myself that he had been drinking, and answered as steadily as I could: "May I go in, sir? Mrs. Brympton has rung for me."

"You may all go in, for what I care," says he, and, pushing by me, walked down the hall to his own bedroom. I looked after him as he went, and to my surprise I saw that he walked as straight as a sober man.

I found my mistress lying very weak and still, but she forced a smile when she saw me, and signed to me to pour out some drops for her. After that she lay without speaking, her breath coming quick, and her eyes closed. Suddenly she groped out with her hand, and "*Emma*," says she, faintly.

"It's Hartley, madam," I said. "Do you want anything?"

She opened her eyes wide and gave me a startled look.

"I was dreaming," she said. "You may go, now, Hartley, and thank you kindly. I'm quite well again, you see." And she turned her face away from me.

3

There was no more sleep for me that night, and I was thankful when daylight came.

Soon afterward, Agnes called me to Mrs. Brympton. I was afraid she was ill again, for she seldom sent for me before nine, but I found her sitting up in bed, pale and drawn-looking, but quite herself.

"Hartley," says she quickly, "will you put on your things at once and go down to the village for me? I want this prescription made up—" here she hesitated a minute and blushed—"and I should like you to be back again before Mr. Brympton is up."

"Certainly, madam," I said.

"And—stay a moment—" she called me back as if an idea had just struck her—"while you're waiting for the mixture, you'll have time to go on to Mr. Ranford's with this note."

It was a two-mile walk to the village, and on my way I had time to turn things over in my mind. It struck me as peculiar that my mistress should wish the prescription made up without Mr. Brympton's knowledge; and, putting this together with the scene of the night before, and with much else that I had noticed and suspected, I began to wonder if the poor lady was weary of her life, and had come to the mad resolve of ending it. The idea took such hold on me that I reached the village on a run, and dropped breathless into a chair before the chemist's counter. The good man, who was just taking down his shutters, stared at me so hard that it brought me to myself.

"Mr. Limmel," I says, trying to speak indifferent, "will you run your eye over this, and tell me if it's quite right?"

He put on his spectacles and studied the prescription.

"Why, it's one of Dr. Walton's," says he. "What should be wrong with it?"

"Well—is it dangerous to take?"

"Dangerous—how do you mean?"

I could have shaken the man for his stupidity.

"I mean—if a person was to take too much of it—by mistake of course—" says I, my heart in my throat.

"Lord bless you, no. It's only lime-water. You might feed it to a baby by the bottleful."

I gave a great sigh of relief, and hurried on to Mr. Ranford's. But on the way another thought struck me. If there was nothing to conceal about my visit to the chemist's, was it my other errand that Mrs. Brympton wished me to keep private? Somehow, that thought frightened me worse than the other. Yet the two gentlemen seemed fast friends, and I would have staked my head on my mistress's goodness. I felt ashamed of my suspicions, and concluded that I was still disturbed by the strange events of the night. I left the note at Mr. Ranford's—and, hurrying back to Brympton, slipped in by a side door without being seen, as I thought.

An hour later, however, as I was carrying in my mistress's breakfast, I was stopped in the hall by Mr. Brympton.

"What were you doing out so early?" he says, looking hard at me.

"Early—me, sir?" I said, in a tremble.

"Come, come," he says, an angry red spot coming out on his forehead, "didn't I see you scuttling home through the shrubbery an hour or more ago?"

I'm a truthful woman by nature, but at that a lie popped out ready-made. "No, sir, you didn't," said I, and looked straight back at him.

He shrugged his shoulders and gave a sullen laugh. "I suppose you think I was drunk last night?" he asked suddenly.

"No, sir, I don't," I answered, this time truthfully enough.

He turned away with another shrug. "A pretty notion my servants have of me!" I heard him mutter as he walked off.

Not till I had settled down to my afternoon's sewing did I realize how the events of the night had shaken me. I couldn't pass that locked door without a shiver. I knew I had heard someone come out of it, and walk down the passage ahead of me. I thought of speaking to Mrs. Blinder or to Mr. Wace, the only two in the house who appeared to have an inkling of what was going on, but I had a feeling that if I questioned them they would deny everything, and that I might learn more by holding my tongue and keeping my eyes open. The idea of spending another night opposite the locked room sickened me, and once I was seized with the notion of packing my trunk and taking the first train to town; but it wasn't in me to throw over a kind mistress in that manner, and I tried to go on with my sewing as if nothing had happened.

I hadn't worked ten minutes before the sewing-machine broke down. It was one I had found in the house, a good machine, but a trifle out of order: Mrs. Blinder said it had never been used since Emma Saxon's death. I stopped to see what was wrong, and as I was working at the machine a drawer which I had never been able to open slid forward and a photograph fell out. I picked it up and sat looking at it in a maze. It was a woman's likeness, and I knew I had seen the face somewhere—the eyes had an asking look that I had felt on me before. And suddenly I remembered the pale woman in the passage.

I stood up, cold all over, and ran out of the room. My heart seemed to be thumping in the top of my head, and I felt as if I should never get away from the look in those eyes. I went straight to Mrs. Blinder. She was taking her afternoon nap, and sat up with a jump when I came in.

"Mrs. Blinder," said I, "who is that?" And I held out the photograph.

She rubbed her eyes and stared.

"Why, Emma Saxon," says she. "Where did you find it?"

I looked hard at her for a minute. "Mrs. Blinder," I said, "I've seen that face before."

Mrs. Blinder got up and walked over to the looking-glass. "Dear me! I must have been asleep," she says. "My front is all over one ear. And now do run along, Miss Hartley, dear, for I hear the clock striking four, and I must go down this very minute and put on the Virginia ham for Mr. Brympton's dinner."

4

To all appearances, things went on as usual for a week or two. The only difference was that Mr. Brympton stayed on, instead of going off as he usually did, and that Mr. Ranford never showed himself. I heard Mr. Brympton remark on this one afternoon when he was sitting in my mistress's room before dinner.

"Where's Ranford?" says he. "He hasn't been near the house for a week. Does he keep away because I'm here?"

Mrs. Brympton spoke so low that I couldn't catch her answer.

"Well," he went on, "two's company and three's trumpery; I'm sorry to be in Ranford's way, and I suppose I shall have to take myself off again in a day or two and give him a show." And he laughed at his own joke.

The very next day, as it happened, Mr. Ranford called. The footman said the three were very merry over their tea in the library, and Mr. Brympton strolled down to the gate with Mr. Ranford when he left.

I have said that things went on as usual; and so they did with the rest of the household; but as for myself, I had never been the same since the night my bell had rung. Night after night I used to lie awake, listening for it to ring again, and for the door of the locked room to open stealthily. But the bell never rang, and I heard no sound across the passage. At last the silence began to be more dreadful to me than the most mysterious sounds. I felt that *someone* were cowering there, behind the locked door, watching and listening as I watched and listened, and I could almost have cried out, "Whoever you are, come out and let me see you face to face, but don't lurk there and spy on me in the darkness!"

Feeling as I did, you may wonder I didn't give warning. Once I very nearly did so; but at the last moment something held me back. Whether it was compassion for my mistress, who had grown more and more dependent on me, or unwillingness to try a new place, or some other feeling that I couldn't put a name to, I lingered on as if spell-bound, though every night was dreadful to me, and the days but little better.

For one thing, I didn't like Mrs. Brympton's looks. She had never been the same since that night, no more than I had. I thought she would brighten up after Mr. Brympton left, but though she seemed easier in her mind, her spirits didn't revive, nor her strength either. She had grown attached to me, and seemed to like to have me about; and Agnes told me one day that, since Emma Saxon's death, I was the only maid her mistress had taken to. This gave me a warm feeling for the poor lady, though after all there was little I could do to help her.

After Mr. Brympton's departure, Mr. Ranford took to coming again, though less often than formerly. I met him once or twice in the grounds, or in the village, and I couldn't but think there was a change in him too; but I set it down to my disordered fancy.

The weeks passed, and Mr. Brympton had now been a month

absent. We heard he was cruising with a friend in the West Indies, and Mr. Wace said that was a long way off, but though you had the wings of a dove and went to the uttermost parts of the earth, you couldn't get away from the Almighty. Agnes said that as long as he stayed away from Brympton, the Almighty might have him and welcome; and this raised a laugh, though Mrs. Blinder tried to look shocked, and Mr. Wace said the bears would eat us.

We were all glad to hear that the West Indies were a long way off, and I remember that, in spite of Mr. Wace's solemn looks, we had a very merry dinner that day in the hall. I don't know if it was because of my being in better spirits, but I fancied Mrs. Brympton looked better too, and seemed more cheerful in her manner. She had been for a walk in the morning, and after luncheon she lay down in her room, and I read aloud to her. When she dismissed me I went to my own room feeling quite bright and happy, and for the first time in weeks walked past the locked door without thinking of it. As I sat down to my work I looked out and saw a few snow-flakes falling. The sight was pleasanter than the eternal rain, and I pictured to myself how pretty the bare gardens would look in their white mantle. It seemed to me as if the snow would cover up all the dreariness, indoors as well as out.

The fancy had hardly crossed my mind when I heard a step at my side. I looked up, thinking it was Agnes.

"Well, Agnes—" said I, and the words froze on my tongue; for there, in the door, stood Emma Saxon.

I don't know how long she stood there. I only know I couldn't stir or take my eyes from her. Afterward I was terribly frightened, but at the time it wasn't fear I felt, but something deeper and quieter. She looked at me long and long, and her face was just one dumb prayer to me—but how in the world was I to help her? Suddenly she turned, and I heard her walk down the passage. This time I wasn't afraid to follow—I felt that I must know what she wanted. I sprang up and ran out. She was at the other end of the passage, and I expected her to take the turn toward my mistress's room; but instead of that she pushed open the door that led to the backstairs. I followed her down the stairs, and across the passageway to the back door.

The kitchen and hall were empty at that hour, the servants being off duty, except for the footman, who was in the pantry. At the door she stood still a moment, with another look at me; then she turned the handle, and stepped out. For a minute I hesitated. Where was she leading me to? The door had closed softly after her, and I opened it and looked out, half-expecting to find that she had disappeared. But I saw her a few yards off, hurrying across the court-yard to the path through the woods. Her figure looked black and lonely in the snow, and for a second my heart failed me and I thought of turning back. But all the while she was drawing me after her; and catching up an old shawl of Mrs. Blinder's I ran out into the open.

Emma Saxon was in the wood-path now. She walked on steadily, and I followed at the same pace, till we passed out of the gates and reached the high-road. Then she struck across the open fields to the village. By this time the ground was white, and as she climbed the slope of a bare hill ahead of me I noticed that she left no foot-prints behind her. At sight of that, my heart shrivelled up within me, and my knees were water. Somehow, it was worse here than indoors. She made the whole countryside seem lonely as the grave, with none but us two in it, and no help in the wide world.

Once I tried to go back; but she turned and looked at me, and it was as if she had dragged me with ropes. After that I followed her like a dog. We came to the village, and she led me through it, past the church and the blacksmith's shop, and down the lane to Mr. Ranford's. Mr. Ranford's house stands close to the road: a plain old-fashioned building, with a flagged path leading to the door between box-borders. The lane was deserted, and as I turned into it, I saw Emma Saxon pause under the old elm by the gate.

And now another fear came over me. I saw that we had reached the end of our journey, and that it was my turn to act. All the way from Brympton I had been asking myself what she wanted of me, but I had followed in a trance, as it were, and not till I saw her stop at Mr. Ranford's gate did my brain begin to clear itself. It stood a little way off in the snow, my heart beating fit to strangle me, and my feet frozen to the ground; and she stood under the elm and watched me.

I knew well enough that she hadn't led me there for nothing. I felt there was something I ought to say or do—but how was I to guess what it was? I had never thought harm of my mistress and Mr. Ranford, but I was sure now that, from one cause or another, some dreadful thing hung over them. *She* knew what it was; she would tell me if she could; perhaps she would answer if I questioned her.

It turned me faint to think of speaking to her; but I plucked up heart and dragged myself across the few yards between us. As I did so, I heard the house-door open, and saw Mr. Ranford approaching. He looked handsome and cheerful, as my mistress had looked that morning, and at sight of him the blood began to flow again in my veins.

"Why, Hartley," said he, "what's the matter? I saw you coming down the lane just now, and came out to see if you had taken root in the snow." He stopped and stared at me. "What are you looking at?" he says.

I turned toward the elm as he spoke, and his eyes followed me; but there was no one there. The lane was empty as far as the eye could reach.

A sense of helplessness came over me. She was gone, and I had not been able to guess what she wanted. Her last look had pierced me to the marrow; and yet it had not told me! All at once, I felt more desolate than when she had stood there watching me. It seemed as if she had left me all alone to carry the weight of the secret I couldn't guess. The snow went round me in great circles, and the ground fell away from me....

A drop of brandy and the warmth of Mr. Ranford's fire soon brought me to, and I insisted on being driven back at once to Brympton. It was nearly dark, and I was afraid my mistress might be wanting me. I explained to Mr. Ranford that I had been out for a walk and had been taken with a fit of giddiness as I passed his gate. This was true enough; yet I never felt more like a liar than when I said it.

When I dressed Mrs. Brympton for dinner she remarked on my pale looks and asked what ailed me. I told her I had a headache, and she said she would not require me again that evening, and advised me to go to bed.

It was a fact that I could scarcely keep on my feet; yet I had no fancy to spend a solitary evening in my room. I sat downstairs in the hall as long as I could hold my head up; but by nine I crept upstairs, too weary to care what happened if I could but get my head on a pillow. The rest of the household went to bed soon afterward; they kept early hours when the master was away, and before ten I heard Mrs. Blinder's door close, and Mr. Wace's soon after.

It was a very still night, earth and air all muffled in snow. Once in bed I felt easier, and lay quiet, listening to the strange noises that come out in a house after dark. Once I thought I heard a door open and close again below: it might have been the glass door that led to the gardens. I got up and peered out of the window; but it was in the dark of the moon, and nothing visible outside but the streaking of snow against the panes.

I went back to bed and must have dozed, for I jumped awake to the furious ringing of my bell. Before my head was clear I had sprung out of bed, and was dragging on my clothes. '*It is going to happen now*,' I heard myself saying; but what I meant I had no notion. My hands seemed to be covered with glue—I thought I should never get into my clothes. At last I opened my door and peered down the passage. As far as my candle-flame carried, I could see nothing unusual ahead of me. I hurried on, breathless; but as I pushed open the baize door leading to the main hall my heart stood still, for there at the head of the stairs was Emma Saxon, peering dreadfully down into the darkness.

For a second I couldn't stir; but my hand slipped from the door, and as it swung shut the figure vanished. At the same instant there came another sound from below stairs—a stealthy mysterious sound, as of a latch-key turning in the house-door. I ran to Mrs. Brympton's room and knocked.

There was no answer, and I knocked again. This time I heard someone moving in the room; the bolt slipped back and my mistress stood before me. To my surprise I saw that she had not undressed for the night. She gave me a startled look.

"What is this, Hartley?" she says in a whisper. "Are you ill? What are you doing here at this hour?"

"I am not ill, madam; but my bell rang."

At that she turned pale, and seemed about to fall.

"You are mistaken," she said harshly; "I didn't ring. You must have been dreaming." I had never heard her speak in such a tone. "Go back to bed," she said, closing the door on me.

But as she spoke I heard sounds again in the hall below: a man's step this time; and the truth leaped out on me.

"Madam," I said, pushing past her, "there is someone in the house—"

"Someone—?"

"Mr. Brympton, I think—I hear his step below—"

A dreadful look came over her, and without a word, she dropped flat at my feet. I fell on my knees and tried to lift her: by the way she breathed I saw it was no common faint. But as I raised her head there came quick steps on the stairs and across the hall: the door was flung open, and there stood Mr. Brympton, in his travelling-clothes, the snow dripping from him. He drew back with a start as he saw me kneeling by my mistress.

"What the devil is this?" he shouted. He was less high-coloured than usual, and the red spot came out on his forehead.

"Mrs. Brympton has fainted, sir," said I.

He laughed unsteadily and pushed by me. "It's a pity she didn't choose a more convenient moment. I'm sorry to disturb her, but—"

I raised myself up, aghast at the man's action.

"Sir," said I, "are you mad? What are you doing?"

"Going to meet a friend," said he, and seemed to make for the dressing-room.

At that my heart turned over. I don't know what I thought or feared; but I sprang up and caught him by the sleeve.

"Sir, sir," said I, "for pity's sake look at your wife!"

He shook me off furiously.

"It seems that's done for me," says he, and caught hold of the dressing-room door.

At that moment I heard a slight noise inside. Slight as it was, he heard it too, and tore the door open; but as he did so he dropped back. On the threshold stood Emma Saxon. All was dark behind her, but I saw her plainly, and so did he. He threw up his hands as if to hide his face from her; and when I looked again she was gone.

He stood motionless, as if the strength had run out of him; and in the stillness my mistress suddenly raised herself, and opening her eyes fixed a look on him. Then she fell back, and I saw the death-flutter pass over her. . . .

We buried her on the third day, in a driving snow-storm. There were few people in the church, for it was bad weather to come from town, and I've a notion my mistress was one that hadn't many near friends. Mr. Ranford was among the last to come, just before they carried her up the aisle. He was in black, of course, being such a friend of the family, and I never saw a gentleman so pale. As he passed me, I noticed that he leaned a trifle on a stick he carried; and I fancy Mr. Brympton noticed it too, for the red spot came out sharp on his forehead, and all through the service he kept staring across the church at Mr. Ranford, instead of following the prayers as a mourner should.

When it was over and we went out to the graveyard, Mr. Ranford had disappeared, and as soon as my poor mistress's body was underground, Mr. Brympton jumped into the carriage nearest the gate and drove off without a word to any of us. I heard him call out, "To the station," and we servants went back alone to the house.

Xingu

1

Mrs. Ballinger is one of the ladies who pursue culture in bands, as though it were dangerous to meet alone. To this end she had founded the Lunch Club, an association composed of herself and several other indomitable huntresses of erudition. The Lunch Club, after three or four winters of lunching and debate, had acquired such local distinction that the entertainment of distinguished strangers became one of its accepted functions; in recognition of which it duly extended to the celebrated "Osric Dane," on the day of her arrival in Hillbridge, an invitation to be present at the next meeting.

The club was to meet at Mrs. Ballinger's. The other members, behind her back, were of one voice in deploring her unwillingness to cede her rights in favour of Mrs. Plinth, whose house made a more impressive setting for the entertainment of celebrities; while, as Mrs. Leveret observed, there was always the picture-gallery to fall back on.

Mrs. Plinth made no secret of sharing this view. She had always regarded it as one of her obligations to entertain the Lunch Club's distinguished guests. Mrs. Plinth was almost as proud of her obligations as she was of her picture-gallery; she was in fact fond of implying that the one possession implied the other, and that only a woman of her wealth could afford to live up to a standard as high as that which she had set herself. An all-round sense of duty, roughly adaptable to various ends, was, in her opinion, all that Providence exacted of the more humbly stationed; but the power which had predestined Mrs. Plinth to keep footmen clearly intended her to maintain an equally specialised staff of responsibilities. It was the more to be regretted that Mrs. Ballinger, whose obligations to society were bounded by the narrow scope of two parlour-maids, should have been so tenacious of the right to entertain Osric Dane.

The question of that lady's reception had for a month past profoundly moved the members of the Lunch Club. It was not that they felt themselves unequal to the task, but that their sense of the opportunity plunged them into the agreeable uncertainty of the lady who weighs the alternatives of a well-stocked wardrobe. If such subsidiary members as Mrs. Leveret were fluttered by the thought of exchanging ideas with the author of *The Wings of Death*, no forebodings of the kind disturbed the conscious adequacy of Mrs. Plinth, Mrs. Ballinger and Miss Van Vluyck.

The Wings of Death had, in fact, at Miss Van Vluyck's suggestion, been chosen as the subject of discussion at the last club meeting, and each member had thus been enabled to express her own opinion or to appropriate whatever seemed most likely to be of use in the comments of the others. Mrs. Roby alone had abstained from profiting by the opportunity thus offered; but it was now openly recognised that, as a member of the Lunch Club, Mrs. Roby was a failure. "It all comes," as Miss Van Vluyck put it, "of accepting a woman on a man's estimation." Mrs. Roby, returning to Hillbridge from a prolonged sojourn in exotic regions—the other ladies no longer took the trouble to remember where—had been emphatically commended by the distinguished biologist, Professor Foreland, as the most agreeable woman he had ever met; and the members of the Lunch Club, awed by an encomium that carried the weight of a diploma, and rashly assuming that the professor's social sympathies would follow the line of his scientific bent, had seized the chance of annexing a biological member.

Their disillusionment was complete. At Miss Van Vluyck's first offhand mention of the pterodactyl Mrs. Roby had confusedly murmured: "I know so little about metres—" and after that painful betrayal of incompetence she had prudently withdrawn from farther participation in the mental gymnastics of the club.

"I suppose she flattered him," Miss Van Vluyck summed up—"or else it's the way she does her hair."

The dimensions of Miss Van Vluyck's dining-room having restricted the membership of the club to six, the non-conductiveness of one member was a serious obstacle to the exchange of ideas, and some wonder had already been expressed that Mrs. Roby should care to live, as it were, on the intellectual bounty of the others. This feeling was augmented by the discovery that she had not yet read *The Wings of Death*. She owned to having heard the name of Osric Dane; but that—incredible as it appeared—was the extent of her acquaintance with the celebrated novelist. The ladies could not conceal their surprise, but Mrs. Ballinger, whose pride in the club made her wish to put even Mrs. Roby in the best possible light, gently insinuated that, though she had not had time to acquaint herself with *The Wings of Death*, she must at least be familiar with its equally remarkable predecessor, *The Supreme Instant*.

Mrs. Roby wrinkled her sunny brows in a conscientious effort of memory, as a result of which she recalled that, oh, yes, she *had* seen the book at her brother's, when she was staying with him in Brazil, and had even carried it off to read one day on a boating party; but they had all got to shying things at each other in the boat, and the book had gone overboard, so she had never had the chance—

The picture evoked by this anecdote did not advance Mrs. Roby's credit with the club, and there was a painful pause, which was broken by Mrs. Plinth's remarking: "I can understand that, with all your other pursuits, you should not find much time for reading; but I should have thought you might at least have got up *The Wings of Death* before Osric Dane's arrival."

Mrs. Roby took this rebuke good-humouredly. She had meant, she owned to glance through the book; but she had been so absorbed in a novel of Trollope's that—

"No one reads Trollope now," Mrs. Ballinger interrupted impatiently.

Mrs. Roby looked pained. "I'm only just beginning," she confessed.

"And does he interest you?" Mrs. Plinth inquired.

"He amuses me."

"Amusement," said Mrs. Plinth sententiously, "is hardly what I look for in my choice of books."

"Oh, certainly, *The Wings of Death* is not amusing," ventured Mrs. Leveret, whose manner of putting forth an opinion was like that of an obliging salesman with a variety of other styles to submit if his first selection does not suit.

"Was it *meant* to be?" enquired Mrs. Plinth, who was fond of asking questions that she permitted no one but herself to answer. "Assuredly not."

"Assuredly not—that is what I was going to say," assented Mrs. Leveret, hastily rolling up her opinion and reaching for another. "It was meant to—to elevate."

Miss Van Vluyck adjusted her spectacles as though they were the black cap of condemnation. "I hardly see," she interposed, "how a book steeped in the bitterest pessimism can be said to elevate, however much it may instruct."

"I meant, of course, to instruct," said Mrs. Leveret, flurried by the unexpected distinction between two terms which she had supposed to be synonymous. Mrs. Leveret's enjoyment of the Lunch Club was frequently marred by such surprises; and not knowing her own value to the other ladies as a mirror for their mental complacency she was sometimes troubled by a doubt of her worthiness to join in their debates. It was only the fact of having a dull sister who thought her clever that saved her from a sense of hopeless inferiority.

"Do they get married in the end?" Mrs. Roby interposed.

"They—who?" the Lunch Club collectively exclaimed.

"Why, the girl and man. It's a novel, isn't it? I always think that's the one thing that matters. If they're parted it spoils my dinner."

Mrs. Plinth and Mrs. Ballinger exchanged scandalised glances, and the latter said: "I should hardly advise you to read *The Wings of Death*, in that spirit. For my part, when there are so many books that one *has* to read, I wonder how anyone can find time for those that are merely amusing."

"The beautiful part of it," Laura Glyde murmured, "is surely just this—that no one can tell *how The Wings of Death* ends. Osric Dane, overcome by the dread significance of her own meaning, has mercifully veiled it—perhaps even from herself—as Apelles, in representing the sacrifice of Iphigenia, veiled the face of Agamemnon."

"What's that? Is it poetry?" whispered Mrs. Leveret nervously to Mrs. Plinth, who, disdaining a definite reply, said coldly: "You should look it up. I always make it a point to look things up." Her tone added—"though I might easily have it done for me by the footman."

"I was about to say," Miss Van Vluyck resumed, "that it must always be a question whether a book *can* instruct unless it elevates."

"Oh—" murmured Mrs. Leveret, now feeling herself hopelessly astray.

"I don't know," said Mrs. Ballinger, scenting in Miss Van Vluyck's tone a tendency to depreciate the coveted distinction of entertaining Osric Dane; "I don't know that such a question can seriously be raised as to a book which has attracted more attention among thoughtful people than any novel since 'Robert Elsmere.'"

"Oh, but don't you see," exclaimed Laura Glyde, "that it's just the dark hopelessness of it all—the wonderful tone-scheme of black on black—that makes it such an artistic achievement? It reminded me so when I read it of Prince Rupert's *maniere noire* . . . the book is etched, not painted, yet one feels the colour values so intensely . . ."

"Who is *he*?" Mrs. Leveret whispered to her neighbour. "Someone she's met abroad?"

"The wonderful part of the book," Mrs. Ballinger conceded, "is that it may be looked at from so many points of view. I hear that as a study of determinism Professor Lupton ranks it with *The Data of Ethics*."

"I'm told that Osric Dane spent ten years in preparatory studies before beginning to write it," said Mrs. Plinth. "She looks up everything—verifies everything. It has always been my principle, as you know. Nothing would induce me, now, to put aside a book before I'd finished it, just because I can buy as many more as I want."

"And what do *you* think of *The Wings of Death?*" Mrs. Roby abruptly asked her.

It was the kind of question that might be termed out of order, and the ladies glanced at each other as though disclaiming any share in such a breach of discipline. They all knew that there was nothing Mrs. Plinth so much disliked as being asked her opinion of a book. Books were written to read; if one read them what more could be expected? To be questioned in detail regarding the contents of a volume seemed to her as great an outrage as being searched for smuggled laces at the Custom House.

The club had always respected this idiosyncrasy of Mrs. Plinth's. Such opinions as she had were imposing and substantial: her mind, like her house, was furnished with monumental "pieces" that were not meant to be suddenly disarranged; and it was one of the unwritten rules of the Lunch Club that, within her own province, each member's habits of thought should be respected. The meeting therefore closed with an increased sense, on the part of the other ladies, of Mrs. Roby's hopeless unfitness to be one of them.

2

Mrs. Leveret, on the eventful day, had arrived early at Mrs. Ballinger's, her volume of *Appropriate Allusions* in her pocket.

It always flustered Mrs. Leveret to be late at the Lunch Club: she liked to collect her thoughts and gather a hint, as the others assembled, of the turn the conversation was likely to take. Today, however, she felt herself completely at a loss; and even the familiar contact of *Appropriate Allusions,* which stuck into her as she sat down, failed to give her any reassurance. It was an admirable little volume, compiled to meet all the social emergencies; so that, whether on the occasion of Anniversaries, joyful or melancholy (as the classification ran), of Banquets, social or municipal, or of Baptisms, Church of England or sectarian, its student need never be at a loss for a pertinent reference. Mrs. Leveret, though she had for years devoutly conned its pages, valued it, however, rather for its moral support than for its practical services; for though in the privacy of her own room she commanded an army of quotations, these invariably deserted her at the critical moment, and the only line she retained—*Canst thou draw out Leviathan with a hook?*—was one she had never yet found the occasion to apply.

Today she felt that even the complete mastery of the volume would hardly have insured her self-possession; for she thought it probable, even if she *did*, in some miraculous way, remember an Allusion, it would be only to find that Osric Dane used a different volume (Mrs. Leveret was convinced that literary people always carried them), and would consequently not recognise her quotations.

Mrs. Leveret's sense of being adrift was intensified by the appearance of Mrs. Ballinger's drawing-room. To a careless eye its aspect was unchanged; but those acquainted with Mrs. Ballinger's way of arranging her books would instantly have detected the marks of recent perturbation. Mrs. Ballinger's province, as a member of the Lunch Club, was the Book of the Day. On that, whatever it was, from a novel to a treatise on experimental psychology, she was confidently, authoritatively "up." What became of last year's books, or last week's even; what she did with the "subjects" she had previously professed with equal authority; no one had ever yet discovered. Her mind was an hotel where facts came and went like transient lodgers, without leaving their address behind, and frequently without paying for their board.

It was Mrs. Ballinger's boast that she was "abreast with the Thought of the Day," and her pride that this advanced position should be expressed by the books on her drawing-room table. These volumes, frequently renewed, and almost always damp from the press, bore names generally unfamiliar to Mrs. Leveret, and giving her, as she furtively scanned them, a disheartening glimpse of new fields of knowledge to be breathlessly traversed in Mrs. Ballinger's wake. But today a number of maturer-looking volumes were adroitly mingled with the primeurs of the press—Karl Marx jostled Professor Bergson, and the "Confessions of St. Augustine" lay beside the last work on *Mendelism*; so that even to Mrs. Leveret's fluttered perceptions it was clear that Mrs.

Ballinger didn't in the least know what Osric Dane was likely to talk about, and had taken measures to be prepared for anything. Mrs. Leveret felt like a passenger on an ocean steamer who is told that there is no immediate danger, but that she had better put on her life-belt.

It was a relief to be roused from these forebodings by Miss Van Vluyck's arrival.

"Well, my dear," the newcomer briskly asked her hostess, "what subjects are we to discuss today?"

Mrs. Ballinger was furtively replacing a volume of Wordsworth by a copy of Verlaine. "I hardly know," she said somewhat nervously. "Perhaps we had better leave that to circumstances."

"Circumstances?" said Miss Van Vluyck drily. "That means, I suppose, that Laura Glyde will take the floor as usual, and we shall be deluged with literature."

Philanthropy and statistics were Miss Van Vluyck's province, and she naturally resented any tendency to divert their guest's attention from these topics.

Mrs. Plinth at this moment appeared.

"Literature?" she protested in a tone of remonstrance. "But this is perfectly unexpected. I understood we were to talk of Osric Dane's novel."

Mrs. Ballinger winced at the discrimination, but let it pass. "We can hardly make that our chief subject—at least not *too* intentionally," she suggested. "Of course we can let our talk *drift* in that direction; but we ought to have some other topic as an introduction, and that is what I wanted to consult you about. The fact is, we know so little of Osric Dane's tastes and interests that it is difficult to make any special preparation."

"It may be difficult," said Mrs. Plinth with decision, "but it is absolutely necessary. I know what that happy-go-lucky principle leads to. As I told one of my nieces the other day, there are certain emergencies for which a lady should always be prepared. It's in shocking taste to wear colours when one pays a visit of condolence, or a last year's dress when there are reports that one's husband is on the wrong side of the market; and so it is with conversation. All I ask is that I should know beforehand what is to be talked about; then I feel sure of being able to say the proper thing."

"I quite agree with you," Mrs. Ballinger anxiously assented; "but—"

And at that instant, heralded by the fluttered parlour-maid, Osric Dane appeared upon the threshold.

Mrs. Leveret told her sister afterward that she had known at a glance what was coming. She saw that Osric Dane was not going to meet them half way. That distinguished personage had indeed entered with an air of compulsion not calculated to promote the easy exercise of hospitality. She looked as though she were about to be photographed for a new edition of her books.

The desire to propitiate a divinity is generally in inverse ratio to its responsiveness, and the sense of discouragement produced by Osric Dane's entrance visibly increased the Lunch Club's eagerness to please her. Any lingering idea that she might consider herself under an obligation to her entertainers was at once dispelled by her manner: as Mrs. Leveret said afterward to her sister, she had a way of looking at you that made you feel as if there was something wrong with your hat. This evidence of greatness produced such an immediate impression on the ladies that a shudder of awe ran through them when Mrs. Roby, as their hostess led the great personage into the dining-room, turned back to whisper to the others: "What a brute she is!"

The hour about the table did not tend to correct this verdict. It was passed by Osric Dane in the silent deglutition of Mrs. Ballinger's menu, and by the members of the club in the emission of tentative platitudes which their guest seemed to swallow as perfunctorily as the successive courses of the luncheon.

Mrs. Ballinger's deplorable delay in fixing a topic had thrown the club into a mental disarray which increased with the return to the drawing-room, where the actual business of discussion was to open. Each lady waited for the other to speak; and there was a general shock of disappointment when their hostess opened the conversation by the painfully commonplace inquiry: "Is this your first visit to Hillbridge?"

Even Mrs. Leveret was conscious that this was a bad beginning; and a vague impulse of deprecation made Miss Glyde interject: "It is a very small place indeed."

Mrs. Plinth bristled. "We have a great many representative people," she said, in the tone of one who speaks for her order.

Osric Dane turned to her thoughtfully. "What do they represent?" she asked.

Mrs. Plinth's constitutional dislike to being questioned was intensified by her sense of unpreparedness; and her reproachful glance passed the question on to Mrs. Ballinger.

"Why," said that lady, glancing in turn at the other members, "as a community I hope it is not too much to say that we stand for culture."

"For art—" Miss Glyde eagerly interjected.

"For art and literature," Mrs. Ballinger emended.

"And for sociology, I trust," snapped Miss Van Vluyck.

"We have a standard," said Mrs. Plinth, feeling herself suddenly secure on the vast expanse of a generalisation: and Mrs. Leveret, thinking there must be room for more than one on so broad a statement, took courage to murmur: "Oh, certainly; we have a standard."

"The object of our little club," Mrs. Ballinger continued, "is to concentrate the highest tendencies of Hillbridge—to centralise and focus its complex intellectual effort."

This was felt to be so happy that the ladies drew an almost audible breath of relief.

"We aspire," the President went on, "to stand for what is highest in art, literature and ethics."

Osric Dane again turned to her. "What ethics?" she asked.

A tremor of apprehension encircled the room. None of the ladies required any preparation to pronounce on a question of morals; but when they were called ethics it was different. The club, when fresh from the *Encyclopaedia Britannica*, the *Reader's Handbook* or Smith's *Classical Dictionary*, could deal confidently with any subject; but when taken unawares it had been known to define agnosticism as a heresy of the Early Church and Professor Froude as a distinguished histologist; and such minor members as Mrs. Leveret still secretly regarded ethics as something vaguely pagan.

Even to Mrs. Ballinger, Osric Dane's question was unsettling, and there was a general sense of gratitude when Laura Glyde leaned forward to say, with her most sympathetic accent: "You must excuse us, Mrs. Dane, for not being able, just at present, to talk of anything but *The Wings of Death*."

"Yes," said Miss Van Vluyck, with a sudden resolve to carry the war into the enemy's camp. "We are so anxious to know the exact purpose you had in mind in writing your wonderful book."

"You will find," Mrs. Plinth interposed, "that we are not superficial readers."

"We are eager to hear from you," Miss Van Vluyck continued, "if the pessimistic tendency of the book is an expression of your own convictions or—"

"Or merely," Miss Glyde hastily thrust in, "a sombre background brushed in to throw your figures into more vivid relief. *Are* you not primarily plastic?"

"I have always maintained," Mrs. Ballinger interposed, "that you represent the purely objective method—"

Osric Dane helped herself critically to coffee. "How do you define objective?" she then inquired.

There was a flurried pause before Laura Glyde intensely murmured: "In reading *you* we don't define, we feel."

Osric Dane smiled. "The cerebellum," she remarked, "is not infrequently the seat of the literary emotions." And she took a second lump of sugar.

The sting that this remark was vaguely felt to conceal was almost neutralised by the satisfaction of being addressed in such technical language.

"Ah, the cerebellum," said Miss Van Vluyck complacently. "The club took a course in psychology last winter."

"Which psychology?" asked Osric Dane.

There was an agonising pause, during which each member of the club secretly deplored the distressing inefficiency of the others. Only Mrs. Roby went on placidly sipping her chartreuse. At last Mrs. Ballinger said, with an attempt at a high tone: "Well, really, you know, it was last year that we took psychology, and this winter we have been so absorbed in—"

She broke off, nervously trying to recall some of the Club's discussions; but her faculties seemed to be paralysed by the petrifying stare of Osric Dane. What *had* the club been absorbed in lately? Mrs. Ballinger, with a vague purpose of gaining time, repeated slowly: "We've been so intensely absorbed in—"

Mrs. Roby put down her liqueur glass and drew near the group with a smile.

"In Xingu?" she gently prompted.

A thrill ran through the other members. They exchanged confused glances, and then, with one accord, turned a gaze of mingled relief and interrogation on their unexpected rescuer. The expression of each denoted a different phase of the same emotion. Mrs. Plinth was the first to compose her features to an air of reassurance: after a moment's hasty adjustment her look almost implied that it was she who had given the word to Mrs. Ballinger.

"Xingu, of course!" exclaimed the latter with her accustomed promptness, while Miss Van Vluyck and Laura Glyde seemed to be plumbing the depths of memory, and Mrs. Leveret, feeling apprehensively for *Appropriate Allusions,* was somehow reassured by the uncomfortable pressure of its bulk against her person.

Osric Dane's change of countenance was no less striking than that of her entertainers. She too put down her coffee-cup, but with a look of distinct annoyance: she too wore, for a brief moment, what Mrs. Roby afterward described as the look of feeling for something in the back of her head; and before she could dissemble these momentary signs of weakness, Mrs. Roby, turning to her with a deferential smile, had said: "And we've been so hoping that today you would tell us just what you think of it."

Osric Dane received the homage of the smile as a matter of course; but the accompanying question obviously embarrassed her, and it became clear to her observers that she was not quick at shifting her facial scenery. It was as though her countenance had so long been set in an expression of unchallenged superiority that the muscles had stiffened, and refused to obey her orders.

"Xingu—" she murmured, as if seeking in her turn to gain time.

Mrs. Roby continued to press her. "Knowing how engrossing the subject is, you will understand how it happens that the club has let everything else go to the wall for the moment. Since we took up Xingu I might almost say—were it not for your books—that nothing else seems to us worth remembering."

Osric Dane's stern features were darkened rather than lit up by an uneasy smile. "I am glad to hear there is one exception," she gave out between narrowed lips.

"Oh, of course," Mrs. Roby said prettily; "but as you have shown us that—so very naturally!—you don't care to talk about your own things, we really can't let you off from telling us exactly what you think about Xingu; especially," she added, with a persuasive smile, "as some people say that one of your last books was simply saturated with it."

It was an *it*, then—the assurance sped like fire through the parched minds of the other members. In their eagerness to gain the least little clue to Xingu they almost forgot the joy of assisting at the discomfiture of Mrs. Dane.

The latter reddened nervously under her antagonist's direct assault. "May I ask," she faltered out in an embarrassed tone, "to which of my books you refer?"

Mrs. Roby did not falter. "That's just what I want you to tell us; because, though I was present, I didn't actually take part."

"Present at what?" Mrs. Dane took her up; and for an instant the trembling members of the Lunch Club thought that the champion Providence had raised up for them had lost a point. But Mrs. Roby explained herself gaily: "At the discussion, of course. And so we're dreadfully anxious to know just how it was that you went into the Xingu."

There was a portentous pause, a silence so big with incalculable dangers that the members with one accord checked the words on their lips, like soldiers dropping their arms to watch a single combat between their leaders. Then Mrs. Dane gave expression to their inmost dread by saying sharply: "Ah—you say *the* Xingu, do you?"

Mrs. Roby smiled undauntedly. "It *is* a shade pedantic, isn't it? Personally, I always drop the article; but I don't know how the other members feel about it."

The other members looked as though they would willingly have dispensed with this deferential appeal to their opinion, and Mrs. Roby, after a bright glance about the group, went on: "They probably think, as I do, that nothing really matters except the thing itself—except Xingu."

No immediate reply seemed to occur to Mrs. Dane, and Mrs. Ballinger gathered courage to say: "Surely everyone must feel that about Xingu."

Mrs. Plinth came to her support with a heavy murmur of assent, and Laura Glyde breathed emotionally: "I have known cases where it has changed a whole life."

"It has done me worlds of good," Mrs. Leveret interjected, seeming to herself to remember that she had either taken it or read it in the winter before.

"Of course," Mrs. Roby admitted, "the difficulty is that one must give up so much time to it. It's very long."

"I can't imagine," said Miss Van Vluyck tartly, "grudging the time given to such a subject."

"And deep in places," Mrs. Roby pursued; (so then it was a book!) "And it isn't easy to skip."

"I never skip," said Mrs. Plinth dogmatically.

"Ah, it's dangerous to, in Xingu. Even at the start there are places where one can't. One must just wade through."

"I should hardly call it *wading*," said Mrs. Ballinger sarcastically.

Mrs. Roby sent her a look of interest. "Ah—you always found it went swimmingly?"

Mrs. Ballinger hesitated. "Of course there are difficult passages," she conceded modestly.

"Yes; some are not at all clear—even," Mrs. Roby added, "if one is familiar with the original."

"As I suppose you are?" Osric Dane interposed, suddenly fixing her with a look of challenge.

Mrs. Roby met it by a deprecating smile. "Oh, it's really not difficult up to a certain point; though some of the branches are very little known, and it's almost impossible to get at the source."

"Have you ever tried?" Mrs. Plinth enquired, still distrustful of Mrs. Roby's thoroughness.

Mrs. Roby was silent for a moment; then she replied with lowered lids: "No—but a friend of mine did; a very brilliant man; and he told me it was best for women—not to . . ."

A shudder ran around the room. Mrs. Leveret coughed so that the parlour-maid, who was handing the cigarettes, should not hear; Miss Van Vluyck's face took on a nauseated expression, and Mrs. Plinth looked as if she were passing someone she did not care to bow to. But the most remarkable result of Mrs. Roby's words was the effect they produced on the Lunch Club's distinguished guest. Osric Dane's impassive features suddenly melted to an expression of the warmest human sympathy, and edging her chair toward Mrs. Roby's she asked: "Did he really? And—did you find he was right?"

Mrs. Ballinger, in whom annoyance at Mrs. Roby's unwonted assumption of prominence was beginning to displace gratitude for the aid she had rendered, could not consent to her being allowed, by such dubious means, to monopolise the attention of their guest. If Osric Dane had not enough self-respect to resent Mrs. Roby's flippancy, at least the Lunch Club would do so in the person of its President.

Mrs. Ballinger laid her hand on Mrs. Roby's arm. "We must not forget," she said with a frigid amiability, "that absorbing as Xingu is to *us*, it may be less interesting to—"

"Oh, no, on the contrary, I assure you," Osric Dane energetically intervened.

"—to others," Mrs. Ballinger finished firmly; "and we must not allow our little meeting to end without persuading Mrs. Dane to say a few words to us on a subject which, today, is much more present in all our thoughts. I refer, of course, to *The Wings of Death*."

The other members, animated by various degrees of the same sentiment, and encouraged by the humanised mien of their redoubtable guest, repeated after Mrs. Ballinger: "Oh, yes, you really *must* talk to us a little about your book."

Osric Dane's expression became as bored, though not as haughty, as when her work had been previously mentioned. But before she could respond to Mrs. Ballinger's request, Mrs. Roby had risen from her seat, and was pulling her veil down over her frivolous nose.

"I'm so sorry," she said, advancing toward her hostess with outstretched hand, "but before Mrs. Dane begins I think I'd better run away. Unluckily, as you know, I haven't read her books, so I should be at a terrible disadvantage among you all; and besides, I've an engagement to play bridge."

If Mrs. Roby had simply pleaded her ignorance of Osric Dane's works as a reason for withdrawing, the Lunch Club, in view of her recent prowess, might have approved such evidence of discretion; but to couple this excuse with the brazen announcement that she was foregoing the privilege for the purpose of joining a bridge-party, was only one more instance of her deplorable lack of discrimination.

The ladies were disposed, however, to feel that her departure-now that she had performed the sole service she was ever likely to render them—would probably make for greater order and dignity in the impending discussion, besides relieving them of the sense of self-distrust which her presence always mysteriously produced. Mrs. Ballinger therefore restricted herself to a formal murmur of regret, and the other members were just grouping themselves comfortably about Osric Dane when the latter, to their dismay, started up from the sofa on which she had been deferentially enthroned.

"Oh wait—do wait, and I'll go with you!" she called out to Mrs. Roby; and, seizing the hands of the disconcerted members, she administered a series of farewell pressures with the mechanical haste of a railway-conductor punching tickets.

"I'm so sorry—I'd quite forgotten—" she flung back at them from the threshold; and as she joined Mrs. Roby, who had turned in surprise at her appeal, the other ladies had the mortification of hearing her say, in a voice which she did not take the pains to lower: "If you'll let me walk a little way with you, I should so like to ask you a few more questions about Xingu . . ."

3

The incident had been so rapid that the door closed on the departing pair before the other members had had time to understand what was happening. Then a sense of the indignity put upon them by Osric

Dane's unceremonious desertion began to contend with the confused feeling that they had been cheated out of their due without exactly knowing how or why.

There was an awkward silence, during which Mrs. Ballinger, with a perfunctory hand, rearranged the skilfully grouped literature at which her distinguished guest had not so much as glanced; then Miss Van Vluyck tartly pronounced: "Well, I can't say that I consider Osric Dane's departure a great loss."

This confession crystallised the fluid resentment of the other members, and Mrs. Leveret exclaimed: "I do believe she came on purpose to be nasty!"

It was Mrs. Plinth's private opinion that Osric Dane's attitude toward the Lunch Club might have been very different had it welcomed her in the majestic setting of the Plinth drawing-rooms; but not liking to reflect on the inadequacy of Mrs. Ballinger's establishment she sought a round-about satisfaction in depreciating her *savoir faire.*

"I said from the first that we ought to have had a subject ready. It's what always happens when you're unprepared. Now if we'd only got up Xingu—"

The slowness of Mrs. Plinth's mental processes was always allowed for by the club; but this instance of it was too much for Mrs. Ballinger's equanimity.

"Xingu!" she scoffed. "Why, it was the fact of our knowing so much more about it than she did—unprepared though we were—that made Osric Dane so furious. I should have thought that was plain enough to everybody!"

This retort impressed even Mrs. Plinth, and Laura Glyde, moved by an impulse of generosity, said: "Yes, we really ought to be grateful to Mrs. Roby for introducing the topic. It may have made Osric Dane furious, but at least it made her civil."

"I am glad we were able to show her," added Miss Van Vluyck, "that a broad and up-to-date culture is not confined to the great intellectual centres."

This increased the satisfaction of the other members, and they began to forget their wrath against Osric Dane in the pleasure of having contributed to her defeat.

Miss Van Vluyck thoughtfully rubbed her spectacles. "What surprised me most," she continued, "was that Fanny Roby should be so up on Xingu."

This frank admission threw a slight chill on the company, but Mrs.

Ballinger said with an air of indulgent irony: "Mrs. Roby always has the knack of making a little go a long way; still, we certainly owe her a debt for happening to remember that she'd heard of Xingu." And this was felt by the other members to be a graceful way of cancelling once for all the Club's obligation to Mrs. Roby.

Even Mrs. Leveret took courage to speed a timid shaft of irony: "I fancy Osric Dane hardly expected to take a lesson in Xingu at Hillbridge!"

Mrs. Ballinger smiled. "When she asked me what we represented-do you remember?—I wish I'd simply said we represented Xingu!"

All the ladies laughed appreciatively at this sally, except Mrs. Plinth, who said, after a moment's deliberation: "I'm not sure it would have been wise to do so."

Mrs. Ballinger, who was already beginning to feel as if she had launched at Osric Dane the retort which had just occurred to her, looked ironically at Mrs. Plinth. "May I ask why?" she enquired.

Mrs. Plinth looked grave. "Surely," she said, "I understood from Mrs. Roby herself that the subject was one it was as well not to go into too deeply?"

Miss Van Vluyck rejoined with precision: "I think that applied only to an investigation of the origin of the—of the—"; and suddenly she found that her usually accurate memory had failed her. "It's a part of the subject I never studied myself," she concluded lamely.

"Nor I," said Mrs. Ballinger.

Laura Glyde bent toward them with widened eyes. "And yet it seems—doesn't it?—the part that is fullest of an esoteric fascination?"

"I don't know on what you base that," said Miss Van Vluyck argumentatively.

"Well, didn't you notice how intensely interested Osric Dane became as soon as she heard what the brilliant foreigner—he *was* a foreigner, wasn't he?—had told Mrs. Roby about the origin—the origin of the rite—or whatever you call it?"

Mrs. Plinth looked disapproving, and Mrs. Ballinger visibly wavered. Then she said in a decisive tone: "It may not be desirable to touch on the—on that part of the subject in general conversation; but, from the importance it evidently has to a woman of Osric Dane's distinction, I feel as if we ought not to be afraid to discuss it among ourselves—without gloves—though with closed doors, if necessary."

"I'm quite of your opinion," Miss Van Vluyck came briskly to her support; "on condition, that is, that all grossness of language is avoided."

"Oh, I'm sure we shall understand without that," Mrs. Leveret tittered; and Laura Glyde added significantly: "I fancy we can read between the lines," while Mrs. Ballinger rose to assure herself that the doors were really closed.

Mrs. Plinth had not yet given her adhesion. "I hardly see," she began, "what benefit is to be derived from investigating such peculiar customs—"

But Mrs. Ballinger's patience had reached the extreme limit of tension. "This at least," she returned; "that we shall not be placed again in the humiliating position of finding ourselves less up on our own subjects than Fanny Roby!"

Even to Mrs. Plinth this argument was conclusive. She peered furtively about the room and lowered her commanding tones to ask: "Have you got a copy?"

"A—a copy?" stammered Mrs. Ballinger. She was aware that the other members were looking at her expectantly, and that this answer was inadequate, so she supported it by asking another question. "A copy of what?"

Her companions bent their expectant gaze on Mrs. Plinth, who, in turn, appeared less sure of herself than usual. "Why, of—of—the book," she explained.

"What book?" snapped Miss Van Vluyck, almost as sharply as Osric Dane.

Mrs. Ballinger looked at Laura Glyde, whose eyes were interrogatively fixed on Mrs. Leveret. The fact of being deferred to was so new to the latter that it filled her with an insane temerity. "Why, Xingu, of course!" she exclaimed.

A profound silence followed this direct challenge to the resources of Mrs. Ballinger's library, and the latter, after glancing nervously toward the Books of the Day, returned in a deprecating voice: "It's not a thing one cares to leave about."

"I should think *not*!" exclaimed Mrs. Plinth.

"It *is* a book, then?" said Miss Van Vluyck.

This again threw the company into disarray, and Mrs. Ballinger, with an impatient sigh, rejoined: "Why—there *is* a book-naturally . . ."

"Then why did Miss Glyde call it a religion?"

Laura Glyde started up. "A religion? I never—"

"Yes, you did," Miss Van Vluyck insisted; "you spoke of rites; and Mrs. Plinth said it was a custom."

Miss Glyde was evidently making a desperate effort to reinforce her statement; but accuracy of detail was not her strongest point. At length she began in a deep murmur: "Surely they used to do something of the kind at the Eleusinian mysteries—"

"Oh—" said Miss Van Vluyck, on the verge of disapproval; and Mrs. Plinth protested: "I understood there was to be no indelicacy!"

Mrs. Ballinger could not control her irritation. "Really, it is too bad that we should not be able to talk the matter over quietly among ourselves. Personally, I think that if one goes into Xingu at all—"

"Oh, so do I!" cried Miss Glyde.

"And I don't see how one can avoid doing so, if one wishes to keep up with the Thought of the Day—"

Mrs. Leveret uttered an exclamation of relief. "There—that's it!" she interposed.

"What's it?" the President curtly took her up.

"Why—it's a—a Thought: I mean a philosophy."

This seemed to bring a certain relief to Mrs. Ballinger and Laura Glyde, but Miss Van Vluyck said dogmatically: "Excuse me if I tell you that you're all mistaken. Xingu happens to be a language."

"A language!" the Lunch Club cried.

"Certainly. Don't you remember Fanny Roby's saying that there were several branches, and that some were hard to trace? What could that apply to but dialects?"

Mrs. Ballinger could no longer restrain a contemptuous laugh. "Really, if the Lunch Club has reached such a pass that it has to go to Fanny Roby for instruction on a subject like Xingu, it had almost better cease to exist!"

"It's really her fault for not being clearer," Laura Glyde put in.

"Oh, clearness and Fanny Roby!" Mrs. Ballinger shrugged. "I daresay we shall find she was mistaken on almost every point."

"Why not look it up?" said Mrs. Plinth.

As a rule this recurrent suggestion of Mrs. Plinth's was ignored in the heat of discussion, and only resorted to afterward in the privacy of each member's home. But on the present occasion the desire to ascribe their own confusion of thought to the vague and contradictory nature of Mrs. Roby's statements caused the members of the Lunch Club to utter a collective demand for a book of reference.

At this point the production of her treasured volume gave Mrs. Leveret, for a moment, the unusual experience of occupying the centre front; but she was not able to hold it long, for *Appropriate Allusions* contained no mention of Xingu.

"Oh, that's not the kind of thing we want!" exclaimed Miss Van Vluyck. She cast a disparaging glance over Mrs. Ballinger's assortment of literature, and added impatiently: "Haven't you any useful books?"

"Of course I have," replied Mrs. Ballinger indignantly; "but I keep them in my husband's dressing-room."

From this region, after some difficulty and delay, the parlourmaid produced the W-Z volume of an *Encyclopaedia* and, in deference to the fact that the demand for it had come from Miss Van Vluyck, laid the ponderous tome before her.

There was a moment of painful suspense while Miss Van Vluyck rubbed her spectacles, adjusted them, and turned to Z; and a murmur of surprise when she said: "It isn't here."

"I suppose," said Mrs. Plinth, "it's not fit to be put in a book of reference."

"Oh, nonsense!" exclaimed Mrs. Ballinger. "Try X."

Miss Van Vluyck turned back through the volume, peering short-sightedly up and down the pages, till she came to a stop and remained motionless, like a dog on a point.

"Well, have you found it?" Mrs. Ballinger enquired, after a considerable delay.

"Yes. I've found it," said Miss Van Vluyck in a queer voice.

Mrs. Plinth hastily interposed: "I beg you won't read it aloud if there's anything offensive."

Miss Van Vluyck, without answering, continued her silent scrutiny.

"Well, what *is* it?" exclaimed Laura Glyde excitedly.

"*Do* tell us!" urged Mrs. Leveret, feeling that she would have something awful to tell her sister.

Miss Van Vluyck pushed the volume aside and turned slowly toward the expectant group.

"It's a river."

"A *river*?"

"Yes: in Brazil. Isn't that where she's been living?"

"Who? Fanny Roby? Oh, but you must be mistaken. You've been reading the wrong thing," Mrs. Ballinger exclaimed, leaning over her to seize the volume.

"It's the only *Xingu* in the *Encyclopaedia*; and she *has* been living in Brazil," Miss Van Vluyck persisted.

"Yes: her brother has a consulship there," Mrs. Leveret eagerly interposed.

"But it's too ridiculous! I—we—why we *all* remember studying

Xingu last year—or the year before last," Mrs. Ballinger stammered.

"I thought I did when *you* said so," Laura Glyde avowed.

"I said so?" cried Mrs. Ballinger.

"Yes. You said it had crowded everything else out of your mind."

"Well, *you* said it had changed your whole life!"

"For that matter, Miss Van Vluyck said she had never grudged the time she'd given it."

Mrs. Plinth interposed: "I made it clear that I knew nothing whatever of the original."

Mrs. Ballinger broke off the dispute with a groan. "Oh, what does it all matter if she's been making fools of us? I believe Miss Van Vluyck's right—she was talking of the river all the while!"

"How could she? It's too preposterous," Miss Glyde exclaimed.

"Listen." Miss Van Vluyck had repossessed herself of the *Encyclopaedia*, and restored her spectacles to a nose reddened by excitement. "'The Xingu, one of the principal rivers of Brazil, rises on the plateau of Mato Grosso, and flows in a northerly direction for a length of no less than one thousand one hundred and eighteen miles, entering the Amazon near the mouth of the latter river. The upper course of the Xingu is auriferous and fed by numerous branches. Its source was first discovered in 1884 by the German explorer von den Steinen, after a difficult and dangerous expedition through a region inhabited by tribes still in the Stone Age of culture.'"

The ladies received this communication in a state of stupefied silence from which Mrs. Leveret was the first to rally. "She certainly *did* speak of its having branches."

The word seemed to snap the last thread of their incredulity. "And of its great length," gasped Mrs. Ballinger.

"She said it was awfully deep, and you couldn't skip—you just had to wade through," Miss Glyde subjoined.

The idea worked its way more slowly through Mrs. Plinth's compact resistances. "How could there be anything improper about a river?" she inquired.

"Improper?"

"Why, what she said about the source—that it was corrupt?"

"Not corrupt, but hard to get at," Laura Glyde corrected. "Someone who'd been there had told her so. I daresay it was the explorer himself—doesn't it say the expedition was dangerous?"

"'Difficult and dangerous,'" read Miss Van Vluyck.

Mrs. Ballinger pressed her hands to her throbbing temples. "There's nothing she said that wouldn't apply to a river—to this river!" She swung about excitedly to the other members. "Why, do you remember her telling us that she hadn't read *The Supreme Instant* because she'd taken it on a boating party while she was staying with her brother, and someone had 'shied' it overboard-'shied' of course was her own expression?"

The ladies breathlessly signified that the expression had not escaped them.

"Well—and then didn't she tell Osric Dane that one of her books was simply saturated with Xingu? Of course it was, if some of Mrs. Roby's rowdy friends had thrown it into the river!"

This surprising reconstruction of the scene in which they had just participated left the members of the Lunch Club inarticulate. At length Mrs. Plinth, after visibly labouring with the problem, said in a heavy tone: "Osric Dane was taken in too."

Mrs. Leveret took courage at this. "Perhaps that's what Mrs. Roby did it for. She said Osric Dane was a brute, and she may have wanted to give her a lesson."

Miss Van Vluyck frowned. "It was hardly worthwhile to do it at our expense."

"At least," said Miss Glyde with a touch of bitterness, "she succeeded in interesting her, which was more than we did."

"What chance had we?" rejoined Mrs. Ballinger. "Mrs. Roby monopolised her from the first. And *that*, I've no doubt, was her purpose—to give Osric Dane a false impression of her own standing in the club. She would hesitate at nothing to attract attention: we all know how she took in poor Professor Foreland."

"She actually makes him give bridge-teas every Thursday," Mrs. Leveret piped up.

Laura Glyde struck her hands together. "Why, this is Thursday, and it's *there* she's gone, of course; and taken Osric with her!"

"And they're shrieking over us at this moment," said Mrs. Ballinger between her teeth.

This possibility seemed too preposterous to be admitted. "She would hardly dare," said Miss Van Vluyck, "confess the imposture to Osric Dane."

"I'm not so sure: I thought I saw her make a sign as she left. If she hadn't made a sign, why should Osric Dane have rushed out after her?"

"Well, you know, we'd all been telling her how wonderful Xingu was, and she said she wanted to find out more about it," Mrs. Leveret said, with a tardy impulse of justice to the absent.

This reminder, far from mitigating the wrath of the other members, gave it a stronger impetus.

"Yes—and that's exactly what they're both laughing over now," said Laura Glyde ironically.

Mrs. Plinth stood up and gathered her expensive furs about her monumental form. "I have no wish to criticise," she said; "but unless the Lunch Club can protect its members against the recurrence of such—such unbecoming scenes, I for one—"

"Oh, so do I!" agreed Miss Glyde, rising also.

Miss Van Vluyck closed the *Encyclopaedia* and proceeded to button herself into her jacket. "My time is really too valuable—" she began.

"I fancy we are all of one mind," said Mrs. Ballinger, looking searchingly at Mrs. Leveret, who looked at the others.

"I always deprecate anything like a scandal—" Mrs. Plinth continued.

"She has been the cause of one today!" exclaimed Miss Glyde.

Mrs. Leveret moaned: "I don't see how she *could*!" and Miss Van Vluyck said, picking up her note-book: "Some women stop at nothing."

"—but if," Mrs. Plinth took up her argument impressively, "anything of the kind had happened in *my* house" (it never would have, her tone implied), "I should have felt that I owed it to myself either to ask for Mrs. Roby's resignation—or to offer mine."

"Oh, Mrs. Plinth—" gasped the Lunch Club.

"Fortunately for me," Mrs. Plinth continued with an awful magnanimity, "the matter was taken out of my hands by our President's decision that the right to entertain distinguished guests was a privilege vested in her office; and I think the other members will agree that, as she was alone in this opinion, she ought to be alone in deciding on the best way of effacing its—its really deplorable consequences."

A deep silence followed this unexpected outbreak of Mrs. Plinth's long-stored resentment.

"I don't see why I should be expected to ask her to resign—" Mrs. Ballinger at length began; but Laura Glyde turned back to remind her: "You know she made you say that you'd got on swimmingly in Xingu."

An ill-timed giggle escaped from Mrs. Leveret, and Mrs. Ballinger energetically continued "—but you needn't think for a moment that

I'm afraid to!"

The door of the drawing-room closed on the retreating backs of the Lunch Club, and the President of that distinguished association, seating herself at her writing-table, and pushing away a copy of *The Wings of Death* to make room for her elbow, drew forth a sheet of the club's note-paper, on which she began to write: "My dear Mrs. Roby—"

The Choice

1

Stilling, that night after dinner, had surpassed himself. He always did, Wrayford reflected, when the small fry from Highfield came to dine. He, Cobham Stilling, who had to find his bearings and keep to his level in the big heedless ironic world of New York, dilated and grew vast in the congenial medium of Highfield. The Red House was the biggest house of the Highfield summer colony, and Cobham Stilling was its biggest man. No one else within a radius of a hundred miles (on a conservative estimate) had as many horses, as many green-houses, as many servants, and assuredly no one else had three motors and a motor-boat for the lake.

The motor-boat was Stilling's latest hobby, and he rode—or steered—it in and out of the conversation all the evening, to the obvious edification of everyone present save his wife and his visitor, Austin Wrayford. The interest of the latter two who, from opposite ends of the drawing-room, exchanged a fleeting glance when Stilling again launched his craft on the thin current of the talk—the interest of Mrs. Stilling and Wrayford had already lost its edge by protracted contact with the subject.

But the dinner-guests—the Rector, Mr. Swordsley, his wife Mrs. Swordsley, Lucy and Agnes Granger, their brother Addison, and young Jack Emmerton from Harvard were all, for divers reasons, stirred to the proper pitch of feeling. Mr. Swordsley, no doubt, was saying to himself: "If my good parishioner here can afford to buy a motor-boat, in addition to all the other expenditures which an establishment like this must entail, I certainly need not scruple to appeal to him again for a contribution for our Galahad Club."

The Granger girls, meanwhile, were evoking visions of lakeside picnics, not unadorned with the presence of young Mr. Emmerton;

while that youth himself speculated as to whether his affable host would let him, when he came back on his next vacation, "learn to run the thing himself"; and Mr. Addison Granger, the elderly bachelor brother of the volatile Lucy and Agnes, mentally formulated the precise phrase in which, in his next letter to his cousin Professor Spildyke of the University of East Latmos, he should allude to "our last delightful trip in my old friend Cobham Stilling's ten-thousand-dollar motor-launch"—for East Latmos was still in that primitive stage of culture on which five figures impinge.

Isabel Stilling, sitting beside Mrs. Swordsley, her bead slightly bent above the needlework with which on these occasions it was her old-fashioned habit to employ herself—Isabel also had doubtless her reflections to make. As Wrayford leaned back in his corner and looked at her across the wide flower-filled drawing-room he noted, first of all—for the how many hundredth time?—the play of her hands above the embroidery-frame, the shadow of the thick dark hair on her forehead, the lids over her somewhat full grey eyes. He noted all this with a conscious deliberateness of enjoyment, taking in unconsciously, at the same time, the particular quality in her attitude, in the fall of her dress and the turn of her head, which had set her for him, from the first day, in a separate world; then he said to himself: "She is certainly thinking: 'Where on earth will Cobham get the money to pay for it?'"

Stilling, cigar in mouth and thumbs in his waistcoat pockets, was impressively perorating from his usual dominant position on the hearth-rug.

"I said: 'If I have the thing at all, I want the best that can be got.' That's my way, you know, Swordsley; I suppose I'm what you'd call fastidious. Always was, about everything, from cigars to wom—" his eye met the apprehensive glance of Mrs. Swordsley, who looked like her husband with his clerical coat cut slightly lower—"so I said: 'If I have the thing at all, I want the best that can be got.' Nothing makeshift for me, no second-best. I never cared for the cheap and showy. I always say frankly to a man: 'If you can't give me a first-rate cigar, for the Lord's sake let me smoke my own.'"

He paused to do so. "Well, if you have my standards, you can't buy a thing in a minute. You must look round, compare, select. I found there were lots of motor-boats on the market, just as there's lots of stuff called champagne. But I said to myself: 'Ten to one there's only one fit to buy, just as there's only one champagne fit for a gentleman to drink.' Argued like a lawyer, eh, Austin?" He tossed this to Wrayford. "Take me for one of your own trade, wouldn't you? Well, I'm not such a fool as I look. I suppose you fellows who are tied to the treadmill—excuse me, Swordsley, but work's work, isn't it?—I suppose you think a man like me has nothing to do but take it easy: loll through life like a woman. By George, sir, I'd like either of you to see the time it takes—I won't say the *brain*—but just the time it takes to pick out a good motor-boat. Why, I went—"

Mrs. Stilling set her embroidery-frame noiselessly on the table at her side, and turned her head toward Wrayford. "Would you mind ringing for the tray?"

The interruption helped Mrs. Swordsley to waver to her feet. "I'm afraid we ought really to be going; my husband has an early service tomorrow."

Her host intervened with a genial protest. "Going already? Nothing of the sort! Why, the night's still young, as the poet says. Long way from here to the rectory? Nonsense! In our little twenty-horse car we do it in five minutes—don't we, Belle? Ah, you're walking, to be sure—" Stilling's indulgent gesture seemed to concede that, in such a case, allowances must be made, and that he was the last man not to make them. "Well, then, Swordsley—" He held out a thick red hand that seemed to exude beneficence, and the clergyman, pressing it, ventured to murmur a suggestion.

"What, that Galahad Club again? Why, I thought my wife—Isabel, didn't we—No? Well, it must have been my mother, then. Of course, you know, anything my good mother gives is—well—virtually—You haven't asked her? Sure? I could have sworn; I get so many of these appeals. And in these times, you know, we have to go cautiously. I'm sure you recognize that yourself, Swordsley. With my obligations—here now, to show you don't bear malice, have a brandy and soda before you go. Nonsense, man! This brandy isn't liquor; it's liqueur. I picked it up last year in London—last of a famous lot from Lord St. Oswyn's cellar. Laid down here, it stood me at—Eh?" he broke off as his wife moved toward him. "Ah, yes, of course. Miss Lucy, Miss Agnes—a drop of soda-water? Look here, Addison, you won't refuse my tipple, I know. Well, take a cigar, at any rate, Swordsley.

"And, by the way, I'm afraid you'll have to go round the long way by the avenue tonight. Sorry, Mrs. Swordsley, but I forgot to tell them to leave the gate into the lane unlocked. Well, it's a jolly night, and I daresay you won't mind the extra turn along the lake. And, by Jove! if the moon's out, you'll have a glimpse of the motorboat. She's moored just out beyond our boat-house; and it's a privilege to look at her, I can tell you!"

The dispersal of his guests carried Stilling out into the hall, where his pleasantries reverberated under the oak rafters while the Granger girls were being muffled for the drive and the carriages summoned from the stables.

By a common impulse Mrs. Stilling and Wrayford had moved together toward the fireplace, which was hidden by a tall screen from the door into the hall. Wrayford leaned his elbow against the mantelpiece, and Mrs. Stilling stood beside him, her clasped hands hanging down before her.

"Have you anything more to talk over with him?" she asked.

"No. We wound it all up before dinner. He doesn't want to talk about it anymore than he can help."

"It's so bad?"

"No; but this time he's got to pull up."

She stood silent, with lowered lids. He listened a moment, catching Stilling's farewell shout; then he moved a little nearer, and laid his hand on her arm.

"In an hour?"

She made an imperceptible motion of assent.

"I'll tell you about it then. The key's as usual?"

She signed another "Yes" and walked away with her long drifting step as her husband came in from the hall.

He went up to the tray and poured himself out a tall glass of brandy and soda.

"The weather is turning queer—black as pitch. I hope the Swordsleys won't walk into the lake—involuntary immersion, eh? He'd come out a Baptist, I suppose. What'd the bishop do in such a case? There's a problem for a lawyer, my boy!"

He clapped his hand on Wrayford's thin shoulder and then walked over to his wife, who was gathering up her embroidery silks and dropping them into her work-bag. Stilling took her by the arms and swung her playfully about so that she faced the lamplight.

"What's the matter with you tonight?"

"The matter?" she echoed, colouring a little, and standing very straight in her desire not to appear to shrink from his touch.

"You never opened your lips. Left me the whole job of entertaining those blessed people. Didn't she, Austin?"

Wrayford laughed and lit a cigarette.

"There! You see even Austin noticed it. What's the matter, I say? Aren't they good enough for you? I don't say they're particularly exciting; but, hang it! I like to ask them here—I like to give people pleasure."

"I didn't mean to be dull," said Isabel.

"Well, you must learn to make an effort. Don't treat people as if they weren't in the room just because they don't happen to amuse you. Do you know what they'll think? They'll think it's because you've got a bigger house and more money than they have. Shall I tell you something? My mother said she'd noticed the same thing in you lately. She said she sometimes felt you looked down on her for living in a small house. Oh, she was half joking, of course; but you see you do give people that impression. I can't understand treating any one in that way. The more I have myself, the more I want to make other people happy."

Isabel gently freed herself and laid the work-bag on her embroidery-frame. "I have a headache; perhaps that made me stupid. I'm going to bed." She turned toward Wrayford and held out her hand. "Goodnight."

"Goodnight," he answered, opening the door for her.

When he turned back into the room, his host was pouring himself a third glass of brandy and soda.

"Here, have a nip, Austin? Gad, I need it badly, after the shaking up you gave me this afternoon." Stilling laughed and carried his glass to the hearth, where he took up his usual commanding position. "Why the deuce don't you drink something? You look as glum as Isabel. One would think you were the chap that had been hit by this business."

Wrayford threw himself into the chair from which Mrs. Stilling had lately risen. It was the one she usually sat in, and to his fancy a faint scent of her clung to it. He leaned back and looked up at Stilling.

"Want a cigar?" the latter continued. "Shall we go into the den and smoke?"

Wrayford hesitated. "If there's anything more you want to ask me about—"

"Gad, no! I had full measure and running over this afternoon. The deuce of it is, I don't see where the money's all gone to. Luckily I've got plenty of nerve; I'm not the kind of man to sit down and snivel because I've been touched in Wall Street."

Wrayford got to his feet again. "Then, if you don't want me, I think I'll go up to my room and put some finishing touches to a brief before

I turn in. I must get back to town tomorrow afternoon."

"All right, then." Stilling set down his empty glass, and held out his hand with a tinge of alacrity. "Goodnight, old man."

They shook hands, and Wrayford moved toward the door.

"I say, Austin—stop a minute!" his host called after him. Wrayford turned, and the two men faced each other across the hearth-rug. Stilling's eyes shifted uneasily.

"There's one thing more you can do for me before you leave. Tell Isabel about that loan; explain to her that she's got to sign a note for it."

Wrayford, in his turn, flushed slightly. "You want me to tell her?"

"Hang it! I'm soft-hearted—that's the worst of me."

Stilling moved toward the tray, and lifted the brandy decanter. "And she'll take it better from you; she'll *have* to take it from you. She's proud. You can take her out for a row tomorrow morning—look here, take her out in the motor-launch if you like. I meant to have a spin in it myself; but if you'll tell her—"

Wrayford hesitated. "All right, I'll tell her."

"Thanks a lot, my dear fellow. And you'll make her see it wasn't my fault, eh? Women are awfully vague about money, and she'll think it's all right if you back me up."

Wrayford nodded. "As you please."

"And, Austin—there's just one more thing. You needn't say anything to Isabel about the other business—I mean about my mother's securities."

"Ah?" said Wrayford, pausing.

Stilling shifted from one foot to the other. "I'd rather put that to the old lady myself. I can make it clear to her. She idolizes me, you know—and, hang it! I've got a good record. Up to now, I mean. My mother's been in clover since I married; I may say she's been my first thought. And I don't want her to hear of this beastly business from Isabel. Isabel's a little harsh at times—and of course this isn't going to make her any easier to live with."

"Very well," said Wrayford.

Stilling, with a look of relief, walked toward the window which opened on the terrace. "Gad! what a queer night! Hot as the kitchen-range. Shouldn't wonder if we had a squall before morning. I wonder if that infernal skipper took in the launch's awnings before he went home."

Wrayford stopped with his hand on the door. "Yes, I saw him do it.

She's shipshape for the night."

"Good! That saves me a run down to the shore."

"Goodnight, then," said Wrayford.

"Goodnight, old man. You'll tell her?"

"I'll tell her."

"And mum about my mother!" his host called after him.

2

The darkness had thinned a little when Wrayford scrambled down the steep path to the shore. Though the air was heavy the threat of a storm seemed to have vanished, and now and then the moon's edge showed above a torn slope of cloud.

But in the thick shrubbery about the boat-house the darkness was still dense, and Wrayford had to strike a match before he could find the lock and insert his key. He left the door unlatched, and groped his way in. How often he had crept into this warm pine-scented obscurity, guiding himself by the edge of the bench along the wall, and hearing the soft lap of water through the gaps in the flooring! He knew just where one had to duck one's head to avoid the two canoes swung from the rafters, and just where to put his hand on the latch of the farther door that led to the broad balcony above the lake.

The boat-house represented one of Stilling's abandoned whims. He had built it some seven years before, and for a time it had been the scene of incessant nautical exploits. Stilling had rowed, sailed, paddled indefatigably, and all Highfield had been impressed to bear him company, and to admire his versatility. Then motors had come in, and he had forsaken aquatic sports for the flying chariot. The canoes of birch-bark and canvas had been hoisted to the roof, the sail-boat had rotted at her moorings, and the movable floor of the boat-house, ingeniously contrived to slide back on noiseless runners, had lain undisturbed through several seasons. Even the key of the boat-house had been mislaid—by Isabel's fault, her husband said—and the locksmith had to be called in to make a new one when the purchase of the motor-boat made the lake once more the centre of Stilling's activity.

As Wrayford entered he noticed that a strange oily odour overpowered the usual scent of dry pine-wood; and at the next step his foot struck an object that rolled noisily across the boards. He lighted another match, and found he had overturned a can of grease which the boatman had no doubt been using to oil the runners of the sliding floor.

Wrayford felt his way down the length of the boathouse, and softly opening the balcony door looked out on the lake. A few yards away, he saw the launch lying at anchor in the veiled moonlight; and just below him, on the black water, was the dim outline of the skiff which the boatman kept to paddle out to her. The silence was so intense that Wrayford fancied he heard a faint rustling in the shrubbery on the high bank behind the boat-house, and the crackle of gravel on the path descending to it.

He closed the door again and turned back into the darkness; and as he did so the other door, on the land-side, swung inward, and he saw a figure in the dim opening. Just enough light entered through the round holes above the respective doors to reveal Mrs. Stilling's cloaked outline, and to guide her to him as he advanced. But before they met she stumbled and gave a little cry.

"What is it?" he exclaimed.

"My foot caught; the floor seemed to give way under me. Ah, of course—" she bent down in the darkness—"I saw the men oiling it this morning."

Wrayford caught her by the arm. "Do take care! It might be dangerous if it slid too easily. The water's deep under here."

"Yes; the water's very deep. I sometimes wish—" She leaned against him without finishing her sentence, and he put both arms about her.

"Hush!" he said, his lips on hers.

Suddenly she threw her head back and seemed to listen.

"What's the matter? What do you hear?"

"I don't know." He felt her trembling. "I'm not sure this place is as safe as it used to be—"

Wrayford held her to him reassuringly. "But the boatman sleeps down at the village; and who else should come here at this hour?"

"Cobham might. He thinks of nothing but the launch.'"

"He won't tonight. I told him I'd seen the skipper put her shipshape, and that satisfied him."

"Ah—he did think of coming, then?"

"Only for a minute, when the sky looked so black half an hour ago, and he was afraid of a squall. It's clearing now, and there's no danger."

He drew her down on the bench, and they sat a moment or two in silence, her hands in his. Then she said: "You'd better tell me."

Wrayford gave a faint laugh. "Yes, I suppose I had. In fact, he asked me to."

"He asked you to?"

"Yes."

She uttered an exclamation of contempt. "He's afraid!"

Wrayford made no reply, and she went on: "I'm not. Tell me everything, please."

"Well, he's chucked away a pretty big sum again—"

"How?"

"He says he doesn't know. He's been speculating, I suppose. The madness of making him your trustee!"

She drew her hands away. "You know why I did it. When we married I didn't want to put him in the false position of the man who contributes nothing and accepts everything; I wanted people to think the money was partly his."

"I don't know what you've made people think; but you've been eminently successful in one respect. *He* thinks it's all his—and he loses it as if it were."

"There are worse things. What was it that he wished you to tell me?"

"That you've got to sign another promissory note—for fifty thousand this time."

"Is that all?"

Wrayford hesitated; then he said: "Yes—for the present."

She sat motionless, her head bent, her hand resting passively in his.

He leaned nearer. "What did you' mean just now, by worse things?"

She hesitated. "Haven't you noticed that he's been drinking a great deal lately?"

"Yes; I've noticed."

They were both silent; then Wrayford broke out, with sudden vehemence: "And yet you won't—"

"Won't?"

"Put an end to it. Good God! Save what's left of your life."

She made no answer, and in the stillness the throb of the water underneath them sounded like the beat of a tormented heart.

"Isabel—" Wrayford murmured. He bent over to kiss her. "Isabel! I can't stand it! listen—"

"No; no. I've thought of everything. There's the boy—the boy's fond of him. He's not a bad father."

"Except in the trifling matter of ruining his son."

"And there's his poor old mother. He's a good son, at any rate; he'd never hurt her. And I know her. If I left him, she'd never take a penny of my money. What she has of her own is not enough to live on; and how could he provide for her? If I put him out of doors, I should be putting his mother out too."

"You could arrange that—there are always ways."

"Not for her! She's proud. And then she believes in him. Lots of people believe in him, you know. It would kill her if she ever found out."

Wrayford made an impatient movement. "It will kill you if you stay with him to prevent her finding out."

She laid her other hand on his. "Not while I have you."

"Have me? In this way?"

"In any way."

"My poor girl—poor child!"

"Unless you grow tired—unless your patience gives out."

He was silent, and she went on insistently: "Don't you suppose I've thought of that too—foreseen it?"

"Well—and then?" he exclaimed.

"I've accepted that too."

He dropped her hands with a despairing gesture. "Then, indeed, I waste my breath!"

She made no answer, and for a time they sat silent again, a little between them. At length he asked: "You're not crying?"

"No."

"I can't see your face, it's grown so dark."

"Yes. The storm must be coming." She made a motion as if to rise.

He drew close and put his arm about her. "Don't leave me yet. You know I must go tomorrow." He broke off with a laugh. "I'm to break the news to you tomorrow morning, by the way; I'm to take you out in the motor-launch and break it to you." He dropped her hands and stood up. "Good God! How can I go and leave you here with him?"

"You've done it often."

"Yes; but each time it's more damnable. And then I've always had a hope—"

She rose also. "Give it up! Give it up!"

"You've none, then, yourself?"

She was silent, drawing the folds of her cloak about her.

"None—none?" he insisted.

He had to bend his head to hear her answer. "Only one!"

"What, my dearest? What?"

"Don't touch me! That he may die!"

They drew apart again, hearing each other's quick breathing

through the darkness.

"You wish that too?" he said.

"I wish it always—every day, every hour, every moment!" She paused, and then let the words break from her. "You'd better know it; you'd better know the worst of me. I'm not the saint you suppose; the duty I do is poisoned by the thoughts I think. Day by day, hour by hour, I wish him dead. When he goes out I pray for something to happen; when he comes back I say to myself: 'Are you here again?' When I hear of people being killed in accidents, I think: 'Why wasn't he there?' When I read the death-notices in the paper I say: 'So-and-so was just his age.'

"When I see him taking such care of his health and his diet—as he does, you know, except when he gets reckless and begins to drink too much—when I see him exercising and resting, and eating only certain things, and weighing himself, and feeling his muscles, and boasting that he hasn't gained a pound, I think of the men who die from overwork, or who throw their lives away for some great object, and I say to myself: 'What can kill a man who thinks only of himself?' And night after night I keep myself from going to sleep for fear I may dream that he's dead. When I dream that, and wake and find him there it's worse than ever—"

She broke off with a sob, and the loud lapping of the water under the floor was like the beat of a rebellious heart.

"There, you know the truth!" she said.

He answered after a pause: "People do die."

"Do they?" She laughed. "Yes—in happy marriages!"

They were silent again, and Isabel turned, feeling her way toward the door. As she did so, the profound stillness was broken by the sound of a man's voice trolling out unsteadily the refrain of a music-hall song.

The two in the boat-house darted toward each other with a simultaneous movement, clutching hands as they met.

"He's coming!" Isabel said.

Wrayford disengaged his hands.

"He may only be out for a turn before he goes to bed. Wait a minute. I'll see." He felt his way to the bench, scrambled up on it, and stretching his body forward managed to bring his eyes in line with the opening above the door.

"It's as black as pitch. I can't see anything."

The refrain rang out nearer.

"Wait! I saw something twinkle. There it is again. It's his cigar. It's coming this way—down the path."

There was a long rattle of thunder through the stillness.

"It's the storm!" Isabel whispered. "He's coming to see about the launch."

Wrayford dropped noiselessly from the bench and she caught him by the arm.

"Isn't there time to get up the path and slip under the shrubbery?"

"No, he's in the path now. He'll be here in two minutes. He'll find us."

He felt her hand tighten on his arm.

"You must go in the skiff, then. It's the only way."

"And let him find you? And hear my oars? Listen—there's something I must say."

She flung her arms about him and pressed her face to his.

"Isabel, just now I didn't tell you everything. He's ruined his mother—taken everything of hers too. And he's got to tell her; it can't be kept from her."

She uttered an incredulous exclamation and drew back.

"Is this the truth? Why didn't you tell me before?"

"He forbade me. You were not to know."

Close above them, in the shrubbery, Stilling warbled:

"*Nita, Juanita,*

Ask thy soul if we must part!"

Wrayford held her by both arms. "Understand this—if he comes in, he'll find us. And if there's a row you'll lose your boy."

She seemed not to hear him. "You—you—you—he'll kill you!" she exclaimed.

Wrayford laughed impatiently and released her, and she stood shrinking against the wall, her hands pressed to her breast. Wrayford straightened himself and she felt that he was listening intently. Then he dropped to his knees and laid his hands against the boards of the sliding floor. It yielded at once, as if with a kind of evil alacrity; and at their feet they saw, under the motionless solid night, another darker night that moved and shimmered. Wrayford threw himself back against the opposite wall, behind the door.

A key rattled in the lock, and after a moment's fumbling the door swung open. Wrayford and Isabel saw a man's black bulk against the obscurity. It moved a step, lurched forward, and vanished out of sight. From the depths beneath them there came a splash and a long cry.

"Go! go!" Wrayford cried out, feeling blindly for Isabel in the blackness.

"Oh—" she cried, wrenching herself away from him.

He stood still a moment, as if dazed; then she saw him suddenly plunge from her side, and heard another splash far down, and a tumult in the beaten water.

In the darkness she cowered close to the opening, pressing her face over the edge, and crying out the name of each of the two men in turn. Suddenly she began to see: the obscurity was less opaque, as if a faint moon-pallor diluted it. Isabel vaguely discerned the two shapes struggling in the black pit below her; once she saw the gleam of a face. She glanced up desperately for some means of rescue, and caught sight of the oars ranged on brackets against the wall. She snatched down the nearest, bent over the opening, and pushed the oar down into the blackness, crying out her husband's name.

The clouds had swallowed the moon again, and she could see nothing below her; but she still heard the tumult in the beaten water.

"Cobham! Cobham!" she screamed.

As if in answer, she felt a mighty clutch on the oar, a clutch that strained her arms to the breaking-point as she tried to brace her knees against the runners of the sliding floor.

"Hold on! Hold on! Hold on!" a voice gasped out from below; and she held on, with racked muscles, with bleeding palms, with eyes straining from their sockets, and a heart that tugged at her as the weight was tugging at the oar.

Suddenly the weight relaxed, and the oar slipped up through her lacerated hands. She felt a wet body scrambling over the edge of the opening, and Stilling's voice, raucous and strange, groaned out, close to her: "God! I thought I was done for."

He staggered to his knees, coughing and sputtering, and the water dripped on her from his streaming clothes.

She flung herself down, again, straining over the pit. Not a sound came up from it.

"Austin! Austin! Quick! Another oar!" she shrieked.

Stilling gave a cry. "My God! Was it Austin? What in hell—Another oar? No, no; untie the skiff, I tell you. But it's no use. Nothing's any use. I felt him lose hold as I came up."

After that she was conscious of nothing till, hours later, as it appeared to her, she became dimly aware of her husband's voice, high, hysterical and important, haranguing a group of scared lantern-struck faces that had sprung up mysteriously about them in the night.

“Poor Austin! Poor Wrayford. . . . terrible loss to me. . . . mysterious dispensation. Yes, I do feel gratitude—miraculous escape—but I wish old Austin could have known that I was saved!”

The Valley of Childish Things and Other Emblems

1

Once upon a time a number of children lived together in the Valley of Childish Things, playing all manner of delightful games, and studying the same lesson-books. But one day a little girl, one of their number, decided that it was time to see something of the world about which the lesson-books had taught her; and as none of the other children cared to leave their games, she set out alone to climb the pass which led out of the valley.

It was a hard climb, but at length she reached a cold, bleak table-land beyond the mountains. Here she saw cities and men, and learned many useful arts, and in so doing grew to be a woman. But the table-land was bleak and cold, and when she had served her apprenticeship she decided to return to her old companions in the Valley of Childish Things, and work with them instead of with strangers.

It was a weary way back, and her feet were bruised by the stones, and her face was beaten by the weather; but half way down the pass she met a man, who kindly helped her over the roughest places. Like herself, he was lame and weather-beaten; but as soon as he spoke she recognised him as one of her old playmates. He too had been out in the world, and was going back to the valley; and on the way they talked together of the work they meant to do there. He had been a dull boy, and she had never taken much notice of him; but as she listened to his plans for building bridges and draining swamps and cutting roads through the jungle, she thought to herself, "Since he has grown into such a fine fellow, what splendid men and women my other playmates must have become!"

But what was her surprise to find, on reaching the valley, that her former companions, instead of growing into men and women, had all remained little children. Most of them were playing the same old games, and the few who affected to be working were engaged in such strenuous occupations as building mud-pies and sailing paper boats in basins. As for the lad who had been the favourite companion of her studies, he was playing marbles with all the youngest boys in the valley.

At first, the children seemed glad to have her back, but soon she saw that her presence interfered with their games; and when she tried to tell them of the great things that were being done on the table-land beyond the mountains, they picked up their toys and went farther down the valley to play.

Then she turned to her fellow-traveller, who was the only grown man in the valley; but he was on his knees before a dear little girl with blue eyes and a coral necklace, for whom he was making a garden out of cockle-shells and bits of glass, and broken flowers stuck in sand.

The little girl was clapping her hands and crowing (she was too young to speak articulately); and when she who had grown to be a woman laid her hand on the man's shoulder, and asked him if he did not want to set to work with her building bridges, draining swamps, and cutting roads through the jungle, he replied that at that particular moment he was too busy.

And as she turned away, he added in the kindest possible way, "Really, my dear, you ought to have taken better care of your complexion."

2

There was once a maiden lady who lived alone in a commodious brick house facing north and south. The lady was very fond of warmth and sunshine, but unfortunately her room was on the north side of the house, so that in winter she had no sun at all.

This distressed her so much that, after long deliberation, she sent for an architect, and asked him if it would be possible to turn the house around so that her room should face the south. The architect replied that anything could be done for money; but the estimated cost of turning the house around was so high that the lady, who enjoyed a handsome income, was obliged to reduce her way of living and sell her securities at a sacrifice to raise money enough for the purpose.

At length, however, the house was turned around, and she felt almost consoled for her impoverishment by the first ray of sunlight which stole through her shutters the next morning.

That very day she received a visit from an old friend who had been absent a year; and this friend, finding her seated at her window in a flood of sunlight, immediately exclaimed:

"My dear, how sensible of you to have moved into a south room! I never could understand why you persisted so long in living on the north side of the house."

And the following day the architect sent in his bill.

3

There was once a little girl who was so very intelligent that her parents feared that she would die.

But an aged aunt, who had crossed the Atlantic in a sailing-vessel, said, "My dears, let her marry the first man she falls in love with, and she will make such a fool of herself that it will probably save her life."

4

A thinly clad man, who was trudging afoot through a wintry and shelterless region, met another wrapped in a big black cloak. The cloak hung heavily on its wearer, and seemed to drag him back, but at least it kept off the cold.

"That's a fine warm cloak you've got," said the first man through his chattering teeth.

"Oh," said the other, "it's none of my choosing, I promise you. It's only my old happiness dyed black and made over into a sorrow; but in this weather a man must wear what he's got."

"To think of some people's luck!" muttered the first man, as the other passed on. "Now I never had enough happiness to make a sorrow out of."

5

There was once a man who married a sweet little wife; but when he set out with her from her father's house, he found that she had never been taught to walk. They had a long way to go, and there was nothing for him to do but to carry her; and as he carried her she grew heavier and heavier.

Then they came to a wide, deep river, and he found that she had never been taught to swim. So he told her to hold fast to his shoulder, and started to swim with her across the river. And as he swam she grew frightened, and dragged him down in her struggles. And the river was deep and wide, and the current ran fast; and once or twice she nearly had him under. But he fought his way through, and landed her safely on the other side; and behold, he found himself in a strange country, beyond all imagining delightful. And as he looked about him and gave thanks, he said to himself:

"Perhaps if I hadn't had to carry her over, I shouldn't have kept up long enough to get here myself."

6

A soul once cowered in a grey waste, and a mighty shape came by. Then the soul cried out for help, saying, "Shall I be left to perish alone in this desert of Unsatisfied Desires?"

"But you are mistaken," the shape replied; "this is the land of Gratified Longings. And, moreover, you are not alone, for the country is full of people; but whoever tarries here grows blind."

7

There was once a very successful architect who made a great name for himself. At length he built a magnificent temple, to which he devoted more time and thought than to any of the other buildings he had erected; and the world pronounced it his masterpiece. Shortly afterward he died, and when he came before the judgment angel he was not asked how many sins he had committed, but how many houses he had built.

He hung his head and said, more than he could count.

The judgment angel asked what they were like, and the architect said that he was afraid they were pretty bad.

"And are you sorry?" asked the angel.

"Very sorry," said the architect, with honest contrition.

"And how about that famous temple that you built just before you died?" the angel continued. "Are you satisfied with that?"

"Oh, no," the architect exclaimed. "I really think it has some good points about it,—I did try my best, you know,—but there's one dreadful mistake that I'd give my soul to go back and rectify."

"Well," said the angel, "you can't go back and rectify it, but you can take your choice of the following alternatives: either we can let the world go on thinking your temple a masterpiece and you the greatest architect that ever lived, or we can send to earth a young fellow we've got here who will discover your mistake at a glance, and point it out so clearly to posterity that you'll be the laughing-stock of all succeeding generations of architects. Which do you choose?"

"Oh, well," said the architect, "if it comes to that, you know -- as long as it suits my clients as it is, I really don't see the use of making such a fuss."

8

A man once married a charming young person who agreed with him on every question. At first they were very happy, for the man thought his wife the most interesting companion he had ever met, and they spent their days telling each other what wonderful people they were. But by and by the man began to find his wife rather tiresome. Wherever he went she insisted upon going; whatever he did, she was sure to tell him that it would have been better to do the opposite; and moreover, it gradually dawned upon him that his friends had never thought so highly of her as he did. Having made this discovery, he naturally felt justified in regarding himself as the aggrieved party; she took the same view of her situation, and their life was one of incessant recrimination.

Finally, after years spent in violent quarrels and short-lived reconciliations, the man grew weary, and decided to divorce his wife.

He engaged an able lawyer, who assured him that he would have no difficulty in obtaining a divorce; but to his surprise, the judge refused to grant it.

"But—" said the man, and he began to recapitulate his injuries.

"That's all very true," said the judge, "and nothing would be easier than for you to obtain a divorce if you had only married another person."

"What do you mean by another person?" asked the man in astonishment.

"Well," replied the judge, "it appears that you inadvertently married yourself; that is a union no court has the power to dissolve."

"Oh, said the man; and he was secretly glad, for in his heart he was already longing to make it up again with his wife.

9

There was once a gentleman who greatly disliked to assume any responsibility. Being possessed of ample means and numerous poor relatives, he might have indulged a variety of tastes and even a few virtues; but since there is no occupation that does not bring a few cares in its train, this gentleman resolutely refrained from doing anything.

He ceased to visit his old mother, who lived in the country, because it made him nervous to catch the train; he subscribed to no charities because it was a bother to write the checks; he received no visits because he did not wish to be under the obligation of returning them; he invited no guests to stay with him, for fear of being bored before they left; he gave no presents because it was so troublesome to choose them; finally, he even gave up asking his friends to dine because it was such a nuisance to tell the cook that they were coming.

This gentleman took an honest pride in his complete detachment from the trivial importunities of life, and was never tired of ridiculing those who complained of the weight of their responsibilities, justly remarking that if they really wished to be their own masters they had only to follow his example.

One day, however, one of his servants carelessly left the front door open, and Death walked in unannounced, and begged the gentleman to come along as quickly as possible, as there were a good many more people to be called for that afternoon.

"But I can't," cried the gentleman, in dismay. "I really can't, you know. I—why, I've asked some people to dine with me this evening."

"That's a little too much," said Death. And the devil carried the gentleman off in a big black bag.

10

There was once a man who had seen the Parthenon, and he wished to build his god a temple like it.

But he was not a skilful man, and, try as he would, he could produce only a mud hut thatched with straw; and he sat down and wept because he could not build a temple for his god.

But one who passed by said to him:

"There are two worse plights than yours. One is to have no god; the other is to build a mud hut and mistake it for the Parthenon."

Velvet Ear-Pads

1

Professor Loring G. Hibbart, of Purewater University, Clio, N.Y., settled himself in the corner of his compartment in the Marseilles-Ventimiglia express, drew his velvet ear-pads from his pocket, slipped them over his ears, and began to think.

It was nearly three weeks since he had been able to indulge undisturbed in this enchanting operation. On the steamer which had brought him from Boston to Marseilles considerable opportunity had in truth been afforded him, for though he had instantly discovered his fellow-passengers to be insinuating and pervasive, an extremely rough passage had soon reduced them to inoffensiveness. Unluckily the same cause had in like manner affected the Professor; and when the ship approached calmer waters, and he began to revive, the others revived also, and proceeded to pervade, to insinuate and even to multiply—since a lady gave birth to twins as they entered the Mediterranean.

As for the tumultuous twenty-four hours since his landing, the Professor preferred not to include them in his retrospect. It was enough that they were over. "All I want is *quiet*," he had said to the doctors who, after his alarming attack of influenza, followed by bronchial pneumonia, had ordered an immediate departure for warmer climes; and they had thrust him onto an excursion-steamer jammed with noisy sight-seers, and shipped him to a port whither all the rest of the world appeared to be bound at the same moment!

His own fault, perhaps? Well—he never could plan or decide in a hurry, and when, still shaken by illness, he had suddenly been told that he must spend six months in a mild climate, and been faced with the alternatives of southern California or southern France, he had chosen the latter because it meant a more complete escape from professional associations and the terror of meeting people one knew. As far as climate went, he understood the chances to be equal; and all he wanted was to recover from his pulmonary trouble and employ his enforced leisure in writing a refutation of Einstein's newly published book on Relativity.

Once the Professor had decided on the south of France, there remained the difficulty of finding, in that populous region, a spot quiet enough to suit him; but after much anxious consultation with colleagues who shared his dread of noise and of promiscuous human intercourse, he had decided on a secluded *pension* high up in the hills, between Monte Carlo and Mentone. In this favoured spot, he was told, no dogs barked, cocks crew or cats courted. There were no waterfalls, or other sonorous natural phenomena, and it was utterly impossible for a motor (even with its muffler knocked off) to ascend the precipitous lane which led to the *pension*. If, in short, it were possible to refute Einstein's theory, it was in just such a place, and there only, that the feat might be accomplished.

Once settled in the train, the Professor breathed more freely. Most of his fellow-passengers had stayed on the ship, which was carrying them on to swarm over a succession of other places as he had just left them swarming over Marseilles. The train he got into was not very crowded, and should other travellers enter the compartment, his ear-pads would secure him from interruption. At last he could revert to the absorbing thought of the book he was planning; could plunge into it like a diver into the ocean. He drew a deep breath and plunged. . . .

Certainly the compartment had been empty when the train left Marseilles—he was sure of that; but he seemed to remember now that a man had got in at a later station, though he couldn't have said where or when; for once he began to think, time vanished from him as utterly as space.

He became conscious of the intruding presence only from the smell of tobacco gradually insinuating itself into his nostrils. Very gradually; for when the Professor had withdrawn into his inner stronghold of Pure Reason, and pulled up the ladder, it was not easy for any appeal to reach him through the channel of the senses. Not that these were defective in him. Far from it: he could smell and see, taste and hear, with any man alive; but for many years past he had refrained from exercising these faculties except in so far as they conduced to the maintenance of life and security. He would have preferred that the world should contain nothing to see, nothing to smell, nothing to hear; and by negativing persistently every superfluous hint of his visual, auditive or olfactory organs he had sheathed himself in a general impenetrability of which the ear-pads were merely a restricted symbol.

His noticing the whiff of tobacco was an accident, a symptom of his still disorganised state; he put the smell resolutely from him, registered "A Man Opposite," and plunged again into the Abstract.

Once—about an hour later, he fancied—the train stopped with a jerk which flung him abruptly out of his corner. His mental balance was disturbed, and for one irritating instant his gaze unwillingly rested on silver groves, purple promontories and a blue sea. "Ugh—*scenery!*" he muttered; and with a renewed effort of the will he dropped his mental curtain between that inconsequent jumble of phenomena and the absolutely featureless area in which the pure intellect thrones. The incident had brought back the smell of his neighbour's cigarette; but the Professor sternly excluded that also, and the train moved on. . . .

Professor Hibbart was in truth a man of passionately excitable nature: no one was ever, by temperament, less adapted to the lofty intellectual labours in which his mind delighted. He asked only to live in the empyrean; but he was perpetually being dragged back to earth by the pity, wrath or contempt excited in him by the slipshod course of human affairs. There were only two objects on which he flattered himself he could always look with a perfectly unseeing eye; and these were a romantic landscape and a pretty woman. And he was not absolutely sure about the landscape.

Suddenly a touch, soft yet peremptory, was laid on his arm. Looking down, he beheld a gloved hand; looking up he saw that the man opposite him was a woman.

To this awkward discovery he was still prepared to oppose the blank wall of the most complete imperception. But a sharp pinch proved that the lady who had taken hold of his arm had done so with the fixed determination to attract his attention, at the cost of whatever pain or inconvenience to himself. As she appeared also to be saying something—probably asking if the next station were the one at which she ought to get out—he formed with soundless lips the word "Deaf," and pointed to his ears. The lady's reply was to release his wrist, and with her free hand flick off an ear-pad.

"Deaf? Oh, no," she said briskly, in fluent but exotic English. "You wouldn't need ear-pads if you were. You don't want to be bothered—that's all. I know the trick; you got it out of Herbert Spencer!"

The assault had nearly disabled the Professor for farther resistance; but he rallied his wits and answered stonily: "I have no time-table.

You'd better consult the guard."

The lady threw her spent cigarette out of the window. As the smoke drifted away from her features he became uneasily aware that they were youthful, and that the muscles about her lips and eyes were contracted into what is currently known as a smile. In another moment, he realized with dismay, he was going to know what she looked like. He averted his eyes.

"I don't want to consult the guard—I want to consult *you*," said the lady.

His ears took reluctant note of an intonation at once gay and appealing, which caressed the "You" as if it were a new pronoun rich in vowels, and the only one of its kind in the world.

"Eeee-you," she repeated.

He shook his averted head. "I don't know the name of a single station on this line."

"Dear me, don't you?" The idea seemed to shock her, to make a peculiar appeal to her sympathy. "But I do—every one of them! With my eyes shut. Listen: I'll begin at the beginning. Paris—"

"But I don't *want* to know them!" he almost screamed.

"Well, neither do I. What I want is to ask you a favour—just one tiny little enormous favour."

The Professor still looked away. "I have been in very bad health until recently," he volunteered.

"Oh, I'm so glad—glad, I mean," she corrected herself hastily, "that you're all right again now! And glad too that you've been ill, since that just confirms it—"

Here the Professor fell. "Confirms what?" he snapped, and saw too late the trap into which he had plunged.

"My belief that you are predestined to help me," replied his neighbour with joyful conviction.

"Oh, but that's quite a mistake—a complete mistake. I never in my life helped anybody, in any way. I've always made it a rule not to."

"Not even a Russian refugee?"

"Never!"

"Oh, yes, you have. You've helped *me!*"

The Professor turned an ireful glance upon her, and she nodded. "I am a Russian refugee."

"You?" he exclaimed. His eyes, by this time, had definitely escaped from his control, and were recording with an irrepressible activity and an exasperating precision the details of her appearance and her dress.

Both were harmonious and opulent. He laughed incredulously.

"Why do you laugh? Can't you see that I'm a refugee; by my clothes, I mean? Who has such pearls but Russian refugees? Or such sables? We have to have them—to sell, of course You don't care to buy my sables, do you? For you they would be only six thousand pounds cash. No, I thought not. It's my duty to ask—but I didn't suppose they would interest you. The Paris and London jewellers farm out the pearls to us; the big dressmakers supply the furs. For of course we've all sold the originals long ago. And really I've been rather successful. I placed two sets of silver fox and a rope of pearls last week at Monte Carlo. Ah, that fatal place! I gambled away the whole of my commission the same night...But I'm forgetting to tell you how you've already helped me. . . ."

She paused to draw breath, and in the pause the Professor, who had kept his hand on his loosened ear-pad, slipped it back over his ear.

"I wear these," he said coldly, "to avoid argument."

With a flick she had it off again. "I wasn't going to argue—I was only going to thank you."

"I can't conceive for what. In any case, I don't want to be thanked."

Her brows gathered resentfully. "Why did you *ask* to be, then?" she snapped; and opening a bejewelled wrist-bag she drew forth from a smother of cigarette-papers and pawn-tickets a slip of paper on which her astonished companion read a phrase written in a pointed feminine hand, but signed with his own name.

"*There!*"

The Professor took the paper and scanned it indignantly.

> This copy of *The Elimination of Phenomena* was presented by Professor Loring G. Hibbart of Purewater University, Clio, N. Y., to the library of the American Y. M. C. A. Refugee Centre at Odessa.
>
> A word of appreciation, sent by any reader to the above address, would greatly gratify Loring G. Hibbart.

"*There!*" she repeated. "Why did you ask to be thanked if you didn't want to be? What else does 'greatly gratify' mean? I couldn't write to you from Odessa because I hadn't the money to buy a stamp; but I've longed ever since to tell you what your book did for me. It simply changed my whole life—books do sometimes, you know. I saw everything differently—even our Refugee Centre! I decided at once to give up my lover and divorce my husband. Those were my two first

Eliminations." She smiled retrospectively. "But you mustn't think I'm a frivolous person. I have my degree as a Doctor of Philosophy—I took it at sixteen, at the University of Moscow. I gave up philosophy the year after for sculpture; the next year I gave up sculpture for mathematics and love. For a year I loved. After that I married Prince Balalatinsky. He was my cousin, and enormously wealthy. I need not have divorced him, as it turned out, for he was soon afterward buried alive by the Bolsheviks. But how could I have foreseen it? And your book had made me feel—"

"Good gracious!" the author of the book interrupted desperately. "You don't suppose *I* wrote that rubbish about wanting to be thanked, do you?"

"Didn't you? How could I tell? Almost all the things sent from America to the refugee camp came with little labels like that. You all seemed to think we were sitting before perfectly appointed desks, with fountain pens and stamp-cases from Bond Street in our pockets. I remember once getting a lipstick and a Bernard Shaw calendar labelled: 'If the refugee who receives these would write a line of thanks to little Sadie Burt of Meropee Junction, Ga., who bought them out of her own savings by giving up chewing-gum for a whole month, it would make a little American girl very happy.' Of course I was sorry not to be able to write to little Sadie." She broke off, and then added: "Do you know, I was sure you were my Professor as soon as I saw your name on your suit-case?"

"Good Lord!" groaned the Professor.

He had forgotten to remove the obligatory steamer-labels! Instinctively he reached out a hand to tear off the offending member; but again a gesture of the Princess's arrested him. "It's too late now. And you can't surely grudge me the pleasure of thanking you for your book?"

"But I *didn't* ask—"

"No; but I wanted to. You see, at that time I had quite discarded philosophy. I was living in the Actual—with a young officer of Preobrajensky—when the war broke out. And of course in our camp at Odessa the Actual was the very thing one wanted to get away from. And your book took me straight back into that other world where I had known my only pure happiness. Purity—what a wonderful thing it is! What a pity it is so hard to keep; like money, and everything else really valuable! But I'm thankful for any little morsel of it that I've had. When I was only ten years old—"

But suddenly she drew back and nestled down into her lustrous furs. "You thought I was going to tell you the story of my life? No. Put your ear-pads on again. I know now why you wear them—because you're planning a new book. Is it not so? You see I can read your thoughts. Go on—do! I would rather assist at the birth of a masterpiece than chatter about my own insignificant affairs."

The Professor smiled. If she thought masterpieces were born in that way—between railway stations, and in a whirl of prattle! Yet he was not wholly angry. Either because it had been unexpectedly agreeable to hear his book praised, or because of that harmonious impression which, now that he actually saw her, a protracted scrutiny confirmed, he began to feel more tolerantly toward his neighbour. Deliberately, his eyes still on hers, he pushed the other ear-pad away.

"Oh—" she said with a little gasp. "Does that mean I may go on talking?" But before he could answer, her face clouded. "I know—it only means that I might as well, now that I've broken in on your meditations. I'm dreadfully penitent; but luckily you won't have me for long, for I'm getting out at Cannes, and Cannes is the next station. And that reminds me of the enormous little favour I have to ask."

The Professor's face clouded also: he had a nervous apprehension of being asked favours. "My fountain pen," he said, regaining firmness of tone, "is broken."

"Ah—you thought I meant to ask for your autograph? Or perhaps for a cheque?" (Lord, how quick she was!) She shook her head. "No, I don't care for compulsory autographs. And I'm not going to ask for money—I'm going to give you some."

He faced her with renewed dismay. Could it be—? After all, he was not more than fifty-seven; and the blameless life he had led had perhaps helped to preserve a certain. . . .at least that was *one* theory. . . . .In these corrupt European societies what might a man not find himself exposed to? With some difficulty he executed a pinched smile.

"*Money?*"

She nodded again. "Oh, don't laugh! Don't think I'm joking. It's your ear-pads," she disconcertingly added.

"Yes. If you hadn't put them on I should never have spoken to you; for it wasn't till afterward that I saw your name on the suitcase. And after that I should have been too shy to break in on the meditations of a Great Philosopher. But you see I have been watching—oh, for years!—for your ear-pads."

He stared at her helplessly. "You want to buy them from me?" he asked in terror, wondering how on earth he would be able to get others in a country of which he did not speak the language.

She burst into a laugh that ran up and down the whole scale of friendly derision and tender mockery.

"Buy them? Gracious, no! I could make myself a better pair in five minutes." She smiled at his visible relief. "But you see I'm ruined—stony broke; isn't that what they call it? I have a young American friend who is always saying that about himself. And once in the Caucasus, years ago, a gipsy told me that if ever I had gambled away my last penny (and I nearly *have*) it would all be won back by a pale intellectual looking man in velvet ear-pads, if only I could induce him to put a stake on the tables for me." She leaned forward and scrutinised him. "You are very pale, you know," she said, "and very intellectual looking. I was sure it was you when you told me you'd been ill."

Professor Loring D. Hibbart looked about him desperately. He knew now that he was shut up with a madwoman. A harmless one, probably; but what if, in the depths of that jewelled bag, a toy revolver lurked under the pawn-tickets and the cigarette papers? The Professor's life had been so guarded from what are known as "exciting situations" that he was not sure of his ability to meet one with becoming tact and energy.

"I suppose I'm a physical coward," he reflected bitterly, an uncomfortable dampness breaking out all over him. "And I *know*," he added in self-extenuation, "that I'm in no condition yet for any sort of a struggle. . . ."

But what did one do with lunatics? If only he could remember! And suddenly he did: one humoured them!

Fortified by the thought, he made shift to glance more kindly toward the Princess Balalatinsky. "So you want me to gamble for you?" he said, in the playful tone he might have adopted in addressing little Sadie Burt of Meropee.

"Oh, how glorious of you! You will? I *knew* you would! But first," she broke off, "you must let me explain—"

"Oh, do explain, of course," he agreed, rapidly calculating that her volubility might make the explanation last until they reached the next station, where, as she had declared, she was to leave the train.

Already her eye was less wild; and he drew an inward breath of relief.

"You angel, you! I *do*," she confessed, "simply love to talk about myself. And I'm sure you'll be interested when I tell you that, if you'll only do as I ask, I shall be able to marry one of your own compatriots—such a beautiful heroic youth! It is for him, for him only, that I long to be wealthy again. If you loved, could you bear to see your beloved threatened with starvation?"

"But I thought," he gently reminded her, "that it was you who were threatened with starvation?"

"We *both* are. Isn't it terrible? You see, when we met and loved, we each had the same thought—to make the other wealthy! It was not possible, at the moment, for either of us to attain our end by the natural expedient of a rich marriage with reasonable prospect of a quick divorce—so we staked our all at those accursed tables, and we both lost! My poor betrothed has only a few hundred *francs* left, and as for me, I have had to take a miserably paid job as a dressmaker's *mannequin* at Cannes. But I see you are going on to Monte Carlo (yes, that's on your luggage too); and as I don't suppose you will spend a night there without visiting the rooms, I—" She was pulling forth the hundred *francs* from her inexhaustible bag when the Professor checked her with dismay. Mad though she might be, he could not even make believe to take her money.

"I'm *not* spending a night at Monte Carlo," he protested. "I'm only getting out there to take a motorbus for a quiet place up in the hills; I've the name written down somewhere; my room is engaged, so I couldn't possibly wait over," he argued gently.

She looked at him with what seemed to his inflamed imagination the craftiness of a maniac. "Don't you know that our train is nearly two hours late? I don't suppose you noticed that we ran over a crowded excursion charabanc near Toulon? Didn't you even hear the ambulances rushing up? Your motorbus will certainly have left Monte Carlo when you arrive, so you'll *have* to spend the night there! And even if you don't," she added persuasively, "the station's only two steps from the Casino, and you surely can't refuse just to nip in for half an hour." She clasped her hands in entreaty. "You wouldn't refuse if you knew my betrothed—your young compatriot! If only we had a few thousands all would go smoothly.

"We should be married at once and go to live on his ancestral estate of Kansas. It appears the climate is that of Africa in summer and of the Government of Omsk in winter; so our plan is to grow oranges and breed sables. You see, we can hardly fail to succeed with two such crops. All we ask is enough money to make a start. And that you will get for me tonight. You have only to stake this hundred *franc* note;

you'll win on the first turn, and you'll go on winning. You'll see!"

With one of her sudden plunges she pried open his contracted fist and pressed into it a banknote wrapped in a torn envelope. "Now listen; this is my address at Cannes. Princess Balala—oh, here's the station. Goodbye, guardian angel. No, "*au revoir*"; I shall see you soon. They call me Betsy at the dressmaker's. . . ."

Before he could open his convulsed fingers, or dash out after her, she had vanished, bag and baggage, in the crowd and confusion of the platform; other people, pushing and chattering and tearing themselves from the embrace of friends, had piled into her place, and were waving from the window, and blocking the way out; and now the train was moving on, and there he sat in his corner, aghast, clutching the banknote. . . .

2

At Monte Carlo the Professor captured a porter and rescued his luggage. Exhausted by this effort, and by the attempt to communicate with the porter, first in Latin and then in French as practised at Purewater, he withdrew to a corner of the waiting-room and fished in his pockets for the address of the quiet *pension* in the hills. He found it at last, and handed it wearily to the porter. The latter threw up his hands. "*Parti! Parti! Autobus* gone." That devil of a woman had been right!

When would there be another, the Professor asked.

Not till tomorrow morning at 8:30. To confirm his statement the porter pointed to a large time-table on the wall of the waiting-room. The Professor scanned it and sat down again with a groan. He was about to consult his companion as to the possibility of finding a night's lodging in a respectable *pension* (fantastic as the idea seemed in such a place); but hardly had he begun: "Can you tell me where—" when, with a nod of comprehension and a wink of complicity, the porter returned in fluent English: "Pretty ladies? Turkish bath? Fottographs?"

The Professor repudiated these suggestions with a shudder, and leaving his bags in the cloak-room set forth on his quest. He had hardly taken two steps when another stranger of obviously doubtful morality offered him a pamphlet which he was indignantly rejecting when he noticed its title: *The Theory of Chance in Roulette.* The theory of chance was deeply interesting to the Professor, and the idea of its application to roulette not without an abstract attraction. He bought the pamphlet and sat down on the nearest bench.

His study was so absorbing that he was roused only by the fall of twilight, and the scattered twinkle of many lamps all radiating up to the central focus of the Casino. The Professor started to his feet, remembering that he had still to find a lodging. "And I must be up early to catch the bus," he reminded himself. He took his way down a wide empty street apparently leading to a quieter and less illuminated quarter. This street he followed for some distance, vainly scrutinizing the houses, which seemed all to be private dwellings, till at length he ran against a slim well-set-up young fellow in tennis flannels, with a bright conversational eye, who was strolling along from the opposite direction.

"Excuse me, sir," said the Professor.

"What for?" rejoined the other, in a pleasant tone made doubly pleasant by the familiar burr of the last word, which he pronounced like *fur*.

"Why, you're an American!" exclaimed the Professor.

"Sher*lock!*" exulted the young man, extending his hand. "I diagnose the same complaint in yourself."

The Professor sighed pleasurably. "Oh, yes. What I want," he added, "is to find a plain quiet boarding-house or family hotel."

"Same as mother used to make 'em?" The young man reflected. "Well, it's a queer place in which to prosecute your search; but there is one at Monte, and I'm about the only person that knows it. My name's Taber Tring. Come along."

For a second the Professor's eye rested doubtfully on Mr. Tring. He knew, of course—even at Purewater it was known—that in the corrupt capitals of Europe one could not always rely implicitly on the information given by strangers casually encountered; no, not even when it was offered with affability, and in the reassuring twang of the Western States. But after all Monte Carlo was not a capital; it was just an absurd little joke of a town crammed on a ledge between sea and mountain; and a second glance at the young man convinced the Professor that he was as harmless as the town.

Mr. Tring, who seemed quick at thought-reading, returned his look with an amused glance.

"Not much like our big and breezy land, is it? These Riviera resorts always remind me of the subway at rush hours; everybody strap-hanging. But my landlady is an old friend, and I know one of her boarders left this morning, because I heard her trying to seize his luggage. He got away; so I don't see why you shouldn't have his room. See?"

The Professor saw. But he became immediately apprehensive of having his own luggage seized, an experience unprecedented in his history.

"Are such things liable to occur in this place?" he enquired.

"What? A scrap with your landlady? Not if you pay up regularly; or if she likes you. I guess she didn't like that other fellow; and I know he was always on the wrong side of the tables."

"The tables—do you refer to the gambling tables?" The Professor stopped short to put the question.

"That's it," said the other.

"And do you yourself sometimes visit the gambling-rooms?" the Professor next enquired.

"Oh, hell," said Taber Tring expressively.

The Professor scrutinized him with growing interest. "And have you a theory of chance?"

The young man met his gaze squarely. "I have; but it can't be put into language that would pass the censor."

"Ah—you refer, no doubt, to your personal experience. But, as regards the theory—"

"Well, the theory has let me down to bedrock; and I came down on it devilish hard." His expression turned from apathy to animation. "I'm stony broke; but if you'd like to lend me a hundred *francs* to have another try—"

"Oh, no," said the Professor hastily; "I don't possess it." And his doubts began to stir again.

Taber Tring laughed. "Of course you don't; not for lending purposes. I was only joking; everybody makes that joke here. Well, here's the house; I'll go ahead and rout out our hostess."

They stopped before a pleasant-looking little house at the end of the street. A palm-tree, a couple of rose-bushes and a gateway surmounted by the word *Arcadie* divided it from the pavement; the Professor drew a breath of relief as a stout lady in an orange wig bustled out to receive him.

In spite of the orange wig her face was so full of a shrewd benevolence that the Professor felt sure he had reached a haven of rest. She welcomed him affably, informed him that she had a room, and offered to lead him up to it. "Only for tonight, though? For it is promised to a Siamese nobleman for tomorrow."

This, the Professor assured her, made no difference, as he would be leaving at daylight. But on the lowest step of the stair he turned and addressed himself to Mr. Tring.

"Perhaps the lady would be good enough to have my bags brought up from the station? If you would kindly explain that I'm going out now to take a little stroll. As I'm leaving so early tomorrow it's my only chance to have a look around."

"That's so; I'll tell her," the young man rejoined sympathetically; and as the Professor's hand was on the gate, he heard Mr. Tring call out, mimicking the stentorian tones of a megaphone man on a sight-seeing motorbus: "Third street to the left, then first right to the tables"; after which he added, in his natural tone: "Say, Arcadia locks up at midnight."

The Professor smiled at the superfluous hint.

3

Having satisfied a polyglot door-keeper as to his nationality, and the fact that he was not a minor, the Professor found himself in the gambling-rooms. They were not particularly crowded for people were beginning to go out for dinner, and he was able to draw fairly near to the first roulette table he encountered.

As he stood looking over the shoulders of the players he understood that no study of abstract theories could be worth the experience acquired by thus observing the humours of the goddess in her very temple. Her caprices, so ably seconded by the inconceivable stupidity, timidity or rashness of her votaries, first amused and finally exasperated the Professor; he began to feel toward her something of the annoyance excited in him by the sight of a pretty woman, or any other vain superfluity, combined with the secret sense that if he chose he could make her dance to his tune, and that it might be mildly amusing to do so. He had felt the same once or twice—but only for a fugitive instant—about pretty women.

None, however, had ever attracted him as strongly as this veiled divinity. The longing to twitch the veil from her cryptic features became violent, irresistible. "Not one of these fools has any idea of the theory of chance," he muttered to himself, elbowing his way to a seat near one of the croupiers. As he did so, he put his hand into his pocket, and found to his disgust that it contained only a single five-*franc* piece and a few *sous*. All the rest of his money—a matter of four or five hundred *francs*—lay locked up in his suit-case at *Arcadie*. He anathematized his luck in expurgated language, and was about to rise from the table when the croupier called out: "*Faites vos jeux, Messieurs.*"

The Professor, with a murmured expletive which was to a real oath what Postum is to coffee, dropped back into his place and flung his five-*franc* piece on the last three numbers. He lost.

Of course—in his excitement he had gone exactly contrary to his own theory! It was on the first three that he had meant to stake his paltry bet. Well; now it was too late. But stay—

Diving into another pocket, he came with surprise on a hundred *franc* note. Could it really be his? But no; he had an exact memorandum of his funds, and he knew this banknote was not to be thus accounted for. He made a violent effort to shake off his abstraction, and finally recalled that the note in question had been pressed into his hand that very afternoon as he left the train. But by whom—?

"*Messieurs, faites vos jeux! Faites vos jeux! Le jeu est fait. Rien ne va plus.*"

The hundred *francs*, escaping from his hand, had fluttered of themselves to a number in the middle of the table. That number came up. Across the green board thirty-six other hundred *franc* notes flew swiftly back in the direction of the Professor. Should he put them all back on the same number? "Yes," he nodded calmly to the croupier's question; and the three-thousand seven hundred *francs* were guided to their place by the croupier's rake.

The number came up again, and another argosy of notes sailed into the haven of the happy gambler's pocket. This time he knew he ought to settle down quietly to his theory; and he did so. He staked a thousand and tripled it, then let the three thousand lie, and won again. He doubled that stake, and began to feel his neighbours watching him with mingled interest and envy as the winnings once more flowed his way. But to whom did this mounting pile really belong?

No time to think of that now; he was fast in the clutches of his theory. It seemed to guide him like some superior being seated at the helm of his intelligence: his private daemon pitted against the veiled goddess! It was exciting, undoubtedly; considerably more so, for example, than taking tea with the President's wife at Purewater. He was beginning to feel like Napoleon, disposing his battalions to right and left, advancing, retreating, reinforcing or redistributing his troops. Ah, the veiled goddess was getting what she deserved for once!

At a late hour of the evening, when the Professor had become the centre of an ever-thickening crowd of fascinated observers, it suddenly came back to him that a woman had given him that original hundred *franc* note. A woman in the train that afternoon. . . .But what did he care for that? He was playing the limit at every stake; and his mind had never worked more clearly and with a more exquisite sense of complete detachment. He was in his own particular seventh heaven of lucidity. He even recalled, at the precise moment when cognisance of the fact became useful, that the doors of Arcadie closed at midnight, and that he had only just time to get back if he wished to sleep with a roof over his head.

As he did wish to, he pocketed his gains quietly and composedly, rose from the table and walked out of the rooms. He felt hungry, cheerful and alert. Perhaps, after all, excitement had been what he needed—pleasurable excitement, that is, not the kind occasioned by the small daily irritations of life, such as the presence of that woman in the train whose name he was still unable to remember. What he would have liked best of all would have been to sit down in one of the brightly lit *cafés* he was passing, before a bottle of beer and a ham sandwich; or perhaps what he had heard spoken of as a Welsh rabbit. But he did not want to sleep on a bench, for the night air was sharp; so he continued self-denyingly on his way to Arcadie.

A sleepy boy in a dirty apron let him in, locked up after him, and led him to a small bare room on the second floor. The stairs creaked and rattled as they mounted, and the rumblings of sleep sounded through the doors of the rooms they passed. Arcadie was a cramped and ramshackle construction, and the Professor hoped to heaven that his *pension* in the hills would be more solidly built and less densely inhabited. However, for one night it didn't matter—or so he imagined.

His guide left him, and he turned on the electric light, threw down on the table the notes with which all his pockets were bulging, and began to unstrap his portmanteaux.

Though he had so little luggage he always found the process of unpacking a long and laborious one; for he never could remember where he had put anything, and invariably passed through all the successive phases of apprehension and despair before he finally discovered his bedroom slippers in his spongebag, and the sponge itself (still dripping) rolled up inside his pyjamas.

But tonight he sought for neither sponge not pyjamas, for as he opened his first suitcase his hand lit on a ream of spotless foolscap—the kind he always used for his literary work. The table on which he had tossed his winnings held a crusty hotel inkstand, and was directly overhung by a vacillating electric bulb. Before it was a chair; through the open window flowed the silence of the night, interwoven with the murmurs of a sleeping sea and hardly disturbed by the occasional far-off hoot of a motor horn. In his own brain was the same nocturnal quiet and serenity. A curious thing had happened to him. His bout with the veiled goddess had sharpened his wits and dragged him suddenly and completely out of the intellectual apathy into which he had been gradually immersed by his illness and the harassing discomforts of the last few weeks. He was no longer thinking now about the gambling tables or the theory of chance; but with all the strength of his freshly stimulated faculties was grappling the mighty monster with whom he meant to try a fall.

"*Einstein!*" he cried, as a Crusader might have shouted his battle-cry. He sat down at the table, shoved aside the banknotes, plunged his pen into the blue mud of the inkstand, and began.

The silence was delicious, mysterious. Link by link the chain of his argument unrolled itself, travelling across his pages with the unending flow of a trail of migratory caterpillars. Not a break; not a hesitation. It was years since his mental machinery had worked with that smooth consecutiveness. He began to wonder whether, after all, it might not be better to give up the idea of a remote and doubtful *pension* in the hills, and settle himself for the winter in a place apparently so propitious to his intellectual activities.

It was then that the noises in the next room suddenly began. First there was the brutal slam of the door, followed by a silly bad-tempered struggle with a reluctant lock. Then a pair of shoes were flung down on the tiled floor. Water was next poured into an unsteady basin, and a water-jug set down with a hideous clatter on a rickety washstand which seemed to be placed against the communicating door between the two rooms. Turbulent ablutions ensued. These over, there succeeded a moment of deceptive calm, almost immediately succeeded by a series of whistled scales, emitted just above the whistler's breath, and merging into the exact though subdued reproduction of various barn-yard gutturals, ending up with the raucous yelp of a parrot proclaiming again and again: "I'm stony broke, I am!"

All the while Professor Hibbart's brain continued to marshal its arguments, and try to press them into the hard mould of words. But the struggle became more and more unequal as the repressed cacophony next door increased. At last he jumped up, rummaged in every pocket for his ear-pads and snapped them furiously over his ears. But this measure, instead of silencing the tenuous insistent noises from the next room, only made him strain for them more attentively through the protecting pads, giving them the supernatural shrillness of sounds heard at midnight in a sleeping house, the secret crackings and creakings against which heaped-up pillows and drawn-up bedclothes are a vain defence.

Finally, the Professor noticed that there was a wide crack under the communicating door. Not till that crack was filled would work be possible. He jumped up again and dived at the washstand for towels. But he found that in the hasty preparation of the room the towels had been forgotten. A newspaper, then—but no; he cast about him in vain for a newspaper. . . .

The noises had now sunk to a whisper, broken by irritating intervals of silence; but in the exasperated state of the Professor's nerves these irregular lulls, and the tension of watching for the sounds that broke them, were more trying than what had gone before. He sent a despairing glance about him, and his eye lit on the pile of banknotes on the table. He sprang up again, seized the notes, and crammed them into the crack.

After that the silence became suddenly and almost miraculously complete, and he went on with his writing.

4

After his first twenty-four hours in the hills the Professor was ready to swear that this final refuge was all he had hoped for. The situation (though he had hardly looked out on it) seemed high yet sheltered; he had a vague impression of sunshine in his room; and when he went down on the first morning, after a deep and curative sleep, he at once found himself in a congenial atmosphere. No effusive compatriots; no bowing and scraping French; only four or five English people, as much in dread of being spoken to as he was of their speaking to him. He consumed the necessary number of square inches of proteins and carbohydrates and withdrew to his room, as stubbornly ignored as if the other guests had all thought he was trying to catch their eyes. An hour later he was lost in his work.

If only life could ever remain on an even keel! But something had made him suspect it from the first: *there was a baby in the house.* Of course everybody denied it: the cook said the bowl of pap left by accident on the stairs was for the cat; the landlady said she had been a widow twenty years, and did he suppose—? And the *bonne* denied that there was a smell of paregoric on the landing, and said that was the way the scent of mimosa sometimes affected people.

That night, after a constitutional in the garden (ear-pads on), the Professor went up to his room to resume his writing. For two hours he wrote uninterruptedly; then he was disturbed by a faint wail. He clapped on the pads, and continued; but the wail, low as it was, pierced them like a corkscrew. Finally, he laid down his pen and listened, furiously. Every five minutes the sound came again. "I suppose they'll say it's a kitten!" he growled. No such pretence could deceive him for a moment; he remembered now that at the moment of entering the house he had noticed a smell of nursery. If only he had turned straight around and gone elsewhere! But where?

The idea of a fresh plunge into the unknown made him feel as weak as in the first stages of convalescence. And then his book had already sunk such talons into him; he could feel it sucking at his brain like some hungry animal. And all those people downstairs had been as cold and stony at dinner as they had at lunch. After two such encounters he was sure they would never bother him. A Paradise indeed, but for that serpent!

The wail continued, and he turned in his chair and looked slowly and desperately about him. The room was small and bare, and had only one door, the one leading into the passage. He vaguely recalled that, two nights before, at Monte Carlo, he had been disturbed in much the same way, and had found means to end the disturbance. What had he done? If only he could remember!

His eye went back to the door. There was a light under it now; no doubt someone was up with the child. Slowly his mind dropped from the empyrean to the level of the crack under the door.

"A couple of towels. . . . Ah, but, there are no towels!" Almost as the words formed themselves, his glance lit on a well-garnished rack. What had made him think there were no towels? Why, he had been reliving the night at Monte Carlo, where in fact, he now remembered, he could find none, and to protect himself from the noise next door had had to. . . .

"Oh, my God!" shouted the Professor. His pen clattered to the floor. He jumped up, and his chair crashed after it. The baby, terror-struck, ceased to cry. There was an awful silence.

"Oh, my God!" shouted the Professor.

Slowly the vision of that other room came back: he saw himself jumping up just as wildly, dashing for towels and finding none, and then seizing a pile of papers and cramming them into the crack under the door. Papers, indeed! "Oh, my God. . . ."

It was money that he had seized that other night: hundreds of hundred *franc* bills; or hundreds of thousands, were they? How furiously he had crushed and crumpled them in his haste to cram enough stuffing into the crack! Money—an unbelievable amount of it. But how in the world had it got there, to whom on earth did it belong?

The Professor sat down on the edge of the bed and took his bursting head between his hands.

Daylight found him still labouring to reconstitute the succession of incredible episodes leading up to his mad act. Of all the piles of notes he had stuffed under the door not one *franc* had belonged to him. Of that he was now sure. He recalled also, but less clearly, that someone had given him a banknote—a hundred *francs*, he thought; was it on the steamer at Marseilles, or in the train?—given it with some mysterious injunction about gambling. . . .that was as far as he could go at present. . . .His mind had come down from the empyrean with a crash, and was still dazed from its abrupt contact with reality. At any rate, not a penny of the money was his, and he had left it all under the door in his hotel bedroom at Monte Carlo. And that was two days ago...

The baby was again crying, but the rest of the house still slept when, unkempt, unshorn, and with as many loose ends to his raiment as Hamlet, Professor Hibbart dashed out past an affrighted *bonne*, who cried after him that he might still catch the autobus if he took the short cut to the village.

To the Professor any abrupt emergence from his work was like coming to after a severe operation. He floated in a world as empty of ideas as of facts, and hemmed with slippery perpendicular walls. All the way to Monte Carlo those walls were made of the faces in the motorbus, blank inscrutable faces, smooth secret surfaces up which his mind struggled to clamber back to the actual. Only one definite emotion survived: hatred of the being—a woman, was it?—who had given him that fatal hundred *franc* note. He clung to that feeling as to a life-belt, waiting doggedly till it should lift him back to reality. If only he could have recalled his enemy's name!

Arrived at Monte Carlo he hailed a taxi and pronounced the one name he did recall: *Arcadie!* But what chance was there that the first chauffeur he met would know the title, or remember the site, of that undistinguished family hotel?

"Arcadie? But, of course! It's the place they're all asking for!" cried the chauffeur, turning without a moment's hesitation in what seemed to his fare to be the right direction. Yet how could that obscure pension be the place "they" were all asking for, and who in the name of madness were "they"?

"Are you sure—?" the Professor faltered.

"Of finding the way? *Allons donc*; we have only to follow the crowd!"

This was a slight exaggeration, for at that early hour the residential quarter of Monte Carlo was hardly more populous than when the Professor had last seen it; but if he had doubted being on the right road his doubt was presently dispelled by the sight of a well-set-up young man in tennis flannels, with a bright conversational eye, who came swinging along from the opposite direction.

"Taber Tring!" cried a voice from the depths of the Professor's subconsciousness; and the Professor nearly flung himself over the side of the taxi in the effort to attract his friend's notice.

Apparently he had been mistaken; for the young man, arrested by his signals, gave back a blank stare from eyes grown suddenly speechless, and then, turning on his heels, disappeared double-quick down a side-street. The Professor, thrown back into his habitual uncertainty, wavered over the question of pursuit; but the taxi was still moving forward, and before he could decide what to do it had worked its way through a throng of gaping people and drawn up before a gate surmounted by the well-remembered Arcadie.

"There you are!" the chauffeur gestured, with the air of a parent humouring a spoilt child.

There he was! The Professor started to jump out, and pushing through the crowd was confronted with a smoking ruin. The garden gate, under its lying inscription, led straight into chaos; and behind where *Arcadie* had stood, other houses, blank unknown houses, were also shouldering up to gape at the disaster.

"But this is not the place!" remonstrated the Professor. "This is a house that has burnt down!"

"*Parbleu*," replied the chauffeur, still humouring him.

The Professor's temples were bursting.

"But was it—*was* it—was *this* the Hotel *Arcadie?*"

The chauffeur shrugged again and pointed to the name.

"When—did it burn?"

"Early yesterday."

"And the landlady—the person who kept it?"

"*Ah, ça. . . .*"

"But how, in the name of pity, can I find out?"

The chauffeur seemed moved by his distress. "Let *Monsieur* reassure himself. There was no loss of life. If *Monsieur* had friends or relations. . . ."

The Professor waved away the suggestion.

"We could, of course, address ourselves to the police," the chauffeur continued.

The police! The mere sound of the word filled his hearer with dismay. Explain to the police about that money? How could he—and in his French? He turned cold at the idea, and in his dread of seeing himself transported to the *commissariat* by the too-sympathetic driver, he hurriedly paid the latter off, and remained alone gazing through the gate at the drenched and smoking monument of his folly.

The money—try to get back the money? It had seemed almost hopeless before; now the attempt could only expose him to all the mysterious perils of an alien law. He saw himself interrogated, investigated, his passport seized, his manuscript confiscated, and every hope of rational repose and work annihilated for months to come. He felt himself curiously eyed by the policeman who was guarding the ruins, and turned from the scene of the disaster almost as hurriedly as the young man whom he had taken—no doubt erroneously—for Taber Tring.

Having reached another quarter of the town, he sat down on a bench to take stock of his situation.

It was exactly what he had done two days before when, on arriving at Monte Carlo, he had found that he had missed the motorbus; and the associations of ideas once more came to his rescue.

Gradually there arose in his mind a faint wavering vision of a young woman, pearled and furred and scented, precipitately descending from his compartment, and, as she did so, cramming a banknote into his hand.

"The Princess. . . .the Princess. . . .*they call me Betsy at the dressmaker's*. . . . "That was as far as the clue went; but presently the Professor remembered that his companion had got out of the train at Cannes, and it became certain to him that his only hope of clearing his overburdened conscience would be to take the train to that place, and there prosecute his almost hopeless search.

5

Not until he found himself seated in the train, and on the point of starting for Cannes, did the full horror of his situation break on the Professor. Then, for an hour, he contemplated it in all its intricate enormity, saw himself as a man dishonoured, ruined (for he now remembered the full amount of the sum he had to account for), and, worse still, severed from his best-loved work for a period incalculably long. For after he had struggled through the preliminary difficulties he would have to settle down to the slow task of reimbursement, and he knew that, to earn enough money to repay what he had lost, he must abandon serious scientific work such as he was now engaged in, and probably stoop—abominable thought!—to writing popular "science" articles in one of the illustrated magazines. Such a job had once been offered him on very handsome terms, and contemptuously rejected; and the best he could now hope was that there was still an opening for him somewhere between the Etiquette Column and the notes on Rachel powder and bathing tights.

Arrived at Cannes, he found his way to what appeared to be the fashionable shopping-street, and exteriorising his attention by an extreme effort of the will he began to go the rounds of the dressmaking establishments.

At every one he was received with distinguished politeness, and every one, by some curious coincidence, had a Betsy to offer him. As the Betsies were all young, fluffy and rosy, considerable offence was caused by his rapid rejection of them, and it was in vain that he tried to close his ears to the crude and disobliging comments which on each occasion attended his retreat. But he had by this time regained a sufficiently clear vision of the Princess to be sure that she was not concealed behind any of the youthful substitutes proposed to him. In despair he issued from the last shop, and again sat himself down to consider.

As he did so, his mind gave a queer click, and the doors of his inner consciousness again swung open. But this time it was only to draw him back into the creative world from which he had been so violently ejected. He had suddenly seen a point to be made in the Einstein controversy, and he began to fumble for a paper on which to jot it down. He found only one, the closely-scribbled flap of a torn envelope on which, during the journey to Cannes, he had calculated and re-calculated the extent of the sum he would have to raise to reimburse the Princess; but possibly there might be a clear space on the other side. He turned it over, and there read, in a tall slanting hand:

Princesse Balalatinsky,
Villa Mon Caprice,
Route de Californie.

He started to his feet, and glanced about him frantically for a taxi. He had no idea where the Route de Californie was, but in his desperate circumstances, it seemed as easy to hire a taxi for a five minutes' transit as for a long expedition. Besides, it was the only way he knew of being sure of reaching his destination; and to do so as soon as possible was now a fixed idea.

The taxi carried him a long way; back through the whole length of the town, out on a flat white dusty road, and then up and up between walls overhung with luxuriant verdure till, at a turn, it stood still with a violent jerk.

The Professor looked out, and saw himself confronted by the expressive countenance of Mr. Taber Tring.

"Oh, my God—you again!" shrieked the young man, turning suddenly white with fury—or was it rather with fear?

"Why do you say *again?*" questioned the Professor; but his interlocutor, taking to his heels with unaccountable velocity, had already disappeared down a verdant by-way.

The Professor leaned back in the taxi in speechless amazement. He was sure now that the "again" referred to their previous encounter that morning at Monte Carlo, and he could only conclude that it had become a fixed habit of Taber Tring's to run away whenever they met, and that he ran a great deal too fast for the Professor ever to hope to overtake him.

"Well," said the driver, "there's a gentleman who isn't pleased. He thought I had no fare, and expected to get a lift up to the top of this mountain."

"I should have been happy to give him a lift," said the Professor rather wistfully; to which the driver replied: "He must be a mile off by this time. He didn't seem to fancy your looks."

There was no controverting this statement, mortifying as it was, and they continued their ascent till a gateway impressively crowned by heraldic lions admitted them to terraced gardens above which a villa of ample proportions looked forth upon the landscape.

The Professor was by this time so steeled to the unexpected that he hardly paused to consider the strange incongruity between the Princess's account of her fortunes and the setting in which she lived. He had read *Mon Caprice* on the gate, and that was the name on the envelope he had found in his pocket. With a resolute hand he rang the bell and asked a resplendent footman if the Princess Balalatinsky were at home.

He was shown through a long succession of drawing-rooms, in the last of which the Princess rose from the depths of a broad divan. She was dressed in black draperies, half-transparent—no, half-translucent; and she stood before the Professor in all the formidable completeness of her beauty.

Instantly his mind clicked again, and a voice shrilled up at him from the depths: "You always knew you could still recognize a beautiful woman when you saw one"; but he closed his ears to the suggestion and advanced toward the lady.

Before he could take more than three steps she was at his side, almost at his feet; her burning clasp was on his wrists, and her eyes were consuming him like coals of fire.

"Master! *Maestro!* Disguise is useless! You choose to come to me unannounced; but I was sure you would answer my appeal, and I should have recognised you anywhere, and among any number of people." She lifted his astonished hand to her lips. "It is the penalty of genius," she breathed.

"But—" gasped the Professor.

A scented finger was laid across his lips. "Hush: not yet. Let me tell you first why I ventured to write to you." She drew him gently down to an arm-chair beside the divan, and herself sank orientally into its pillows. "I thought I had exhausted all the emotions of life. At *my* age—is it not a tragedy? But I was mistaken. It is true that I had tried philosophy, marriage, mathematics, divorce, sculpture and love; but I had never attempted the stage. How long it sometimes takes to discover one's real vocation! No doubt you may have gone through the same uncertainties yourself. At any rate, my gift for the drama did not reveal itself till three months ago, and I have only just completed my play, *The Scarlet Cataract*, a picture of my life, as the title suggests—and which, my friends tell me, is not without dramatic merit. In fact, if I were to listen to them. . . ."

The Professor struggled from his seat. His old fear of her madness had returned. He began very mildly: "It is quite natural that you should mistake me for someone else—"

With an inimitable gesture she waved the interruption aside. "But what I want to explain is that, of course, the leading role can have but one interpreter—Myself. The things happened to *Me*: who else could possibly know how to act them? Therefore, if I appeal to you—on my knees, Illustrious *Impresario!*—it is in my double character as dramatist and *tragédienne*; for in spite of appearances my life *has* been a tragedy, as you will acknowledge if you will let me outline its principal events in a few words. . . ."

But here she had to pause a second for breath, and the Professor, on his feet, actually shouted his protest. "Madam, I cannot let you go on another moment, first because I've heard the story of your life already, and secondly because I'm not the man you suppose."

The Princess turned deadly pale. "Impostor!" she hissed, and reached for an embroidered bell-rope.

Her agitation had the curious effect of calming the Professor. "You had better not send me away," he said, "till you learn why I am here. I am the unhappy man to whom, the day before yesterday, you entrusted a hundred *franc* note which you asked him to stake for you at Monte Carlo. Unfortunately, I could not recall your name or address, and I have been hunting for you through all the dressmakers' establishments in Cannes."

The instant lighting-up of her face was a sight so lovely that he almost forgot his apprehensions and his shame.

"The dressmakers' shops? Ah—in search of 'Betsy'! It is true, I was obliged to act as a *mannequin* for one day; but since then my fortunes have miraculously changed—changed thanks to you; for now," the Princess continued with enthusiasm, "I do at last recognise my good angel, my benefactor of the other day, and ask myself how I could have failed to know you again, how I could have taken you for a vulgar theatrical manager, you, a man of genius and a Philosopher. Can you ever forgive me? For I owe you everything—everything—everything!" she sobbed out, again almost at his knees.

His self-possession continued to increase in proportion to her agitation. He actually risked laying a hand on her arm and pressing her mildly back among her cushions.

"Only a change of pronouns," he said sighing, "is necessary to the complete accuracy of your last statement."

But she was off again on a new tack. "That blessed hundred *franc* note! From the moment when you took it from me, as I got out of the train, my luck miraculously and completely changed. I knew you were going to win some money for me; but how could I have imagined the extent of the fortune you were to heap at my feet?"

A cold sweat broke out over the Professor. She knew, then—once again her infernal intuition had pierced his secret! In the train had she not discovered his name, identified him as the author of *The Elimination of Phenomena*, and guessed that he was actually engaged in the composition of another work? At the moment he had fancied that there was a plausible explanation for each of these discoveries; but he now felt that her powers of divination were in need of no outward aid. She had risen from her seat and was once more in possession of his hands.

"You have come to be thanked—and I do thank you!" Her heavy lashes glittered with tears which threatened to merge with the drops of moisture rolling down the Professor's agonized brow.

"Don't—don't, I beg!" He freed himself and shrank back. "If you'll only let me speak...let me explain. . . ."

She raised a reproachful finger. "Let you belittle yourself? Let you reject my gratitude? No—no! Nothing that you can say can make any difference. The gipsy in the Caucasus told me long ago what you were going to do for me. And now that you have done it you want to stifle the thanks on my lips!"

"But you have nothing to thank me for. I have made no money for you—on the contrary, I—"

"Hush, hush! Such words are blasphemy. Look about you at all this luxury, this beauty. I expected to have to leave it tomorrow. And thanks to you, wealth has poured in on me at the moment when I thought I was face to face with ruin."

"Madam, you must let me undeceive you. I don't know who can have brought you such an erroneous report." The Professor glanced about him in acute distress, seeking to escape from her devouring scrutiny. "It is true that I did make a considerable sum for you, but I—I afterward lost it. To my shame be it said."

The Princess hardly appeared to hear him. Tears of gratitude still rained down her face. "Lost it? A little more, a little less—what does it matter? In my present pecuniary situation nothing of that sort counts. I am rich—rich for life! I should, in fact," she continued with a gush of candour, "be an absolutely happy woman if I could only find an *impresario* who would stage my play." She lifted her enchanting eyes to his. "I wonder, by the way, dear friend," she proposed, "if you would let me read it to you now?"

"Oh, no, no," the Professor protested; and then, becoming aware of the offence his words were likely to give, he added precipitately: "Before we turn to any other subject you must really let me tell you just how much money I owe you, and what were the unfortunate circumstances in which. . . ."

But he was conscious that the Princess was no longer listening to him. A new light had dawned in her face, and the glow of it was already drying her tears. Slim, palpitating and girlish, she turned toward one of the tall French windows opening upon the terrace.

"My *fiancé*—your young compatriot! Here he is! Oh, how happy I am to bring you together!" she exclaimed.

The Professor followed her glance with a stare of fresh amazement. Through the half-open window, a young man in tennis flannels had strolled into the room.

"My Taber," the Princess breathed, "this is my benefactor—*our* benefactor—this is. . . ."

Taber Tring gently removed the perfect arms which were already tightening about his neck. "I know who he is," he said in a hard high tone. "That's why I've been running away from him ever since early this morning."

His good-humoured boyish face was absolutely decomposed by distress. Without vouchsafing the least attention to the Princess he stood pallidly but resolutely facing her visitor.

"I've been running for all I was worth; at least till a quarter of an hour ago. Then I suddenly pulled up short and said to myself: 'Taber Tring, this won't do. You were born in the Middle West, but your parents came from New England, and now's the time to prove it if you're ever going to. Stern and rockbound coast, and *Mayflower* and all the rest of it. If there's anything in it, it ought to come out now.' And, by George it *did*; and here I am, ready to make a clean breast of it."

He drew a silk handkerchief from his pocket, and wiped his brow, which was as damp with agony as the Professor's. But the Professor's patience had reached its final limit, and he was determined, whatever happened, to hold all interrupters at bay till he had made a clean breast of his own.

"I don't know, sir," he said, "why you avoided my presence this morning nor why you now seek it; but since you are connected with this lady by so close a tie, there is no reason why I should not continue in your presence what I had begun to tell her. I repeat then, Madam, that with your hundred *franc* note in my hand, I approached a table and staked the sum with results so unexpectedly and incredibly favourable that I left the gaming-rooms just before midnight in possession of—"

"Ninety-nine thousand seven hundred *francs* and no *centimes*," Taber Tring interposed.

The Professor received this with a gasp of astonishment; but everything which was happening was so foreign to all the laws of probability as experienced at Purewater that it did not long arrest his attention.

"You have stated the sum accurately," he said; "but you do not know that I am no longer in possession of a penny of it."

"Oh, don't I?" groaned Taber Tring, wiping a fresh outbreak of moisture from his forehead.

The Professor stopped short. "You do know? Ah, but to be sure. You were yourself a fellow-boarder at Arcadie. You were perhaps under its roof when that disastrous fire broke out and destroyed the whole of the large sum of money I had so negligently left—"

"Under the door!" shrieked Taber Tring. "Under the door of your room, which happened to be the one next to mine."

A light began to dawn on the Professor. "Is it possible that you were the neighbour whose unseasonable agitation during the small hours of the night caused me, in the total absence of towels or other available material, to stuff the money in question under the crack of the door in order to continue my intellectual labours undisturbed?"

"That's me," said Taber Tring sullenly.

But the Princess, who had been listening to the Professor's disquisition with a look of lovely bewilderment gradually verging on boredom, here intervened with a sudden flash of attention.

"What sort of noises proceeded from my Taber's room at that advanced hour of the night?" she inquisitorially demanded of the Professor.

"Oh, shucks," said her betrothed in a weary tone. "Aren't they all alike, every one of 'em?" He turned to the Professor. "I daresay I *was* making a noise. I was about desperate. Stony broke, and didn't know which way to turn next. I guess *you'd* have made a noise in my place."

The Professor felt a stirring of sympathy for the stricken youth. "I'm sorry for you—very sorry," he said. "If I had known your situation I should have tried to master my impatience, and should probably not have crammed the money under the door; in which case it would not have been destroyed in the fire. . . ."

("How like the reflexions of a Chinese *sage!*" the Princess admiringly murmured.)

"Destroyed in the fire? It wasn't," said Taber Tring.

The Professor reeled back and was obliged to support himself upon the nearest chair. "It wasn't?"

"Trust me," said the young man. "I was there, and I stole it."

"You stole it—his money?" The Princess instantly flung herself on his bosom. "To save your beloved from ruin? Oh, how Christlike—how Dostoyevskian!" She addressed herself with streaming eyes to the Professor. "Oh, spare him, sir, for heaven's sake spare him! What shall I do to avert your vengeance? Shall I prostitute myself in the streets of Cannes? I will do anything to atone to you for his heroic gesture in stealing your money—"

Taber Tring again put her gently aside. "Do drop it, Betsy. This is not a woman's job. I stole that money in order to gamble with it, and I've got to pay it back, and all that I won with it too." He paused and faced about on the Professor. "Isn't that so, sir?" he questioned. "I've been puzzling over it day and night for the last two days, and I can't figure it out any other way. Hard on you, Betsy, just as we thought our fortune was made; but my firm conviction, Professor Hibbart, as a man of New England stock, is that at this moment I owe you the sum of one million seven hundred and fifty thousand *francs*."

"My God," screamed the Professor, "what system did you play?"

Mr. Tring's open countenance snapped shut like a steel trap. "That's my secret," he said politely; and the Professor had to acknowledge that it was.

"I must ask you," the young man pursued, "to be good enough either to disprove or to confirm my estimate of my indebtedness to you. How much should you consider that you owed if you had stolen anybody's money and made a lot more with it? Only the sum stolen or the whole amount? There's my point."

"But I did! I have!" cried the Professor. "Did what?"

"Exactly what you have done. Stole—that is, gambled with a sum of money entrusted to me for the purpose, and won the large amount you have correctly stated. It is true," the Professor continued, "that I had no intention of appropriating a penny of it; but, believing that my culpable negligence had caused the whole sum to be destroyed by fire, I considered myself—"

"Well?" panted Taber Tring.

"As indebted for the entire amount to this lady here—"

Taber Tring's face became illuminated with sudden comprehension.

"Holy Moses! You don't mean to say all that money under the door belonged to Betsy?"

"Every cent of it, in my opinion," said the Professor firmly; and the two men stood and stared at each other.

"But, good gracious," the Princess intervened, "then nobody has stolen anything!"

The load which had crushed the Professor to earth rolled from his shoulders, and he lifted the head of a free man. "So it would seem."

But Taber Tring could only ejaculate once again: "Holy Moses!"

"Then we are rich once more—is it not so, my Taber?" The Princess leaned a thoughtful head upon her hand. "Do you know, I could almost regret it? Yes, I regret, dear friends, that you are both blameless, and that no sacrifice will be demanded of me. It would have been so beautiful if you had both sinned, and I had also had to sin to save you. But, on the other hand," she reflected, with lifted eyes and a smile like heaven, "I shall now be able to have my play brought out at my own expense. And for that," she cried, again possessing herself of Professor Hibbart's hands, "for that too I have to thank you! And this is the only way I know of doing it."

She flung her arms around his neck and lifted her lips to his; and the exonerated and emancipated Professor took what she offered like a man.

"And now," she cried, "for my other hero!" and caught her betrothed to her heart. These effusions were interrupted by the entrance of the resplendent footman, who surveyed them without surprise or disapproval.

"There is at the door," he announced, "a young lady of the name of Betsy who is asking for *Monsieur*." He indicated the Professor. "She would give no other name; she said that was enough. She knows *Monsieur* has been seeking her everywhere in Cannes, and she is in despair at having missed him; but at the time she was engaged with another client."

The Professor turned pale, and Taber Tring's left lid sketched a tentative wink.

But the Princess intervened in her most princely manner. "Of course! My name is Betsy, and you were seeking for *me* at all the dressmakers'!" She turned to the footman with her smile of benediction. "Tell the young lady," she said, "that *Monsieur* in his turn is engaged with another client, who begs her to accept this slight compensation for her trouble." She slipped from her wrist a hoop of jade and brilliants, and the footman withdrew with the token.

"And now," said the Princess, "as it is past three o'clock, we ought really to be thinking of *zakouska*."

The Bolted Door

1

Hubert Granice, pacing the length of his pleasant lamp-lit library, paused to compare his watch with the clock on the chimney-piece.

Three minutes to eight.

In exactly three minutes Mr. Peter Ascham, of the eminent legal firm of Ascham and Pettilow, would have his punctual hand on the door-bell of the flat. It was a comfort to reflect that Ascham was so punctual—the suspense was beginning to make his host nervous. And the sound of the door-bell would be the beginning of the end—after that there'd be no going back, by God—no going back!

Granice resumed his pacing. Each time he reached the end of the room opposite the door he caught his reflection in the Florentine mirror above the fine old walnut *credence* he had picked up at Dijon—saw himself spare, quick-moving, carefully brushed and dressed, but furrowed, grey about the temples, with a stoop which he corrected by a spasmodic straightening of the shoulders whenever a glass confronted him: a tired middle-aged man, baffled, beaten, worn out.

As he summed himself up thus for the third or fourth time the door opened and he turned with a thrill of relief to greet his guest. But it was only the man-servant who entered, advancing silently over the mossy surface of the old Turkey rug.

"Mr. Ascham telephones, sir, to say he's unexpectedly detained and can't be here till eight-thirty."

Granice made a curt gesture of annoyance. It was becoming harder and harder for him to control these reflexes. He turned on his heel, tossing to the servant over his shoulder: "Very good. Put off dinner."

Down his spine he felt the man's injured stare. Mr. Granice had always been so mild-spoken to his people—no doubt the odd change in his manner had already been noticed and discussed below stairs.

And very likely they suspected the cause. He stood drumming on the writing-table till he heard the servant go out; then he threw himself into a chair, propping his elbows on the table and resting his chin on his locked hands.

Another half hour alone with it!

He wondered irritably what could have detained his guest. Some professional matter, no doubt—the punctilious lawyer would have allowed nothing less to interfere with a dinner engagement, more especially since Granice, in his note, had said: "I shall want a little business chat afterward."

But what professional matter could have come up at that unprofessional hour? Perhaps some other soul in misery had called on the lawyer; and, after all, Granice's note had given no hint of his own need! No doubt Ascham thought he merely wanted to make another change in his will. Since he had come into his little property, ten years earlier, Granice had been perpetually tinkering with his will.

Suddenly another thought pulled him up, sending a flush to his sallow temples. He remembered a word he had tossed to the lawyer some six weeks earlier, at the Century Club.

> Yes—my play's as good as taken. I shall be calling on you soon
> to go over the contract. Those theatrical chaps are so slippery—
> I won't trust anybody but you to tie the knot for me!

That, of course, was what Ascham would think he was wanted for. Granice, at the idea, broke into an audible laugh—a queer stage-laugh, like the cackle of a baffled villain in a melodrama. The absurdity, the unnaturalness of the sound abashed him, and he compressed his lips angrily. Would he take to soliloquy next?

He lowered his arms and pulled open the upper drawer of the writing-table. In the right-hand corner lay a thick manuscript, bound in paper folders, and tied with a string beneath which a letter had been slipped. Next to the manuscript was a small revolver. Granice stared a moment at these oddly associated objects; then he took the letter from under the string and slowly began to open it. He had known he should do so from the moment his hand touched the drawer. Whenever his eye fell on that letter some relentless force compelled him to re-read it.

It was dated about four weeks back, under the letter-head of "The Diversity Theatre."

My Dear Mr. Granice:

I have given the matter my best consideration for the last month, and it's no use—the play won't do. I have talked it over with Miss Melrose—and you know there isn't a gamer artist on our stage—and I regret to tell you she feels just as I do about it. It isn't the poetry that scares her—or me either. We both want to do all we can to help along the poetic drama—we believe the public's ready for it, and we're willing to take a big financial risk in order to be the first to give them what they want. *But we don't believe they could be made to want this.* The fact is, there isn't enough drama in your play to the allowance of poetry—the thing drags all through. You've got a big idea, but it's not out of swaddling clothes.

If this was your first play I'd say: *Try again.* But it has been just the same with all the others you've shown me. And you remember the result of *The Lee Shore,*' where you carried all the expenses of production yourself, and we couldn't fill the theatre for a week. Yet *The Lee Shore* was a modern problem play—much easier to swing than blank verse. It isn't as if you hadn't tried all kinds—

Granice folded the letter and put it carefully back into the envelope. Why on earth was he re-reading it, when he knew every phrase in it by heart, when for a month past he had seen it, night after night, stand out in letters of flame against the darkness of his sleepless lids?

It has been just the same with all the others you've shown me.

That was the way they dismissed ten years of passionate unremitting work!

You remember the result of The Lee Shore.

Good God—as if he were likely to forget it! He relived it all now in a drowning flash: the persistent rejection of the play, his sudden resolve to put it on at his own cost, to spend ten thousand dollars of his inheritance on testing his chance of success—the fever of preparation, the dry-mouthed agony of the "first night," the flat fall, the stupid press, his secret rush to Europe to escape the condolence of his friends!

It isn't as if you hadn't tried all kinds.

No—he had tried all kinds: comedy, tragedy, prose and verse, the light curtain-raiser, the short sharp drama, the bourgeois-realistic and the lyrical-romantic—finally deciding that he would no longer "prostitute his talent" to win popularity, but would impose on the public his own theory of art in the form of five acts of blank verse. Yes, he had offered them everything—and always with the same result.

Ten years of it—ten years of dogged work and unrelieved failure. The ten years from forty to fifty—the best ten years of his life! And if one counted the years before, the silent years of dreams, assimilation, preparation—then call it half a man's life-time: half a man's life-time thrown away!

And what was he to do with the remaining half? Well, he had settled that, thank God! He turned and glanced anxiously at the clock. Ten minutes past eight—only ten minutes had been consumed in that stormy rush through his whole past! And he must wait another twenty minutes for Ascham. It was one of the worst symptoms of his case that, in proportion as he had grown to shrink from human company, he dreaded more and more to be alone. . . . But why the devil was he waiting for Ascham? Why didn't he cut the knot himself? Since he was so unutterably sick of the whole business, why did he have to call in an outsider to rid him of this nightmare of living?

He opened the drawer again and laid his hand on the revolver. It was a small slim ivory toy—just the instrument for a tired sufferer to give himself a "hypodermic" with. Granice raised it slowly in one hand, while with the other he felt under the thin hair at the back of his head, between the ear and the nape. He knew just where to place the muzzle: he had once got a young surgeon to show him. And as he found the spot, and lifted the revolver to it, the inevitable phenomenon occurred.

The hand that held the weapon began to shake, the tremor communicated itself to his arm, his heart gave a wild leap which sent up a wave of deadly nausea to his throat, he smelt the powder, he sickened at the crash of the bullet through his skull, and a sweat of fear broke out over his forehead and ran down his quivering face. . . .

He laid away the revolver with an oath and, pulling out a cologne-scented handkerchief, passed it tremulously over his brow and temples. It was no use—he knew he could never do it in that way. His attempts at self-destruction were as futile as his snatches at fame! He couldn't make himself a real life, and he couldn't get rid of the life he had. And that was why he had sent for Ascham to help him. . . .

The lawyer, over the Camembert and Burgundy, began to excuse himself for his delay.

"I didn't like to say anything while your man was about—but the fact is, I was sent for on a rather unusual matter—"

"Oh, it's all right," said Granice cheerfully. He was beginning to feel the usual reaction that food and company produced. It was not any recovered pleasure in life that he felt, but only a deeper withdrawal into himself. It was easier to go on automatically with the social gestures than to uncover to any human eye the abyss within him.

"My dear fellow, it's sacrilege to keep a dinner waiting—especially the production of an artist like yours." Mr. Ascham sipped his Burgundy luxuriously. "But the fact is, Mrs. Ashgrove sent for me."

Granice raised his head with a quick movement of surprise. For a moment he was shaken out of his self-absorption.

"*Mrs. Ashgrove?*"

Ascham smiled. "I thought you'd be interested; I know your passion for *causes celebres*. And this promises to be one. Of course it's out of our line entirely—we never touch criminal cases. But she wanted to consult me as a friend. Ashgrove was a distant connection of my wife's. And, by Jove, it *is* a queer case!" The servant re-entered, and Ascham snapped his lips shut.

Would the gentlemen have their coffee in the dining-room?

"No—serve it in the library," said Granice, rising. He led the way back to the curtained confidential room. He was really curious to hear what Ascham had to tell him.

While the coffee and cigars were being served he fidgeted about the library, glancing at his letters—the usual meaningless notes and bills—and picking up the evening paper. As he unfolded it a headline caught his eye.

ROSE MELROSE WANTS TO PLAY POETRY.
THINKS SHE HAS FOUND HER POET.

He read on with a thumping heart—found the name of a young author he had barely heard of, saw the title of a play, a "poetic drama," dance before his eyes, and dropped the paper, sick, disgusted. It was true, then—she *was* "game"—it was not the manner but the matter she mistrusted!

Granice turned to the servant, who seemed to be purposely lingering. "I shan't need you this evening, Flint. I'll lock up myself."

He fancied the man's acquiescence implied surprise. What was going on, Flint seemed to wonder, that Mr. Granice should want him out of the way? Probably he would find a pretext for coming back to see.

Granice suddenly felt himself enveloped in a network of espionage.

As the door closed he threw himself into an armchair and leaned forward to take a light from Ascham's cigar.

"Tell me about Mrs. Ashgrove," he said, seeming to himself to speak stiffly, as if his lips were cracked.

"Mrs. Ashgrove? Well, there's not much to *tell*."

"And you couldn't if there were?" Granice smiled.

"Probably not. As a matter of fact, she wanted my advice about her choice of counsel. There was nothing especially confidential in our talk."

"And what's your impression, now you've seen her?"

"My impression is, very distinctly, *that nothing will ever be known*."

"Ah—?" Granice murmured, puffing at his cigar.

"I'm more and more convinced that whoever poisoned Ashgrove knew his business, and will consequently never be found out. That's a capital cigar you've given me."

"You like it? I get them over from Cuba." Granice examined his own reflectively. "Then you believe in the theory that the clever criminals never *are* caught?"

"Of course I do. Look about you—look back for the last dozen years—none of the big murder problems are ever solved." The lawyer ruminated behind his blue cloud. "Why, take the instance in your own family: I'd forgotten I had an illustration at hand! Take old Joseph Lenman's murder—do you suppose that will ever be explained?"

As the words dropped from Ascham's lips his host looked slowly about the library, and every object in it stared back at him with a stale unescapable familiarity. How sick he was of looking at that room! It was as dull as the face of a wife one has wearied of. He cleared his throat slowly; then he turned his head to the lawyer and said: "I could explain the Lenman murder myself."

Ascham's eye kindled: he shared Granice's interest in criminal cases.

"By Jove! You've had a theory all this time? It's odd you never mentioned it. Go ahead and tell me. There are certain features in the Lenman case not unlike this Ashgrove affair, and your idea may be a help."

Granice paused and his eye reverted instinctively to the table drawer in which the revolver and the manuscript lay side by side. What if he were to try another appeal to Rose Melrose? Then he looked at the notes and bills on the table, and the horror of taking up again the lifeless routine of life—of performing the same automatic gestures another day—displaced his fleeting vision.

"I haven't a theory. I *know* who murdered Joseph Lenman."

Ascham settled himself comfortably in his chair, prepared for enjoyment.

"You *know?* Well, who did?" he laughed.

"I did," said Granice, rising.

He stood before Ascham, and the lawyer lay back staring up at him. Then he broke into another laugh.

"Why, this is glorious! You murdered him, did you? To inherit his money, I suppose? Better and better! Go on, my boy! Unbosom yourself! Tell me all about it! Confession is good for the soul."

Granice waited till the lawyer had shaken the last peal of laughter from his throat; then he repeated doggedly: "I murdered him."

The two men looked at each other for a long moment, and this time Ascham did not laugh.

"Granice!"

"I murdered him—to get his money, as you say."

There was another pause, and Granice, with a vague underlying sense of amusement, saw his guest's look change from pleasantry to apprehension.

"What's the joke, my dear fellow? I fail to see."

"It's not a joke. It's the truth. I murdered him." He had spoken painfully at first, as if there were a knot in his throat; but each time he repeated the words he found they were easier to say.

Ascham laid down his extinct cigar.

"What's the matter? Aren't you well? What on earth are you driving at?"

"I'm perfectly well. But I murdered my cousin, Joseph Lenman, and I want it known that I murdered him."

"*You want it known?*"

"Yes. That's why I sent for you. I'm sick of living, and when I try to kill myself I funk it." He spoke quite naturally now, as if the knot in his throat had been untied.

"Good Lord—good Lord," the lawyer gasped.

"But I suppose," Granice continued, "there's no doubt this would be murder in the first degree? I'm sure of the chair if I own up?"

Ascham drew a long breath; then he said slowly: "Sit down, Granice. Let's talk."

2.

Granice told his story simply, connectedly.

He began by a quick survey of his early years—the years of drudgery and privation. His father, a charming man who could never say "no," had so signally failed to say it on certain essential occasions that when he died he left an illegitimate family and a mortgaged estate. His lawful kin found themselves hanging over a gulf of debt, and young Granice, to support his mother and sister, had to leave Harvard and bury himself at eighteen in a broker's office. He loathed his work, and he was always poor, always worried and in ill-health. A few years later his mother died, but his sister, an ineffectual neurasthenic, remained on his hands. His own health gave out, and he had to go away for six months, and work harder than ever when he came back.

He had no knack for business, no head for figures, no dimmest insight into the mysteries of commerce. He wanted to travel and write—those were his inmost longings. And as the years dragged on, and he neared middle-age without making any more money, or acquiring any firmer health, a sick despair possessed him. He tried writing, but he always came home from the office so tired that his brain could not work.

For half the year he did not reach his dim up-town flat till after dark, and could only "brush up" for dinner, and afterward lie on the lounge with his pipe, while his sister droned through the evening paper. Sometimes he spent an evening at the theatre; or he dined out, or, more rarely, strayed off with an acquaintance or two in quest of what is known as "pleasure." And in summer, when he and Kate went to the sea-side for a month, he dozed through the days in utter weariness. Once he fell in love with a charming girl—but what had he to offer her, in God's name? She seemed to like him, and in common decency he had to drop out of the running. Apparently no one replaced him, for she never married, but grew stoutish, greyish, philanthropic—yet how sweet she had been when he had first kissed her! One more wasted life, he reflected...

But the stage had always been his master-passion. He would have sold his soul for the time and freedom to write plays! It was *in him*—he could not remember when it had not been his deepest-seated instinct. As the years passed it became a morbid, a relentless obsession—yet with every year the material conditions were more and more against it. He felt himself growing middle-aged, and he watched the reflection of the process in his sister's wasted face. At eighteen she had been pretty, and as full of enthusiasm as he.

Now she was sour, trivial, insignificant—she had missed her chance of life. And she had no resources, poor creature, was fashioned simply for the primitive functions she had been denied the chance to fulfil! It exasperated him to think of it—and to reflect that even now a little travel, a little health, a little money, might transform her, make her young and desirable. . . . The chief fruit of his experience was that there is no such fixed state as age or youth—there is only health as against sickness, wealth as against poverty; and age or youth as the outcome of the lot one draws.

At this point in his narrative Granice stood up, and went to lean against the mantel-piece, looking down at Ascham, who had not moved from his seat, or changed his attitude of rigid fascinated attention.

******

"Then came the summer when we went to Wrenfield to be near old Lenman—my mother's cousin, as you know. Some of the family always mounted guard over him—generally a niece or so. But that year they were all scattered, and one of the nieces offered to lend us her cottage if we'd relieve her of duty for two months. It was a nuisance for me, of course, for Wrenfield is two hours from town; but my mother, who was a slave to family observances, had always been good to the old man, so it was natural we should be called on—and there was the saving of rent and the good air for Kate. So we went.

"You never knew Joseph Lenman? Well, picture to yourself an amoeba or some primitive organism of that sort, under a Titan's microscope. He was large, undifferentiated, inert—since I could remember him he had done nothing but take his temperature and read the *Churchman*. Oh, and cultivate melons—that was his hobby. Not vulgar, out-of-door melons—his were grown under glass. He had miles of it at Wrenfield—his big kitchen-garden was surrounded by blinking battalions of green-houses. And in nearly all of them melons were grown—early melons and late, French, English, domestic—dwarf melons and monsters: every shape, colour and variety.

"They were petted and nursed like children—a staff of trained attendants waited on them. I'm not sure they didn't have a doctor to take their temperature—at any rate the place was full of thermometers. And they didn't sprawl on the ground like ordinary melons; they were trained against the glass like nectarines, and each melon hung in a net which sustained its weight and left it free on all sides to the sun and air . . .

"It used to strike me sometimes that old Lenman was just like one of his own melons—the pale-fleshed English kind. His life, apathetic and motionless, hung in a net of gold, in an equable warm ventilated atmosphere, high above sordid earthly worries. The cardinal rule of his existence was not to let himself be 'worried.' . . . I remember his advising me to try it myself, one day when I spoke to him about Kate's bad health, and her need of a change. 'I never let myself worry,' he said complacently. 'It's the worst thing for the liver—and you look to me as if you had a liver. Take my advice and be cheerful. You'll make yourself happier and others too.' And all he had to do was to write a cheque, and send the poor girl off for a holiday!

"The hardest part of it was that the money half-belonged to us already. The old skin-flint only had it for life, in trust for us and the others. But his life was a good deal sounder than mine or Kate's—and one could picture him taking extra care of it for the joke of keeping us waiting. I always felt that the sight of our hungry eyes was a tonic to him.

"Well, I tried to see if I couldn't reach him through his vanity. I flattered him, feigned a passionate interest in his melons. And he was taken in, and used to discourse on them by the hour. On fine days he was driven to the green-houses in his pony-chair, and waddled through them, prodding and leering at the fruit, like a fat Turk in his *seraglio*. When he bragged to me of the expense of growing them I was reminded of a hideous old Lothario bragging of what his pleasures cost. And the resemblance was completed by the fact that he couldn't eat as much as a mouthful of his melons—had lived for years on buttermilk and toast. 'But, after all, it's my only hobby—why shouldn't I indulge it?' he said sentimentally. As if I'd ever been able to indulge any of mine! On the keep of those melons Kate and I could have lived like gods. . . .

"One day toward the end of the summer, when Kate was too unwell to drag herself up to the big house, she asked me to go and spend the afternoon with cousin Joseph. It was a lovely soft September afternoon—a day to lie under a Roman stone-pine, with one's eyes on the sky, and let the cosmic harmonies rush through one. Perhaps the vision was suggested by the fact that, as I entered cousin Joseph's hideous black walnut library, I passed one of the under-gardeners, a handsome full-throated Italian, who dashed out in such a hurry that he nearly knocked me down. I remember thinking it queer that the fellow, whom I had often seen about the melon-houses, did not bow to me, or even seem to see me.

"Cousin Joseph sat in his usual seat, behind the darkened windows, his fat hands folded on his protuberant waistcoat, the last number of the *Churchman* at his elbow, and near it, on a huge dish, a fat melon—the fattest melon I'd ever seen. As I looked at it I pictured the ecstasy of contemplation from which I must have roused him, and congratulated myself on finding him in such a mood, since I had made up my mind to ask him a favour. Then I noticed that his face, instead of looking as calm as an egg-shell, was distorted and whimpering—and without stopping to greet me he pointed passionately to the melon.

"'Look at it, look at it—did you ever see such a beauty? Such firmness—roundness—such delicious smoothness to the touch?' It was as if he had said 'she' instead of 'it,' and when he put out his senile hand and touched the melon I positively had to look the other way.

"Then he told me what had happened. The Italian under-gardener, who had been specially recommended for the melon-houses—though it was against my cousin's principles to employ a Papist—had been assigned to the care of the monster: for it had revealed itself, early in its existence, as destined to become a monster, to surpass its plumpest, pulpiest sisters, carry off prizes at agricultural shows, and be photographed and celebrated in every gardening paper in the land. The Italian had done well—seemed to have a sense of responsibility. And that very morning he had been ordered to pick the melon, which was to be shown next day at the county fair, and to bring it in for Mr. Lenman to gaze on its blonde virginity. But in picking it, what had the damned scoundrelly Jesuit done but drop it—drop it crash on the sharp spout of a watering-pot, so that it received a deep gash in its firm pale rotundity, and was henceforth but a bruised, ruined, fallen melon?

"The old man's rage was fearful in its impotence—he shook, spluttered and strangled with it. He had just had the Italian up and had sacked him on the spot, without wages or character—had threatened to have him arrested if he was ever caught prowling about Wrenfield. 'By God, and I'll do it—I'll write to Washington—I'll have the pauper scoundrel deported! I'll show him what money can do!' As likely as not there was some murderous Black-hand business under it—it would be found that the fellow was a member of a 'gang.' Those Italians would murder you for a quarter. He meant to have the police look into it. . . . And then he grew frightened at his own excitement.

'But I must calm myself,' he said. He took his temperature, rang for his drops, and turned to the *Churchman*. He had been reading an article on Nestorianism when the melon was brought in. He asked me to go on with it, and I read to him for an hour, in the dim close room, with a fat fly buzzing stealthily about the fallen melon.

"All the while one phrase of the old man's buzzed in my brain like the fly about the melon. '*I'll show him what money can do!*' Good heaven! If *I* could but show the old man! If I could make him see his power of giving happiness as a new outlet for his monstrous egotism! I tried to tell him something about my situation and Kate's—spoke of my ill-health, my unsuccessful drudgery, my longing to write, to make myself a name—I stammered out an entreaty for a loan. 'I can guarantee to repay you, sir—I've a half-written play as security. . . .'

"I shall never forget his glassy stare. His face had grown as smooth as an egg-shell again—his eyes peered over his fat cheeks like sentinels over a slippery rampart.

"'A half-written play—a play of *yours* as security?' He looked at me almost fearfully, as if detecting the first symptoms of insanity. 'Do you understand anything of business?' he enquired mildly. I laughed and answered: 'No, not much.'

"He leaned back with closed lids. 'All this excitement has been too much for me,' he said. 'If you'll excuse me, I'll prepare for my nap.' And I stumbled out of the room, blindly, like the Italian."

★★★★★★

Granice moved away from the mantel-piece, and walked across to the tray set out with decanters and soda-water. He poured himself a tall glass of soda-water, emptied it, and glanced at Ascham's dead cigar.

"Better light another," he suggested.

The lawyer shook his head, and Granice went on with his tale. He told of his mounting obsession—how the murderous impulse had waked in him on the instant of his cousin's refusal, and he had muttered to himself: "By God, if you won't, I'll make you." He spoke more tranquilly as the narrative proceeded, as though his rage had died down once the resolve to act on it was taken. He applied his whole mind to the question of how the old man was to be "disposed of." Suddenly he remembered the outcry: "Those Italians will murder you for a quarter!" But no definite project presented itself: he simply waited for an inspiration.

Granice and his sister moved to town a day or two after the incident of the melon. But the cousins, who had returned, kept them informed of the old man's condition. One day, about three weeks later, Granice, on getting home, found Kate excited over a report from Wrenfield. The Italian had been there again—had somehow slipped into the house, made his way up to the library, and "used threatening language." The house-keeper found cousin Joseph gasping, the whites of his eyes showing "something awful." The doctor was sent for, and the attack warded off; and the police had ordered the Italian from the neighbourhood.

But Cousin Joseph, thereafter, languished, had "nerves," and lost his taste for toast and butter-milk. The doctor called in a colleague, and the consultation amused and excited the old man—he became once more an important figure. The medical men reassured the family—too completely!—and to the patient they recommended a more varied diet: advised him to take whatever "tempted him." And so one day, tremulously, prayerfully, he decided on a tiny bit of melon. It was brought up with ceremony, and consumed in the presence of the housekeeper and a hovering cousin; and twenty minutes later he was dead. . . .

"But you remember the circumstances," Granice went on; "how suspicion turned at once on the Italian? In spite of the hint the police had given him he had been seen hanging about the house since 'the scene.' It was said that he had tender relations with the kitchen-maid, and the rest seemed easy to explain. But when they looked round to ask him for the explanation he was gone—gone clean out of sight. He had been 'warned' to leave Wrenfield, and he had taken the warning so to heart that no one ever laid eyes on him again."

Granice paused. He had dropped into a chair opposite the lawyer's, and he sat for a moment, his head thrown back, looking about the familiar room. Everything in it had grown grimacing and alien, and each strange insistent object seemed craning forward from its place to hear him.

"It was I who put the stuff in the melon," he said. "And I don't want you to think I'm sorry for it. This isn't 'remorse,' understand. I'm glad the old skin-flint is dead—I'm glad the others have their money. But mine's no use to me anymore. My sister married miserably, and died. And I've never had what I wanted."

Ascham continued to stare; then he said: "What on earth was your object, then?"

"Why, to *get* what I wanted—what I fancied was in reach! I wanted change, rest, *life*, for both of us—wanted, above all, for myself, the chance to write! I travelled, got back my health, and came home to tie myself up to my work. And I've slaved at it steadily for ten years without reward—without the most distant hope of success! Nobody will look at my stuff. And now I'm fifty, and I'm beaten, and I know it." His chin dropped forward on his breast. "I want to chuck the whole business," he ended.

3.

It was after midnight when Ascham left.

His hand on Granice's shoulder, as he turned to go—"District Attorney be hanged; see a doctor, see a doctor!" he had cried; and so, with an exaggerated laugh, had pulled on his coat and departed.

Granice turned back into the library. It had never occurred to him that Ascham would not believe his story. For three hours he had explained, elucidated, patiently and painfully gone over every detail—but without once breaking down the iron incredulity of the lawyer's eye.

At first Ascham had feigned to be convinced—but that, as Granice now perceived, was simply to get him to expose himself, to entrap him into contradictions. And when the attempt failed, when Granice triumphantly met and refuted each disconcerting question, the lawyer dropped the mask suddenly, and said with a good-humoured laugh: "By Jove, Granice you'll write a successful play yet. The way you've worked this all out is a marvel."

Granice swung about furiously—that last sneer about the play inflamed him. Was all the world in a conspiracy to deride his failure?

"I did it, I did it," he muttered sullenly, his rage spending itself against the impenetrable surface of the other's mockery; and Ascham answered with a smile: "Ever read any of those books on hallucination? I've got a fairly good medico-legal library. I could send you one or two if you like. . . ."

Left alone, Granice cowered down in the chair before his writing-table. He understood that Ascham thought him off his head.

"Good God—what if they all think me crazy?"

The horror of it broke out over him in a cold sweat—he sat there and shook, his eyes hidden in his icy hands. But gradually, as he began to rehearse his story for the thousandth time, he saw again how incontrovertible it was, and felt sure that any criminal lawyer would believe him.

"That's the trouble—Ascham's not a criminal lawyer. And then he's a friend. What a fool I was to talk to a friend! Even if he did believe me, he'd never let me see it—his instinct would be to cover the whole thing up.. . . . But in that case—if he *did* believe me—he might think it a kindness to get me shut up in an asylum. . . ." Granice began to tremble again. "Good heaven! If he should bring in an expert—one of those damned alienists! Ascham and Pettilow can do anything—their word always goes. If Ascham drops a hint that I'd better be shut up, I'll be in a strait-jacket by tomorrow! And he'd do it from the kindest motives—be quite right to do it if he thinks I'm a murderer!"

The vision froze him to his chair. He pressed his fists to his bursting temples and tried to think. For the first time he hoped that Ascham had not believed his story.

"But he did—he did! I can see it now—I noticed what a queer eye he cocked at me. Good God, what shall I do—what shall I do?"

He started up and looked at the clock. Half-past one. What if Ascham should think the case urgent, rout out an alienist, and come back with him? Granice jumped to his feet, and his sudden gesture brushed the morning paper from the table. Mechanically he stooped to pick it up, and the movement started a new train of association.

He sat down again, and reached for the telephone book in the rack by his chair.

"Give me three-o-ten . . . . yes."

The new idea in his mind had revived his flagging energy. He would act—act at once. It was only by thus planning ahead, committing himself to some unavoidable line of conduct, that he could pull himself through the meaningless days. Each time he reached a fresh decision it was like coming out of a foggy weltering sea into a calm harbour with lights. One of the queerest phases of his long agony was the intense relief produced by these momentary lulls.

"That the office of the *Investigator?* Yes? Give me Mr. Denver, please. . . . Hallo, Denve. . . . Yes, Hubert Granice. . . . . Just caught you? Going straight home? Can I come and see you . . . . yes, now ... have a talk? It's rather urgent ... yes, might give you some first-rate 'copy.' . . . All right!" He hung up the receiver with a laugh. It had been a happy thought to call up the editor of the *Investigator*—Robert Denver was the very man he needed. . . .

Granice put out the lights in the library—it was odd how the automatic gestures persisted!—went into the hall, put on his hat and overcoat, and let himself out of the flat. In the hall, a sleepy elevator boy blinked at him and then dropped his head on his folded arms.

Granice passed out into the street. At the corner of Fifth Avenue he hailed a crawling cab, and called out an up-town address. The long thoroughfare stretched before him, dim and deserted, like an ancient avenue of tombs. But from Denver's house a friendly beam fell on the pavement; and as Granice sprang from his cab the editor's electric turned the corner.

The two men grasped hands, and Denver, feeling for his latch-key, ushered Granice into the brightly-lit hall.

"Disturb me? Not a bit. You might have, at ten tomorrow morning . . . . but this is my liveliest hour . . . . you know my habits of old."

Granice had known Robert Denver for fifteen years—watched his rise through all the stages of journalism to the Olympian pinnacle of the *Investigator's* editorial office. In the thick-set man with grizzling hair there were few traces left of the hungry-eyed young reporter who, on his way home in the small hours, used to "bob in" on Granice, while the latter sat grinding at his plays. Denver had to pass Granice's flat on the way to his own, and it became a habit, if he saw a light in the window, and Granice's shadow against the blind, to go in, smoke a pipe, and discuss the universe.

"Well—this is like old times—a good old habit reversed." The editor smote his visitor genially on the shoulder. "Reminds me of the nights when I used to rout you out. . . . How's the play, by the way? There *is* a play, I suppose? It's as safe to ask you that as to say to some men: 'How's the baby?'"

Denver laughed good-naturedly, and Granice thought how thick and heavy he had grown. It was evident, even to Granice's tortured nerves, that the words had not been uttered in malice—and the fact gave him a new measure of his insignificance. Denver did not even know that he had been a failure! The fact hurt more than Ascham's irony.

"Come in—come in." The editor led the way into a small cheerful room, where there were cigars and decanters. He pushed an armchair toward his visitor, and dropped into another with a comfortable groan.

"Now, then—help yourself. And let's hear all about it."

He beamed at Granice over his pipe-bowl, and the latter, lighting his cigar, said to himself: "Success makes men comfortable, but it makes them stupid."

Then he turned, and began: "Denver, I want to tell you—"

The clock ticked rhythmically on the mantel-piece. The room was gradually filled with drifting blue layers of smoke, and through them the editor's face came and went like the moon through a moving sky. Once the hour struck—then the rhythmical ticking began again. The atmosphere grew denser and heavier, and beads of perspiration began to roll from Granice's forehead.

"Do you mind if I open the window?"

"No. It *is* stuffy in here. Wait—I'll do it myself." Denver pushed down the upper sash, and returned to his chair. "Well—go on," he said, filling another pipe. His composure exasperated Granice.

"There's no use in my going on if you don't believe me."

The editor remained unmoved. "Who says I don't believe you? And how can I tell till you've finished?"

Granice went on, ashamed of his outburst. "It was simple enough, as you'll see. From the day the old man said to me, 'Those Italians would murder you for a quarter,' I dropped everything and just worked at my scheme. It struck me at once that I must find a way of getting to Wrenfield and back in a night—and that led to the idea of a motor. A motor—that never occurred to you? You wonder where I got the money, I suppose. Well, I had a thousand or so put by, and I nosed around till I found what I wanted—a second-hand racer.

"I knew how to drive a car, and I tried the thing and found it was all right. Times were bad, and I bought it for my price, and stored it away. Where? Why, in one of those no-questions-asked garages where they keep motors that are not for family use. I had a lively cousin who had put me up to that dodge, and I looked about till I found a queer hole where they took in my car like a baby in a foundling asylum..... Then I practiced running to Wrenfield and back in a night. I knew the way pretty well, for I'd done it often with the same lively cousin—and in the small hours, too. The distance is over ninety miles, and on the third trial I did it under two hours. But my arms were so lame that I could hardly get dressed the next morning.....

"Well, then came the report about the Italian's threats, and I saw I must act at once . . . I meant to break into the old man's room, shoot him, and get away again. It was a big risk, but I thought I could manage it. Then we heard that he was ill—that there'd been a consultation. Perhaps the fates were going to do it for me! Good Lord, if that could only be!. . . . "

Granice stopped and wiped his forehead: the open window did not seem to have cooled the room.

"Then came word that he was better; and the day after, when I came up from my office, I found Kate laughing over the news that he was to try a bit of melon. The house-keeper had just telephoned her—all Wrenfield was in a flutter. The doctor himself had picked out the melon, one of the little French ones that are hardly bigger than a large tomato—and the patient was to eat it at his breakfast the next morning.

"In a flash I saw my chance. It was a bare chance, no more. But I knew the ways of the house—I was sure the melon would be brought in overnight and put in the pantry ice-box. If there were only one melon in the icebox I could be fairly sure it was the one I wanted. Melons didn't lie around loose in that house—everyone was known, numbered, catalogued. The old man was beset by the dread that the servants would eat them, and he took a hundred mean precautions to prevent it. Yes, I felt pretty sure of my melon. . . . and poisoning was much safer than shooting. It would have been the devil and all to get into the old man's bedroom without his rousing the house; but I ought to be able to break into the pantry without much trouble.

"It was a cloudy night, too—everything served me. I dined quietly, and sat down at my desk. Kate had one of her usual headaches, and went to bed early. As soon as she was gone I slipped out. I had got together a sort of disguise—red beard and queer-looking ulster. I shoved them into a bag, and went round to the garage. There was no one there but a half-drunken machinist whom I'd never seen before. That served me, too. They were always changing machinists, and this new fellow didn't even bother to ask if the car belonged to me. It was a very easy-going place. . . . .

"Well, I jumped in, ran up Broadway, and let the car go as soon as I was out of Harlem. Dark as it was, I could trust myself to strike a sharp pace. In the shadow of a wood I stopped a second and got into the beard and ulster. Then away again—it was just eleven-thirty when I got to Wrenfield.

"I left the car in a dark lane behind the Lenman place, and slipped through the kitchen-garden. The melon-houses winked at me through the dark—I remember thinking that they knew what I wanted to know. . . . . By the stable a dog came out growling—but he nosed me out, jumped on me, and went back. . . . The house was as dark as the grave. I knew everybody went to bed by ten. But there might be a prowling servant—the kitchen-maid might have come down to let in her Italian. I had to risk that, of course. I crept around by the back door and hid in the shrubbery. Then I listened. It was all as silent as death. I crossed over to the house, pried open the pantry window and climbed in. I had a little electric lamp in my pocket, and shielding it with my cap I groped my way to the ice-box, opened it—and there was the little French melon. . . . . only one.

"I stopped to listen—I was quite cool. Then I pulled out my bottle of stuff and my syringe, and gave each section of the melon a hypodermic. It was all done inside of three minutes—at ten minutes to twelve I was back in the car. I got out of the lane as quietly as I could, struck a back road that skirted the village, and let the car out as soon as I was beyond the last houses. I only stopped once on the way in, to drop the beard and ulster into a pond. I had a big stone ready to weight them with and they went down plump, like a dead body—and at two o'clock I was back at my desk."

Granice stopped speaking and looked across the smoke-fumes at his listener; but Denver's face remained inscrutable.

At length he said: "Why did you want to tell me this?"

The question startled Granice. He was about to explain, as he had explained to Ascham; but suddenly it occurred to him that if his motive had not seemed convincing to the lawyer it would carry much less weight with Denver. Both were successful men, and success does not understand the subtle agony of failure. Granice cast about for another reason.

"Why, I—the thing haunts me. . . . remorse, I suppose you'd call it. . . . ."

Denver struck the ashes from his empty pipe.

"Remorse? Bosh!" he said energetically.

Granice's heart sank. "You don't believe in—*remorse?*"

"Not an atom: in the man of action. The mere fact of your talking of remorse proves to me that you're not the man to have planned and put through such a job."

Granice groaned. "Well—I lied to you about remorse. I've never felt any."

Denver's lips tightened sceptically about his freshly-filled pipe. "What was your motive, then? You must have had one."

"I'll tell you—" And Granice began again to rehearse the story of his failure, of his loathing for life. "Don't say you don't believe me this time . . . . . that this isn't a real reason!" he stammered out piteously as he ended.

Denver meditated. "No, I won't say that. I've seen too many queer things. There's always a reason for wanting to get out of life—the wonder is that we find so many for staying in!"

Granice's heart grew light. "Then you *do* believe me?" he faltered.

"Believe that you're sick of the job? Yes. And that you haven't the nerve to pull the trigger? Oh, yes—that's easy enough, too. But all that doesn't make you a murderer—though I don't say it proves you could never have been one."

"I *have* been one, Denver—I swear to you."

"Perhaps." He meditated. "Just tell me one or two things."

"Oh, go ahead. You won't stump me!" Granice heard himself say with a laugh.

"Well—how did you make all those trial trips without exciting your sister's curiosity? I knew your night habits pretty well at that time, remember. You were very seldom out late. Didn't the change in your ways surprise her?"

"No; because she was away at the time. She went to pay several visits in the country soon after we came back from Wrenfield, and was only in town for a night or two before—before I did the job."

"And that night she went to bed early with a headache?"

"Yes—blinding. She didn't know anything when she had that kind. And her room was at the back of the flat."

Denver again meditated. "And when you got back—she didn't hear you? You got in without her knowing it?"

"Yes. I went straight to my work—took it up at the word where I'd left off—*why, Denver, don't you remember?*" Granice suddenly, passionately interjected.

"Remember—?"

"Yes; how you found me—when you looked in that morning, between two and three. ... your usual hour . . . . ?"

"Yes," the editor nodded.

Granice gave a short laugh. "In my old coat—with my pipe: looked as if I'd been working all night, didn't I? Well, I hadn't been in my chair ten minutes!"

Denver uncrossed his legs and then crossed them again. "I didn't know whether *you* remembered that."

"What?"

"My coming in that particular night—or morning."

Granice swung round in his chair. "Why, man alive! That's why I'm here now. Because it was you who spoke for me at the inquest, when they looked round to see what all the old man's heirs had been doing that night—you who testified to having dropped in and found me at my desk as usual. . . . . I thought *that* would appeal to your journalistic sense if nothing else would!"

Denver smiled. "Oh, my journalistic sense is still susceptible enough—and the idea's picturesque, I grant you: asking the man who proved your alibi to establish your guilt."

"That's it—that's it!" Granice's laugh had a ring of triumph.

"Well, but how about the other chap's testimony—I mean that young doctor: what was his name? Ned Ranney. Don't you remember my testifying that I'd met him at the elevated station, and told him I was on my way to smoke a pipe with you, and his saying: 'All right; you'll find him in. I passed the house two hours ago, and saw his shadow against the blind, as usual.' And the lady with the toothache in the flat across the way: she corroborated his statement, you remember."

"Yes; I remember."

"Well, then?"

"Simple enough. Before starting I rigged up a kind of manikin with old coats and a cushion—something to cast a shadow on the blind. All you fellows were used to seeing my shadow there in the small hours—I counted on that, and knew you'd take any vague outline as mine."

"Simple enough, as you say. But the woman with the toothache saw the shadow move—you remember she said she saw you sink forward, as if you'd fallen asleep."

"Yes; and she was right. It *did* move. I suppose some extra-heavy dray must have jolted by the flimsy building—at any rate, something gave my manikin a jar, and when I came back he had sunk forward, half over the table."

There was a long silence between the two men. Granice, with a throbbing heart, watched Denver refill his pipe. The editor, at any rate, did not sneer and flout him. After all, journalism gave a deeper insight than the law into the fantastic possibilities of life, prepared one better to allow for the incalculableness of human impulses.

"Well?" Granice faltered out.

Denver stood up with a shrug. "Look here, man—what's wrong with you? Make a clean breast of it! Nerves gone to smash? I'd like to take you to see a chap I know—an ex-prize-fighter—who's a wonder at pulling fellows in your state out of their hole—"

"Oh, oh—" Granice broke in. He stood up also, and the two men eyed each other. "You don't believe me, then?"

"This yarn—how can I? There wasn't a flaw in your alibi."

"But haven't I filled it full of them now?"

Denver shook his head. "I might think so if I hadn't happened to know that you *wanted* to. There's the hitch, don't you see?"

Granice groaned. "No, I didn't. You mean my wanting to be found guilty—?"

"Of course! If somebody else had accused you, the story might have been worth looking into. As it is, a child could have invented it. It doesn't do much credit to your ingenuity."

Granice turned sullenly toward the door. What was the use of arguing? But on the threshold a sudden impulse drew him back. "Look here, Denver—I daresay you're right. But will you do just one thing to prove it? Put my statement in the *Investigator*, just as I've made it. Ridicule it as much as you like. Only give the other fellows a chance at it—men who don't know anything about me. Set them talking and looking about. I don't care a damn whether *you* believe me—what I want is to convince the Grand Jury! I oughtn't to have come to a man who knows me—your cursed incredulity is infectious. I don't put my case well, because I know in advance it's discredited, and I almost end by not believing it myself. That's why I can't convince *you*. It's a vicious circle." He laid a hand on Denver's arm. "Send a stenographer, and put my statement in the paper."

But Denver did not warm to the idea. "My dear fellow, you seem to forget that all the evidence was pretty thoroughly sifted at the time, every possible clue followed up. The public would have been ready enough then to believe that you murdered old Lenman—you or anybody else. All they wanted was a murderer—the most improbable would have served. But your alibi was too confoundedly complete. And nothing you've told me has shaken it." Denver laid his cool hand over the other's burning fingers. "Look here, old fellow, go home and work up a better case—then come in and submit it to the *Investigator*."

4.

The perspiration was rolling off Granice's forehead. Every few minutes he had to draw out his handkerchief and wipe the moisture from his haggard face.

For an hour and a half, he had been talking steadily, putting his case to the district attorney. Luckily he had a speaking acquaintance with Allonby, and had obtained, without much difficulty, a private audience on the very day after his talk with Robert Denver. In the interval between he had hurried home, got out of his evening clothes, and gone forth again at once into the dreary dawn. His fear of Ascham and the alienist made it impossible for him to remain in his rooms. And it seemed to him that the only way of averting that hideous peril was by establishing, in some sane impartial mind, the proof of his guilt. Even if he had not been so incurably sick of life, the electric chair seemed now the only alternative to the strait-jacket.

As he paused to wipe his forehead he saw the district attorney glance at his watch. The gesture was significant, and Granice lifted an appealing hand. "I don't expect you to believe me now—but can't you put me under arrest, and have the thing looked into?"

Allonby smiled faintly under his heavy greyish moustache. He had a ruddy face, full and jovial, in which his keen professional eyes seemed to keep watch over impulses not strictly professional.

"Well, I don't know that we need lock you up just yet. But of course I'm bound to look into your statement—"

Granice rose with an exquisite sense of relief. Surely Allonby wouldn't have said that if he hadn't believed him!

"That's all right. Then I needn't detain you. I can be found at any time at my apartment." He gave the address.

The district attorney smiled again, more openly. "What do you say to leaving it for an hour or two this evening? I'm giving a little supper at Rector's—quiet, little affair, you understand: just Miss Melrose—I think you know her—and a friend or two; and if you'll join us. . . . ."

Granice stumbled out of the office without knowing what reply he had made.

He waited for four days—four days of concentrated horror. During the first twenty-four hours the fear of Ascham's alienist dogged him; and as that subsided, it was replaced by the exasperating sense that his avowal had made no impression on the district attorney. Evidently, if he had been going to look into the case, Allonby would have been heard from before now. . . . . . And that mocking invitation to supper showed clearly enough how little the story had impressed him!

Granice was overcome by the futility of any farther attempt to inculpate himself. He was chained to life—a "prisoner of consciousness." Where was it he had read the phrase? Well, he was learning what it meant. In the glaring night-hours, when his brain seemed ablaze, he was visited by a sense of his fixed identity, of his irreducible, inexpungable *selfness*, keener, more insidious, more unescapable, than any sensation he had ever known. He had not guessed that the mind was capable of such intricacies of self-realization, of penetrating so deep into its own dark windings. Often he woke from his brief snatches of sleep with the feeling that something material was clinging to him, was on his hands and face, and in his throat—and as his brain cleared he understood that it was the sense of his own loathed personality that stuck to him like some thick viscous substance.

Then, in the first morning hours, he would rise and look out of his window at the awakening activities of the street—at the street-cleaners, the ash-cart drivers, and the other dingy workers flitting hurriedly by through the sallow winter light. Oh, to be one of them—any of them—to take his chance in any of their skins! They were the toilers—the men whose lot was pitied—the victims wept over and ranted about by altruists and economists; and how gladly he would have taken up the load of any one of them, if only he might have shaken off his own! But, no—the iron circle of consciousness held them too: each one was handcuffed to his own hideous ego. Why wish to be any one man rather than another? The only absolute good was not to be. . . . And Flint, coming in to draw his bath, would ask if he preferred his eggs scrambled or poached that morning?

On the fifth day he wrote a long urgent letter to Allonby; and for the succeeding two days he had the occupation of waiting for an answer. He hardly stirred from his rooms, in his fear of missing the letter by a moment; but would the district attorney write, or send a representative: a policeman, a "secret agent," or some other mysterious emissary of the law?

On the third morning Flint, stepping softly—as if, confound it! his master were ill—entered the library where Granice sat behind an unread newspaper, and proffered a card on a tray.

Granice read the name—J. B. Hewson—and underneath, in pencil, "From the District Attorney's office." He started up with a thumping heart, and signed an assent to the servant.

Mr. Hewson was a slight sallow nondescript man of about fifty—the kind of man of whom one is sure to see a specimen in any crowd. "Just the type of the successful detective," Granice reflected as he shook hands with his visitor.

And it was in that character that Mr. Hewson briefly introduced himself. He had been sent by the District Attorney to have "a quiet talk" with Mr. Granice—to ask him to repeat the statement he had made about the Lenman murder.

His manner was so quiet, so reasonable and receptive, that Granice's self-confidence returned. Here was a sensible man—a man who knew his business—it would be easy enough to make *him* see through that ridiculous alibi! Granice offered Mr. Hewson a cigar, and lighting one himself—to prove his coolness—began again to tell his story.

He was conscious, as he proceeded, of telling it better than ever before. Practice helped, no doubt; and his listener's detached, impartial attitude helped still more. He could see that Hewson, at least, had not decided in advance to disbelieve him, and the sense of being trusted made him more lucid and more consecutive. Yes, this time his words would certainly carry conviction. . . . .

5.

Despairingly, Granice gazed up and down the shabby street. Beside him stood a young man with bright prominent eyes, a smooth but not too smoothly-shaven face, and an Irish smile. The young man's nimble glance followed Granice's.

"Sure of the number, are you?" he asked briskly.

"Oh, yes—it was 104."

"Well, then, the new building has swallowed it up—that's certain."

He tilted his head back and surveyed the half-finished front of a brick and limestone flat-house that reared its flimsy elegance above a row of tottering tenements and stables.

"Dead sure?" he repeated.

"Yes," said Granice, discouraged. "And even if I hadn't been, I know the garage was just opposite Leffler's over there." He pointed across the street to a tumble-down stable with a blotched sign on which the words "Livery and Boarding" were still faintly discernible.

The young man dashed across to the opposite pavement. "Well, that's something—may get a clue there. Leffler's—same name there, anyhow. You remember that name?"

"Yes—distinctly."

Granice had felt a return of confidence since he had enlisted the interest of the *Explorer's* "smartest" reporter. If there were moments when he hardly believed his own story, there were others when it seemed impossible that everyone should not believe it; and young Peter McCarren, peering, listening, questioning, jotting down notes, inspired him with an exquisite sense of security. McCarren had fastened on the case at once, "like a leech," as he phrased it—jumped at it, thrilled to it, and settled down to "draw the last drop of fact from it, and had not let go till he had." No one else had treated Granice in that way—even Allonby's detective had not taken a single note. And though a week had elapsed since the visit of that authorized official, nothing had been heard from the District Attorney's office: Allonby had apparently dropped the matter again. But McCarren wasn't going to drop it—not he! He positively hung on Granice's footsteps. They had spent the greater part of the previous day together, and now they were off again, running down clues.

But at Leffler's they got none, after all. Leffler's was no longer a stable. It was condemned to demolition, and in the respite between sentence and execution it had become a vague place of storage, a hospital for broken-down carriages and carts, presided over by a blear-eyed old woman who knew nothing of Flood's garage across the way—did not even remember what had stood there before the new flat-house began to rise.

"Well—we may run Leffler down somewhere; I've seen harder jobs done," said McCarren, cheerfully noting down the name.

As they walked back toward Sixth Avenue he added, in a less sanguine tone: "I'd undertake now to put the thing through if you could only put me on the track of that cyanide."

Granice's heart sank. Yes—there was the weak spot; he had felt it from the first! But he still hoped to convince McCarren that his case was strong enough without it; and he urged the reporter to come back to his rooms and sum up the facts with him again.

"Sorry, Mr. Granice, but I'm due at the office now. Besides, it'd be no use till I get some fresh stuff to work on. Suppose I call you up tomorrow or next day?"

He plunged into a trolley and left Granice gazing desolately after him.

Two days later he reappeared at the apartment, a shade less jaunty in demeanour.

"Well, Mr. Granice, the stars in their courses are against you, as the bard says. Can't get a trace of Flood, or of Leffler either. And you say you bought the motor through Flood, and sold it through him, too?"

"Yes," said Granice wearily.

"Who bought it, do you know?"

Granice wrinkled his brows. "Why, Flood—yes, Flood himself. I sold it back to him three months later."

"Flood? The devil! And I've ransacked the town for Flood. That kind of business disappears as if the earth had swallowed it."

Granice, discouraged, kept silence.

"That brings us back to the poison," McCarren continued, his note-book out. "Just go over that again, will you?"

And Granice went over it again. It had all been so simple at the time—and he had been so clever in covering up his traces! As soon as he decided on poison he looked about for an acquaintance who manufactured chemicals; and there was Jim Dawes, a Harvard classmate, in the dyeing business—just the man. But at the last moment it occurred to him that suspicion might turn toward so obvious an opportunity, and he decided on a more tortuous course. Another friend, Carrick Venn, a student of medicine whom irremediable ill-health had kept from the practice of his profession, amused his leisure with experiments in physics, for the exercise of which he had set up a simple laboratory.

Granice had the habit of dropping in to smoke a cigar with him on Sunday afternoons, and the friends generally sat in Venn's workshop, at the back of the old family house in Stuyvesant Square. Off this work-shop was the cupboard of supplies, with its row of deadly bottles. Carrick Venn was an original, a man of restless curious tastes, and his place, on a Sunday, was often full of visitors: a cheerful crowd of journalists, scribblers, painters, experimenters in divers forms of expression. Coming and going among so many, it was easy enough to pass unperceived; and one afternoon Granice, arriving before Venn had returned home, found himself alone in the work-shop, and quickly slipping into the cupboard, transferred the drug to his pocket.

But that had happened ten years ago; and Venn, poor fellow, was long since dead of his dragging ailment. His old father was dead, too, the house in Stuyvesant Square had been turned into a boarding-house, and the shifting life of New York had passed its rapid sponge over every trace of their obscure little history. Even the optimistic McCarren seemed to acknowledge the hopelessness of seeking for proof in that direction.

"And there's the third door slammed in our faces." He shut his note-book, and throwing back his head, rested his bright inquisitive eyes on Granice's furrowed face.

"Look here, Mr. Granice—you see the weak spot, don't you?"

The other made a despairing motion. "I see so many!"

"Yes: but the one that weakens all the others. Why the deuce do you want this thing known? Why do you want to put your head into the noose?"

Granice looked at him hopelessly, trying to take the measure of his quick light irreverent mind. No one so full of a cheerful animal life would believe in the craving for death as a sufficient motive; and

Granice racked his brain for one more convincing. But suddenly he saw the reporter's face soften, and melt to a naive sentimentalism.

"Mr. Granice—has the memory of it always haunted you?"

Granice stared a moment, and then leapt at the opening. "That's it—the memory of it . . . . always . . . ."

McCarren nodded vehemently. "Dogged your steps, eh? Wouldn't let you sleep? The time came when you *had* to make a clean breast of it?"

"I had to. Can't you understand?"

The reporter struck his fist on the table. "God, sir! I don't suppose there's a human being with a drop of warm blood in him that can't picture the deadly horrors of remorse—"

The Celtic imagination was aflame, and Granice mutely thanked him for the word. What neither Ascham nor Denver would accept as a conceivable motive the Irish reporter seized on as the most adequate; and, as he said, once one could find a convincing motive, the difficulties of the case became so many incentives to effort.

"Remorse—*remorse*," he repeated, rolling the word under his tongue with an accent that was a clue to the psychology of the popular drama; and Granice, perversely, said to himself: "If I could only have struck that note I should have been running in six theatres at once."

He saw that from that moment McCarren's professional zeal would be fanned by emotional curiosity; and he profited by the fact to propose that they should dine together, and go on afterward to some music-hall or theatre. It was becoming necessary to Granice to feel himself an object of pre-occupation, to find himself in another mind. He took a kind of grey penumbral pleasure in riveting McCarren's attention on his case; and to feign the grimaces of moral anguish became a passionately engrossing game. He had not entered a theatre for months; but he sat out the meaningless performance in rigid tolerance, sustained by the sense of the reporter's observation.

Between the acts, McCarren amused him with anecdotes about the audience: he knew everyone by sight, and could lift the curtain from every physiognomy. Granice listened indulgently. He had lost all interest in his kind, but he knew that he was himself the real centre of McCarren's attention, and that every word the latter spoke had an indirect bearing on his own problem.

"See that fellow over there—the little dried-up man in the third row, pulling his moustache? *His* memoirs would be worth publishing," McCarren said suddenly in the last *entr'acte*.

Granice, following his glance, recognised the detective from Allonby's office. For a moment he had the thrilling sense that he was being shadowed.

"Caesar, if *he* could talk—!" McCarren continued. "Know who he is, of course? Dr. John B. Stell, the biggest alienist in the country—"

Granice, with a start, bent again between the heads in front of him. "*That* man—the fourth from the aisle? You're mistaken. That's not Dr. Stell."

McCarren laughed. "Well, I guess I've been in court enough to know Stell when I see him. He testifies in nearly all the big cases where they plead insanity."

A cold shiver ran down Granice's spine, but he repeated obstinately: "That's not Dr. Stell."

"Not Stell? Why, man, I *know* him. Look—here he comes. If it isn't Stell, he won't speak to me."

The little dried-up man was moving slowly up the aisle. As he neared McCarren he made a slight gesture of recognition.

"How'do, Doctor Stell? Pretty slim show, ain't it?" the reporter cheerfully flung out at him. And Mr. J. B. Hewson, with a nod of amicable assent, passed on.

Granice sat benumbed. He knew he had not been mistaken—the man who had just passed was the same man whom Allonby had sent to see him: a physician disguised as a detective. Allonby, then, had thought him insane, like the others—had regarded his confession as the maundering of a maniac. The discovery froze Granice with horror—he seemed to see the mad-house gaping for him.

"Isn't there a man a good deal like him—a detective named J. B. Hewson?"

But he knew in advance what McCarren's answer would be. "Hewson? J. B. Hewson? Never heard of him. But that was J. B. Stell fast enough—I guess he can be trusted to know himself, and you saw he answered to his name."

6.

Some days passed before Granice could obtain a word with the district attorney: he began to think that Allonby avoided him.

But when they were face to face Allonby's jovial countenance showed no sign of embarrassment. He waved his visitor to a chair, and leaned across his desk with the encouraging smile of a consulting physician.

Granice broke out at once: "That detective you sent me the other day—"

Allonby raised a deprecating hand.

"—I know: it was Stell the alienist. Why did you do that, Allonby?"

The other's face did not lose its composure. "Because I looked up your story first—and there's nothing in it."

"Nothing in it?" Granice furiously interposed.

"Absolutely nothing. If there is, why the deuce don't you bring me proofs? I know you've been talking to Peter Ascham, and to Denver, and to that little ferret McCarren of the *Explorer*. Have any of them been able to make out a case for you? No. Well, what am I to do?"

Granice's lips began to tremble. "Why did you play me that trick?"

"About Stell? I had to, my dear fellow: it's part of my business. Stell *is* a detective, if you come to that—every doctor is."

The trembling of Granice's lips increased, communicating itself in a long quiver to his facial muscles. He forced a laugh through his dry throat. "Well—and what did he detect?"

"In you? Oh, he thinks it's overwork—overwork and too much smoking. If you look in on him some day at his office he'll show you the record of hundreds of cases like yours, and advise you what treatment to follow. It's one of the commonest forms of hallucination. Have a cigar, all the same."

"But, Allonby, I killed that man!"

The district attorney's large hand, outstretched on his desk, had an almost imperceptible gesture, and a moment later, as if an answer to the call of an electric bell, a clerk looked in from the outer office.

"Sorry, my dear fellow—lot of people waiting. Drop in on Stell some morning," Allonby said, shaking hands.

McCarren had to own himself beaten: there was absolutely no flaw in the alibi. And since his duty to his journal obviously forbade his wasting time on insoluble mysteries, he ceased to frequent Granice, who dropped back into a deeper isolation. For a day or two after his visit to Allonby he continued to live in dread of Dr. Stell. Why might not Allonby have deceived him as to the alienist's diagnosis? What if he were really being shadowed, not by a police agent but by a mad-doctor? To have the truth out, he suddenly determined to call on Dr. Stell.

The physician received him kindly, and reverted without embarrassment to the conditions of their previous meeting. "We have to do that occasionally, Mr. Granice; it's one of our methods. And you had given Allonby a fright."

Granice was silent. He would have liked to reaffirm his guilt, to produce the fresh arguments which had occurred to him since his last talk with the physician; but he feared his eagerness might be taken for a symptom of derangement, and he affected to smile away Dr. Stell's allusion.

"You think, then, it's a case of brain-fag—nothing more?"

"Nothing more. And I should advise you to knock off tobacco. You smoke a good deal, don't you?"

He developed his treatment, recommending massage, gymnastics, travel, or any form of diversion that did not—that in short—

Granice interrupted him impatiently. "Oh, I loathe all that—and I'm sick of travelling."

"H'm. Then some larger interest—politics, reform, philanthropy? Something to take you out of yourself."

"Yes. I understand," said Granice wearily.

"Above all, don't lose heart. I see hundreds of cases like yours," the doctor added cheerfully from the threshold.

On the doorstep Granice stood still and laughed. Hundreds of cases like his—the case of a man who had committed a murder, who confessed his guilt, and whom no one would believe! Why, there had never been a case like it in the world. What a good figure Stell would have made in a play: the great alienist who couldn't read a man's mind any better than that!

Granice saw huge comic opportunities in the type.

But as he walked away, his fears dispelled, the sense of listlessness returned on him. For the first time since his avowal to Peter Ascham he found himself without an occupation, and understood that he had been carried through the past weeks only by the necessity of constant action. Now his life had once more become a stagnant backwater, and as he stood on the street corner watching the tides of traffic sweep by, he asked himself despairingly how much longer he could endure to float about in the sluggish circle of his consciousness.

The thought of self-destruction recurred to him; but again his flesh recoiled. He yearned for death from other hands, but he could never take it from his own. And, aside from his insuperable physical reluctance, another motive restrained him. He was possessed by the dogged desire to establish the truth of his story. He refused to be swept aside as an irresponsible dreamer—even if he had to kill himself in the end, he would not do so before proving to society that he had deserved death from it.

He began to write long letters to the papers; but after the first had been published and commented on, public curiosity was quelled by a brief statement from the district attorney's office, and the rest of his communications remained unprinted. Ascham came to see him, and begged him to travel. Robert Denver dropped in, and tried to joke him out of his delusion; till Granice, mistrustful of their motives, began to dread the reappearance of Dr. Stell, and set a guard on his lips. But the words he kept back engendered others and still others in his brain. His inner self became a humming factory of arguments, and he spent long hours reciting and writing down elaborate statements of his crime, which he constantly retouched and developed.

Then gradually his activity languished under the lack of an audience, the sense of being buried beneath deepening drifts of indifference. In a passion of resentment, he swore that he would prove himself a murderer, even if he had to commit another crime to do it; and for a sleepless night or two the thought flamed red on his darkness. But daylight dispelled it. The determining impulse was lacking and he hated too promiscuously to choose his victim... So he was thrown back on the unavailing struggle to impose the truth of his story. As fast as one channel closed on him he tried to pierce another through the sliding sands of incredulity. But every issue seemed blocked, and the whole human race leagued together to cheat one man of the right to die.

Thus viewed, the situation became so monstrous that he lost his last shred of self-restraint in contemplating it. What if he were really the victim of some mocking experiment, the centre of a ring of holiday-makers jeering at a poor creature in its blind dashes against the solid walls of consciousness? But, no—men were not so uniformly cruel: there were flaws in the close surface of their indifference, cracks of weakness and pity here and there. . . .

Granice began to think that his mistake lay in having appealed to persons more or less familiar with his past, and to whom the visible conformities of his life seemed a final disproof of its one fierce secret deviation. The general tendency was to take for the whole of life the slit seen between the blinders of habit: and in his walk down that narrow *vista* Granice cut a correct enough figure. To a vision free to follow his whole orbit his story would be more intelligible: it would be easier to convince a chance idler in the street than the trained intelligence hampered by a sense of his antecedents. This idea shot up in him with the tropic luxuriance of each new seed of thought, and he began to walk the streets, and to frequent out-of-the-way chop-houses and bars in his search for the impartial stranger to whom he should disclose himself.

At first every face looked encouragement; but at the crucial moment he always held back. So much was at stake, and it was so essential that his first choice should be decisive. He dreaded stupidity, timidity, intolerance. The imaginative eye, the furrowed brow, were what he sought. He must reveal himself only to a heart versed in the tortuous motions of the human will; and he began to hate the dull benevolence of the average face. Once or twice, obscurely, allusively, he made a beginning—once sitting down at a man's side in a basement chop-house, another day approaching a lounger on an east-side wharf. But in both cases the premonition of failure checked him on the brink of avowal. His dread of being taken for a man in the clutch of a fixed idea gave him an unnatural keenness in reading the expression of his interlocutors, and he had provided himself in advance with a series of verbal alternatives, trapdoors of evasion from the first dart of ridicule or suspicion.

He passed the greater part of the day in the streets, coming home at irregular hours, dreading the silence and orderliness of his apartment, and the critical scrutiny of Flint. His real life was spent in a world so remote from this familiar setting that he sometimes had the mysterious sense of a living metempsychosis, a furtive passage from one identity to another—yet the other as unescapably himself!

One humiliation he was spared: the desire to live never revived in him. Not for a moment was he tempted to a shabby pact with existing conditions. He wanted to die, wanted it with the fixed unwavering desire which alone attains its end. And still the end eluded him! It would not always, of course—he had full faith in the dark star of his destiny. And he could prove it best by repeating his story, persistently and indefatigably, pouring it into indifferent ears, hammering it into dull brains, till at last it kindled a spark, and some one of the careless millions paused, listened, believed. . . .

It was a mild March day, and he had been loitering on the west-side docks, looking at faces. He was becoming an expert in physiognomies: his eagerness no longer made rash darts and awkward recoils. He knew now the face he needed, as clearly as if it had come to him in a vision; and not till he found it would he speak. As he walked eastward through the shabby reeking streets he had a premonition that he should find it that morning. Perhaps it was the promise of spring in the air—certainly he felt calmer than for many days. . . .

He turned into Washington Square, struck across it obliquely, and walked up University Place. Its heterogeneous passers always allured him—they were less hurried than in Broadway, less enclosed and classified than in Fifth Avenue. He walked slowly, watching for his face. At Union Square he felt a sudden relapse into discouragement, like a votary who has watched too long for a sign from the altar. Perhaps, after all, he should never find his face. . . . The air was languid, and he felt tired.

He walked between the bald grass-plots and the twisted trees, making for an empty seat. Presently he passed a bench on which a girl sat alone, and something as definite as the twitch of a cord made him stop before her.

He had never dreamed of telling his story to a girl, had hardly looked at the women's faces as they passed. His case was man's work: how could a woman help him? But this girl's face was extraordinary—quiet and wide as a clear evening sky. It suggested a hundred images of space, distance, mystery, like ships he had seen, as a boy, quietly berthed by a familiar wharf, but with the breath of far seas and strange harbours in their shrouds. . . . . Certainly this girl would understand. He went up to her quietly, lifting his hat, observing the forms—wishing her to see at once that he was "a gentleman."

"I am a stranger to you," he began, sitting down beside her, "but your face is so extremely intelligent that I fee. . . . . I feel it is the face I've waited for. . . . . looked for everywhere; and I want to tell you—"

The girl's eyes widened: she rose to her feet. She was escaping him!

In his dismay he ran a few steps after her, and caught her roughly by the arm.

"Here—wait—listen! Oh, don't scream, you fool!" he shouted out.

He felt a hand on his own arm; turned and confronted a policeman. Instantly he understood that he was being arrested, and something hard within him was loosened and ran to tears.

"Ah, you know—you *know* I'm guilty!"

He was conscious that a crowd was forming, and that the girl's frightened face had disappeared. But what did he care about her face? It was the policeman who had really understood him. He turned and followed, the crowd at his heels. . . . .

7.

In the charming place in which he found himself there were so many sympathetic faces that he felt more than ever convinced of the certainty of making himself heard.

It was a bad blow, at first, to find that he had not been arrested for murder; but Ascham, who had come to him at once, explained that he needed rest, and the time to "review" his statements; it appeared that reiteration had made them a little confused and contradictory. To this end he had willingly acquiesced in his removal to a large quiet establishment, with an open space and trees about it, where he had found a number of intelligent companions, some, like himself, engaged in preparing or reviewing statements of their cases, and others ready to lend an interested ear to his own recital.

For a time, he was content to let himself go on the tranquil current of this existence; but although his auditors gave him for the most part an encouraging attention, which, in some, went the length of really brilliant and helpful suggestion, he gradually felt a recurrence of his old doubts. Either his hearers were not sincere, or else they had less power to aid him than they boasted. His interminable conferences resulted in nothing, and as the benefit of the long rest made itself felt, it produced an increased mental lucidity which rendered inaction more and more unbearable.

At length he discovered that on certain days visitors from the outer world were admitted to his retreat; and he wrote out long and logically constructed relations of his crime, and furtively slipped them into the hands of these messengers of hope.

This occupation gave him a fresh lease of patience, and he now lived only to watch for the visitors' days, and scan the faces that swept by him like stars seen and lost in the rifts of a hurrying sky.

Mostly, these faces were strange and less intelligent than those of his companions. But they represented his last means of access to the world, a kind of subterranean channel on which he could set his "statements" afloat, like paper boats which the mysterious current might sweep out into the open seas of life.

One day, however, his attention was arrested by a familiar contour, a pair of bright prominent eyes, and a chin insufficiently shaved. He sprang up and stood in the path of Peter McCarren.

The journalist looked at him doubtfully, then held out his hand with a startled deprecating, "*Why—?*"

"You didn't know me? I'm so changed?" Granice faltered, feeling the rebound of the other's wonder.

"Why, no; but you're looking quieter—smoothed out," McCarren smiled.

"Yes: that's what I'm here for—to rest. And I've taken the opportunity to write out a clearer statement—"

Granice's hand shook so that he could hardly draw the folded paper from his pocket. As he did so he noticed that the reporter was accompanied by a tall man with grave compassionate eyes. It came to Granice in a wild thrill of conviction that this was the face he had waited for. . . . . .

"Perhaps your friend—he *is* your friend?—would glance over it—or I could put the case in a few words if you have time?" Granice's voice shook like his hand. If this chance escaped him he felt that his last hope was gone. McCarren and the stranger looked at each other, and the former glanced at his watch.

"I'm sorry we can't stay and talk it over now, Mr. Granice; but my friend has an engagement, and we're rather pressed—"

Granice continued to proffer the paper. "I'm sorry—I think I could have explained. But you'll take this, at any rate?"

The stranger looked at him gently. "Certainly—I'll take it." He had his hand out. "Goodbye."

"Goodbye," Granice echoed.

He stood watching the two men move away from him through the long light hall; and as he watched them a tear ran down his face. But as soon as they were out of sight he turned and walked hastily toward his room, beginning to hope again, already planning a new statement.

Outside the building the two men stood still, and the journalist's companion looked up curiously at the long monotonous rows of barred windows.

"So that was Granice?"

"Yes—that was Granice, poor devil," said McCarren.

"Strange case! I suppose there's never been one just like it? He's still absolutely convinced that he committed that murder?"

"Absolutely. Yes."

The stranger reflected. "And there was no conceivable ground for the idea? No one could make out how it started? A quiet conventional sort of fellow like that—where do you suppose he got such a delusion? Did you ever get the least clue to it?"

McCarren stood still, his hands in his pockets, his head cocked up in contemplation of the barred windows. Then he turned his bright hard gaze on his companion.

"That was the queer part of it. I've never spoken of it—but I *did* get a clue."

"By Jove! That's interesting. What was it?"

McCarren formed his red lips into a whistle. "Why—that it wasn't a delusion."

He produced his effect—the other turned on him with a pallid stare.

"He murdered the man all right. I tumbled on the truth by the merest accident, when I'd pretty nearly chucked the whole job."

"He murdered him—murdered his cousin?"

"Sure as you live. Only don't split on me. It's about the queerest business I ever ran into. . . . *Do about it?* Why, what was I to do? I couldn't hang the poor devil, could I? Lord, but I was glad when they collared him, and had him stowed away safe in there!"

The tall man listened with a grave face, grasping Granice's statement in his hand.

"Here—take this; it makes me sick," he said abruptly, thrusting the paper at the reporter; and the two men turned and walked in silence to the gates.

The House of the Dead Hand

1

"Above all," the letter ended, "don't leave Siena without seeing Doctor Lombard's Leonardo. Lombard is a queer old Englishman, a mystic or a madman (if the two are not synonymous), and a devout student of the Italian Renaissance. He has lived for years in Italy, exploring its remotest corners, and has lately picked up an undoubted Leonardo, which came to light in a farmhouse near Bergamo. It is believed to be one of the missing pictures mentioned by Vasari, and is at any rate, according to the most competent authorities, a genuine and almost untouched example of the best period.

"Lombard is a queer stick, and jealous of showing his treasures; but we struck up a friendship when I was working on the Sodomas in Siena three years ago, and if you will give him the enclosed line you may get a peep at the Leonardo. Probably not more than a peep, though, for I hear he refuses to have it reproduced. I want badly to use it in my monograph on the Windsor drawings, so please see what you can do for me, and if you can't persuade him to let you take a photograph or make a sketch, at least jot down a detailed description of the picture and get from him all the facts you can. I hear that the French and Italian governments have offered him a large advance on his purchase, but that he refuses to sell at any price, though he certainly can't afford such luxuries; in fact, I don't see where he got enough money to buy the picture. He lives in the Via Papa Giulio."

Wyant sat at the *table d'hote* of his hotel, re-reading his friend's letter over a late luncheon. He had been five days in Siena without having found time to call on Doctor Lombard; not from any indifference to the opportunity presented, but because it was his first visit to the strange red city and he was still under the spell of its more conspicuous wonders—the brick palaces flinging out their wrought-iron torch-holders with a gesture of arrogant suzerainty; the great council-chamber emblazoned with civic allegories; the pageant of Pope Julius on the Library walls; the Sodomas smiling balefully through the dusk of mouldering chapels—and it was only when his first hunger was appeased that he remembered that one course in the banquet was still untasted.

He put the letter in his pocket and turned to leave the room, with a nod to its only other occupant, an olive-skinned young man with lustrous eyes and a low collar, who sat on the other side of the table, perusing the Fanfulla di Domenica. This gentleman, his daily *vis-a-vis,* returned the nod with a Latin eloquence of gesture, and Wyant passed on to the ante-chamber, where he paused to light a cigarette. He was just restoring the case to his pocket when he heard a hurried step behind him, and the lustrous-eyed young man advanced through the glass doors of the dining- room.

"Pardon me, sir," he said in measured English, and with an intonation of exquisite politeness; "you have let this letter fall."

Wyant, recognising his friend's note of introduction to Doctor Lombard, took it with a word of thanks, and was about to turn away when he perceived that the eyes of his fellow diner remained fixed on him with a gaze of melancholy interrogation.

"Again pardon me," the young man at length ventured, "but are you by chance the friend of the illustrious Doctor Lombard?"

"No," returned Wyant, with the instinctive Anglo-Saxon distrust of foreign advances. Then, fearing to appear rude, he said with a guarded politeness: "Perhaps, by the way, you can tell me the number of his house. I see it is not given here."

The young man brightened perceptibly. "The number of the house is thirteen; but anyone can indicate it to you—it is well known in Siena. It is called," he continued after a moment, "the House of the Dead Hand."

Wyant stared. "What a queer name!" he said.

"The name comes from an antique hand of marble which for many hundred years has been above the door."

Wyant was turning away with a gesture of thanks, when the other added: "If you would have the kindness to ring twice."

"To ring twice?"

"At the doctor's." The young man smiled. "It is the custom."

It was a dazzling March afternoon, with a shower of sun from the mid-blue, and a marshalling of slaty clouds behind the umber-coloured hills. For nearly an hour Wyant loitered on the Lizza, watching the shadows race across the naked landscape and the thunder blacken in the west; then he decided to set out for the House of the Dead Hand. The map in his guidebook showed him that the Via Papa Giulio was one of the streets which radiate from the *Piazza*, and thither he bent his course, pausing at every other step to fill his eye with some fresh image of weather-beaten beauty.

The clouds had rolled upward, obscuring the sunshine and hanging like a funereal baldachin above the projecting cornices of Doctor Lombard's street, and Wyant walked for some distance in the shade of the beetling palace fronts before his eye fell on a doorway surmounted by a sallow marble hand. He stood for a moment staring up at the strange emblem. The hand was a woman's—a dead drooping hand, which hung there convulsed and helpless, as though it had been thrust forth in denunciation of some evil mystery within the house, and had sunk struggling into death.

A girl who was drawing water from the well in the court said that the English doctor lived on the first floor, and Wyant, passing through a glazed door, mounted the damp degrees of a vaulted stairway with a plaster Æsculapius mouldering in a niche on the landing. Facing the Æsculapius was another door, and as Wyant put his hand on the bell-rope he remembered his unknown friend's injunction, and rang twice.

His ring was answered by a peasant woman with a low forehead and small close-set eyes, who, after a prolonged scrutiny of himself, his card, and his letter of introduction, left him standing in a high, cold ante-chamber floored with brick. He heard her wooden pattens click down an interminable corridor, and after some delay she returned and told him to follow her.

They passed through a long saloon, bare as the ante-chamber, but loftily vaulted, and frescoed with a seventeenth-century Triumph of Scipio or Alexander—martial figures following Wyant with the filmed melancholy gaze of shades in limbo. At the end of this apartment he was admitted to a smaller room, with the same atmosphere of mortal cold, but showing more obvious signs of occupancy. The walls were covered with tapestry which had faded to the grey-brown tints of decaying vegetation, so that the young man felt as though he were entering a sunless autumn wood. Against these hangings stood a few tall cabinets on heavy gilt feet, and at a table in the window three persons were seated: an elderly lady who was warming her hands over a brazier, a girl bent above a strip of needle-work, and an old man.

As the latter advanced toward Wyant, the young man was conscious of staring with unseemly intentness at his small round-backed figure, dressed with shabby disorder and surmounted by a wonderful head, lean, vulpine, eagle-beaked as that of some art-loving despot of the Renaissance: a head combining the venerable hair and large prominent eyes of the humanist with the greedy profile of the adventurer. Wyant, in musing on the Italian portrait-medals of the fifteenth century, had often fancied that only in that period of fierce individualism could types so paradoxical have been produced; yet the subtle craftsmen who committed them to the bronze had never drawn a face more strangely stamped with contradictory passions than that of Doctor Lombard.

"I am glad to see you," he said to Wyant, extending a hand which seemed a mere framework held together by knotted veins. "We lead a quiet life here and receive few visitors, but any friend of Professor Clyde's is welcome." Then, with a gesture which included the two women, he added dryly: "My wife and daughter often talk of Professor Clyde."

"Oh yes—he used to make me such nice toast; they don't understand toast in Italy," said Mrs. Lombard in a high plaintive voice.

It would have been difficult, from Doctor Lombard's manner and appearance to guess his nationality; but his wife was so inconsciently and ineradicably English that even the silhouette of her cap seemed a protest against Continental laxities. She was a stout fair woman, with pale cheeks netted with red lines. A brooch with a miniature portrait sustained a bogwood watch-chain upon her bosom, and at her elbow lay a heap of knitting and an old copy of *The Queen*.

The young girl, who had remained standing, was a slim replica of her mother, with an apple-cheeked face and opaque blue eyes. Her small head was prodigally laden with braids of dull fair hair, and she might have had a kind of transient prettiness but for the sullen droop of her round mouth. It was hard to say whether her expression implied ill-temper or apathy; but Wyant was struck by the contrast between the fierce vitality of the doctor's age and the inanimateness of his daughter's youth.

Seating himself in the chair which his host advanced, the young man tried to open the conversation by addressing to Mrs. Lombard some random remark on the beauties of Siena. The lady murmured a resigned assent, and Doctor Lombard interposed with a smile: "My dear sir, my wife considers Siena a most salubrious spot, and is favourably impressed by the cheapness of the marketing; but she deplores the total absence of muffins and cannel coal, and cannot resign herself to the Italian method of dusting furniture."

"But they don't, you know—they don't dust it!" Mrs. Lombard protested, without showing any resentment of her husband's manner.

"Precisely—they don't dust it. Since we have lived in Siena we have not once seen the cobwebs removed from the battlements of the Mangia. Can you conceive of such housekeeping? My wife has never yet dared to write it home to her aunts at Bonchurch." Mrs. Lombard accepted in silence this remarkable statement of her views, and her husband, with a malicious smile at Wyant's embarrassment, planted himself suddenly before the young man. "And now," said he, "do you want to see my Leonardo?"

"*Do* I?" cried Wyant, on his feet in a flash.

The doctor chuckled. "Ah," he said, with a kind of crooning deliberation, "that's the way they all behave—that's what they all come for." He turned to his daughter with another variation of mockery in his smile. "Don't fancy it's for your *beaux yeux*, my dear; or for the mature charms of Mrs. Lombard," he added, glaring suddenly at his wife, who had taken up her knitting and was softly murmuring over the number of her stitches.

Neither lady appeared to notice his pleasantries, and he continued, addressing himself to Wyant: "They all come—they all come; but many are called and few are chosen." His voice sank to solemnity. "While I live," he said, "no unworthy eye shall desecrate that picture. But I will not do my friend Clyde the injustice to suppose that he would send an unworthy representative. He tells me he wishes a description of the picture for his book; and you shall describe it to him—if you can."

Wyant hesitated, not knowing whether it was a propitious moment to put in his appeal for a photograph.

"Well, sir," he said, "you know Clyde wants me to take away all I can of it."

Doctor Lombard eyed him sardonically. "You're welcome to take away all you can carry," he replied; adding, as he turned to his daughter: "That is, if he has your permission, Sybilla."

The girl rose without a word, and laying aside her work, took a key from a secret drawer in one of the cabinets, while the doctor continued in the same note of grim jocularity: "For you must know that the picture is not mine—it is my daughter's."

He followed with evident amusement the surprised glance which

Wyant turned on the young girl's impassive figure.

"Sybilla," he pursued, "is a votary of the arts; she has inherited her fond father's passion for the unattainable. Luckily, however, she also recently inherited a tidy legacy from her grandmother; and having seen the Leonardo, on which its discoverer had placed a price far beyond my reach, she took a step which deserves to go down to history: she invested her whole inheritance in the purchase of the picture, thus enabling me to spend my closing years in communion with one of the world's masterpieces. My dear sir, could Antigone do more?"

The object of this strange eulogy had meanwhile drawn aside one of the tapestry hangings, and fitted her key into a concealed door.

"Come," said Doctor Lombard, "let us go before the light fails us."

Wyant glanced at Mrs. Lombard, who continued to knit impassively.

"No, no," said his host, "my wife will not come with us. You might not suspect it from her conversation, but my wife has no feeling for art—Italian art, that is; for no one is fonder of our early Victorian school."

"Frith's Railway Station, you know," said Mrs. Lombard, smiling. "I like an animated picture."

Miss Lombard, who had unlocked the door, held back the tapestry to let her father and Wyant pass out; then she followed them down a narrow stone passage with another door at its end. This door was iron-barred, and Wyant noticed that it had a complicated patent lock. The girl fitted another key into the lock, and Doctor Lombard led the way into a small room. The dark panelling of this apartment was irradiated by streams of yellow light slanting through the disbanded thunder clouds, and in the central brightness hung a picture concealed by a curtain of faded velvet.

"A little too bright, Sybilla," said Doctor Lombard. His face had grown solemn, and his mouth twitched nervously as his daughter drew a linen drapery across the upper part of the window.

"That will do—that will do." He turned impressively to Wyant. "Do you see the pomegranate bud in this rug? Place yourself there—keep your left foot on it, please. And now, Sybilla, draw the cord."

Miss Lombard advanced and placed her hand on a cord hidden behind the velvet curtain.

"Ah," said the doctor, "one moment: I should like you, while looking at the picture, to have in mind a few lines of verse. Sybilla—"

Without the slightest change of countenance, and with a promptness which proved her to be prepared for the request, Miss Lombard began to recite, in a full round voice like her mother's, St. Bernard's invocation to the Virgin, in the thirty-third *canto* of the Paradise.

"Thank you, my dear," said her father, drawing a deep breath as she ended. "That unapproachable combination of vowel sounds prepares one better than anything I know for the contemplation of the picture."

As he spoke the folds of velvet slowly parted, and the Leonardo appeared in its frame of tarnished gold:

From the nature of Miss Lombard's recitation Wyant had expected a sacred subject, and his surprise was therefore great as the composition was gradually revealed by the widening division of the curtain.

In the background a steel-coloured river wound through a pale calcareous landscape; while to the left, on a lonely peak, a crucified Christ hung livid against indigo clouds. The central figure of the foreground, however, was that of a woman seated in an antique chair of marble with *bas-reliefs* of dancing *maenads*. Her feet rested on a meadow sprinkled with minute wild-flowers, and her attitude of smiling majesty recalled that of Dosso Dossi's Circe. She wore a red robe, flowing in closely fluted lines from under a fancifully embroidered cloak.

Above her high forehead the crinkled golden hair flowed sideways beneath a veil; one hand drooped on the arm of her chair; the other held up an inverted human skull, into which a young Dionysus, smooth, brown and sidelong as the St. John of the Louvre, poured a stream of wine from a high-poised flagon. At the lady's feet lay the symbols of art and luxury: a flute and a roll of music, a platter heaped with grapes and roses, the torso of a Greek statuette, and a bowl overflowing with coins and jewels; behind her, on the chalky hilltop, hung the crucified Christ. A scroll in a corner of the foreground bore the legend: *Lux Mundi*.

Wyant, emerging from the first plunge of wonder, turned inquiringly toward his companions. Neither had moved. Miss Lombard stood with her hand on the cord, her lids lowered, her mouth drooping; the doctor, his strange Thoth-like profile turned toward his guest, was still lost in rapt contemplation of his treasure.

Wyant addressed the young girl.

"You are fortunate," he said, "to be the possessor of anything so perfect."

"It is considered very beautiful," she said coldly.

"Beautiful—*Beautiful*!" the doctor burst out. "Ah, the poor, worn out, over-worked word! There are no adjectives in the language fresh enough to describe such pristine brilliancy; all their brightness has been worn off by misuse. Think of the things that have been called beautiful, and then look at *that*!"

"It is worthy of a new vocabulary," Wyant agreed.

"Yes," Doctor Lombard continued, "my daughter is indeed fortunate. She has chosen what Catholics call the higher life— the counsel of perfection. What other private person enjoys the same opportunity of understanding the master? Who else lives under the same roof with an untouched masterpiece of Leonardo's? Think of the happiness of being always under the influence of such a creation; of living *into* it; of partaking of it in daily and hourly communion! This room is a chapel; the sight of that picture is a sacrament. What an atmosphere for a young life to unfold itself in! My daughter is singularly blessed. Sybilla, point out some of the details to Mr. Wyant; I see that he will appreciate them."

The girl turned her dense blue eyes toward Wyant; then, glancing away from him, she pointed to the canvas.

"Notice the modelling of the left hand," she began in a monotonous voice; "it recalls the hand of the Mona Lisa. The head of the naked genius will remind you of that of the St. John of the Louvre, but it is more purely pagan and is turned a little less to the right. The embroidery on the cloak is symbolic: you will see that the roots of this plant have burst through the vase. This recalls the famous definition of Hamlet's character in Wilhelm Meister. Here are the mystic rose, the flame, and the serpent, emblem of eternity. Some of the other symbols we have not yet been able to decipher."

Wyant watched her curiously; she seemed to be reciting a lesson. "And the picture itself?" he said. "How do you explain that? *Lux Mundi*—what a curious device to connect with such a subject! What can it mean?"

Miss Lombard dropped her eyes: the answer was evidently not included in her lesson.

"What, indeed?" the doctor interposed. "What does life mean? As one may define it in a hundred different ways, so one may find a hundred different meanings in this picture. Its symbolism is as many-faceted as a well-cut diamond. Who, for instance, is that divine lady? Is it she who is the true *Lux Mundi*—the light reflected from jewels and young eyes, from polished marble and clear waters and statues of bronze? Or is that the Light of the World, extinguished on yonder stormy hill, and is this lady the Pride of Life, feasting blindly on the wine of iniquity, with her back turned to the light which has shone for her in vain? Something of both these meanings may be traced in the picture; but to me it symbolizes rather the central truth of existence: that all that is raised in in corruption is sown in corruption; art, beauty, love, religion; that all our wine is drunk out of skulls, and poured for us by the mysterious genius of a remote and cruel past."

The doctor's face blazed: his bent figure seemed to straighten itself and become taller.

"Ah," he cried, growing more dithyrambic, "how lightly you ask what it means! How confidently you expect an answer! Yet here am I who have given my life to the study of the Renaissance; who have violated its tomb, laid open its dead body, and traced the course of every muscle, bone, and artery; who have sucked its very soul from the pages of poets and humanists; who have wept and believed with Joachim of Flora, smiled and doubted with Æneas Sylvius Piccolomini; who have patiently followed to its source the least inspiration of the masters, and groped in Neolithic caverns and Babylonian ruins for the first unfolding tendrils of the arabesques of Mantegna and Crivelli; and I tell you that I stand abashed and ignorant before the mystery of this picture. It means nothing—it means all things. It may represent the period which saw its creation; it may represent all ages past and to come. There are volumes of meaning in the tiniest emblem on the lady's cloak; the blossoms of its border are rooted in the deepest soil of myth and tradition. Don't ask what it means, young man, but bow your head in thankfulness for having seen it!"

Miss Lombard laid her hand on his arm.

"Don't excite yourself, father," she said in the detached tone of a professional nurse.

He answered with a despairing gesture. "Ah, it's easy for you to talk. You have years and years to spend with it; I am an old man, and every moment counts!"

"It's bad for you," she repeated with gentle obstinacy.

The doctor's sacred fury had in fact burnt itself out. He dropped into a seat with dull eyes and slackening lips, and his daughter drew the curtain across the picture.

Wyant turned away reluctantly. He felt that his opportunity was slipping from him, yet he dared not refer to Clyde's wish for a photograph. He now understood the meaning of the laugh with which

Doctor Lombard had given him leave to carry away all the details he could remember. The picture was so dazzling, so unexpected, so crossed with elusive and contradictory suggestions, that the most alert observer, when placed suddenly before it, must lose his coordinating faculty in a sense of confused wonder. Yet how valuable to Clyde the record of such a work would be! In some ways it seemed to be the summing up of the master's thought, the key to his enigmatic philosophy.

The doctor had risen and was walking slowly toward the door. His daughter unlocked it, and Wyant followed them back in silence to the room in which they had left Mrs. Lombard. That lady was no longer there, and he could think of no excuse for lingering. He thanked the doctor, and turned to Miss Lombard, who stood in the middle of the room as though awaiting farther orders.

"It is very good of you," he said, "to allow one even a glimpse of such a treasure."

She looked at him with her odd directness. "You will come again?" she said quickly; and turning to her father she added: "You know what Professor Clyde asked. This gentleman cannot give him any account of the picture without seeing it again."

Doctor Lombard glanced at her vaguely; he was still like a person in a trance.

"Eh?" he said, rousing himself with an effort.

"I said, father, that Mr. Wyant must see the picture again if he is to tell Professor Clyde about it," Miss Lombard repeated with extraordinary precision of tone.

Wyant was silent. He had the puzzled sense that his wishes were being divined and gratified for reasons with which he was in no way connected

"Well, well," the doctor muttered, "I don't say no—I don't say no. I know what Clyde wants—I don't refuse to help him." He turned to Wyant. "You may come again—you may make notes," he added with a sudden effort. "Jot down what occurs to you. I'm willing to concede that."

Wyant again caught the girl's eye, but its emphatic message perplexed him.

"You're very good," he said tentatively, "but the fact is the picture is so mysterious—so full of complicated detail—that I'm afraid no notes I could make would serve Clyde's purpose as well as—as a photograph, say. If you would allow me—"

Miss Lombard's brow darkened, and her father raised his head furiously.

"A photograph? A photograph, did you say? Good God, man, not ten people have been allowed to set foot in that room! A *photograph*?"

Wyant saw his mistake, but saw also that he had gone too far to retreat.

"I know, sir, from what Clyde has told me, that you object to having any reproduction of the picture published; but he hoped you might let me take a photograph for his personal use—not to be reproduced in his book, but simply to give him something to work by. I should take the photograph myself, and the negative would of course be yours. If you wished it, only one impression would be struck off, and that one Clyde could return to you when he had done with it."

Doctor Lombard interrupted him with a snarl. "When he had done with it? Just so: I thank thee for that word! When it had been re-photographed, drawn, traced, autotyped, passed about from hand to hand, defiled by every ignorant eye in England, vulgarized by the blundering praise of every art-scribbler in Europe! Bah! I'd as soon give you the picture itself: why don't you ask for that?"

"Well, sir," said Wyant calmly, "if you will trust me with it, I'll engage to take it safely to England and back, and to let no eye but Clyde's see it while it is out of your keeping." The doctor received this remarkable proposal in silence; then he burst into a laugh.

"Upon my soul!" he said with sardonic good humour.

It was Miss Lombard's turn to look perplexedly at Wyant. His last words and her father's unexpected reply had evidently carried her beyond her depth.

"Well, sir, am I to take the picture?" Wyant smilingly pursued.

"No, young man; nor a photograph of it. Nor a sketch, either; mind that,—nothing that can be reproduced. Sybilla," he cried with sudden passion, "swear to me that the picture shall never be reproduced! No photograph, no sketch—now or afterward. Do you hear me?"

"Yes, father," said the girl quietly.

"The vandals," he muttered, "the desecrators of beauty; if I thought it would ever get into their hands I'd burn it first, by God!" He turned to Wyant, speaking more quietly. "I said you might come back—I never retract what I say. But you must give me your word that no one but Clyde shall see the notes you make." Wyant was growing warm.

"If you won't trust me with a photograph I wonder you trust me not to show my notes!" he exclaimed.

The doctor looked at him with a malicious smile.

"Humph!" he said; "would they be of much use to anybody?"

Wyant saw that he was losing ground and controlled his impatience.

"To Clyde, I hope, at any rate," he answered, holding out his hand. The doctor shook it without a trace of resentment, and Wyant added: "When shall I come, sir?"

"Tomorrow—tomorrow morning," cried Miss Lombard, speaking suddenly.

She looked fixedly at her father, and he shrugged his shoulders.

"The picture is hers," he said to Wyant.

In the ante-chamber the young man was met by the woman who had admitted him. She handed him his hat and stick, and turned to unbar the door. As the bolt slipped back he felt a touch on his arm.

"You have a letter?" she said in a low tone.

"A letter?" He stared. "What letter?"

She shrugged her shoulders, and drew back to let him pass.

2

As Wyant emerged from the house he paused once more to glance up at its scarred brick facade. The marble hand drooped tragically above the entrance: in the waning light it seemed to have relaxed into the passiveness of despair, and Wyant stood musing on its hidden meaning. But the Dead Hand was not the only mysterious thing about Doctor Lombard's house. What were the relations between Miss Lombard and her father? Above all, between Miss Lombard and her picture? She did not look like a person capable of a disinterested passion for the arts; and there had been moments when it struck Wyant that she hated the picture.

The sky at the end of the street was flooded with turbulent yellow light, and the young man turned his steps toward the church of San Domenico, in the hope of catching the lingering brightness on Sodoma's St. Catherine.

The great bare aisles were almost dark when he entered, and he had to grope his way to the chapel steps. Under the momentary evocation of the sunset, the saint's figure emerged pale and swooning from the dusk, and the warm light gave a sensual tinge to her ecstasy. The flesh seemed to glow and heave, the eyelids to tremble; Wyant stood fascinated by the accidental collaboration of light and colour.

Suddenly he noticed that something white had fluttered to the ground at his feet. He stooped and picked up a small thin sheet of note-paper, folded and sealed like an old-fashioned letter, and bearing the superscription:-

To the Count Ottaviano Celsi.

Wyant stared at this mysterious document. Where had it come from? He was distinctly conscious of having seen it fall through the air, close to his feet. He glanced up at the dark ceiling of the chapel; then he turned and looked about the church. There was only one figure in it, that of a man who knelt near the high altar.

Suddenly Wyant recalled the question of Doctor Lombard's maid-servant. Was this the letter she had asked for? Had he been unconsciously carrying it about with him all the afternoon? Who was Count Ottaviano Celsi, and how came Wyant to have been chosen to act as that nobleman's ambulant letter-box?

Wyant laid his hat and stick on the chapel steps and began to explore his pockets, in the irrational hope of finding there some clue to the mystery; but they held nothing which he had not himself put there, and he was reduced to wondering how the letter, supposing some unknown hand to have bestowed it on him, had happened to fall out while he stood motionless before the picture.

At this point he was disturbed by a step on the floor of the aisle, and turning, he saw his lustrous-eyed neighbour of the *table d'hote.*

The young man bowed and waved an apologetic hand.

"I do not intrude?" he inquired suavely.

Without waiting for a reply, he mounted the steps of the chapel, glancing about him with the affable air of an afternoon caller.

"I see," he remarked with a smile, "that you know the hour at which our saint should be visited."

Wyant agreed that the hour was indeed felicitous.

The stranger stood beamingly before the picture.

"What grace! What poetry!" he murmured, apostrophizing the St. Catherine, but letting his glance slip rapidly about the chapel as he spoke.

Wyant, detecting the manoeuvre, murmured a brief assent.

"But it is cold here—mortally cold; you do not find it so?" The intruder put on his hat. "It is permitted at this hour—when the church is empty. And you, my dear sir—do you not feel the dampness? You are an artist, are you not? And to artists it is permitted to cover the head when they are engaged in the study of the paintings."

He darted suddenly toward the steps and bent over Wyant's hat.

"Permit me—cover yourself!" he said a moment later, holding out the hat with an ingratiating gesture.

A light flashed on Wyant.

"Perhaps," he said, looking straight at the young man, "you will tell me your name. My own is Wyant."

The stranger, surprised, but not disconcerted, drew forth a coroneted card, which he offered with a low bow. On the card was engraved:—

Il Conte Ottaviano Celsi.

"I am much obliged to you," said Wyant; "and I may as well tell you that the letter which you apparently expected to find in the lining of my hat is not there, but in my pocket."

He drew it out and handed it to its owner, who had grown very pale.

"And now," Wyant continued, "you will perhaps be good enough to tell me what all this means."

There was no mistaking the effect produced on Count Ottaviano by this request. His lips moved, but he achieved only an ineffectual smile.

"I suppose you know," Wyant went on, his anger rising at the sight of the other's discomfiture, "that you have taken an unwarrantable liberty. I don't yet understand what part I have been made to play, but it's evident that you have made use of me to serve some purpose of your own, and I propose to know the reason why."

Count Ottaviano advanced with an imploring gesture.

"Sir," he pleaded, "you permit me to speak?"

"I expect you to," cried Wyant. "But not here," he added, hearing the clank of the verger's keys. "It is growing dark, and we shall be turned out in a few minutes."

He walked across the church, and Count Ottaviano followed him out into the deserted square.

"Now," said Wyant, pausing on the steps.

The count, who had regained some measure of self-possession, began to speak in a high key, with an accompaniment of conciliatory gesture.

"My dear sir—my dear Mr. Wyant—you find me in an abominable position—that, as a man of honour, I immediately confess. I have taken advantage of you—yes! I have counted on your amiability, your chivalry—too far, perhaps? I confess it! But what could I do? It was to oblige a lady"—he laid a hand on his heart—"a lady whom I would die to serve!" He went on with increasing volubility, his deliberate English swept away by a torrent of Italian, through which Wyant, with some difficulty, struggled to a comprehension of the case.

Count Ottaviano, according to his own statement, had come to Siena some months previously, on business connected with his mother's property; the paternal estate being near Orvieto, of which ancient city his father was syndic. Soon after his arrival in Siena the young count had met the incomparable daughter of Doctor Lombard, and falling deeply in love with her, had prevailed on his parents to ask her hand in marriage. Doctor Lombard had not opposed his suit, but when the question of settlements arose it became known that Miss Lombard, who was possessed of a small property in her own right, had a short time before invested the whole amount in the purchase of the Bergamo Leonardo. Thereupon Count Ottaviano's parents had politely suggested that she should sell the picture and thus recover her independence; and this proposal being met by a curt refusal from Doctor Lombard, they had withdrawn their consent to their son's marriage.

The young lady's attitude had hitherto been one of passive submission; she was horribly afraid of her father, and would never venture openly to oppose him; but she had made known to Ottaviano her intention of not giving him up, of waiting patiently till events should take a more favourable turn. She seemed hardly aware, the count said with a sigh, that the means of escape lay in her own hands; that she was of age, and had a right to sell the picture, and to marry without asking her father's consent. Meanwhile her suitor spared no pains to keep himself before her, to remind her that he, too, was waiting and would never give her up.

Doctor Lombard, who suspected the young man of trying to persuade Sybilla to sell the picture, had forbidden the lovers to meet or to correspond; they were thus driven to clandestine communication, and had several times, the count ingenuously avowed, made use of the doctor's visitors as a means of exchanging letters.

"And you told the visitors to ring twice?" Wyant interposed.

The young man extended his hands in a deprecating gesture. Could Mr. Wyant blame him? He was young, he was ardent, he was enamoured! The young lady had done him the supreme honour of avowing her attachment, of pledging her unalterable fidelity; should he suffer his devotion to be outdone? But his purpose in writing to her, he admitted, was not merely to reiterate his fidelity; he was trying by every means in his power to induce her to sell the picture. He had organized a plan of action; every detail was complete; if she would but have the courage to carry out his instructions he would answer for the result. His idea was that she should secretly retire to a convent of which his aunt was the Mother Superior, and from that stronghold should transact the sale of the Leonardo.

He had a purchaser ready, who was willing to pay a large sum; a sum, Count Ottaviano whispered, considerably in excess of the young lady's original inheritance; once the picture sold, it could, if necessary, be removed by force from Doctor Lombard's house, and his daughter, being safely in the convent, would be spared the painful scenes incidental to the removal. Finally, if Doctor Lombard were vindictive enough to refuse his consent to her marriage, she had only to make a *sommation respectueuse*, and at the end of the prescribed delay no power on earth could prevent her becoming the wife of Count Ottaviano.

Wyant's anger had fallen at the recital of this simple romance.

It was absurd to be angry with a young man who confided his secrets to the first stranger he met in the streets, and placed his hand on his heart whenever he mentioned the name of his betrothed. The easiest way out of the business was to take it as a joke. Wyant had played the wall to this new Pyramus and Thisbe, and was philosophic enough to laugh at the part he had unwittingly performed.

He held out his hand with a smile to Count Ottaviano.

"I won't deprive you any longer," he said, "of the pleasure of reading your letter."

"Oh, sir, a thousand thanks! And when you return to the *casa* Lombard, you will take a message from me—the letter she expected this afternoon?"

"The letter she expected?" Wyant paused. "No, thank you. I thought you understood that where I come from we don't do that kind of thing—knowingly."

"But, sir, to serve a young lady!"

"I'm sorry for the young lady, if what you tell me is true"—the count's expressive hands resented the doubt—"but remember that if I am under obligations to anyone in this matter, it is to her father, who has admitted me to his house and has allowed me to see his picture."

"*His* picture? Hers!"

"Well, the house is his, at all events."

"Unhappily—since to her it is a dungeon!"

"Why doesn't she leave it, then?" exclaimed Wyant impatiently. The count clasped his hands. "Ah, how you say that—with what force, with what virility! If you would but say it to *her* in that tone—you, her countryman! She has no one to advise her; the mother is an idiot; the father is terrible; she is in his power; it is my belief that he would kill her if she resisted him. Mr. Wyant, I tremble for her life while she remains in that house!"

"Oh, come," said Wyant lightly, "they seem to understand each other well enough. But in any case, you must see that I can't interfere—at least you would if you were an Englishman," he added with an escape of contempt.

3

Wyant's affiliations in Siena being restricted to an acquaintance with his land-lady, he was forced to apply to her for the verification of Count Ottaviano's story.

The young nobleman had, it appeared, given a perfectly correct account of his situation. His father, Count Celsi-Mongirone, was a man of distinguished family and some wealth. He was syndic of Orvieto, and lived either in that town or on his neighbouring estate of Mongirone. His wife owned a large property near Siena, and Count Ottaviano, who was the second son, came there from time to time to look into its management. The eldest son was in the army, the youngest in the Church; and an aunt of Count Ottaviano's was Mother Superior of the Visitandine convent in Siena.

At one time it had been said that Count Ottaviano, who was a most amiable and accomplished young man, was to marry the daughter of the strange Englishman, Doctor Lombard, but difficulties having arisen as to the adjustment of the young lady's dower, Count Celsi-Mongirone had very properly broken off the match. It was sad for the young man, however, who was said to be deeply in love, and to find frequent excuses for coming to Siena to inspect his mother's estate.

Viewed in the light of Count Ottaviano's personality the story had a tinge of opera *bouffe*; but the next morning, as Wyant mounted the stairs of the House of the Dead Hand, the situation insensibly assumed another aspect. It was impossible to take Doctor Lombard lightly; and there was a suggestion of fatality in the appearance of his gaunt dwelling. Who could tell amid what tragic records of domestic tyranny and fluttering broken purposes the little drama of Miss Lombard's fate was being played out? Might not the accumulated influences of such a house modify the lives within it in a manner unguessed by the inmates of a suburban villa with sanitary plumbing and a telephone? One person, at least, remained unperturbed by such fanciful problems; and that was Mrs. Lombard, who, at Wyant's entrance, raised a placidly wrinkled brow from her knitting. The morning was mild, and her chair had been wheeled into a bar of sunshine near the window, so that she made a cheerful spot of prose in the poetic gloom of her surroundings.

"What a nice morning!" she said; "it must be delightful weather at Bonchurch."

Her dull blue glance wandered across the narrow street with its threatening house fronts, and fluttered back baffled, like a bird with clipped wings. It was evident, poor lady, that she had never seen beyond the opposite houses.

Wyant was not sorry to find her alone. Seeing that she was surprised at his reappearance he said at once: "I have come back to study Miss Lombard's picture."

"Oh, the picture—" Mrs. Lombard's face expressed a gentle disappointment, which might have been boredom in a person of acuter sensibilities. "It's an original Leonardo, you know," she said mechanically.

"And Miss Lombard is very proud of it, I suppose? She seems to have inherited her father's love for art."

Mrs. Lombard counted her stitches, and he went on: "It's unusual in so young a girl. Such tastes generally develop later."

Mrs. Lombard looked up eagerly. "That's what I say! I was quite different at her age, you know. I liked dancing, and doing a pretty bit of fancy-work. Not that I couldn't sketch, too; I had a master down from London. My aunts have some of my crayons hung up in their drawing-room now—I did a view of Kenilworth which was thought pleasing. But I liked a picnic, too, or a pretty walk through the woods with young people of my own age. I say it's more natural, Mr. Wyant; one may have a feeling for art, and do crayons that are worth framing, and yet not give up everything else. I was taught that there were other things."

Wyant, half-ashamed of provoking these innocent confidences, could not resist another question. "And Miss Lombard cares for nothing else?"

Her mother looked troubled.

"Sybilla is so clever—she says I don't understand. You know how self-confident young people are! My husband never said that of me, now—he knows I had an excellent education. My aunts were very particular; I was brought up to have opinions, and my husband has always respected them. He says himself that he wouldn't for the world miss hearing my opinion on any subject; you may have noticed that he often refers to my tastes. He has always respected my preference for living in England; he likes to hear me give my reasons for it. He is so much interested in my ideas that he often says he knows just what I am going to say before I speak. But Sybilla does not care for what I think—"

At this point Doctor Lombard entered. He glanced sharply at Wyant. "The servant is a fool; she didn't tell me you were here." His eye turned to his wife. "Well, my dear, what have you been telling Mr. Wyant? About the aunts at Bonchurch, I'll be bound!"

Mrs. Lombard looked triumphantly at Wyant, and her husband rubbed his hooked fingers, with a smile.

"Mrs. Lombard's aunts are very superior women. They subscribe to the circulating library, and borrow *Good Words* and the *Monthly Packet* from the curate's wife across the way. They have the rector to tea twice a year, and keep a page-boy, and are visited by two baronets' wives. They devoted themselves to the education of their orphan niece, and I think I may say without boasting that Mrs. Lombard's conversation shows marked traces of the advantages she enjoyed."

Mrs. Lombard coloured with pleasure.

"I was telling Mr. Wyant that my aunts were very particular."

"Quite so, my dear; and did you mention that they never sleep in anything but linen, and that Miss Sophia puts away the furs and blankets every spring with her own hands? Both those facts are interesting to the student of human nature." Doctor Lombard glanced at his watch. "But we are missing an incomparable moment; the light is perfect at this hour."

Wyant rose, and the doctor led him through the tapestried door and down the passageway.

The light was, in fact, perfect, and the picture shone with an inner radiancy, as though a lamp burned behind the soft screen of the lady's flesh. Every detail of the foreground detached itself with jewel-like precision. Wyant noticed a dozen accessories which had escaped him on the previous day.

He drew out his note-book, and the doctor, who had dropped his sardonic grin for a look of devout contemplation, pushed a chair forward, and seated himself on a carved settle against the wall. "Now, then," he said, "tell Clyde what you can; but the letter killeth."

He sank down, his hands hanging on the arm of the settle like the claws of a dead bird, his eyes fixed on Wyant's notebook with the obvious intention of detecting any attempt at a surreptitious sketch.

Wyant, nettled at this surveillance, and disturbed by the speculations which Doctor Lombard's strange household excited, sat motionless for a few minutes, staring first at the picture and then at the blank pages of the note-book. The thought that Doctor Lombard was enjoying his discomfiture at length roused him, and he began to write.

He was interrupted by a knock on the iron door. Doctor Lombard rose to unlock it, and his daughter entered.

She bowed hurriedly to Wyant, without looking at him.

"Father, had you forgotten that the man from Monte Amiato was to come back this morning with an answer about the *bas-relief?* He is here now; he says he can't wait."

"The devil!" cried her father impatiently. "Didn't you tell him—"

"Yes; but he says he can't come back. If you want to see him you must come now.

"Then you think there's a chance?—"

She nodded.

He turned and looked at Wyant, who was writing assiduously.

"You will stay here, Sybilla; I shall be back in a moment."

He hurried out, locking the door behind him.

Wyant had looked up, wondering if Miss Lombard would show any surprise at being locked in with him; but it was his turn to be surprised, for hardly had they heard the key withdrawn when she moved close to him, her small face pale and tumultuous.

"I arranged it—I must speak to you," she gasped. "He'll be back in five minutes."

Her courage seemed to fail, and she looked at him helplessly.

Wyant had a sense of stepping among explosives. He glanced about him at the dusky vaulted room, at the haunting smile of the strange picture overhead, and at the pink-and-white girl whispering of conspiracies in a voice meant to exchange platitudes with a curate.

"How can I help you?" he said with a rush of compassion.

"Oh, if you would! I never have a chance to speak to anyone; it's so difficult—he watches me—he'll be back immediately."

"Try to tell me what I can do."

"I don't dare; I feel as if he were behind me." She turned away, fixing her eyes on the picture. A sound startled her. "There he comes, and I haven't spoken! It was my only chance; but it bewilders me so to be hurried."

"I don't hear any one," said Wyant, listening. "Try to tell me."

"How can I make you understand? It would take so long to explain." She drew a deep breath, and then with a plunge—"Will you come here again this afternoon—at about five?" she whispered.

"Come here again?"

"Yes—you can ask to see the picture,—make some excuse. He will come with you, of course; I will open the door for you—and—and lock you both in"—she gasped.

"Lock us in?"

"You see? You understand? It's the only way for me to leave the house—if I am ever to do it"— She drew another difficult breath. "The key will be returned—by a safe person—in half an hour,—perhaps sooner—"

She trembled so much that she was obliged to lean against the settle for support.

"Wyant looked at her steadily; he was very sorry for her.

"I can't, Miss Lombard," he said at length.

"You can't?"

"I'm sorry; I must seem cruel; but consider—"

He was stopped by the futility of the word: as well ask a hunted rabbit to pause in its dash for a hole!

Wyant took her hand; it was cold and nerveless.

"I will serve you in any way I can; but you must see that this way is impossible. Can't I talk to you again? Perhaps—"

"Oh," she cried, starting up, "there he comes!"

Doctor Lombard's step sounded in the passage.

Wyant held her fast. "Tell me one thing: he won't let you sell the picture?"

"No—hush!"

"Make no pledges for the future, then; promise me that."

"The future?"

"In case he should die: your father is an old man. You haven't promised?"

She shook her head.

"Don't, then; remember that."

She made no answer, and the key turned in the lock.

As he passed out of the house, its scowling cornice and facade of ravaged brick looked down on him with the startlingness of a strange face, seen momentarily in a crowd, and impressing itself on the brain as part of an inevitable future. Above the doorway, the marble hand reached out like the cry of an imprisoned anguish.

Wyant turned away impatiently.

"Rubbish!" he said to himself. "*She* isn't walled in; she can get out if she wants to."

4

Wyant had any number of plans for coming to Miss Lombard's aid: he was elaborating the twentieth when, on the same afternoon, he stepped into the express train for Florence. By the time the train reached Certaldo he was convinced that, in thus hastening his departure, he had followed the only reasonable course; at Empoli, he began to reflect that the priest and the Levite had probably justified themselves in much the same manner.

A month later, after his return to England, he was unexpectedly relieved from these alternatives of extenuation and approval. A paragraph in the morning paper announced the sudden death of Doctor Lombard, the distinguished English dilettante who had long resided in Siena. Wyant's justification was complete. Our blindest impulses become evidence of perspicacity when they fall in with the course of events.

Wyant could now comfortably speculate on the particular complications from which his foresight had probably saved him. The climax was unexpectedly dramatic. Miss Lombard, on the brink of a step which, whatever its issue, would have burdened her with retrospective compunction, had been set free before her suitor's ardour could have had time to cool, and was now doubtless planning a life of domestic felicity on the proceeds of the Leonardo. One thing, however, struck Wyant as odd—he saw no mention of the sale of the picture. He had scanned the papers for an immediate announcement of its transfer to one of the great museums; but presently concluding that Miss Lombard, out of filial piety, had wished to avoid an appearance of unseemly haste in the disposal of her treasure, he dismissed the matter from his mind. Other affairs happened to engage him; the months slipped by, and gradually the lady and the picture dwelt less vividly in his mind.

It was not till five or six years later, when chance took him again to Siena, that the recollection started from some inner fold of memory. He found himself, as it happened, at the head of Doctor Lombard's street, and glancing down that grim thoroughfare, caught an oblique glimpse of the doctor's house front, with the Dead Hand projecting above its threshold. The sight revived his interest, and that evening, over an admirable frittata, he questioned his landlady about Miss Lombard's marriage.

"The daughter of the English doctor? But she has never married, *signore*."

"Never married? What, then, became of Count Ottaviano?"

"For a long time he waited; but last year he married a noble lady of the Maremma."

"But what happened—why was the marriage broken?"

The landlady enacted a pantomime of baffled interrogation.

"And Miss Lombard still lives in her father's house?"

"Yes, *signore*; she is still there."

"And the Leonardo—"

"The Leonardo, also, is still there."

The next day, as Wyant entered the House of the Dead Hand, he remembered Count Ottaviano's injunction to ring twice, and smiled mournfully to think that so much subtlety had been vain. But what could have prevented the marriage? If Doctor Lombard's death had been long delayed, time might have acted as a dissolvent, or the young lady's resolve have failed; but it seemed impossible that the white heat of ardour in which Wyant had left the lovers should have cooled in a few short weeks.

As he ascended the vaulted stairway the atmosphere of the place seemed a reply to his conjectures. The same numbing air fell on him, like an emanation from some persistent will-power, a something fierce and imminent which might reduce to impotence every impulse within its range. Wyant could almost fancy a hand on his shoulder, guiding him upward with the ironical intent of confronting him with the evidence of its work.

A strange servant opened the door, and he was presently introduced to the tapestried room, where, from their usual seats in the window, Mrs. Lombard and her daughter advanced to welcome him with faint ejaculations of surprise.

Both had grown oddly old, but in a dry, smooth way, as fruits might shrivel on a shelf instead of ripening on the tree. Mrs. Lombard was still knitting, and pausing now and then to warm her swollen hands above the brazier; and Miss Lombard, in rising, had laid aside a strip of needle-work which might have been the same on which Wyant had first seen her engaged

Their visitor inquired discreetly how they had fared in the interval, and learned that they had thought of returning to England, but had somehow never done so.

"I am sorry not to see my aunts again," Mrs. Lombard said resignedly; "but Sybilla thinks it best that we should not go this year."

"Next year, perhaps," murmured Miss Lombard, in a voice which seemed to suggest that they had a great waste of time to fill.

She had returned to her seat, and sat bending over her work. Her hair enveloped her head in the same thick braids, but the rose colour of her cheeks had turned to blotches of dull red, like some pigment which has darkened in drying.

"And Professor Clyde—is he well?" Mrs. Lombard asked affably; continuing, as her daughter raised a startled eye: "Surely, Sybilla, Mr. Wyant was the gentleman who was sent by Professor Clyde to see the Leonardo?"

Miss Lombard was silent, but Wyant hastened to assure the elder lady of his friend's well-being.

"Ah—perhaps, then, he will come back some day to Siena," she said, sighing. Wyant declared that it was more than likely; and there ensued a pause, which he presently broke by saying to Miss Lombard: "And you still have the picture?"

She raised her eyes and looked at him. "Should you like to see it?" she asked.

On his assenting, she rose, and extracting the same key from the same secret drawer, unlocked the door beneath the tapestry. They walked down the passage in silence, and she stood aside with a grave gesture, making Wyant pass before her into the room. Then she crossed over and drew the curtain back from the picture. The light of the early afternoon poured full on it: its surface appeared to ripple and heave with a fluid splendour. The colours had lost none of their warmth, the outlines none of their pure precision; it seemed to Wyant like some magical flower which had burst suddenly from the mould of darkness and oblivion.

He turned to Miss Lombard with a movement of comprehension.

"Ah, I understand—you couldn't part with it, after all!" he cried.

"No—I couldn't part with it," she answered.

"It's too beautiful,—too *beautiful*,"—he assented.

"Too beautiful?" She turned on him with a curious stare. "I have never thought it beautiful, you know."

He gave back the stare. "You have never—"

She shook her head. "It's not that. I hate it; I've always hated it. But he wouldn't let me—he will never let me now."

Wyant was startled by her use of the present tense. Her look surprised him, too: there was a strange fixity of resentment in her innocuous eye. Was it possible that she was labouring under some delusion? Or did the pronoun not refer to her father?

"You mean that Doctor Lombard did not wish you to part with the picture?"

"No—he prevented me; he will always prevent me."

There was another pause. "You promised him, then, before his death—"

"No; I promised nothing. He died too suddenly to make me." Her voice sank to a whisper. "I was free—perfectly free—or I thought I was till I tried."

"Till you tried?"

"To disobey him—to sell the picture. Then I found it was impossible. I tried again and again; but he was always in the room with me."

She glanced over her shoulder as though she had heard a step; and to Wyant, too, for a moment, the room seemed full of a third presence.

"And you can't"—he faltered, unconsciously dropping his voice to the pitch of hers.

She shook her head, gazing at him mystically. "I can't lock him out; I can never lock him out now. I told you I should never have another chance."

Wyant felt the chill of her words like a cold breath in his hair.

"Oh"—he groaned; but she cut him off with a grave gesture.

"It is too late," she said; "but you ought to have helped me that day."

The Mission of Jane

1

Lethbury, surveying his wife across the dinner table, found his transient conjugal glance arrested by an indefinable change in her appearance.

"How smart you look! Is that a new gown?" he asked.

Her answering look seemed to deprecate his charging her with the extravagance of wasting a new gown on him, and he now perceived that the change lay deeper than any accident of dress. At the same time, he noticed that she betrayed her consciousness of it by a delicate, almost frightened blush. It was one of the compensations of Mrs. Lethbury's protracted childishness that she still blushed as prettily as at eighteen. Her body had been privileged not to outstrip her mind, and the two, as it seemed to Lethbury, were destined to travel together through an eternity of girlishness.

"I don't know what you mean," she said.

Since she never did, he always wondered at her bringing this out as a fresh grievance against him; but his wonder was unresentful, and he said good-humouredly: "You sparkle so that I thought you had on your diamonds."

She sighed and blushed again.

"It must be," he continued, "that you've been to a dressmaker's opening. You're absolutely brimming with illicit enjoyment."

She stared again, this time at the adjective. His adjectives always embarrassed her: their unintelligibleness savoured of impropriety.

"In short," he summed up, "you've been doing something that you're thoroughly ashamed of."

To his surprise she retorted: "I don't see why I should be ashamed of it!"

Lethbury leaned back with a smile of enjoyment. When there was nothing better going he always liked to listen to her explanations.

"Well—?" he said.

She was becoming breathless and ejaculatory. "Of course you'll laugh—you laugh at everything!"

"That rather blunts the point of my derision, doesn't it?" he interjected; but she rushed on without noticing:

"It's so easy to laugh at things."

"Ah," murmured Lethbury with relish, "that's Aunt Sophronia's, isn't it?"

Most of his wife's opinions were heirlooms, and he took a quaint pleasure in tracing their descent. She was proud of their age, and saw no reason for discarding them while they were still serviceable. Some, of course, were so fine that she kept them for state occasions, like her great-grandmother's Crown Derby; but from the lady known as Aunt Sophronia she had inherited a stout set of every-day prejudices that were practically as good as new; whereas her husband's, as she noticed, were always having to be replaced.

In the early days she had fancied there might be a certain satisfaction in taxing him with the fact; but she had long since been silenced by the reply: "My dear, I'm not a rich man, but I never use an opinion twice if I can help it."

She was reduced, therefore, to dwelling on his moral deficiencies; and one of the most obvious of these was his refusal to take things seriously. On this occasion, however, some ulterior purpose kept her from taking up his taunt.

"I'm not in the least ashamed!" she repeated, with the air of shaking a banner to the wind; but the domestic atmosphere being calm, the banner drooped unheroically.

"That," said Lethbury judicially, "encourages me to infer that you ought to be, and that, consequently, you've been giving yourself the unusual pleasure of doing something I shouldn't approve of."

She met this with an almost solemn directness. "No," she said. "You won't approve of it. I've allowed for that."

"Ah," he exclaimed, setting down his liqueur-glass. "You've worked out the whole problem, eh?"

"I believe so."

"That's uncommonly interesting. And what is it?"

She looked at him quietly. "A baby."

If it was seldom given her to surprise him, she had attained the distinction for once.

"A baby?"

"Yes."

"A—human baby?"

"Of course!" she cried, with the virtuous resentment of the woman who has never allowed dogs in the house.

Lethbury's puzzled stare broke into a fresh smile. "A baby I sha'n't approve of? Well, in the abstract I don't think much of them, I admit. Is this an abstract baby?"

Again she frowned at the adjective; but she had reached a pitch of exaltation at which such obstacles could not deter her.

"It's the loveliest baby—" she murmured.

"Ah, then it's concrete. It exists. In this harsh world it draws its breath in pain—"

"It's the healthiest child I ever saw!" she indignantly corrected.

"You've seen it, then?"

Again the accusing blush suffused her. "Yes—I've seen it."

"And to whom does the paragon belong?"

And here indeed she confounded him. "To me—I hope," she declared.

He pushed his chair back with an inarticulate murmur. "To *you*—?"

"To *us*," she corrected.

"Good Lord!" he said. If there had been the least hint of hallucination in her transparent gaze—but no: it was as clear, as shallow, as easily fathomable as when he had first suffered the sharp surprise of striking bottom in it.

It occurred to him that perhaps she was trying to be funny: he knew that there is nothing more cryptic than the humour of the unhumorous.

"Is it a joke?" he faltered.

"Oh, I hope not. I want it so much to be a reality—"

He paused to smile at the limitations of a world in which jokes were not realities, and continued gently: "But since it is one already—"

"To us, I mean: to you and me. I want—" her voice wavered, and her eyes with it. "I have always wanted so dreadfully...it has been such a disappointment. . . .not to. . . ."

"I see," said Lethbury slowly.

But he had not seen before. It seemed curious, now, that he had never thought of her taking it in that way, had never surmised any hidden depths beneath her outspread obviousness. He felt as though he had touched a secret spring in her mind.

There was a moment's silence, moist and tremulous on her part, awkward and slightly irritated on his.

"You've been lonely, I suppose?" he began. It was odd, having suddenly to reckon with the stranger who gazed at him out of her trivial eyes.

"At times," she said.

"I'm sorry."

"It was not your fault. A man has so many occupations; and women who are clever—or very handsome—I suppose that's an occupation too. Sometimes I've felt that when dinner was ordered I had nothing to do till the next day."

"Oh," he groaned.

"It wasn't your fault," she insisted. "I never told you—but when I chose that rose-bud paper for the front room upstairs, I always thought—"

"Well—?"

"It would be such a pretty paper—for a baby—to wake up in. That was years ago, of course; but it was rather an expensive paper. . . . .and it hasn't faded in the least. . . ." she broke off incoherently.

"It hasn't faded?"

"No—and so I thought...as we don't use the room for anything ... now that Aunt Sophronia is dead. . . .I thought I might. . . .you might. . . .oh, Julian, if you could only have seen it just waking up in its crib!"

"Seen what—where? You haven't got a baby upstairs?"

"Oh, no—not *yet*," she said, with her rare laugh—the girlish bubbling of merriment that had seemed one of her chief graces in the early days. It occurred to him that he had not given her enough things to laugh about lately. But then she needed such very elementary things: it was as difficult to amuse her as a savage. He concluded that he was not sufficiently simple.

"Alice," he said, almost solemnly, "what *do* you mean?"

She hesitated a moment: he saw her gather her courage for a supreme effort. Then she said slowly, gravely, as though she were pronouncing a sacramental phrase:

"I'm so lonely without a little child—and I thought perhaps you'd let me adopt one. . . .It's at the hospital. . . .its mother is dead. . . .and I could. . . .pet it, and dress it, and do things for it. . . . .and it's such a good baby. . . .you can ask any of the nurses. . . .it would never, *never* bother you by crying. . . ."

2

Lethbury accompanied his wife to the hospital in a mood of chastened wonder. It did not occur to him to oppose her wish. He knew, of course, that he would have to bear the brunt of the situation: the jokes at the club, the inquiries, the explanations. He saw himself in the comic role of the adopted father, and welcomed it as an expiation. For in his rapid reconstruction of the past he found himself cutting a shabbier figure than he cared to admit. He had always been intolerant of stupid people, and it was his punishment to be convicted of stupidity. As his mind traversed the years between his marriage and this unexpected assumption of paternity, he saw, in the light of an overheated imagination, many signs of unwonted crassness. It was not that he had ceased to think his wife stupid: she *was* stupid, limited, inflexible; but there was a pathos in the struggles of her swaddled mind, in its blind reachings toward the primal emotions.

He had always thought she would have been happier with a child; but he had thought it mechanically, because it had so often been thought before, because it was in the nature of things to think it of every woman, because his wife was so eminently one of a species that she fitted into all the generalisations on the sex. But he had regarded this generalization as merely typical of the triumph of tradition over experience. Maternity was no doubt the supreme function of primitive woman, the one end to which her whole organism tended; but the law of increasing complexity had operated in both sexes, and he had not seriously supposed that, outside the world of Christmas fiction and anecdotic art, such truisms had any special hold on the feminine imagination. Now he saw that the arts in question were kept alive by the vitality of the sentiments they appealed to.

Lethbury was in fact going through a rapid process of readjustment. His marriage had been a failure, but he had preserved toward his wife the exact fidelity of act that is sometimes supposed to excuse any divagation of feeling; so that, for years, the tie between them had consisted mainly in his abstaining from making love to other women. The abstention had not always been easy, for the world is surprisingly well-stocked with the kind of woman one ought to have married but did not; and Lethbury had not escaped the solicitation of such alternatives. His immunity had been purchased at the cost of taking refuge in the somewhat rarified atmosphere of his perceptions; and his world being thus limited, he had given unusual care to its details, compensating himself for the narrowness of his horizon by the minute finish of his foreground.

It was a world of fine shadings and the nicest proportions, where impulse seldom set a blundering foot, and the feast of reason was undisturbed by an intemperate flow of soul. To such a banquet his wife naturally remained uninvited. The diet would have disagreed with her, and she would probably have objected to the other guests. But Lethbury, miscalculating her needs, had hitherto supposed that he had made ample provision for them, and was consequently at liberty to enjoy his own fare without any reproach of mendicancy at his gates. Now he beheld her pressing a starved face against the windows of his life, and in his imaginative reaction he invested her with a pathos borrowed from the sense of his own shortcomings.

In the hospital, the imaginative process continued with increasing force. He looked at his wife with new eyes. Formerly she had been to him a mere bundle of negations, a labyrinth of dead walls and bolted doors. There was nothing behind the walls, and the doors led nowhither: he had sounded and listened often enough to be sure of that. Now he felt like a traveller who, exploring some ancient ruin, comes on an inner cell, intact amid the general dilapidation, and painted with images which reveal the forgotten uses of the building.

His wife stood by a white crib in one of the wards. In the crib lay a child, a year old, the nurse affirmed, but to Lethbury's eye a mere dateless fragment of humanity projected against a background of conjecture. Over this anonymous particle of life Mrs. Lethbury leaned, such ecstasy reflected in her face as strikes up, in Correggio's *Night-piece,* from the child's body to the mother's countenance. It was a light that irradiated and dazzled her. She looked up at an inquiry of Lethbury's, but as their glances met he perceived that she no longer saw him, that he had become as invisible to her as she had long been to him. He had to transfer his question to the nurse.

"What is the child's name?" he asked.

"We call her Jane," said the nurse.

3

Lethbury, at first, had resisted the idea of a legal adoption; but when he found that his wife's curiously limited imagination prevented her regarding the child as hers till it had been made so by process of law, he promptly withdrew his objection. On one point only he remained inflexible; and that was the changing of the waif's name. Mrs. Lethbury, almost at once, had expressed a wish to rechristen it: she fluctuated between Muriel and Gladys, deferring the moment of decision like a lady wavering between two bonnets. But Lethbury was unyielding. In the general surrender of his prejudices this one alone held out.

"But Jane is so dreadful," Mrs. Lethbury protested.

"Well, we don't know that *she* won't be dreadful. She may grow up a Jane."

His wife exclaimed reproachfully. "The nurse says she's the loveliest—"

"Don't they always say that?" asked Lethbury patiently. He was prepared to be inexhaustibly patient now that he had reached a firm foothold of opposition.

"It's cruel to call her Jane," Mrs. Lethbury pleaded.

"It's ridiculous to call her Muriel."

"The nurse is *sure* she must be a lady's child."

Lethbury winced: he had tried, all along, to keep his mind off the question of antecedents.

"Well, let her prove it," he said, with a rising sense of exasperation. He wondered how he could ever have allowed himself to be drawn into such a ridiculous business; for the first time he felt the full irony of it. He had visions of coming home in the afternoon to a house smelling of linseed and paregoric, and of being greeted by a chronic howl as he went upstairs to dress for dinner. He had never been a club-man, but he saw himself becoming one now.

The worst of his anticipations were unfulfilled. The baby was surprisingly well and surprisingly quiet. Such infantile remedies as she absorbed were not potent enough to be perceived beyond the nursery; and when Lethbury could be induced to enter that sanctuary, there was nothing to jar his nerves in the mild pink presence of his adopted daughter. Jars there were, indeed: they were probably inevitable in the disturbed routine of the household; but they occurred between Mrs. Lethbury and the nurses, and Jane contributed to them only a placid stare which might have served as a rebuke to the combatants.

In the reaction from his first impulse of atonement, Lethbury noted with sharpened perceptions the effect of the change on his wife's character. He saw already the error of supposing that it could work any transformation in her. It simply magnified her existing qualities. She was like a dried sponge put in water: she expanded, but she did not change her shape. From the stand-point of scientific observation it was curious to see how her stored instincts responded to the pseudo-maternal call. She overflowed with the petty maxims of the occasion.

One felt in her the epitome, the consummation, of centuries of animal maternity, so that this little woman, who screamed at a mouse and was nervous about burglars, came to typify the cave-mother rending her prey for her young.

It was less easy to regard philosophically the practical effects of her borrowed motherhood. Lethbury found with surprise that she was becoming assertive and definite. She no longer represented the negative side of his life; she showed, indeed, a tendency to inconvenient affirmations. She had gradually expanded her assumption of motherhood till it included his own share in the relation, and he suddenly found himself regarded as the father of Jane.

This was a contingency he had not foreseen, and it took all his philosophy to accept it; but there were moments of compensation. For Mrs. Lethbury was undoubtedly happy for the first time in years; and the thought that he had tardily contributed to this end reconciled him to the irony of the means.

At first he was inclined to reproach himself for still viewing the situation from the outside, for remaining a spectator instead of a participant. He had been allured, for a moment, by the vision of severed hands meeting over a cradle, as the whole body of domestic fiction bears witness to their doing; and the fact that no such conjunction took place he could explain only on the ground that it was a borrowed cradle. He did not dislike the little girl. She still remained to him a hypothetical presence, a query rather than a fact; but her nearness was not unpleasant, and there were moments when her tentative utterances, her groping steps, seemed to loosen the dry accretions enveloping his inner self.

But even at such moments—moments which he invited and caressed—she did not bring him nearer to his wife. He now perceived that he had made a certain place in his life for Mrs. Lethbury, and that she no longer fitted into it. It was too late to enlarge the space, and so she overflowed and encroached. Lethbury struggled against the sense of submergence. He let down barrier after barrier, yielded privacy after privacy; but his wife's personality continued to dilate. She was no longer herself alone: she was herself and Jane. Gradually, in a monstrous fusion of identity, she became herself, himself and Jane; and instead of trying to adapt her to a spare crevice of his character, he found himself carelessly squeezed into the smallest compartment of the domestic economy.

4

He continued to tell himself that he was satisfied if his wife was happy; and it was not till the child's tenth year that he felt a doubt of her happiness.

Jane had been a preternaturally good child. During the eight years of her adoption she had caused her foster-parents no anxiety beyond those connected with the usual succession of youthful diseases. But her unknown progenitors had given her a robust constitution, and she passed unperturbed through measles, chicken-pox and whooping-cough. If there was any suffering it was endured vicariously by Mrs. Lethbury, whose temperature rose and fell with the patient's, and who could not hear Jane sneeze without visions of a marble angel weeping over a broken column. But though Jane's prompt recoveries continued to belie such premonitions, though her existence continued to move forward on an even keel of good health and good conduct, Mrs. Lethbury's satisfaction showed no corresponding advance. Lethbury, at first, was disposed to add her disappointment to the long list of feminine inconsistencies with which the sententious observer of life builds up his favourite induction; but circumstances presently led him to take a kindlier view of the case.

Hitherto his wife had regarded him as a negligible factor in Jane's evolution. Beyond providing for his adopted daughter, and effacing himself before her, he was not expected to contribute to her well-being. But as time passed he appeared to his wife in a new light. It was he who was to educate Jane. In matters of the intellect, Mrs. Lethbury was the first to declare her deficiencies—to proclaim them, even, with a certain virtuous superiority. She said she did not pretend to be clever, and there was no denying the truth of the assertion. Now, however, she seemed less ready, not to own her limitations, but to glory in them. Confronted with the problem of Jane's instruction, she stood in awe of the child.

"I have always been stupid, you know," she said to Lethbury with a new humility, "and I'm afraid I sha'n't know what is best for Jane. I'm sure she has a wonderfully good mind, and I should reproach myself if I didn't give her every opportunity." She looked at him helplessly. "You must tell me what ought to be done."

Lethbury was not unwilling to oblige her. Somewhere in his mental lumber-room there rusted a theory of education such as usually lingers among the impedimenta of the childless. He brought this out, refurbished it, and applied it to Jane. At first he thought his wife had not overrated the quality of the child's mind. Jane seemed extraordinarily intelligent. Her precocious definiteness of mind was encouraging to her inexperienced preceptor. She had no difficulty in fixing her attention, and he felt that every fact he imparted was being etched in metal. He helped his wife to engage the best teachers, and for a while continued to take an ex-official interest in his adopted daughter's studies. But gradually his interest waned. Jane's ideas did not increase with her acquisitions. Her young mind remained a mere receptacle for facts: a kind of cold-storage from which anything that had been put there could be taken out at a moment's notice, intact but congealed.

She developed, moreover, an inordinate pride in the capacity of her mental storehouse, and a tendency to pelt her public with its contents. She was overheard to jeer at her nurse for not knowing when the Saxon Heptarchy had fallen, and she alternately dazzled and depressed Mrs. Lethbury by the wealth of her chronological allusions. She showed no interest in the significance of the facts she amassed: she simply collected dates as another child might have collected stamps or marbles. To her foster-mother she seemed a prodigy of wisdom; but Lethbury saw, with a secret movement of sympathy, how the aptitudes in which Mrs. Lethbury gloried were slowly estranging her from their possessor.

"She is getting too clever for me," his wife said to him, after one of Jane's historical flights, "but I am so glad that she will be a companion to you."

Lethbury groaned in spirit. He did not look forward to Jane's companionship. She was still a good little girl: but there was something automatic and formal in her goodness, as though it were a kind of moral calisthenics that she went through for the sake of showing her agility. An early consciousness of virtue had moreover constituted her the natural guardian and adviser of her elders. Before she was fifteen she had set about reforming the household. She took Mrs. Lethbury in hand first; then she extended her efforts to the servants, with consequences more disastrous to the domestic harmony; and lastly she applied herself to Lethbury.

She proved to him by statistics that he smoked too much, and that it was injurious to the optic nerve to read in bed. She took him to task for not going to church more regularly, and pointed out to him the evils of desultory reading. She suggested that a regular course of study encourages mental concentration, and hinted that inconsecutiveness of thought is a sign of approaching age.

To her adopted mother her suggestions were equally pertinent. She instructed Mrs. Lethbury in an improved way of making beef stock, and called her attention to the unhygienic qualities of carpets. She poured out distracting facts about *bacilli* and vegetable mould, and demonstrated that curtains and picture-frames are a hot-bed of animal organisms. She learned by heart the nutritive ingredients of the principal articles of diet, and revolutionized the cuisine by an attempt to establish a scientific average between starch and phosphates. Four cooks left during this experiment, and Lethbury fell into the habit of dining at his club.

Once or twice, at the outset, he had tried to check Jane's ardour; but his efforts resulted only in hurting his wife's feelings. Jane remained impervious, and Mrs. Lethbury resented any attempt to protect her from her daughter. Lethbury saw that she was consoled for the sense of her own inferiority by the thought of what Jane's intellectual companionship must be to him; and he tried to keep up the illusion by enduring with what grace he might the blighting edification of Jane's discourse.

5

As Jane grew up, he sometimes avenged himself by wondering if his wife was still sorry that they had not called her Muriel. Jane was not ugly; she developed, indeed, a kind of categorical prettiness that might have been a projection of her mind. She had a creditable collection of features, but one had to take an inventory of them to find out that she was good-looking. The fusing grace had been omitted.

Mrs. Lethbury took a touching pride in her daughter's first steps in the world. She expected Jane to take by her complexion those whom she did not capture by her learning. But Jane's rosy freshness did not work any perceptible ravages. Whether the young men guessed the axioms on her lips and detected the encyclopaedia in her eye, or whether they simply found no intrinsic interest in these features, certain it is, that, in spite of her mother's heroic efforts, and of incessant calls on Lethbury's purse, Jane, at the end of her first season, had dropped hopelessly out of the running. A few duller girls found her interesting, and one or two young men came to the house with the object of meeting other young women; but she was rapidly becoming one of the social supernumeraries who are asked out only because they are on people's lists.

The blow was bitter to Mrs. Lethbury; but she consoled herself with the idea that Jane had failed because she was too clever. Jane probably shared this conviction; at all events she betrayed no consciousness of failure. She had developed a pronounced taste for society, and went out, unweariedly and obstinately, winter after winter, while Mrs. Lethbury toiled in her wake, showering attentions on oblivious hostesses.

To Lethbury there was something at once tragic and exasperating in the sight of their two figures, the one conciliatory, the other dogged, both pursuing with unabated zeal the elusive prize of popularity. He even began to feel a personal stake in the pursuit, not as it concerned Jane, but as it affected his wife. He saw that the latter was the victim of Jane's disappointment: that Jane was not above the crude satisfaction of "taking it out" of her mother. Experience checked the impulse to come to his wife's defence; and when his resentment was at its height, Jane disarmed him by giving up the struggle.

Nothing was said to mark her capitulation; but Lethbury noticed that the visiting ceased, and that the dressmaker's bills diminished. At the same time, Mrs. Lethbury made it known that Jane had taken up charities; and before long Jane's conversation confirmed this announcement. At first Lethbury congratulated himself on the change; but Jane's domesticity soon began to weigh on him. During the day she was sometimes absent on errands of mercy; but in the evening she was always there. At first she and Mrs. Lethbury sat in the drawing-room together, and Lethbury smoked in the library; but presently Jane formed the habit of joining him there, and he began to suspect that he was included among the objects of her philanthropy.

Mrs. Lethbury confirmed the suspicion. "Jane has grown very serious-minded lately," she said. "She imagines that she used to neglect you, and she is trying to make up for it. Don't discourage her," she added innocently.

Such a plea delivered Lethbury helpless to his daughter's ministrations: and he found himself measuring the hours he spent with her by the amount of relief they must be affording her mother. There were even moments when he read a furtive gratitude in Mrs. Lethbury's eye.

But Lethbury was no hero, and he had nearly reached the limit of vicarious endurance when something wonderful happened. They never quite knew afterward how it had come about, or who first perceived it; but Mrs. Lethbury one day gave tremulous voice to their inferences.

"Of course," she said, "he comes here because of Elise." The young lady in question, a friend of Jane's, was possessed of attractions which had already been found to explain the presence of masculine visitors.

Lethbury risked a denial. "I don't think he does," he declared.

"But Elise is thought very pretty," Mrs. Lethbury insisted.

"I can't help that," said Lethbury doggedly.

He saw a faint light in his wife's eyes; but she remarked carelessly: "Mr. Budd would be a very good match for Elise."

Lethbury could hardly repress a chuckle: he was so exquisitely aware that she was trying to propitiate the gods.

For a few weeks neither said a word; then Mrs. Lethbury once more reverted to the subject.

"It is a month since Elise went abroad," she said.

"Is it?"

"And Mr. Budd seems to come here just as often—"

"Ah," said Lethbury with heroic indifference; and his wife hastily changed the subject.

Mr. Winstanley Budd was a young man who suffered from an excess of manner. Politeness gushed from him in the driest seasons. He was always performing feats of drawing-room chivalry, and the approach of the most unobtrusive female threw him into attitudes which endangered the furniture. His features, being of the cherubic order, did not lend themselves to this role; but there were moments when he appeared to dominate them, to force them into compliance with an aquiline ideal. The range of Mr. Budd's social benevolence made its object hard to distinguish. He spread his cloak so indiscriminately that one could not always interpret the gesture, and Jane's impassive manner had the effect of increasing his demonstrations: she threw him into paroxysms of politeness.

At first he filled the house with his amenities; but gradually it became apparent that his most dazzling effects were directed exclusively to Jane. Lethbury and his wife held their breath and looked away from each other. They pretended not to notice the frequency of Mr. Budd's visits, they struggled against an imprudent inclination to leave the young people too much alone. Their conclusions were the result of indirect observation, for neither of them dared to be caught watching Mr. Budd: they behaved like naturalists on the trail of a rare butterfly.

In his efforts not to notice Mr. Budd, Lethbury centred his attentions on Jane; and Jane, at this crucial moment, wrung from him a reluctant admiration. While her parents went about dissembling their emotions, she seemed to have none to conceal. She betrayed neither eagerness nor surprise; so complete was her unconcern that there were moments when Lethbury feared it was obtuseness, when he could hardly help whispering to her that now was the moment to lower the net.

Meanwhile the velocity of Mr. Budd's gyrations increased with the ardour of courtship: his politeness became incandescent, and Jane found herself the centre of a pyrotechnical display culminating in the "set piece" of an offer of marriage.

Mrs. Lethbury imparted the news to her husband one evening after their daughter had gone to bed. The announcement was made and received with an air of detachment, as though both feared to be betrayed into unseemly exultation; but Lethbury, as his wife ended, could not repress the inquiry, "Have they decided on a day?"

Mrs. Lethbury's superior command of her features enabled her to look shocked. "What can you be thinking of? He only offered himself at five!"

"Of course—of course—" stammered Lethbury—"but nowadays people marry after such short engagements—"

"Engagement!" said his wife solemnly. "There is no engagement."

Lethbury dropped his cigar. "What on earth do you mean?"

"Jane is thinking it over."

"Thinking it over?"

"She has asked for a month before deciding."

Lethbury sank back with a gasp. Was it genius or was it madness? He felt incompetent to decide; and Mrs. Lethbury's next words showed that she shared his difficulty.

"Of course I don't want to hurry Jane—"

"Of course not," he acquiesced.

"But I pointed out to her that a young man of Mr. Budd's impulsive temperament might—might be easily discouraged—"

"Yes; and what did she say?"

"She said that if she was worth winning she was worth waiting for."

6

The period of Mr. Budd's probation could scarcely have cost him as much mental anguish as it caused his would-be parents-in-law.

Mrs. Lethbury, by various ruses, tried to shorten the ordeal, but Jane remained inexorable; and each morning Lethbury came down to breakfast with the certainty of finding a letter of withdrawal from her discouraged suitor.

When at length the decisive day came, and Mrs. Lethbury, at its close, stole into the library with an air of chastened joy, they stood for a moment without speaking; then Mrs. Lethbury paid a fitting tribute to the proprieties by faltering out: "It will be dreadful to have to give her up—"

Lethbury could not repress a warning gesture; but even as it escaped him, he realised that his wife's grief was genuine.

"Of course, of course," he said, vainly sounding his own emotional shallows for an answering regret. And yet it was his wife who had suffered most from Jane!

He had fancied that these sufferings would be effaced by the milder atmosphere of their last weeks together; but felicity did not soften Jane. Not for a moment did she relax her dominion: she simply widened it to include a new subject. Mr. Budd found himself under orders with the others; and a new fear assailed Lethbury as he saw Jane assume prenuptial control of her betrothed. Lethbury had never felt any strong personal interest in Mr. Budd; but, as Jane's prospective husband, the young man excited his sympathy. To his surprise, he found that Mrs. Lethbury shared the feeling.

"I'm afraid he may find Jane a little exacting," she said, after an evening dedicated to a stormy discussion of the wedding arrangements. "She really ought to make some concessions. If he *wants* to be married in a black frock-coat instead of a dark grey one—" She paused and looked doubtfully at Lethbury.

"What can I do about it?" he said.

"You might explain to him—tell him that Jane isn't always—"

Lethbury made an impatient gesture. "What are you afraid of? His finding her out or his not finding her out?"

Mrs. Lethbury flushed. "You put it so dreadfully!"

Her husband mused for a moment; then he said with an air of cheerful hypocrisy: "After all, Budd is old enough to take care of himself."

But the next day Mrs. Lethbury surprised him. Late in the afternoon she entered the library, so breathless and inarticulate that he scented a catastrophe.

"I've done it!" she cried.

"Done what?"

"Told him." She nodded toward the door. "He's just gone. Jane is out, and I had a chance to talk to him alone."

Lethbury pushed a chair forward and she sank into it.

"What did you tell him? That she is *not* always—"

Mrs. Lethbury lifted a tragic eye. "No; I told him that she always *is*—"

"Always *is*—?"

"Yes."

There was a pause. Lethbury made a call on his hoarded philosophy. He saw Jane suddenly reinstated in her evening seat by the library fire; but an answering chord in him thrilled at his wife's heroism.

"Well—what did he say?"

Mrs. Lethbury's agitation deepened. It was clear that the blow had fallen.

"He. . . .he said. . . .that we. . . .had never understood Jane. . . .or appreciated her. . . ." The final syllables were lost in her handkerchief, and she left him marvelling at the mechanism of a woman.

After that, Lethbury faced the future with an undaunted eye. They had done their duty—at least his wife had done hers—and they were reaping the usual harvest of ingratitude with a zest seldom accorded to such reaping. There was a marked change in Mr. Budd's manner, and his increasing coldness sent a genial glow through Lethbury's system. It was easy to bear with Jane in the light of Mr. Budd's disapproval.

There was a good deal to be borne in the last days, and the brunt of it fell on Mrs. Lethbury. Jane marked her transition to the married state by an appropriate but incongruous display of nerves. She became sentimental, hysterical and reluctant. She quarrelled with her betrothed and threatened to return the ring. Mrs. Lethbury had to intervene, and Lethbury felt the hovering sword of destiny. But the blow was suspended. Mr. Budd's chivalry was proof against all his bride's caprices, and his devotion throve on her cruelty. Lethbury feared that he was too faithful, too enduring, and longed to urge him to vary his tactics. Jane presently reappeared with the ring on her finger, and consented to try on the wedding-dress; but her uncertainties, her reactions, were prolonged till the final day.

When it dawned, Lethbury was still in an ecstasy of apprehension. Feeling reasonably sure of the principal actors, he had centred his fears on incidental possibilities. The clergyman might have a stroke, or the church might burn down, or there might be something wrong with the license. He did all that was humanly possible to avert such contingencies, but there remained that incalculable factor known as the hand of God. Lethbury seemed to feel it groping for him.

In the church it almost had him by the nape. Mr. Budd was late; and for five immeasurable minutes Lethbury and Jane faced a churchful of conjecture. Then the bridegroom appeared, flushed but chivalrous, and explaining to his father-in-law under cover of the ritual that he had torn his glove and had to go back for another.

"You'll be losing the ring next," muttered Lethbury; but Mr. Budd produced this article punctually, and a moment or two later was bearing its wearer captive down the aisle.

At the wedding-breakfast Lethbury caught his wife's eye fixed on him in mild disapproval, and understood that his hilarity was exceeding the bounds of fitness. He pulled himself together, and tried to subdue his tone; but his jubilation bubbled over like a champagne-glass perpetually refilled. The deeper his draughts, the higher it rose.

It was at the brim when, in the wake of the dispersing guests, Jane came down in her travelling-dress and fell on her mother's neck.

"I can't leave you!" she wailed, and Lethbury felt as suddenly sobered as a man under a *douche*. But if the bride was reluctant her captor was relentless. Never had Mr. Budd been more dominant, more aquiline. Lethbury's last fears were dissipated as the young man snatched Jane from her mother's bosom and bore her off to the brougham.

The brougham rolled away, the last milliner's girl forsook her post by the awning, the red carpet was folded up, and the house door closed. Lethbury stood alone in the hall with his wife. As he turned toward her, he noticed the look of tired heroism in her eyes, the deepened lines of her face. They reflected his own symptoms too accurately not to appeal to him. The nervous tension had been horrible. He went up to her, and an answering impulse made her lay a hand on his arm. He held it there a moment.

"Let us go off and have a jolly little dinner at a restaurant," he proposed.

There had been a time when such a suggestion would have surprised her to the verge of disapproval; but now she agreed to it at once.

"Oh, that would be so nice," she murmured with a great sigh of relief and assuagement.

Jane had fulfilled her mission after all: she had drawn them together at last.

The Moving Finger

1

The news of Mrs. Grancy's death came to me with the shock of an immense blunder—one of fate's most irretrievable acts of vandalism. It was as though all sorts of renovating forces had been checked by the clogging of that one wheel. Not that Mrs. Grancy contributed any perceptible momentum to the social machine: her unique distinction was that of filling to perfection her special place in the world. So many people are like badly-composed statues, over-lapping their niches at one point and leaving them vacant at another. Mrs. Grancy's niche was her husband's life; and if it be argued that the space was not large enough for its vacancy to leave a very big gap, I can only say that, at the last resort, such dimensions must be determined by finer instruments than any ready-made standard of utility.

Ralph Grancy's was in short a kind of disembodied usefulness: one of those constructive influences that, instead of crystallizing into definite forms, remain as it were a medium for the development of clear thinking and fine feeling. He faithfully irrigated his own dusty patch of life, and the fruitful moisture stole far beyond his boundaries. If, to carry on the metaphor, Grancy's life was a sedulously-cultivated enclosure, his wife was the flower he had planted in its midst—the embowering tree, rather, which gave him rest and shade at its foot and the wind of dreams in its upper branches.

We had all—his small but devoted band of followers—known a moment when it seemed likely that Grancy would fail us. We had watched him pitted against one stupid obstacle after another—ill-health, poverty, misunderstanding and, worst of all for a man of his texture, his first wife's soft insidious egotism. We had seen him sinking under the leaden embrace of her affection like a swimmer in a drowning clutch; but just as we despaired he had always come to the surface again, blinded, panting, but striking out fiercely for the shore. When at last her death released him it became a question as to how much of the man she had carried with her. Left alone, he revealed numb withered patches, like a tree from which a parasite has been stripped. But gradually he began to put out new leaves; and when he met the lady who was to become his second wife—his one *real* wife, as his friends reckoned—the whole man burst into flower.

The second Mrs. Grancy was past thirty when he married her, and it was clear that she had harvested that crop of middle joy which is rooted in young despair. But if she had lost the surface of eighteen she had kept its inner light; if her cheek lacked the gloss of immaturity her eyes were young with the stored youth of half a life-time. Grancy had first known her somewhere in the East—I believe she was the sister of one of our consuls out there—and when he brought her home to New York she came among us as a stranger. The idea of Grancy's remarriage had been a shock to us all.

After one such calcining most men would have kept out of the fire; but we agreed that he was predestined to sentimental blunders, and we awaited with resignation the embodiment of his latest mistake. Then Mrs. Grancy came—and we understood. She was the most beautiful and the most complete of explanations. We shuffled our defeated omniscience out of sight and gave it hasty burial under a prodigality of welcome. For the first time in years we had Grancy off our minds. "He'll do something great now!" the least sanguine of us prophesied; and our sentimentalist emended: "He *has* done it—in marrying her!"

It was Claydon, the portrait-painter, who risked this hyperbole; and who soon afterward, at the happy husband's request, prepared to defend it in a portrait of Mrs. Grancy. We were all—even Claydon—ready to concede that Mrs. Grancy's unwontedness was in some degree a matter of environment. Her graces were complementary and it needed the mate's call to reveal the flash of colour beneath her neutral-tinted wings. But if she needed Grancy to interpret her, how much greater was the service she rendered him! Claydon professionally described her as the right frame for him; but if she defined she also enlarged, if she threw the whole into perspective she also cleared new ground, opened fresh vistas, reclaimed whole areas of activity that had run to waste under the harsh husbandry of privation.

This interaction of sympathies was not without its visible expression. Claydon was not alone in maintaining that Grancy's presence—or indeed the mere mention of his name—had a perceptible effect on his wife's appearance. It was as though a light were shifted, a curtain drawn back, as though, to borrow another of Claydon's metaphors, Love the indefatigable artist were perpetually seeking a happier "pose" for his model. In this interpretative light Mrs. Grancy acquired the charm which makes some women's faces like a book of which the last page is never turned. There was always something new to read in her eyes. What Claydon read there—or at least such scattered hints of the ritual as reached him through the sanctuary doors—his portrait in due course declared to us. When the picture was exhibited it was at once acclaimed as his masterpiece; but the people who knew Mrs. Grancy smiled and said it was flattered. Claydon, however, had not set out to paint *their* Mrs. Grancy—or ours even—but Ralph's; and Ralph knew his own at a glance. At the first confrontation he saw that Claydon had understood. As for Mrs. Grancy, when the finished picture was shown to her she turned to the painter and said simply: "Ah, you've done me facing the east!"

The picture, then, for all its value, seemed a mere incident in the unfolding of their double destiny, a foot-note to the illuminated text of their lives. It was not till afterward that it acquired the significance of last words spoken on a threshold never to be recrossed. Grancy, a year after his marriage, had given up his town house and carried his bliss an hour's journey away, to a little place among the hills. His various duties and interests brought him frequently to New York but we necessarily saw him less often than when his house had served as the rallying-point of kindred enthusiasms. It seemed a pity that such an influence should be withdrawn, but we all felt that his long arrears of happiness should be paid in whatever coin he chose.

The distance from which the fortunate couple radiated warmth on us was not too great for friendship to traverse; and our conception of a glorified leisure took the form of Sundays spent in the Grancys' library, with its sedative rural outlook, and the portrait of Mrs. Grancy illuminating its studious walls. The picture was at its best in that setting; and we used to accuse Claydon of visiting Mrs. Grancy in order to see her portrait. He met this by declaring that the portrait *was* Mrs. Grancy; and there were moments when the statement seemed unanswerable. One of us, indeed—I think it must have been the novelist—said that Clayton had been saved from falling in love with Mrs. Grancy only by falling in love with his picture of her; and it was noticeable that he, to whom his finished work was no more than the shed husk of future effort, showed a perennial tenderness for this one achievement.

We smiled afterward to think how often, when Mrs. Grancy was in the room, her presence reflecting itself in our talk like a gleam of sky in a hurrying current, Claydon, averted from the real woman, would sit as it were listening to the picture. His attitude, at the time, seemed only a part of the unusualness of those picturesque afternoons, when the most familiar combinations of life underwent a magical change. Some human happiness is a landlocked lake; but the Grancys' was an open sea, stretching a buoyant and illimitable surface to the voyaging interests of life. There was room and to spare on those waters for all our separate ventures; and always beyond the sunset, a mirage of the fortunate isles toward which our prows bent.

2

It was in Rome that, three years later, I heard of her death. The notice said "suddenly"; I was glad of that. I was glad too—basely perhaps—to be away from Grancy at a time when silence must have seemed obtuse and speech derisive.

I was still in Rome when, a few months afterward, he suddenly arrived there. He had been appointed secretary of legation at Constantinople and was on the way to his post. He had taken the place, he said frankly, "to get away." Our relations with the Porte held out a prospect of hard work, and that, he explained, was what he needed. He could never be satisfied to sit down among the ruins. I saw that, like most of us in moments of extreme moral tension, he was playing a part, behaving as he thought it became a man to behave in the eye of disaster. The instinctive posture of grief is a shuffling compromise between defiance and prostration; and pride feels the need of striking a worthier attitude in face of such a foe.

Grancy, by nature musing and retrospective, had chosen the *rôle* of the man of action, who answers blow for blow and opposes a mailed front to the thrusts of destiny; and the completeness of the equipment testified to his inner weakness. We talked only of what we were not thinking of, and parted, after a few days, with a sense of relief that proved the inadequacy of friendship to perform, in such cases, the office assigned to it by tradition.

Soon afterward my own work called me home, but Grancy remained several years in Europe. International diplomacy kept its promise of giving him work to do, and during the year in which he acted as *chargé d'affaires* he acquitted himself, under trying conditions, with conspicuous zeal and discretion. A political redistribution of matter removed him from office just as he had proved his usefulness to the government; and the following summer I heard that he had come home and was down at his place in the country.

On my return to town I wrote him and his reply came by the next post. He answered as it were in his natural voice, urging me to spend the following Sunday with him, and suggesting that I should bring down any of the old set who could be persuaded to join me. I thought this a good sign, and yet—shall I own it?—I was vaguely disappointed. Perhaps we are apt to feel that our friends' sorrows should be kept like those historic monuments from which the encroaching ivy is periodically removed.

That very evening at the club I ran across Claydon. I told him of Grancy's invitation and proposed that we should go down together; but he pleaded an engagement. I was sorry, for I had always felt that he and I stood nearer Ralph than the others, and if the old Sundays were to be renewed I should have preferred that we two should spend the first alone with him. I said as much to Claydon and offered to fit my time to his; but he met this by a general refusal.

"I don't want to go to Grancy's," he said bluntly. I waited a moment, but he appended no qualifying clause.

"You've seen him since he came back?" I finally ventured.

Claydon nodded.

"And is he so awfully bad?"

"Bad? No: he's all right."

"All right? How can he be, unless he's changed beyond all recognition?"

"Oh, you'll recognize *him*," said Claydon, with a puzzling deflection of emphasis.

His ambiguity was beginning to exasperate me, and I felt myself shut out from some knowledge to which I had as good a right as he.

"You've been down there already; I suppose?"

"Yes; I've been down there."

"And you've done with each other—the partnership is dissolved?"

"Done with each other? I wish to God we had!" He rose nervously and tossed aside the review from which my approach had diverted him. "Look here," he said, standing before me, "Ralph's the best fellow going and there's nothing under heaven I wouldn't do for him—short of going down there again." And with that he walked out of the room.

Claydon was incalculable enough for me to read a dozen different meanings into his words; but none of my interpretations satisfied me.

I determined, at any rate, to seek no farther for a companion; and the next Sunday I travelled down to Grancy's alone. He met me at the station and I saw at once that he had changed since our last meeting. Then he had been in fighting array, but now if he and grief still housed together it was no longer as enemies. Physically the transformation was as marked but less reassuring.

If the spirit triumphed the body showed its scars. At five-and-forty he was grey and stooping, with the tired gait of an old man. His serenity, however, was not the resignation of age. I saw that he did not mean to drop out of the game. Almost immediately he began to speak of our old interests; not with an effort, as at our former meeting, but simply and naturally, in the tone of a man whose life has flowed back into its normal channels. I remembered, with a touch of self-reproach, how I had distrusted his reconstructive powers; but my admiration for his reserved force was now tinged by the sense that, after all, such happiness as his ought to have been paid with his last coin. The feeling grew as we neared the house and I found how inextricably his wife was interwoven with my remembrance of the place: how the whole scene was but an extension of that vivid presence.

Within doors nothing was changed, and my hand would have dropped without surprise into her welcoming clasp. It was luncheon-time, and Grancy led me at once to the dining-room, where the walls, the furniture, the very plate and porcelain, seemed a mirror in which a moment since her face had been reflected. I wondered whether Grancy, under the recovered tranquillity of his smile, concealed the same sense of her nearness, saw perpetually between himself and the actual her bright unappeasable ghost. He spoke of her once or twice, in an easy incidental way, and her name seemed to hang in the air after he had uttered it, like a chord that continues to vibrate. If he felt her presence it was evidently as an enveloping medium, the moral atmosphere in which he breathed. I had never before known how completely the dead may survive.

After luncheon we went for a long walk through the autumnal fields and woods, and dusk was falling when we re-entered the house. Grancy led the way to the library, where, at this hour, his wife had always welcomed us back to a bright fire and a cup of tea. The room faced the west, and held a clear light of its own after the rest of the house had grown dark. I remembered how young she had looked in this pale gold light, which irradiated her eyes and hair, or silhouetted her girlish outline as she passed before the windows. Of all the rooms the library was most peculiarly hers; and here I felt that her nearness might take visible shape.

Then, all in a moment, as Grancy opened the door, the feeling vanished and a kind of resistance met me on the threshold. I looked about me. Was the room changed? Had some desecrating hand effaced the traces of her presence? No; here too the setting was undisturbed. My feet sank into the same deep-piled Daghestan; the bookshelves took the firelight on the same rows of rich subdued bindings; her armchair stood in its old place near the tea-table; and from the opposite wall her face confronted me.

Her face—but *was* it hers? I moved nearer and stood looking up at the portrait. Grancy's glance had followed mine and I heard him move to my side.

"You see a change in it?" he said.

"What does it mean?" I asked.

"It means—that five years have passed."

"Over *her*?"

"Why not?—Look at me!" He pointed to his grey hair and furrowed temples. "What do you think kept *her* so young? It was happiness! But now—" he looked up at her with infinite tenderness. "I like her better so," he said. "It's what she would have wished."

"Have wished?"

"That we should grow old together. Do you think she would have wanted to be left behind?"

I stood speechless, my gaze travelling from his worn grief-beaten features to the painted face above. It was not furrowed like his; but a veil of years seemed to have descended on it. The bright hair had lost its elasticity, the cheek its clearness, the brow its light: the whole woman had waned.

Grancy laid his hand on my arm. "You don't like it?" he said sadly.

"Like it? I— I've lost her!" I burst out.

"And I've found her," he answered.

"In *that*?" I cried with a reproachful gesture.

"Yes; in that." He swung round on me almost defiantly. "The other had become a sham, a lie! This is the way she would have looked—does look, I mean. Claydon ought to know, oughtn't he?"

I turned suddenly. "Did Claydon do this for you?"

Grancy nodded.

"Since your return?"

"Yes. I sent for him after I'd been back a week—." He turned away and gave a thrust to the smouldering fire. I followed, glad to leave the picture behind me. Grancy threw himself into a chair near the hearth, so that the light fell on his sensitive variable face. He leaned his head back, shading his eyes with his hand, and began to speak.

3

"You fellows knew enough of my early history to A guess what my second marriage meant to me. I say guess, because no one could understand—really. I've always had a feminine streak in me, I suppose: the need of a pair of eyes that should see with me, of a pulse that should keep time with mine. Life is a big thing, of course; a magnificent spectacle; but I got so tired of looking at it alone! Still, it's always good to live, and I had plenty of happiness—of the evolved kind. What I'd never had a taste of was the simple inconscient sort that one breathes in like the air. . . .

"Well—I met her. It was like finding the climate in which I was meant to live. You know what she was—how indefinitely she multiplied one's points of contact with life, how she lit up the caverns and bridged the abysses! Well, I swear to you (though I suppose the sense of all that was latent in me) that what I used to think of on my way home at the end of the day, was simply that when I opened this door she'd be sitting over there, with the lamp-light falling in a particular way on one little curl in her neck. . . . When Claydon painted her he caught just the look she used to lift to mine when I came in—I've wondered, sometimes, at his knowing how she looked when she and I were alone.—How I rejoiced in that picture! I used to say to her, 'You're my prisoner now—I shall never lose you. If you grew tired of me and left me you'd leave your real self there on the wall!' It was always one of our jokes that she was going to grow tired of me—

"Three years of it—and then she died. It was so sudden that there was no change, no diminution. It was as if she had suddenly become fixed, immovable, like her own portrait: as if Time had ceased at its happiest hour, just as Claydon had thrown down his brush one day and said, 'I can't do better than that.'

"I went away, as you know, and stayed over there five years. I worked as hard as I knew how, and after the first black months a little light stole in on me. From thinking that she would have been interested in what I was doing I came to feel that she *was* interested—that she was there and that she knew. I'm not talking any psychical jargon—I'm simply trying to express the sense I had that an influence so full, so abounding as hers couldn't pass like a spring shower. We had so lived into each other's hearts and minds that the consciousness of what she would have thought and felt illuminated all I did. At first she used to come back shyly, tentatively, as though not sure of finding me; then she stayed longer and longer, till at last she became again the very air I breathed. . . . There were bad moments, of course, when her nearness mocked me with the loss of the real woman; but gradually the distinction between the two was effaced and the mere thought of her grew warm as flesh and blood.

"Then I came home. I landed in the morning and came straight down here. The thought of seeing her portrait possessed me and my heart beat like a lover's as I opened the library door. It was in the afternoon and the room was full of light. It fell on her picture—the picture of a young and radiant woman. She smiled at me coldly across the distance that divided us. I had the feeling that she didn't even recognise me. And then I caught sight of myself in the mirror over there—a grey-haired broken man whom she had never known!

"For a week we two lived together—the strange woman and the strange man. I used to sit night after night and question her smiling face; but no answer ever came. What did she know of me, after all? We were irrevocably separated by the five years of life that lay between us. At times, as I sat here, I almost grew to hate her; for her presence had driven away my gentle ghost, the real wife who had wept, aged, struggled with me during those awful years. . . . It was the worst loneliness I've ever known. Then, gradually, I began to notice a look of sadness in the picture's eyes; a look that seemed to say: 'Don't you see that *I* am lonely too?'

"And all at once it came over me how she would have hated to be left behind! I remembered her comparing life to a heavy book that could not be read with ease unless two people held it together; and I thought how impatiently her hand would have turned the pages that divided us!—So the idea came to me: 'It's the picture that stands between us; the picture that is dead, and not my wife. To sit in this room is to keep watch beside a corpse.' As this feeling grew on me the portrait became like a beautiful mausoleum in which she had been buried alive: I could hear her beating against the painted walls and crying to me faintly for help. . . .

"One day I found I couldn't stand it any longer and I sent for Claydon. He came down and I told him what I'd been through and what I wanted him to do. At first he refused point-blank to touch the picture. The next morning, I went off for a long tramp, and when I came home I found him sitting here alone. He looked at me sharply for a moment and then he said: 'I've changed my mind; I'll do it.' I arranged one of the north rooms as a studio and he shut himself up there for a day; then he sent for me. The picture stood there as you see it now—it was as though she'd met me on the threshold and taken me in her arms! I tried to thank him, to tell him what it meant to me, but he cut me short.

"'There's an up train at five, isn't there?' he asked. 'I'm booked for a dinner tonight. I shall just have time to make a bolt for the station and you can send my traps after me.' I haven't seen him since.

"I can guess what it cost him to lay hands on his masterpiece; but, after all, to him it was only a picture lost, to me it was my wife regained!"

4

After that, for ten years or more, I watched the strange spectacle of a life of hopeful and productive effort based on the structure of a dream. There could be no doubt to those who saw Grancy during this period that he drew his strength and courage from the sense of his wife's mystic participation in his task. When I went back to see him a few months later I found the portrait had been removed from the library and placed in a small study upstairs, to which he had transferred his desk and a few books. He told me he always sat there when he was alone, keeping the library for his Sunday visitors. Those who missed the portrait of course made no comment on its absence, and the few who were in his secret respected it. Gradually all his old friends had gathered about him and our Sunday afternoons regained something of their former character; but Claydon never reappeared among us.

As I look back now I see that Grancy must have been failing from the time of his return home. His invincible spirit belied and disguised the signs of weakness that afterward asserted themselves in my remembrance of him. He seemed to have an inexhaustible fund of life to draw on, and more than one of us was a pensioner on his superfluity.

Nevertheless, when I came back one summer from my European holiday and heard that he had been at the point of death, I understood at once that we had believed him well only because he wished us to.

I hastened down to the country and found him midway in a slow convalescence. I felt then that he was lost to us and he read my thought at a glance.

"Ah," he said, "I'm an old man now and no mistake. I suppose we shall have to go half-speed after this; but we shan't need towing just yet!"

The plural pronoun struck me, and involuntarily I looked up at Mrs. Grancy's portrait. Line by line I saw my fear reflected in it. It was the face of a woman who knows that her husband is dying. My heart stood still at the thought of what Claydon had done.

Grancy had followed my glance. "Yes, it's changed her," he said quietly. "For months, you know, it was touch and go with me—we had a long fight of it, and it was worse for her than for me." After a pause he added: "Claydon has been very kind; he's so busy nowadays that I seldom see him, but when I sent for him the other day he came down at once."

I was silent and we spoke no more of Grancy's illness; but when I took leave it seemed like shutting him in alone with his death-warrant.

The next time I went down to see him he looked much better. It was a Sunday and he received me in the library, so that I did not see the portrait again. He continued to improve and toward spring we began to feel that, as he had said, he might yet travel a long way without being towed.

One evening, on returning to town after a visit which had confirmed my sense of reassurance, I found Claydon dining alone at the club. He asked me to join him and over the coffee our talk turned to his work.

"If you're not too busy," I said at length, "you ought to make time to go down to Grancy's again."

He looked up quickly. "Why?" he asked.

"Because he's quite well again," I returned with a touch of cruelty. "His wife's prognostications were mistaken."

Claydon stared at me a moment. "Oh, *she* knows," he affirmed with a smile that chilled me.

"You mean to leave the portrait as it is then?" I persisted.

He shrugged his shoulders. "He hasn't sent for me yet!"

A waiter came up with the cigars and Claydon rose and joined another group.

It was just a fortnight later that Grancy's housekeeper telegraphed for me. She met me at the station with the news that he had been "taken bad" and that the doctors were with him. I had to wait for some time in the deserted library before the medical men appeared.

They had the baffled manner of empirics who have been superseded by the great Healer; and I lingered only long enough to hear that Grancy was not suffering and that my presence could do him no harm.

I found him seated in his armchair in the little study. He held out his hand with a smile.

"You see she was right after all," he said.

"She?" I repeated, perplexed for the moment.

"My wife." He indicated the picture. "Of course I knew she had no hope from the first. I saw that"—he lowered his voice—"after Claydon had been here. But I wouldn't believe it at first!"

I caught his hands in mine. "For God's sake don't believe it now!" I adjured him.

He shook his head gently. "It's too late," he said. "I might have known that she knew."

"But, Grancy, listen to me," I began; and then I stopped. What could I say that would convince him? There was no common ground of argument on which we could meet; and after all it would be easier for him to die feeling that she *had* known. Strangely enough, I saw that Claydon had missed his mark. . . .

5

Grancy's will named me as one of his executors; and my associate, having other duties on his hands, begged me to assume the task of carrying out our friend's wishes. This placed me under the necessity of informing Claydon that the portrait of Mrs. Grancy had been bequeathed to him; and he replied by the next post that he would send for the picture at once. I was staying in the deserted house when the portrait was taken away; and as the door closed on it I felt that Grancy's presence had vanished too. Was it his turn to follow her now, and could one ghost haunt another?

After that, for a year or two, I heard nothing more of the picture, and though I met Claydon from time to time we had little to say to each other. I had no definable grievance against the man and I tried to remember that he had done a fine thing in sacrificing his best picture to a friend; but my resentment had all the tenacity of unreason.

One day, however, a lady whose portrait he had just finished begged me to go with her to see it. To refuse was impossible, and I went with the less reluctance that I knew I was not the only friend she had invited. The others were all grouped around the easel when I entered, and after contributing my share to the chorus of approval I turned away and began to stroll about the studio. Claydon was something of a collector and his things were generally worth looking at. The studio was a long tapestried room with a curtained archway at one end. The curtains were looped back, showing a smaller apartment, with books and flowers and a few fine bits of bronze and porcelain. The tea-table standing in this inner room proclaimed that it was open to inspection, and I wandered in.

A *bleu poudré* vase first attracted me; then I turned to examine a slender bronze Ganymede, and in so doing found myself face to face with Mrs. Grancy's portrait. I stared up at her blankly and she smiled back at me in all the recovered radiance of youth. The artist had effaced every trace of his later touches and the original picture had reappeared. It throned alone on the panelled wall, asserting a brilliant supremacy over its carefully-chosen surroundings. I felt in an instant that the whole room was tributary to it: that Claydon had heaped his treasures at the feet of the woman he loved. Yes—it was the woman he had loved and not the picture; and my instinctive resentment was explained.

Suddenly I felt a hand on my shoulder.

"Ah, how could you?" I cried, turning on him.

"How could I?" he retorted. "How could I *not*? Doesn't she belong to me now?"

I moved away impatiently.

"Wait a moment," he said with a detaining gesture. "The others have gone and I want to say a word to you.—Oh, I know what you've thought of me—I can guess! You think I killed Grancy, I suppose?"

I was startled by his sudden vehemence. "I think you tried to do a cruel thing," I said.

"Ah—what a little way you others see into life!" he murmured. "Sit down a moment—here, where we can look at her—and I'll tell you."

He threw himself on the ottoman beside me and sat gazing up at the picture, with his hands clasped about his knee.

"Pygmalion," he began slowly, "turned his statue into a real woman; *I* turned my real woman into a picture. Small compensation, you think—but you don't know how much of a woman belongs to you after you've painted her!—Well, I made the best of it, at any rate—I gave her the best I had in me; and she gave me in return what such a woman gives by merely being. And after all she rewarded me enough by making me paint as I shall never paint again! There was one side of her, though, that was mine alone, and that was her beauty; for no one else understood it. To Grancy even it was the mere expression of herself—what language is to thought. Even when he saw the picture he didn't guess my secret—he was so sure she was all his! As though a man should think he owned the moon because it was reflected in the pool at his door—

"Well—when he came home and sent for me to change the picture it was like asking me to commit murder. He wanted me to make an old woman of her—of her who had been so divinely, unchangeably young! As if any man who really loved a woman would ask her to sacrifice her youth and beauty for his sake! At first I told him I couldn't do it—but afterward, when he left me alone with the picture, something queer happened. I suppose it was because I was always so confoundedly fond of Grancy that it went against me to refuse what he asked. Anyhow, as I sat looking up at her, she seemed to say, 'I'm not yours but his, and I want you to make me what he wishes." And so I did it. I could have cut my hand off when the work was done—I daresay he told you I never would go back and look at it. He thought I was too busy—he never understood. . . .

"Well—and then last year he sent for me again—you remember. It was after his illness, and he told me he'd grown twenty years older and that he wanted her to grow older too—he didn't want her to be left behind. The doctors all thought he was going to get well at that time, and he thought so too; and so did I when I first looked at him. But when I turned to the picture—ah, now I don't ask you to believe me; but I swear it was *her* face that told me he was dying, and that she wanted him to know it! She had a message for him and she made me deliver it."

He rose abruptly and walked toward the portrait; then he sat down beside me again.

"Cruel? Yes, it seemed so to me at first; and this time, if I resisted, it was for *his* sake and not for mine. But all the while I felt her eyes drawing me, and gradually she made me understand. If she'd been there in the flesh (she seemed to say) wouldn't she have seen before any of us that he was dying? Wouldn't he have read the news first in her face? And wouldn't it be horrible if now he should discover it instead in strange eyes?—Well—that was what she wanted of me and I did it—I kept them together to the last!" He looked up at the picture again. "But now she belongs to me," he repeated. . . .

www.ingramcontent.com/pod-product-compliance
Lightning Source LLC
Chambersburg PA
CBHW022147010726
47493CB00002B/372
* 9 7 8 1 7 8 2 8 2 5 5 0 0 *